PROOF

With *Proof*, the incomparable *New York Times* bestselling author offers a compelling tale of fine living, fast horses, and shattering suspense.

Wine merchant Tony Beach has expertly catered his latest society soiree, but the fun's over when a team of hit men crashes the party . . . literally. The event leaves Tony with a bitter aftertaste of suspicion—and sets off a mystery that's an intoxicating blend of deception, intrigue, and murder . . .

continued . . .

PROOF

DICK
FRANCIS

BERKLEY BOOKS, NEW YORK

THE BERKLEY PUBLISHING GROUP
Published by the Penguin Group
Penguin Group (USA) Inc.
375 Hudson Street, New York, New York 10014, USA
Penguin Group (Canada), 90 Eglinton Avenue East, Suite 700, Toronto, Ontario M4P 2Y3, Canada
(a division of Pearson Penguin Canada Inc.)
Penguin Books Ltd., 80 Strand, London WC2R 0RL, England
Penguin Group Ireland, 25 St. Stephen's Green, Dublin 2, Ireland (a division of Penguin Books Ltd.)
Penguin Group (Australia), 250 Camberwell Road, Camberwell, Victoria 3124, Australia
(a division of Pearson Australia Group Pty. Ltd.)
Penguin Books India Pvt. Ltd., 11 Community Centre, Panchsheel Park, New Delhi—110 017, India
Penguin Group (NZ), 67 Apollo Drive, Rosedale, North Shore 0632, New Zealand
(a division of Pearson New Zealand Ltd.)
Penguin Books (South Africa) (Pty.) Ltd., 24 Sturdee Avenue, Rosebank, Johannesburg 2196,
South Africa

Penguin Books Ltd., Registered Offices: 80 Strand, London WC2R 0RL, England

This is a work of fiction. Names, characters, places, and incidents either are the product of the author's imagination or are used fictitiously, and any resemblance to actual persons, living or dead, business establishments, events, or locales is entirely coincidental.

PROOF

A Berkley Book / published by arrangement with the author

PRINTING HISTORY
G. P. Putnam's Sons hardcover edition / March 1985
Fawcett Crest edition / April 1986
Jove mass-market edition / July 1997
Berkley mass-market edition / July 2005

Copyright © 1985 by Dick Francis.
The Edgar® name is a registered service mark of the Mystery Writers of America, Inc.
Cover illustration by Greg Montgomery.
Cover design by Steven Ferlauto.

ISBN: 978-0-425-20393-4

BERKLEY®
Berkley Books are published by The Berkley Publishing Group,
a division of Penguin Group (USA) Inc.,
375 Hudson Street, New York, New York 10014.
BERKLEY® is a registered trademark of Penguin Group (USA) Inc.
The "B" design is a trademark belonging to Penguin Group (USA) Inc.

PRINTED IN THE UNITED STATES OF AMERICA

10   9   8   7   6   5   4   3   2

My thanks to
MARGARET GILES
of
PANGBOURNE WINES,
who taught me her business

and to
BARRY MACKANESS
and
my brother-in-law
DICK YORKE,
wineshippers

and to
LEN LIVINGSTONE-LEARMONTH,
long-time friend.

PROOF

ONE

AGONY IS SOCIALLY UNACCEPTABLE. ONE IS NOT SUP posed to weep. Particularly is one not supposed to weep when one is moderately presentable and thirty-two. When one's wife has been dead six months and everyone else has done grieving.

Ah well, they say: He'll get over it. There's always another pretty lady. Time's a great healer, they say. He'll marry again one day, they say.

No doubt they're right.

But oh dear God . . . the emptiness in my house. The devastating, weary, ultimate loneliness. The silence where there used to be laughter, the cold hearth that used to leap with fire for my return, the permanent blank in my bed.

Six months into unremitting ache I felt that my own immediate death would be no great disaster. Half of myself had gone; the fulfilled joyful investment of six years' loving, gone into darkness. What was left simply suffered . . . and looked normal.

Habit kept me checking both ways when I crossed the road; and meanwhile I tended my shop and sold my wines, and smiled and smiled and smiled at the customers.

ONE

TWO

Customers came in all possible shapes, from the schoolchildren who bought potato chips and cola because I was near the bus stop, to the sergeants' mess of the local barracks: from pensioners saving for apologetic half bottles of gin to the knowledgeably lavish laying down port. Customers came once a year and daily, with ignorance and expertise, for happiness and comfort, in gloom and insobriety. Customers ranged from syrup to bitters, like their drinks.

My foremost customer, one Sunday morning that cold October, was a racehorse trainer splashing unstinted fizz over a hundred or so guests in his more or less annual celebration of the Flat races his stable had won during the passing season. Each autumn as his name came high on the winners' list he gave thanks by inviting his owners, his jockeys, his ramifications of friends to share his satisfaction for joys past and to look forward and make plans for starting all over again the following spring.

Each September he would telephone in his perpetual state of rush. "Tony? Three weeks on Sunday, right?

Just the usual, in the tent. You'll do the glasses? And sale or return, of course, right?"

"Right," I would say, and he'd be gone before I could draw breath. It would be his wife, Flora, who later came to the shop smilingly with details.

Accordingly on that Sunday I drove to his place at ten o'clock and parked as close as I could to the large once-white marquee rising tautly from his back lawn. He came bustling out of his house the moment I stopped, as if he'd been looking out for me, which perhaps he had: Jack Hawthorn, maybe sixty, short, plump and shrewd.

"Tony. Well done." He patted me lightly on the shoulder, his usual greeting, as he habitually avoided the social custom of shaking hands. Not, as I had originally guessed, because he feared to catch other people's contagious germs but because, as an avid racing lady had enlightened me, he had "a grip like a defrosting jellyfish" and hated to see people rub their palms on their clothes after touching him.

"A good day for it," I said.

He glanced briefly at the clear sky. "We need rain. The ground's like concrete." Racehorse trainers, like farmers, were never satisfied with the weather. "Did you bring any soft drinks? The Sheik's coming, with his whole teetotaling entourage. Forgot to tell you."

I nodded. "Champagne, soft drinks and a box of oddments."

"Good. Right. I'll leave you to it. The waitresses will be here at eleven, guests at twelve. And you'll stay yourself, of course? My guest, naturally. I take it for granted."

"Your secretary sent me an invitation."

"Did he? Good heavens. How efficient. Right then. Anything you want, come and find me."

I nodded and he hurried away, taking his life as usual at a trot. Notwithstanding the secretary, a somewhat languid man with a supercilious nose and an indefatigable capacity for accurate detailed work, Jack never quite caught up with what he wanted to do. Flora, his placid wife, had told me, "It's Jimmy (the secretary) who enters the horses for the races, Jimmy who sends out the bills, Jimmy who runs all the paperwork single-handed, and Jack never so much as has to pick up a postage stamp. It's habit, all this rushing. Just habit." But she'd spoken fondly, as everyone did, more or less, of Jack Hawthorn: and maybe it was actually the staccato energy of the man that communicated to his horses and set them winning.

He always invited me to his celebrations, either formally or not, partly no doubt so that I should be on the spot to solve any booze-flow problems immediately, but also because I had myself been born into a section of the racing world and was still considered part of it, despite my inexplicable defection into retail liquor.

"Not his father's son," was how the uncharitable put it. Or more plainly, "Lacks the family guts."

My father, a soldier, had won both the Distinguished Service Order and the Military Gold Cup, dashing as valiantly into steeplechase fences as he had into enemy territory. His bravery on all battlefields had been awe-inspiring, and he died from a broken neck on Sandown Park racecourse when I was eleven, and watching.

He had been forty-seven at the time and remained, of course, at that age in the racing world's memory, a tall, straight, laughing, reckless man, untouched, it still seemed to me, by the world's woes. No matter that he was not an ideal shape for jockeyship, he had resolutely followed in the wake of his own father, my grandfather, a distant Titan who had finished second one year in the Grand National before covering himself with military glory in World War I. My grandfather's Victoria Cross lay beside my father's D.S.O. in the display case I had inherited. It was their dash, their flair, their daredevilment that they had not passed on.

"Are you going to grow up like your father, then?" had been said to me in friendly, expectant fashion countless times through my childhood, and it had only slowly dawned on everyone, as on me, that no, I wasn't. I learned to ride, but without distinction. I went to Wellington, the school for soldiers' sons, but not in turn to Sandhurst to put on uniform myself. My mother too often said "Never mind, dear," suffering many disappointments nobly; and I developed deep powerful feelings of inferiority, which still lingered, defying common sense.

Only with Emma had they retreated to insignificance, but now that she had gone, faint but persistent, they were back. A discarded habit of mind insidiously creeping into unguarded corners. Miserable.

Jimmy, the secretary, never helped. He sauntered out of the house, hands in pockets, and watched as I lugged three galvanized washtubs from the rear of my van.

"What are those for?" he said. He couldn't help looking down that nose, I supposed, as he topped six feet four. It was just that his tone of voice matched.

"Ice," I said.

He said, "Oh," or rather "Ay-oh," as a diphthong.

I carried the tubs into the tent, which contained a row of trestle tables with tablecloths near one end and clusters of potted chrysanthemums round the bases of the two main supporting poles. The living grass of the lawn had been covered with serviceable fawn matting, and bunches of red and gold ribbons decorated the streaky grayish canvas walls at regular intervals. In one far corner stood a blower-heater, unlit. The day was marginally not cold enough. The tent was almost festive. Almost. Jack and Flora, and who could blame them, never wasted good cash on unnecessaries.

There was no tremble in the air. No shudder. No premonition at all of the horror soon to happen there. All was quiet and peaceful; expectant certainly, but benign. I remembered it particularly, after.

Jimmy continued to watch while I carted in a case of champagne and unpacked the bottles, standing them upright in one of the tubs on the floor by the tent wall behind the tables. I didn't actually have to do this part of the job, but for Jack Hawthorn, somehow, it was easy to give service beyond contract.

I was working in shirtsleeves, warmed by a pale blue V-necked sleeveless pullover (typical racing world clothes) with my jacket waiting in the van for the metamorphosis to guest. Jimmy was understatedly resplendent in thin fawn polo-necked sweater under a navy-blue blazer; plain brass buttons, no crests, no pretensions. That was the trouble. If he'd had any pretensions I could perhaps have despised him instead of suspecting it was the other way round.

I fetched a second box of champagne and began unpacking it. Jimmy bent from his great height and picked up one of the bottles, staring at the foil and the label as if he'd never seen such things before.

"What's this muck?" he said. "Never heard of it."

"It's the real thing," I said mildly. "It comes from Epernay."

"So I see."

"Flora's choice," I said.

He said "Ay-oh" in complete understanding and put the bottle back. I fetched ice cubes in large black plastic bags and poured them over and round the standing bottles.

"Did you bring any scotch?" he asked.

"Front seat of the van."

He strolled off on the search and came back with an unopened bottle.

"Glass?" he inquired.

For reply I went out to the van and fetched a box containing sixty.

"Help yourself."

Without comment he opened the box, which I'd set on a table, and removed one of the all-purpose goblets.

"Is this ice drinkable?" he said dubiously.

"Pure tap water."

He put ice and whisky in the glass and sipped the result.

"Very prickly this morning, aren't you," he said.

I glanced at him, surprised. "Sorry."

"Someone knocked off a whole load of this stuff in Scotland yesterday, did you know?"

"Champagne?"

"No. Scotch."

I shrugged. "Well . . . it happens."

I fetched a third case and unpacked the bottles. Jimmy watched, clinking his ice.

"How much do you know about whisky, Tony?" he said.

"Well . . . some."

"Would you know one from another?"

"I'm better at wine." I straightened from filling the second tub. "Why?"

"Would you know for certain," he said with a bad stab at casualness, "if you asked for a malt and got sold an ordinary standard, like this?" He raised his glass, nodding to it.

"They taste quite different."

He relaxed slightly, betraying an inner tension I hadn't until then been aware of. "Could you tell one malt from another?"

I looked at him assessingly. "What's this all about?"

"Could you?" He was insistent.

"No," I said. "Not this morning. Not to name them. I'd have to practice. Maybe then. Maybe not."

"But . . . if you learned one particular taste, could you pick it out again from a row of samples? Or say if it wasn't there?"

"Perhaps," I said. I looked at him, waiting, but he was taking his own troubled time, consulting some inner opinion. Shrugging, I went to fetch more ice, pouring it into the second tub, and then carried in and ripped open the fourth case of champagne.

"It's very awkward," he said suddenly.

"What is?"

"I wish you'd stop fiddling with those bottles and listen to me."

His voice was a mixture of petulance and anxiety, and I slowly straightened from putting bottles into the third tub and took notice.

"Tell me, then," I said.

He was older than me by a few years, and our acquaintanceship had mostly been limited to my visits to the Hawthorn house, both as drinks supplier and as occasional guest. His usual manner to me had been fairly civil but without warmth, as no doubt mine to him. He was the third son of the fourth son of a racehorse-owning earl, which gave him an aristocratic name but no fortune, and his job with Jack Hawthorn resulted directly, it was said, from lack of enough brain to excel in the City. It was a judgment I would have been content to accept were it not for Flora's admiration of him, but I hadn't cared enough one way or the other to give it much thought.

"One of Jack's owners has a restaurant," he said. "The Silver Moondance, near Reading. Not aimed at top class. Dinner dances. A singer sometimes. Mass market." His voice was fastidious but without scorn: stating a fact, not an attitude.

I waited noncommittally.

"He invited Jack and Flora and myself to dinner there last week."

"Decent of him," I said.

"Yes." Jimmy looked at me down the nose. "Quite." He paused slightly. "The food was all right, but the drinks . . . Look, Tony, Larry Trent is one of Jack's good owners. He has five horses here. Pays his bills on the nail. I don't want to upset him, but what it says on the label of at least one of the bottles in his restaurant is not what they pour out of it."

He spoke with pained disgust, at which I almost smiled.

"That's not actually unusual," I said.

"But it's illegal." He was indignant.

"Sure it's illegal. Are you certain?"

"Yes. Well yes, I think so. But I wondered if perhaps, before I said anything to Larry Trent, you could taste their stuff? I mean, suppose his staff are ripping him off? I mean, er . . . he could be prosecuted, couldn't he?"

I said, "Why didn't you mention it to him that evening, while you were there?"

Jimmy looked startled. "But we were his guests! It would have been terribly bad form. Surely you can see that."

"Hm," I said dryly. "Then why don't you just tell him now, and privately, what you thought about his drinks? He might be grateful. He would certainly be warned. Anyway, I can't see him whisking his five horses away in a huff."

Jimmy made a pained noise and drank some scotch. "I mentioned this to Jack. He said I must be mistaken. But I'm not, you know. I'm pretty sure I'm not."

I considered him.

"Why does it bother you so much?" I asked.

"What?" He was surprised. "Well, I say, a fraud's a fraud, isn't it? It annoys one."

"Yes." I sighed. "What were these drinks supposed to be?"

"I thought the wine wasn't much, considering its label, but you know how it is, you don't suspect anything . . . but there was the Laphroaig."

I frowned. "The malt from Islay?"

"That's right," Jimmy said. "Heavy malt whisky. My grandfather liked it. He used to give me sips when I was small, much to my mother's fury. Funny how you never forget tastes you learn as a child . . . and of course I've had it since . . . so there it was, on the trolley of drinks they rolled round with the coffee, and I thought I would have some. Nostalgia, and all that."

"And it wasn't Laphroaig?"

"No."

"What was it?"

He looked uncertain. "I thought that you, actually,

might know. If you drank some, I mean.''

I shook my head. "You'd need a proper expert.''

He looked unhappy. "I thought myself, you see, that it was just an ordinary blend, just ordinary, not even pure malt.''

"You'd better tell Mr. Trent," I said. "Let him deal with it himself.''

He said doubtfully, "He'll be here this morning.''

"Easy," I said.

"I don't suppose . . . er . . . that you yourself . . . er . . . could have a word with him?''

"No, I certainly couldn't," I said positively. "From you it could be a friendly warning, from me it would be a deadly insult. Sorry, Jimmy, but honestly, no.''

With resignation he said, "I thought you wouldn't. But worth a try.'' He poured himself more scotch and again put ice into it, and I thought in passing that true whisky aficionados thought ice an abomination, and wondered about the trustworthiness of his perception of Laphroaig.

Flora, rotund and happy in cherry-red wool, came into the tent, looking around and nodding in satisfaction.

"Looks quite bright, doesn't it, Tony dear?''

"Splendid," I said.

"When it's filled with guests . . .''

"Yes," I agreed.

She was conventional, well-intentioned and cozy, mother of three children (not Jack's) who telephoned her regularly. She liked to talk about them on her occasional visits to my shop and tended to place larger orders when the news of them was good. Jack was her second husband, mellowing still under her wing but reportedly jealous of her offspring. Amazing the things people told their wine merchants. I knew a great deal about a lot of people's lives.

Flora peered into the tubs. "Four cases on ice?"

I nodded. "More in the van, if you need it."

"Let's hope not." She smiled sweetly. "But my dear, I wouldn't bet on it. Jimmy love, you don't need to drink whisky. Open some champagne. I'd like a quick glass before everyone swamps us."

Jimmy obliged with languid grace, easing out the cork without explosion, containing the force in his hand. Flora smilingly watched the plume of released gas float from the bottle and tilted a glass forward to catch the first bubbles. At her insistence both Jimmy and I drank also, but from Jimmy's expression it didn't go well with his scotch.

"Lovely!" Flora said appreciatively, sipping; and I thought the wine as usual a bit too thin and fizzy, but sensible enough for those quantities. I sold a great deal of it for weddings.

Flora took her glass and wandered down the marquee to the entrance through which the guests would come, the entrance that faced away from the house, toward the field where the cars would be parked. Jack Hawthorn's house and stableyard were built in a hollow high on the eastern end of the Berkshire Downs, in a place surrounded by hills, invisible until one was close. Most people would arrive by the main road over the hill that faced the rear of the house, parking in the field, and continuing the downward journey on foot through a gate in the low-growing rose hedge, and onto the lawn. After several such parties, Flora had brought crowd control to a fine art: and besides, this way, no one upset the horses.

Flora suddenly exclaimed loudly and came hurrying back.

"It's really too bad of him. The Sheik is here already. His car's coming over the hill. Jimmy, run and meet him. Jack's still changing. Take the Sheik round the yard. Anything. Really, it's too bad. Tell Jack he's here."

Jimmy nodded, put down his glass without haste and ambled off to intercept the oil-rich prince and his retinue. Flora hovered indecisively, not following, talking crossly with maximum indiscretion.

"I don't like that particular Sheik. I can't help it. He's fat and horrible and he behaves as if he owns the place, which he doesn't. And I don't like the way he looks at me with those half-shut eyes, as if I were of no account . . . and Tony, dear, I haven't said any of those things, you understand? I don't like the way Arabs treat women."

"And his horses win races," I said.

"Yes," Flora sighed. "It's not all sweetness and light being a trainer's wife. Some of the owners make me sick." She gave me a brief half-smile and went away to the house, and I finished the unloading with things like orange juice and cola.

Up on the hill the uniformed chauffeur parked the elongated black-windowed Mercedes, which was so identifiably the Sheik's, with its nose pointing to the marquee, and gradually more cars arrived to swell the row there, bringing waitresses and other helpers, and finally, in a steady stream, the hundred-and-something guests.

They came by Rolls, by Range Rover, by Mini and by Ford. One couple arrived in a horse trailer, another by motorcycle. Some brought children, some brought dogs, most of which were left with the cars. In cashmere and cords, in checked shirts and tweeds, in elegance and pearls they walked chatteringly down the grassy slope, through the gate in the rose hedge, across a few steps of lawn, into the beckoning tent. A promising Sunday morning jollification ahead, most troubles left behind.

As always with racing-world parties, everyone there knew somebody else. The decibel count rose rapidly to ear-aching levels and only round the very walls could one talk without shouting. The Sheik, dressed in full Arab robes and flanked by his wary-eyed entourage, was one, I noticed, who stood resolutely with his back to the canvas, holding his orange juice before him and surveying the crush with his half-shut eyes. Jimmy was doing his noble best to amuse, rewarded by unsmiling nods, and gradually and separately other guests stopped to talk to the solid figure in the banded white headgear, but none of them with complete naturalness, and none of them women.

Jimmy after a while detached himself and I found him at my elbow.

"Sticky going, the Sheik?" I said.

"He's not such a bad fellow," Jimmy said loyally. "No social graces in Western gatherings and absolutely paranoid about being assassinated. Never even sits in the dentist's chair, I'm told, without all those bodyguards being right there in the surgery, but he does know about horses. Loves them. You should have seen him just now, going round the yard, those bored eyes came right to life." He looked round the gathering and suddenly exclaimed, "See that man talking to Flora? That's Larry Trent."

"Of the absent Laphroaig?"

Jimmy nodded, wrinkled his brow in indecision and moved off in another direction altogether, and I for a few moments watched the man with Flora, a middle-

aged, dark-haired man with a moustache, one of the few
people wearing a suit, in his case a navy pinstripe with
the coat buttoned, a line of silk handkerchief showing in
the top pocket. The crowd shifted and I lost sight of
him, and I talked, as one does, to a succession of familiar
half-known people, seen once a year or less, with whom
one took on as one had left off, as if time hadn't existed
in between. It was one of those, with best intentions,
who said inevitably, "And how's Emma? How's your
pretty wife?"

I thought I would never get used to it, that jab like a
spike thrust into a jumpy nerve, that positively physical
pain. Emma . . . dear God.

"She's dead," I said, shaking my head slightly,
breaking it to him gently, absolving him from embar-
rassment. I'd had to say it like that often: far too often.
I knew how to do it now without causing discomfort.
Bitter, extraordinary skill of the widowed, taking the dis-
tress away from others, hiding one's own.

"I'm so sorry," he said, meaning it intensely for the
moment, as they do. "I'd no idea. None at all. Er . . .
when?"

"Six months ago," I said.

"Oh." He adjusted his sympathy level suitably. "I'm
really very sorry."

I nodded. He sighed. The world went on. Transaction
over, until next time. Always a next time. And at least
he hadn't asked "How?" and I hadn't had to tell him,
hadn't had to think of the pain and the coma and the
child who had died with her, unborn.

A fair few of Jack's guests were also my customers,
so that even in that racing gathering I found myself talking as much about wine as horses, and it was while an
earnest elderly lady was soliciting my views on Côtes

du Rhone versus Côte de Nuits that I saw Jimmy finally
talking to Larry Trent. He spotted me too and waved for
me to come over, but the earnest lady would buy the
better wine by the caseful if convinced, and I tele-
graphed "later" gestures to Jimmy, to which he flipped
a forgiving hand.

Waitresses wove through the throng carrying dishes
of canapes and sausages on sticks, and I reckoned that
many more than a hundred throats had turned up and
that at the present rate of enthusiasm the forty-eight original bottles would be emptied at any minute. I had already begun to make my way to the tent's service
entrance near the house when Jack himself pounced at
me, clutching my sleeve.

"We'll need more champagne and the waitresses say
your van is locked." His voice was hurried. "The
party's going well, wouldn't you say?"

"Yes, very."

"Great. Good. I'll leave it to you, then." He turned
away, patting shoulders in greeting, enjoying his role as
host.

I checked the tubs, now empty but for two standing
bottles in a sea of melting ice, and went onward out to
the van, fishing in my pocket for the keys. For a moment
I glanced up the hill to where all the cars waited, to the
Range Rover, the horse trailer, the Sheik's Mercedes.
No gaps in the line: no one had yet gone home. There
was a child up there, playing with a dog.

I unlocked the rear door of my van and leaned in to
pull forward the three spare cases that were roughly
cooling under more black bags of ice. I threw one of the
bags out onto the grass, and I picked up one of the cases.

Movement on the edge of my vision made me turn

my head, and in a flash of a second that ordinary day became a nightmare.

The horse trailer was rolling forward down the hill.

Pointing straight at the marquee, gathering speed.

It was already only feet from the rose hedge. It smashed its way through the fragile plants, flattening the last pink flowers of autumn. It advanced inexorably onto the grass.

I leaped to the doorway of the tent screaming a warning, which nobody heard above the din, and which was anyway far too late.

For a frozen infinitesimal moment I saw the party still intact, a packed throng of people smiling, drinking, living and unaware.

Then the horse trailer ploughed into the canvas, and changed many things forever.

THREE

Total communal disbelief lasted through about five seconds of silence, then someone screamed and went on screaming, a high commentary of hysteria on so much horror.

The horse trailer had steamrollered on over the canvas side-wall, burying people beneath; and it had plunged forward into one of the main supporting poles, which snapped under the weight. The whole of the end of the tent nearest me had collapsed inward so that I stood on the edge of it with the ruin at my feet.

Where I had seen the guests, I now in absolute shock saw expanses of heavy gray canvas with countless bulges heaving desperately beneath.

The horse trailer itself stood there obscenely in the middle, huge, dark green, unharmed, impersonal and frightful. There seemed to be no one behind the driving wheel; and to reach the cab one would have had to walk over the shrouded lumps of the living and the dead.

Beyond the horse trailer, at the far end of the tent, in the still erect section, people were fighting their way out through the remains of the entrance and rips in the walls, emerging one by one, staggering and falling like figures in a frieze.

I noticed vaguely that I was still holding the case of champagne. I put it down where I stood, and turned and ran urgently to the telephone in the house.

So quiet in there. So utterly normal. My hands were shaking as I held the receiver.

Police and ambulances to Jack Hawthorn's stables. A doctor. And lifting gear. Coming, they said. All coming. At once.

I went back outside, meeting others with stretched eyes intent on the same errand.

"They're coming," I said. "Coming."

Everyone was trembling, not just myself.

The screaming had stopped, but many were shouting, husbands trying to find their wives, wives their husbands, a mother her son. All the faces were white, all the mouths open, all breaths coming in gasps. People had begun making slits in the canvas with penknives to free those trapped underneath. A woman with small scissors was methodically cutting the lacings of a section of side-wall, tears streaming down her face. The efforts all looked puny, the task immense.

Flora and Jack and Jimmy, I knew, had all been in the part of the tent that had collapsed.

A horse was whinnying nearby and kicking wood, and it was with fresh shock that I realized that the noise was coming from the horse trailer itself. There was a horse in there. Inside.

With stiff legs I went along to the standing section of tent, going in through a gap where other people had come out. The second pole still stood upright, the potted chrysanthemums bright round its foot. There were many scattered and broken glasses, and a few people trying to lift up the folds of the heavily fallen roof, to let the trapped crawl from under.

"We might make a tunnel," I said to one man, and he nodded in understanding, and by lifting one section only, but together, and advancing, he and I and several others made a wide head-high passage forward into the collapsed half, through which about thirty struggling people, dazedly getting to their feet, made their way out upright. Many of their faces and hands were bleeding from glass cuts. Few of them knew what had happened. Two of them were children.

One of the farthest figures we reached that way was Flora. I saw the red wool of her dress on the ground under a flap of canvas and bent down to help her: she was half unconscious with her face to the matting, suffocating.

I pulled her out and carried her down to the free end, and from there gave her to someone outside, and went back. The tunnel idea gradually extended until there was a ring of humans instead of tent poles holding up a fair section of roof, one or two helpers exploring continuously into the edges until as far as we could tell all the people not near the horse trailer itself were outside, walking and alive.

The horse trailer . . .

Into that area no one wanted to go, but my original tunneler and I looked at each other for a long moment and told everyone to leave if they wanted to. Some did, but three or four of us made a new, shorter and lower tunnel, working toward the side of the horse trailer facing the standing section of the tent, lifting tautly stretched canvas to free people still pinned underneath.

Almost the first person we came to was one of the Arabs, who was fiercely vigorous and at any other time would have seemed comic, because as soon as he was released and mobile he began shouting unintelligibly, producing a repeating rifle from his robes and waving it menacingly about.

All we wanted, I thought: a spray of terrified bullets.

The Sheik, I thought . . . Standing against the side-wall, so that his back should be safe.

We found two more people alive on that side, both women, both beyond speech, both white-faced, in torn clothes, bleeding from glass cuts, one with a broken arm. We passed them back into comfort, and went on.

Crawling forward I came then to a pair of feet, toes upward, then to trouser legs, unmoving. Through the canvas-filtered daylight they were easily recognizable; pinstripe cloth, navy blue.

I lifted more space over him until I could see along to the buttoned jacket and the silk handkerchief and a hand flung sideways holding a glass in fragments. And beyond, where a weight pressed down where his neck should have been, there was a line of crimson pulp.

I let the canvas fall back, feeling sick.

"No good," I said to the man behind me. "I think his head's under the front wheel. He's dead."

He gave me a look as shattered as my own, and we moved slowly sideways toward the horse trailer's rear, making our tunnel with difficulty on hands and knees.

Above us, inside the trailer, the horse kicked franti-cally and squealed, restless, excited and alarmed no doubt by the smell; horses were always upset by blood. I could see no prospect all the same of anyone lowering the ramps to let him out.

We found another Arab, alive, flat on his back, an arm bleeding, praying to Allah. We pulled him out and afterward found his rifle lying blackly where he'd been.

"They're mad," said my companion.

"It didn't save their master," I said.

On our knees we both looked in silence at what we could see of the Sheik, which was his head, still in its white headdress with its gold cords. A fold of reddened canvas lay over the rest of him, and my companion, gripping my wrist, said, "Leave it. Don't look. What's the point?"

I thought fleetingly of the policemen and the ambulancemen who would soon be forced to look, but I did as he asked. We made our way silently back to the standing section and began a new tunnel round to the other side of the horse trailer.

It was there that we came to Jack and also Jimmy, both with pulses, though both were unconscious and pinned to the ground by the thick main tent pole, which lay across Jack's legs and Jimmy's chest. We scarcely touched the pole ourselves, but the tremor of our movements brought Jack up to semiconsciousness and to groaning pain.

My companion said "Hell" through his teeth, and I said, "I'll stay here if you go and get something to keep the canvas off them," and he nodded and disappeared, the heavy material falling behind, closing me in.

Jimmy looked dreadful; eyes shut above the long nose, a thread of blood trickling from his mouth.

Jack went on groaning. I held up a bit of tent on my shoulders like Atlas, and presently my fellow tunneler returned, bringing two further helpers and a trestle table for a makeshift roof.

"What do we do?" the first tunneler said, irresolutely.

"Lift the pole," I said. "It may hurt Jack . . . but it may be killing Jimmy."

Everyone agreed. We slowly, carefully, took the

weight off the two injured men and laid the pole on the ground. Jack lapsed into silence. Jimmy lay still like a log. But they were both shallowly breathing: I felt their wrists again, one after the other, with relief.

We stood the trestle table over them and gingerly crawled on, and came to a girl lying on her back with one arm up over her face. Her skirt had been ripped away, and the flesh on the outer side of her left thigh had been torn open and was sagging away from the bone from hip to knee. I lifted the canvas away from her face and saw that she was to some extent conscious.

"Hello," I said inadequately.

She looked at me vaguely. "What's happening?" she said.

"There was an accident."

"Oh?" She seemed sleepy, but when I touched her cheek it was icy.

"We'll get another table," the first tunneler said.

"And a rug, if you can," I said. "She's far too cold."

He nodded and said "Shock," and they all went away, as it needed the three of them to drag the tables through.

I looked at the girl's leg. She was fairly plump, and inside the long widely gaping wound one could easily identify the cream-colored bubbly fat tissue and the dense red muscle, open like a jagged book to inspection. I'd never seen anything like it: and extraordinarily she wasn't bleeding a great deal, certainly not as much as one would have expected.

The body shutting down, I thought. The effects of trauma, as deadly as injury itself.

There was little I could do for her, but I did have a penknife in my pocket incorporating a tiny pair of scissors. With a sigh I pulled up my jersey and cut and tore one side from my shirt, stopping a few inches below the collar and cutting across so that from in front it looked as if I had a whole shirt under my sweater; and I thought that my doing that was ridiculous, but all the same I did it.

Torn into two wide strips the shirt front made reasonable bandages. I slid both pieces under her leg and pulled the flesh back into position, tying her leg together round the bone like trussing a joint of meat. I looked anxiously several times at the girl's face, but if she felt what I was doing it must have been remotely. She lay with her eyes open, her elbow bent over her head, and all she said at one point was "Where is this?" and later, "I don't understand."

"It's all right," I said.

"Oh. Is it? Good."

The tunnelers returned with a table and a traveling rug and also a towel.

"I thought we might wrap that wound together, with this," said the first tunneler, "but I see you've done it."

We put the towel round her leg anyway for extra protection, and then wrapped her in the rug and left her with the table holding up the roof and crawled apprehensively on; but we found no one else we could help. We found one of the waitresses, dead, lying over a tray of canapes, her smooth young face frosty white, and we found the protruding legs of another Arab; and somewhere underneath the horse trailer there were dreadful red shapes we couldn't reach even if we'd wanted to.

In accord the four of us retreated, hearing as we emerged into the blessed fresh air the bells and sirens of the official rescuers as they poured over the hill.

I walked along to where Flora was sitting on a kitchen chair that someone had brought out for her: there were women beside her offering comfort, but her eyes were dark and staring into far spaces, and she was shivering.

"Jack's all right," I said. "The pole knocked him out. One leg is maybe broken, but he's all right."

She looked at me blindly. I took my jacket off and wrapped it round her. "Flora, Jack's alive."

"All those people . . . all our guests . . ." Her voice was faint. "Are you sure about Jack?"

There was no real consolation. I said yes and hugged her, rocking her in my arms like a baby, and she put her head silently on my shoulder, still too stunned for tears.

Things ran after that into a blur, time passing at an enormous rate but not seeming to.

The police had brought a good deal of equipment and after a while had cut away the marquee from an area round the horse trailer, and had set up a head-high ring of screens to hide the shambles there.

Jack, fully conscious, lay on a stretcher with painkiller taking the worst off, protesting weakly that he couldn't go to hospital, he couldn't leave his guests, he couldn't leave his horses, he couldn't leave his wife to cope with everything on her own. Still objecting, he was lifted into an ambulance and, beside a still unconscious Jimmy, slowly driven away.

The guests drifted into the house or sat in their cars and wanted to go home: but there was an enormous fuss going on somewhere over telephone wires because of the death of the Sheik, and the uniformed police had been instructed not to let anyone leave until other investigators had arrived.

The fuss was nonsense, really, I thought. No one could possibly have told where the Sheik would stand in that tent. No one could possibly have aimed the horse trailer deliberately. The brakes had given way and it had rolled down the hill as selective in its victims as an earthquake.

The distraught young couple who had come in it and parked it were both in tears, and I heard the man saying helplessly, "But I left it in gear, with the brakes on . . . I know I did . . . I'm always careful . . . How could it have happened, how could it?" A uniformed policeman was questioning them, his manner less than sympathetic.

I wandered back to my van, to where I'd dumped the case of champagne. It had gone. So had the sixth and seventh cases from inside. So had the back-up gin and whisky from the front seat.

Disgusting, I thought; and shrugged. After carnage, thieves. Human grade-ten sour age-old behavior. It didn't seem to matter, except that I would rather have given it away than that.

Flora was indoors, lying down. Someone brought my coat back. It had blood on the sleeves, I noticed. Blood on my shirt cuffs, blood on my pale blue sweater. Blood, dry, on my hands.

A large crane on caterpillar tracks came grinding slowly over the hill and was maneuvered into position near the horse trailer; and in time, with chains, the heavy green vehicle was lifted a few inches into the air, and, after a pause, lifted higher and swung away onto a stretch of cleared grass.

The horse, still intermittently kicking, was finally released down a ramp and led away by one of Jack's lads, and, closing the trailer again, two policemen took up stances to deter the inquisitive.

There was a small dreadful group of people waiting, unmoving, staring silently at the merciful screens. They knew, they had to know, that those they sought were dead, yet they stood with dry eyes, their faces haggard with persisting hope. Five tons of metal had smashed into a close-packed crowd, yet they hoped.

One of them turned his head and saw me, and walked unsteadily toward me as if his feet were obeying different orders from his legs. He was dressed in jeans and a dirty T-shirt, and he neither looked nor sounded like one of the guests. More like one of Jack's lads on his Sunday off.

"You went in there, didn't you?" he said. "You're the guy who brings the drinks, aren't you? Someone said you went in . . ." He gestured vaguely toward the remains of the tent. "Did you see my wife? Was she in there? Is she?"

"I don't know." I shook my head.

"She was carrying things round. Drinks and such. She likes doing that . . . Seeing people."

One of the waitresses. He saw the movement in my face, and interpreted it unerringly.

"She's there, isn't she?" I didn't answer for a moment, and he said with pride and despair inextricably mixed, "She's pretty, you know. So pretty."

I nodded and swallowed. "She's pretty."

"Oh, no . . ." He let the grief out in a tearing wail. "Oh, no . . ."

I said helplessly, "My own wife died . . . not long ago. I do know . . . I'm so . . . so appallingly sorry."

He looked at me blankly and went back to the others to stare at the screens, and I felt useless and inadequate and swamped with pity.

The horse trailer had hit at shortly before one-thirty: it was after five before the new investigators would let anyone leave. Messages were eventually passed round that all could go, but that each car would have to stop at the gate for the passengers to give their names.

Tired, hungry, disheveled, many with bandaged cuts, the guests who had trooped so expectantly down the hill climbed slowly, silently up. Like refugees, I thought. An exodus. One could hear the engines starting in a chorus, and see the first movement of wheels.

A man touched my arm: the fellow tunneler. A tall man, going gray, with intelligent eyes.

"What's your name?" he asked.

"Tony Beach."

"Mine's McGregor. Gerard McGregor." He pronounced the G of Gerard soft, like a J, in a voice that was remotely but detectably Scots. "Glad to know you," he said. He held out his hand, which I shook.

We smiled slightly at each other, acknowledging our shared experience; then he turned away and put his arm round the shoulders of a good-looking woman at his side, and I watched them thread their way across to the gate through the roses. Pleasant man, I thought; and that was all.

I went into the house to see if there was anything I could do for Flora before I left, and found a shambles of a different sort. Every downstairs room, now empty, looked as if a full-scale army had camped there, which in a way it had. Every cup and saucer in the place must have been pressed into service, and every glass. The bottles on the drinks tray were all empty, open-necked. Ashtrays overflowed. Crumbs of food lay on plates. Cushions were squashed flat.

In the kitchen, locustlike, the lunchless guests had eaten everything to hand. Empty soup tins littered the worktops, eggshells lay in the sink, a chicken carcass, picked clean, jostled gutted packets of biscuits and crackers.

Everything edible had gone from the refrigerator and saucepans lay dirty on the stove.

There was a faint exclamation from the doorway, and I turned to see Flora there, her face heavy and gray above the creased red dress. I made a frustrated gesture at the mess, but she looked at it all without emotion.

"They had to eat," she said. "It's all right."

"I'll straighten it."

"No. Leave it. Tomorrow will do." She came into the room and sat wearily on one of the wooden chairs. "It simply doesn't matter. I told them to help themselves."

"They might have cleaned up afterward," I said.

"You should know the racing world better."

"Is there anything I can do, then?"

"No, nothing." She sighed deeply. "Do you know how many of them are dead?" Her voice itself was lifeless, drained by too much horror.

I shook my head. "The Sheik and one of his men. Larry Trent. And one of the waitresses, married, I think, to one of your lads. Some others. I don't know who."

"Not Janey," Flora said, distressed.

"I don't know."

"Young and pretty. Married Tom Wickens in the summer. Not her."

"I think so."

"Oh, dear." Flora grew if anything paler. "I don't care about the Sheik. It's a wicked thing to say, and we'll lose those horses, but I've known about him for hours and I simply don't care. But Janey . . ."

"I think you would help Tom Wickens," I said.

She stared at me for a moment, then rose to her feet and walked out into the garden, and through the window I saw her go over to the man in the T-shirt and put her arms round him. He turned and hugged her desperately in return, and I wondered fleetingly which of them felt the most released.

I chucked all the worst of the litter into the dustbin, but left the rest of it, as she'd said. Then I went out to the van to go home, and found a very young constable by my side as I opened the door.

"Excuse me, sir," he said, holding pen and notebook ready.

"Yes?"

"Name, sir?"

I gave it, and my address, which he wrote down.

"Where were you in the marquee, sir, when the incident occurred?"

The *incident*, ye gods.

"I wasn't in the marquee," I said. "I was here by the van."

"Oh!" His eyes widened slightly. "Then would you wait here, sir?" He hurried away and returned presently with a man out of uniform who walked slowly, with hunched shoulders.

"Mr. . . . er . . . Beach?" the newcomer said. A shortish man, not young. No aggression.

I nodded. "Yes."

"You were outside, here, is that right, when this happened?"

"Yes."

"And did you . . . by any chance . . . see the horse trailer on its way down the hill?" He had a quiet voice and pronounced every syllable carefully, as if talking to a lip-reader.

I nodded again. He said "Ah," with deep satisfaction, as if that were the answer he had long been seeking, and he smiled on me with favor and suggested we go into the house (where it would be warmer), accompanied by the constable, to take notes.

Among the litter in the drawing room we sat while I answered his questions.

His name was Wilson, he said. He was disappointed that I hadn't seen the horse trailer start down the hill, and he was disappointed that I hadn't seen anyone in or near it before it rolled.

"I'll tell you one thing for certain, though," I said. "It was not parked in any prearranged place. I watched quite a few of the cars arrive. I could see them coming over the hill, the horse trailer among them. They parked in a row just as they arrived, in the same order." I paused, then said, "The Sheik came to the stables a good hour before the other guests, which is why his Mercedes is first in the row. When he arrived he went to look round the yard, to see his horses. Then when several other guests came, he joined them in the marquee. No one maneuvered him into any particular place. I was in there when he came. He was walking with Jack Hawthorn and Jimmy—Jack's secretary. It was just chance he stood where he did. And he didn't of course stand totally still all the time. He must have moved several yards during the hour he was there."

I stopped. There was a small silence.

"Did you get all that, constable?" Wilson asked.

"Yes, sir."

"According to your van, you are a wine merchant, Mr. Beach? And you supplied the drinks for the party?"

"Yes," I agreed.

"And you are observant." His voice was dry, on the edge of dubious.

"Well . . ."

"Could you describe the position of any other of the guests so accurately, Mr. Beach?"

"Yes, some. But one tends to notice a Sheik. And I do notice where people are when I'm anywhere on business. The hosts, and so on, in case they want me."

He watched my face without comment, and presently asked, "What did the Sheik drink?"

"Orange juice with ice and mineral water."

"And his followers?"

"One had fizzy lemonade, the other two, Coca-Cola."

"Did you get that, constable?"

"Yes, sir."

Wilson stared for a while at his toecaps, then took a deep breath as if reaching a decision.

"If I described some clothes to you, Mr. Beach," he said, "could you tell me who was wearing them?"

"Uh, if I knew them."

"Navy pinstripe suit . . ."

I listened to the familiar description. "A man called Larry Trent," I said. "One of Jack Hawthorn's owners. He has . . . had . . . a restaurant; the Silver Moondance, near Reading."

"Got that, constable?"

"Yes, sir."

"And also, Mr. Beach, a blue tweed skirt and jacket with a light blue woolen shirt, pearls round the neck, and pearl earrings?"

I concentrated, trying to remember, and he said, "Greenish slightly hairy trousers, olive-colored sweater over a mustard shirt. Brown tie with mustard stripes."

"Oh . . ."

"You know him?"

"Both of them. Colonel and Mrs. Fulham. I was talking to them. I sell them wine."

"Sold, Mr. Beach," Wilson said regretfully. "That's all, then. I'm afraid all the others have been identified, poor people."

I swallowed. "How many?"

"Altogether? Eight dead, I'm afraid. It could have been worse. Much worse." He rose to his feet and perfunctorily shook my hand. "There may be political repercussions. I can't tell whether you may be needed for more answers. I will put in my report. Good day, Mr. Beach."

He went out in his slow hunched way, followed by the constable, and I walked after them into the garden.

It was growing dark, with lights coming on in places.

The square of screens had been taken down, and two ambulances were preparing to back through the gap the horse trailer had made in the hedge. A row of seven totally covered stretchers lay blackly on the horribly bloodstained matting, with the eighth set apart. In that, I suppose, lay the Sheik, as two living Arabs stood there, one at the head, one at the foot, still tenaciously guarding their prince.

In the dusk the small haggard group of people, all hope gone now, watched silently, with Flora among them, as ambulancemen lifted the seven quiet burdens one by one to bear them away; and I went slowly to my van and sat in it until they had done. Until only the Sheik remained, aloof in death as in life, awaiting a nobler hearse.

I switched on lights and engine and followed the two ambulances over the hill, and in depression drove down to the valley, to my house.

Dark house. Empty house.

I let myself in and went upstairs to change my clothes,

but when I reached the bedroom I just went and lay on the bed without switching on the lamps; and from exhaustion, from shock, from pity, from loneliness and from grief . . . I wept.

FOUR

MONDAY MORNINGS I ALWAYS SPENT IN THE SHOP RE-
stocking the shelves after the weekend's sales and drawing up lists of what I would need as replacements.
Monday afternoons I drove the van to the wholesalers
for spirits, soft drinks, cigarettes, sweets and potato
chips, putting some directly into the shop on my return,
and the reserves into the storeroom.

Mondays also I took stock of the cases of wines
stacked floor to shoulder level in the storeroom and telephoned shippers for more. Mondays the storeroom got
tidied by 5:00 P.M., checked and ready for the week
ahead. Mondays were always hard work.

That particular Monday morning, heavy with the dead
feeling of aftermath, I went drearily to work sliding Gor-
don's gin into neat green rows and slotting Liebfrau-
milch into its rack; tidying the Teacher's, counting the
Bell's, noticing we were out of Moulin-à-Vent. All of it
automatic, my mind still with the Hawthorns, wondering
how Jack was, and Jimmy, and how soon I should telephone to find out.

When I first had the shop I had just met Emma, and

we had run it together with a sense of adventure that had never quite left us. Nowadays I had more prosaic help in the shape of a Mrs. Palissey and also her nephew, Brian, who had willing enough muscles but couldn't read.

Mrs. Palissey, generous as to both bosom and gossip, arrived punctually at nine-thirty and told me wide-eyed that she'd seen on the morning television news about the Sheik being killed at the party.

"You were there, Mr. Beach, weren't you?" She was agog for gory details and waited expectantly, and with an inward sigh I satisfied at least some of her curiosity. Brian loomed over her, six feet tall, listening intently with his mouth open. Brian did most things with his mouth open, outward sign of inward retardation. Brian worked for me because his aunt had begged me piteously. "It's giving my sister a nervous breakdown having him mooning round the house all day every day, and he could lift things here for me when you're out, and he'll be no trouble, I'll see to that."

At first I feared I had simply transferred the imminent breakdown from the sister to myself, but when one got used to Brian's heavy breathing and permanent state of anxiety, one could count on the plus side that he would shift heavy cases of bottles all day without complaining, and didn't talk much.

"All those poor people!" exclaimed Mrs. Palissey, enjoying the drama. "That poor Mrs. Hawthorn. Such a nice lady, I always think."

"Yes," I said, agreeing: and life did, I supposed, have to go on. Automatic, pointless life, like asking Brian to go into the storeroom and fetch another case of White Satin.

He nodded without closing the mouth and went off

on the errand, returning unerringly with the right thing. He might not be able to read, but I had found he could recognize the general appearance of a bottle and label if I told him three or four times what it was, and he now knew all the regular items by sight. Mrs. Palissey said at least once a week that she was ever so proud of him, considering.

Mrs. Palissey and I remained by common consent on formal terms of Mrs. and Mr. More dignified, she said. By nature she liked to please and was in consequence a good saleswoman, making genuinely helpful suggestions to irresolute customers. "Don't know their own minds, do they, Mr. Beach?" she would say when they'd gone and I would agree truthfully that no, they often didn't. Mrs. Palissey and I tended to have the same conversations over and over and slightly too often.

She was honest in all major ways and unscrupulous in minor. She would never cheat me through the till, but Brian ate his way through a lot more potato chips and Mars bars than I gave him myself, and spare light bulbs and half-full jars of Nescafé tended to go home with Mrs. P. if she was short. Mrs. Palissey considered such things "perks" but would have regarded taking a bottle of sherry as stealing. I respected the distinction and was grateful for it, and paid her a little over the norm.

Whenever we were both there together, Mrs. Palissey served the shop customers while I sat in the tiny office within earshot taking orders over the telephone and doing the paperwork, ready to help her if necessary. Some customers, particularly men, came for the wine-chat as much as the product, and her true knowledge there was sweet, dry, cheap, expensive, popular.

It was a man's voice I could hear saying "Is Mr. Beach himself in?" and Mrs. Palissey's helpfully answering, "Yes, sir, he'll be right with you," and I rose and took the few steps into his sight.

The man there, dressed in a belted fawn raincoat, was perhaps a shade older than myself and had a noticeably authoritative manner. Without enormous surprise I watched him reach into an inner pocket for a badge of office and introduce himself as Detective Sergeant Ridger, Thames Valley police. He hoped I might be able to help him with his inquiries.

My mind did one of those quick half-guilty canters round everything possible I might have done wrong before I came to the more sensible conclusion that his presence must have something to do with the accident. And so it had, in a way, but not how I could have expected.

"Do you know a Mr. d'Alban, sir?" He consulted his memory. "The Honorable James d'Alban, sir?"

"Yes I do," I said. "He was injured yesterday at the Hawthorn party. He's not . . . dying?" I shied at the last minute away from "dead."

"No, sir, he's not. As far as I know he's in Battle Hospital with broken ribs, a pierced lung, and concussion."

Enough to be going on with, I thought ironically. Poor Jimmy.

Ridger had a short over-neat haircut, watchful brown eyes, a calculator-wristwatch bristling with knobs and no gift for public relations. He said impersonally, "Mr. d'Alban woke up to some extent in the ambulance taking him to hospital and began talking disjointedly but repeatedly about a man called Larry Trent and some unpronounceable whisky that wasn't what it ought to be, and you, sir, who would know for certain if you tasted it."

I just waited.

Ridger went on. "There was a uniformed policeman in the ambulance with Mr. d'Alban, and the constable reported the substance of those remarks to us, as he was aware we had reason to be interested in them. Mr. d'Alban, he said, was totally unable to answer any questions yesterday and indeed appeared not to know he was being addressed."

I wished vaguely that Ridger would talk more naturally, not as if reading from a notebook. Mrs. Palissey was listening hard though pretending not to, with Brian frowning uncomprehendingly beside her. Ridger glanced at them a shade uneasily and asked if we could talk somewhere in private.

I took him into the minuscule office, large enough only for a desk, two chairs and a heater: about five feet square. He sat in the visitors' chair without waste of time and said, "We've tried to interview Mr. d'Alban this morning but he is in intensive care and the doctor refused us entry." He shrugged. "They say to try tomorrow, but for our purposes tomorrow may be too late."

"And your purposes are . . . what?" I asked.

For the first time he seemed to look at me as a person, not just as an aid to inquiries: but I wasn't sure I liked the change because in his warming interest there was also a hint of manipulation. I had dealt in my time with dozens of salesmen seeking business, and Ridger's was the same sort of approach. He needed something from me that called for persuasion.

"Do you verify, sir, that Mr. d'Alban did talk to you about this whisky?"

"Yes, he did, yesterday morning."

Ridger looked almost smug with satisfaction.

"You may not know, sir," he said, "that Mr. Larry Trent died in yesterday's accident."

"Yes, I did know."

"Well, sir," he discreetly cleared his throat, lowering his voice for the sales pitch, softening the natural bossiness in his face. "To be frank, we've had other complaints about the Silver Moondance. On two former occasions investigations have been carried out there, both times by the Office of Weights and Measures, and by Customs and Excise. On neither occasion was any infringement found."

He paused.

"But this time?" I prompted obligingly.

"This time we think that in view of Mr. Trent's death, it might be possible to make another inspection this morning."

"Ah."

I wasn't sure that he liked the dry understanding in my voice, but he soldiered on. "We have reason to believe that in the past someone at the Silver Moondance, possibly Mr. Trent himself, has been tipped off in advance that the investigations were in hand. So this time my superiors in the C.I.D. would like to make some preliminary inquiries of our own, assisted, if you are agreeable, by yourself, as an impartial expert."

"Um," I said, doubtfully, "this morning, did you say?"

"Now, sir, if you would be so good."

"This very minute?"

"We think, sir, the quicker the better."

"You must surely have your own experts," I said.

It appeared . . . er . . . that there was no official expert available at such short notice, and that as time was all-important . . . would I go?

I could see no real reason why not to, so I said briefly "All right," and told Mrs. Palissey I'd be back as soon as I could. Ridger drove us in his car, and I wondered on the way just how much of an expert the delirious Jimmy had made me out to be, and whether I would be of any use at all, when it came to the point.

The Silver Moondance, along the valley from the small Thames-side town where I had my shop, had originally been a sprawlingly ugly house built on the highest part of a field sloping up from the river. It had over the years metamorphosed successively into school, nursing home, and general boarding house, adding inappropriate wings at every change. Its most recent transformation had been also the most radical, so that little could now be seen of the original shiny yellow-gray bricks for glossier expanses of plate glass. At night from the river the place looked like Blackpool fully illuminated, and even by day, from the road, one could see "Silver Moondance" blinking on and off in white letters over the doorway.

"Do they know you here, sir?" Ridger belatedly asked as we turned into the drive.

I shook my head. "Shouldn't think so. The last time I came here it was the Riverland Guest Home, full of old retired people. I used to deliver their drinks."

Dears, they had been, I remembered nostalgically, and great topers, on the whole, taking joy in their liquid pleasures.

Ridger grunted without much interest and parked on an acre or two of unpopulated tarmac. "They should just be open," he said with satisfaction, locking the car doors. "Ready, sir?"

"Yes," I said. "And, Sergeant ... um ... let me do the talking."

"But ..."

"Best not to alarm them," I said, persuasively, "if

you don't want them pouring the Laphroaig down the sink.''

"The what?''

"What we're looking for.''

"Oh.'' He thought. "Very well.''

I said "Fine'' without emphasis and we walked through the flashing portal into the ritzy plush of the entrance hall.

There were lights on everywhere, but no one in sight. A reception desk; unattended. A flat air of nothing happening and nothing expected.

Ridger and I walked toward a wrought iron and drift-wood sign announcing "Silver Moondance Saloon,'' and pushed through Western-style swing doors into the room beyond. It was red, black and silver, very large and uninhabited. There were many tables, each with four bent-wood chairs set neatly round, and an orthodox bar at one end, open for business.

No bartender.

Ridger walked purposefully across and rapped on the counter, I following him more slowly.

No one came. Ridger rapped again, louder and longer, and was presently rewarded by a youngish fair-haired man coming through another swing door at the back of the bar area, sweating visibly and struggling into a white jacket.

"Give us a chance,'' he said crossly. "We've only been open five minutes.'' He wiped his damp forehead with his fingers and buttoned his coat. "What can I get you?''

"Is the restaurant open?'' I said.

"What? Not yet. They don't start serving before twelve.''

"And the wine waiter, would he be here?''

The barman looked at the clock and shook his head.

"What do you want him for? Whatever drinks you want, I'll get them."

"The wine list," I said humbly. "Could I see it?"

He shrugged, reached under the bar, and produced a padded crimson folder. "Help yourself," he said, handing it across.

He was not actively rude, I thought, just thrown off the rails by the boss's demise. Practiced, a touch effeminate, with unfortunate pimples and a silver identification bracelet inscribed with Tom. I could feel Ridger beginning to bristle beside me, so I said mildly, "Could I have a scotch, please?"

The barman gave a half-exasperated glance at the wine list in my hand but turned away and thrust a regulation glass against the optic measure on a standard-sized bottle of Bell's.

"Something for you?" I said to Ridger.

"Tomato juice. Without Worcester sauce."

The barman put my whisky on the counter. "Anything in yours?" he asked.

"No, thanks."

I paid for the two drinks and we went to sit at one of the tables farthest from the bar.

"This isn't what we came for," Ridger said protestingly.

"First things first," I said, smelling the whisky. "Start at the bottom and work up. Good wine-tasting tactics."

"But . . . ." He thought better of it, and shrugged. "All right, then. Your way. But don't take too long."

I sucked a very small amount of whisky into my mouth and let it wander over my tongue. One can't judge whisky with the taste buds at the tip, up by the front teeth, but only along the sides of the tongue and at the back, and I let everything that was there in the way of flavor develop to the full before I swallowed, and then waited a while for aftertaste.

"Well?" said Ridger. "What now?"

"For a start," I said. "This isn't Bell's."

Ridger looked unexpectedly startled. "Are you sure?"

"Do you know anything about whisky?" I asked.

"No. I'm a beer man, myself. Drink the odd whisky and ginger now and then, that's all."

"Do you want to know?" I flicked a finger at the glass. "I mean, shall I explain?"

"Will it take long?"

"No."

"Go on, then."

"Scotch whisky is made of barley," I said. "You can malt barley, as is done for beer. You let the grains start to grow, to form shoots about an inch or two long. Then for whisky you smoke the shoots, which are called malts, over burning peat, until they pick up the peat and smoke flavors and are crisp. Then you make a mash of the malts with water and let it ferment, then you distill it and put the distillation in wooden casks to age for several years, and that's pure malt whisky, full of overtones of various tastes."

"Right," Ridger said, nodding, his crisp haircut clearly concentrating.

"It's much cheaper," I said, "to make the barley into a mash without going through the malting and smoking stages, and much quicker because the aging process is years shorter, and that sort of whisky is called grain whisky and is a great deal plainer on the tongue."

"O.K.," he said, "go on."

"Good standard scotches like Bell's are a mixture of

malt and grain whiskies. The more malt, the more varied and subtle the flavor. This in this glass has very little or no malt, which doesn't matter at all if you want to mix it with ginger, because you'd kill the malt flavor anyway.''

Ridger looked round the empty room. ''With this place full, with smoke and perfume and ginger ale, who's to know the difference?''

''It would take a brave man,'' I said, smiling.

''What next, then?''

''We might hide the scotch in your tomato juice.'' I poured the one into the other, to his horror. ''I can't drink it,'' I explained. ''Do you want a drunk expert? No good at all.''

''I suppose not,'' he said, weakly for him, and I went over to the bar and asked the barman if he had any malts.

''Sure,'' he said, waving a hand along a row of bottles. ''Glenfiddich, down at the other end there.''

''Mm,'' I said doubtfully. ''Do you have any Laphroaig?''

''La-what?''

''Laphroaig. A friend of mine had some here. He said it was great. He said as I liked malts I should definitely try it.''

The barman looked at his stock, but shook his head.

''Perhaps it's in the restaurant,'' I said. ''I think he did mention drinking it after dinner. Perhaps it's on the drinks trolley.'' I pulled out my wallet and opened it expectantly, and with a considering glance at the notes in sight the barman decided to go on the errand. He returned quite soon with a genuine Laphroaig bottle and charged me outrageously for a nip, which I paid without demur, giving him a tip on top.

I carried the glass to the far table to join Ridger.

"What do you do now?" I asked. "Pray?"

"Taste it," he said tersely.

I smelled it first, however, and tasted it slowly as before, Ridger sitting forward tensely in his chair.

"Well?" he demanded.

"It's not Laphroaig."

"Are you certain?"

"Absolutely positive. Laphroaig is as smoky as you can get. Pure malt. There's almost no malt at all in what I've just tasted. It's the same whisky as before."

"Thanks very much, Mr. Beach," he said with deep satisfaction. "That's great."

He stood up, walked over to the bar and asked to see the bottle from which his friend had just drunk. The bartender obligingly pushed it across the counter, and Ridger picked it up. Then with his other hand he pulled out his identification, and the barman, angry, started shouting.

Ridger proved to have a radio inside his jacket. He spoke to some unseen headquarters, received a tinny reply, and told the bartender the police would be prohibiting the sale of all alcohol at the Silver Moondance for that day at least, while tests were made on the stock.

"You're barmy," the bartender yelled, and to me, viciously, "Creep."

His loud voice brought colleagues in the shape of a worried man in a dark suit who looked junior and ineffective, and a girl in a short pert waitress uniform, long fawn legs below a scarlet tunic, scarlet headband over her hair.

Ridger took stock of the opposition and found himself very much in charge. The ineffective junior announced himself to be the assistant manager, which drew looks of scorn and amazement from the waitress and the barman. Assistant to the assistant, I rather gathered. Ridger explained forcibly again that no liquor was to be sold pending investigations, and all three of them said they knew nothing about anything, and we would have to talk to . . . er . . . talk to . . .

"The management?" I suggested.

They nodded dumbly.

"Let's do that," I said. "Where's the manager?"

The assistant to the assistant manager finally said that the manager was on holiday and the assistant manager was ill. Head office were sending someone to take over as soon as possible.

"Head office?" I said. "Didn't Larry Trent own the place?"

"Er . . ." said the assistant unhappily. "I really don't know. Mr. Trent never said he didn't, I mean, I thought he did. But when I got here this morning the telephone was ringing, and it was head office. That's what he said, anyway. He wanted to speak to the manager, and when I explained he said he would send someone along straightaway."

"Who ran things last night?" Ridger demanded.

"What? Oh, we're closed, Sunday nights."

"And yesterday lunchtime?"

"The assistant manager was here, but he'd got flu. He went home to bed as soon as we closed. And of course Mr. Trent had been here until after opening time, seeing that everything was all right before he went to Mr. Hawthorn's party."

All three looked demoralized but at the same time slightly defiant, seeing the policeman as their natural enemy. Relations scarcely improved when Ridger's reinforcements rolled up: two uniformed constables bringing tape and labels for sealing all the bottles.

I diffidently suggested to Ridger that he should extend his suspicions to the wines.

"Wines?" he frowned. "Yes, if you like, but we've got enough with the spirits."

"All the same," I murmured, and Ridger told the assistant to show me where they kept the wine, and to help me and one of his constables bring any bottles I wanted into the bar. The assistant, deciding that helpfulness would establish his driven-snow innocence, put no obstacles in my way, and in due course, and after consulting the wine list, the assistant, the constable and I returned to the bar carrying two large baskets full of bottles.

The spirits bottles all having been sealed, there was at our return a lull of activity in the Silver Moondance Saloon. I unloaded the bottles onto two tables, six white wine on one, six red on another, and from my jacket pocket produced my favorite corkscrew.

"Hey," the barman protested. "You can't do that."

"Every bottle I open will be paid for," I said, matter-of-factly. "And what's it to you?"

The barman shrugged. "Give me twelve glasses," I said, "and one of those pewter tankards," and he did. I opened the six bottles of varying white wines and under the interested gaze of six pairs of eyes poured a little of the first into a glass. Niersteiner, it said on the label: and Niersteiner it was. I spat the tasted mouthful into the pewter tankard, to disgusted reaction from the audience.

"Do you want him to get drunk?" Ridger demanded, belatedly understanding. "The evidence of a drunk taster wouldn't be acceptable."

I tasted the second white. Chablis; as it should have been.

The third was similarly O.K., a Pouilly Fuissé.

By the time I'd finished the sixth, a Sauternes, the barman had greatly relaxed.

"Nothing wrong with them?" Ridger asked, not worried.

"Nothing," I agreed, stuffing the corks back. "I'll try the reds."

The reds were a St. Emilion, a St. Estèphe, a Mâcon, a Valpolicella, a Volnay and a Nuits St. Georges, all dated 1979. I smelled and tasted each one carefully, spitting and waiting a few moments in between sips so that each wine should be fresh on the tongue, and by the time I'd finished everyone else was restive.

"Well," Ridger demanded, "are they all right?"

"They're quite pleasant," I said, "but they're all the same."

"What do you mean?"

"I mean," I said, "that notwithstanding all those pretty labels, the wine in all of these bottles is none of them. It's a blend. Mostly Italian, I would say, mixed with some French and possibly Yugoslav, but it could be anything."

"You don't know what you're talking about," the barman said impatiently. "We have people every day saying how good the wines are."

"Mm," I said neutrally. "Perhaps you do."

"Are you positive?" Ridger asked me. "They're all the same?"

"Yes."

He nodded as if that settled it and instructed the constables to seal and label the six reds with the date, time and place of confiscation. Then he told the barman to find two boxes to hold all the labeled bottles, which brought a toss of the head, a mulish petulance and a slow and grudging compliance.

I kept my word and paid for all the wine, the only action of mine that pleased the barman from first to last. I got him to itemize every bottle on a Silver Moondance billhead and sign it "Received in full," and then I paid him by credit card, tucking away the receipts.

Ridger seemed to think paying was unnecessary, but then shrugged, and he and the constable began putting the wine into one of the boxes and the whiskies into the other; and into this sullenly orderly scene erupted the man from head office.

FIVE

THE MAN FROM HEAD OFFICE WAS NOT AT FIRST SIGHT intimidating. Short, fortyish, dark-haired, of medium build and wearing glasses, he walked inquiringly into the saloon in a gray worsted business suit as if not sure of the way.

Ridger, taking him, as I did, for a customer, raised his voice and said, "The bar is closed, sir."

The man took no notice but advanced more purposefully until he stood near enough to see the bottles in the boxes. He frowned at them and glanced at the policemen, and I could see in him a distinct change of mental gear. A tightening of muscles; a sharpening of attention: cruise to overdrive in three seconds.

"I'm a police officer," said Ridger firmly, producing his authorization. "The bar is closed until further notice."

"Is it indeed?" said the newcomer ominously. "Be so good as to explain why." The first impression was wrong, I thought. This man could intimidate quite easily.

Ridger blinked. "It's a police matter," he said. "It's no concern of yours."

"Every concern," said the man shortly. "I've come from head office to take over. So just what exactly is going on?" His voice had the edge of one not simply used to command but used to instant action when he spoke. His accent, so far as he had one, was straight-forward business-English, devoid of both regional vowels and swallowed consonants, but also without timbre. Good plain grain, I thought; not malt.

"Your name, sir?" asked Ridger stolidly, ignoring the sharp tone as if he hadn't heard it, which I was sure he had.

The man from head office looked him up and down, assessing the altogether statement of brushed hair, belted raincoat, polished shoes. Ridger reacted to that aggressively, his spine stiffening, the desire to be the dominator growing unmistakably in the set of his jaw. Interesting, I thought.

The man from head office allowed the pause to lengthen until it was clear to everyone that he was giving his name as a result of thought, not out of obedience to Ridger.

"My name is Paul Young," he said finally, with weight. "I represent the company of which this restaurant is a subsidiary. And now, what exactly is going on here?"

Ridger's manner remained combative as he began announcing in his notebook terminology that the Silver Moondance would be prosecuted for contraventions of the Sale of Goods Act.

Paul Young from head office interrupted brusquely. "Cut the jargon and be precise."

Ridger glared at him. Paul Young grew impatient. Neither would visibly defer to the other, but Ridger did in the end explain what he was removing in the boxes.

Paul Young listened with fast growing anger, but this time not aiming it at Ridger himself. He turned his glare instead on the barman (who did his best to shelter behind his pimples) and thunderously demanded to know who was responsible for selling substitutions. From the barman, the waitress and the assistant assistant in turn he got weak disclaiming shakes of the head and none of the defiance they had shown to Ridger.

"And who are you?" he inquired rudely, giving me the up and down inspection. "Another policeman?"

"A customer," I said mildly.

Seeing nothing in me to detain him he returned his forceful attention to Ridger, assuring him authoritatively that head office had had no knowledge of the substitutions and that the fraud must have originated right here in this building. The police could be assured that head office would discover the guilty person and prosecute him themselves, insuring that nothing of this sort could happen again.

It was perfectly clear to Ridger as to everyone else present that Paul Young was in fact badly jolted and surprised by the existence of the fraud, but Ridger with smothered satisfaction said that the outcome would be for the police and the courts to decide, and that meanwhile Mr. Young could give him the address and telephone number of head office, for future reference.

I watched Paul Young while he wrote the required information onto another billhead provided by the barman and wondered vaguely why he didn't carry business cards to save himself that sort of bother. He had large hands, I noticed, full-fleshed, with pale skin, and as he bent his head over the paper I saw the discreet pink hearing aid tucked behind his right ear, below the frame of his glasses. One could get hearing aids built in with the earpieces of eyeglass frames, I thought, and wondered why he didn't.

What a mess, I thought, for a parent company to walk into unawares. And who, I wondered, had been on the fiddle—the manager, the wine waiter, or Larry Trent himself? Not that I wondered at all deeply. The culprit's identity was to me less interesting than the crime, and the crime itself was hardly unique.

The six corks from the bottles of red were lying where I'd left them on the small table, the constables having sealed the open necks with wide wrappings of sticky tape instead of trying to ram back the original plugs, and I picked the corks up almost absentmindedly and put them in my pocket, tidy-minded out of habit.

Paul Young straightened from his writing and handed the sheet of paper to the assistant assistant, who handed it to me, who passed it on to Ridger, who glanced at it, folded it, and tucked it into some inner pocket below the raincoat.

"And now, sir," he said, "close the bar."

The barman looked to Paul Young for instructions and got a shrug and an unwilling nod, and presently an ornamental grille unrolled from ceiling to bar-top, imprisoning the barman in his cage. He clicked a few locks into place and went out through the rear door, not returning to the saloon.

Ridger and Paul Young argued for a while about how soon the Silver Moondance could resume full business, each still covertly maneuvering for domination. I reckoned it came out about quits, because they finally backed off from each other inconclusively, both still in aggressive postures, more snarl than teeth.

Ridger removed his constables, the boxes and myself to the carpark leaving Paul Young to deal with his helpless helpers, and the last I saw of the man from head office, in a backward glance as I went through the Western swing doors, was the businesslike glasses turning to survey his large empty tabled discontinued asset in black and scarlet, the colors of roulette.

RIDGER MUTTERED UNDER HIS BREATH SEVERAL TIMES AS he drove me back to my shop and broke out into plain exasperation when I asked him for a receipt for the case of wines, which he was transporting in the trunk.

"Those twelve bottles do belong to me," I pointed out. "I paid for them, and I want them back. You said yourself that you'd got enough with the whisky to prosecute. The wines were my own idea."

He grudgingly admitted it and gave me a receipt.

"Where do I find you?" I asked.

He told me the address of his station and without the least gratitude for the help he had solicited, drove brusquely away. Between him and Paul Young, I thought, definitely not much to choose.

In the shop Mrs. Palissey had had a veritable barrage of customers, as sometimes happened on Monday mornings, and was showing signs of wear.

"Go to lunch," I said, although it was early, and with gratitude she put on her coat, took Brian in tow, and departed to the local café for fish and chips and a gossip with her constant friend, the traffic warden.

The customers kept coming and I served them with automatic ease, smiling, giving pleasure to the pleasure-seekers. For years, with Emma, I had positively enjoyed the selling, finding my own satisfaction in giving it to others. Without her the warmth I had felt had grown shallow, so that now I dispensed only a surface sympathy, nodding and smiling and hardly listening, hearing only sometimes, not always, the unsaid things in the shopping voices. The power I'd once had had drained away, and I didn't really care.

During a short lull I wrote the list for the wholesaler, planning to go as soon as Mrs. Palissey returned, and noticed that Brian, unasked by me, had swept and straightened the storeroom. The telephone rang three times with good substantial orders and the till, when consulted, showed a healthy profit margin on the morning's trading. Ironic, the whole thing.

Two customers came in together, and I served the woman first, a middle-aged frightened lady who called every day for a bottle of the cheapest gin, tucking it away secretively in a large handbag while taking furtive glances out of the window for passing neighbors. Why didn't she buy it by the case, I'd once long ago asked her teasingly, as it was cheaper by the case, but she'd been alarmed and said no, she enjoyed the walk; and the loneliness had looked out of her eyes along with the fear of being called alcoholic, which she wasn't quite, and I'd felt remorse for being heartless, because I'd known perfectly well why she bought one bottle at a time.

"Nice day, Mr. Beach," she said breathlessly, her glance darting to the street.

"Not too bad, Mrs. Chance."

She gave me the exact money, coins warmed by her palm, notes carefully counted, watching nervously while I wrapped her comfort in tissue.

"Thank you, Mrs. Chance."

She nodded dumbly, gave me a half smile, pushed the bottle into her handbag and departed, pausing at the door to reconnoiter. I put the money in the till and looked inquiringly at the man waiting patiently to be served next, and found myself face to face with no customer but the investigator Wilson from the day before.

"Mr. Beach," he said.

"Mr. Wilson."

Externally he wore exactly the same clothes, as if he had never been to bed or showered and shaved, which he had. He looked rested and clean, and moved comfortably in his slow hunchbacked fashion with the knowing eyes and the noncommunicating face.

"Do you always know what your customers want without asking them?" he said.

"Quite often," I nodded, "but usually I wait for them to say."

"More polite?"

"Infinitely."

He paused. "I came to ask you one or two questions. Is there anywhere we can talk?"

"Just talk," I said apologetically. "Would you like a chair?"

"Are you alone here?"

"Yes."

I fetched the spare chair for him from the office and put it by the counter, and had no sooner done so than three people came in for Cinzano, beer and sherry. Wilson waited through the sales without doing much more than blink, and when the door closed for the third time he stirred without impatience and said, "Yesterday, during the party, were you at any time talking to the Sheik?"

I smiled involuntarily. "No, I wasn't."

"Why does the idea amuse you?"

"Well, the Sheik considers all this . . ." I waved a hand around the bottle-lined walls, ". . . as being positively sinful. Forbidden. Pernicious. Much as we regard cocaine. To him I'm a pusher. In his own country I'd

be in jail, or worse. I wouldn't have introduced myself
to him. Not unless I wanted to invite contempt.''

''I see,'' he said, almost nodding, contemplating the
Islamic view. Then he slightly pursed his lips, approaching, I guessed, the question he had really come to ask.

''Think back,'' he said, ''to when you were outside
the tent, when the horse trailer rolled.''

''Yes.''

''Why were you out there?''

I told him about fetching more champagne.

''And when you went out, the horse trailer was already rolling?''

''No,'' I said. ''When I went out I glanced up at the
cars and everything was all right. I remember noting that
no one had yet left and hoped I'd taken enough champagne to last out.''

''Was there anyone near the trailer?''

''No.''

''You're certain?''

''Yes. No one that I could see.''

''You've consulted your memory . . . before this moment?''

I half smiled. ''Yes. You might say so.''

He sighed. ''Did you see anyone at all anywhere near
any of the cars?''

''No. Except . . . only a child with a dog.''

''Child?''

''They weren't near the trailer. Nearer the Sheik's
Mercedes, really.''

''Can you describe the child?''

''Well . . .'' I frowned. ''A boy.''

''Clothes?''

I looked away from him, gazing vacantly at the racks

of wine, thinking back. "Dark trousers . . . perhaps jeans . . . and a dark blue sweater."

"Hair?"

"Um . . . light brown, I suppose. Not blond, not black."

"Age?"

I pondered, looking again at the patient questioner. "Young. Small. Four, I should think."

"Why are you so definite?"

"I'm not. His head was still big in proportion to his body."

Wilson's eyes glimmered deeply. "What sort of dog?" he said.

I stared vaguely once more into the distance, seeing the child on the hill. "A whippet," I said.

"On a leash?"

"No, running and turning back toward the boy."

"What sort of shoes did the boy have?"

"For God's sake," I said. "I only saw him for a couple of seconds."

His mouth twitched. He looked down at his hands and then up again. "No one else?"

"No."

"How about the Sheik's chauffeur?"

I shook my head. "He might have been sitting in the car, but one couldn't tell. It had tinted windows, as you saw."

He stirred and said thank you and began to get to his feet.

"Incidentally," I said. "Someone stole three cases of champagne and some other bottles out of my van sometime after the accident. I need to report the theft to the police before I claim insurance. May I report it to you?"

He gave me a small smile. "I will note that you have reported it."

"Thanks."

He held his hand out to me over the counter and I shook it. "It's I who thank you, Mr. Beach," he said.

"I haven't been much help."

He smiled his small uncommunicative smile, nodded benignly, and went away.

Good grief, I thought inconsequentially, watching his hunched departing back, one hundred and fifty goblets were lying in splinters in the Hawthorns' back garden, and it was all very well talking of insurance, I was due to supply those very glasses to the Thames Ladies Christmas Charities fund-raising wine and cheese party on the following day, Tuesday, which I had forgotten clean about.

Tentatively I rang the Hawthorns' number, not wanting to overload Flora but to ask all the same how many glasses if any remained intact, and I got not Flora but an answering machine with Jimmy's voice, loud, healthy and languid, inviting me to leave my name, number and message.

I complied, wondering how Jimmy was doing in intensive care, and when Mrs. Palissey came back I took Brian with me to the wholesalers, where he helped me shift umpteen cases from the stores onto trolleys, and from those trolleys to other trolleys at the pay desk, for rolling out to the van, and from the second trolleys into the van, and, back at the shop, from the van into the storeroom. My own muscles, after roughly twelve years of such exercise, would have rivaled a fork-lift truck, and Brian's, too, were coming along nicely. He grinned while he worked. He enjoyed lifting the cases. Two-at-a-time he had begun to scorn; he liked me to pile him with three.

Brian never talked much, which I appreciated. He sat

placidly beside me in the van on the way back, lips apart as usual, and I wondered what went on in that big vacant head, and how much one could teach him if one tried. He'd learned quite a lot in the three or so months he'd been with me, I reflected. He was brilliantly useful compared with day one.

He unloaded the van by himself when we returned and put everything in the right places in the storeroom, which I had arranged with much more method since his arrival. Mrs. Palissey had taken two more orders on the telephone, and I spent some time making up those and the ones from earlier in the day, collecting all the various items together into boxes for Brian to carry out to the van. Being a wine merchant, I often thought, was not a gentle artistic occupation, but thoroughly, backbreakingly physical.

The telephone rang yet again while I was sitting in the office writing the bills to go out with the orders and I stretched out one hand for the receiver with my eyes on my work.

"Tony?" a woman's voice said tentatively. "It's Flora."

"Dear Flora," I said. "How are you? How's Jack? How's everything?"

"Oh . . ." She seemed tired beyond bearing. "Everything's so awful. I know I shouldn't say that, but . . . oh, dear."

"I'll come and fetch the glasses," I said, hearing the appeal she hadn't uttered. "I'll come practically at once."

"There . . . there aren't many left whole . . . but yes, do come."

"Half an hour," I said.

She said "Thank you" faintly and disconnected.

I looked at my watch. Four-thirty. Most often at about that time on Mondays Mrs. Palissey and Brian set off in the van to do any deliveries that lay roughly on their way home, finishing the round the following morning. Mrs. Palissey's ability to drive had been the chief reason I'd originally hired her, and she on her part had been pleased to be given the use of the shop's second-string wheels, an elderly capacious Rover estate car. We swapped the two vehicles around as required, so I said I would do the deliveries that day, if she would stay until five to close the shop, and go home again in the car.

"By all means, Mr. Beach." She was graciously obliging. "And I'll be here at nine-thirty, then, in the morning."

I nodded my thanks and took the bills, the orders, van and myself off up the hill to Jack Hawthorn's stable, where not a great deal had changed since the day before.

I saw, as I came over the hill, that the great green horse trailer still stood on the lawn, with, beyond it, the heaped canvas remains of the marquee. The Sheik had gone, and his bodyguards. The mute bloodstained expanse of fawn matting was scattered with trestle tables and sections of tent pole, and glittering here and there in the rays of late afternoon sunshine lay a million pieces of glass.

I parked as before outside the kitchen entrance and locked the van with a sigh. Flora came slowly out of the house to greet me, dressed in a gray skirt and a green cardigan, dark smudges under exhausted eyes.

I gave her a small hug and a kiss on the cheek. We had never before been on that sort of terms, but disasters could work wonders in that area.

"How's Jack?" I said.

"They've just now set his leg. Pinned it, they say. He's still unconscious, but I saw him this morning . . . before." Her voice was quavery, as it had been on the telephone. "He was very down. So depressed. It made me so miserable." The last word came out on a gasp as her face crumpled into tears. "Oh, dear . . . Oh, dear . . ."

I put my arm round her shaking shoulders. "Don't worry," I said. "He'll be all right. Truly."

She nodded mutely, sniffing and fumbling in a pocket for a handkerchief, and after a while, through gulps, said, "He's alive, and I should be grateful for that, and they say he'll be home quite soon. It's just . . . everything . . . everything . . ."

I nodded. "Just too much."

She nodded also and dried her eyes with a reemergence of spirit, and I asked whether any of her children might not come to help her through this patch.

"They're all so busy, I told them not to. And Jack, you know, he's jealous of them really, he wouldn't want them here when he's away, though I shouldn't say that, only I do seem to tell you things, Tony dear, and I don't know why."

"Like telling the wallpaper," I said.

She smiled very faintly, a considerable advance.

"How's Jimmy?" I asked.

"I didn't see him. He's conscious, they say, and no worse. I don't know what we'll do if he isn't well soon. He runs everything, you know, and without them both, I feel so lost. I can't help it."

"Anything I can do?" I said.

"Oh, yes," she said instantly. "I was hoping . . . I mean, when you said you'd come . . . Have you got time?"

"For what?" I asked.

"Um . . . Tony dear, I don't know how much I can ask of you, but would you . . . could you possibly . . . walk round the yard with me?"

"Well, of course," I said, surprised. "If you want."

"It's evening stables," she explained in a rush. "Jack was so insistent I walked round. He wants me to tell him how everything is, because we've a new head lad, he came only last week, and Jack says he's not sure of him in spite of his references, and he made me promise I'd walk round. And he knows, he really does, that I don't know enough about horses, but he wanted me to promise . . . and he was so depressed that I did."

"No problem at all," I said. "We'll walk round together, and we'll both listen, and afterward we'll make notes for you to relay to Jack."

She sighed with relief and looked at her watch. "It's time now, I should think."

"O.K.," I said, and we walked round the house to the stables and to the sixty or so equine inmates.

In Jack's yard there were two big old quadrangles, built of wood mostly, with a preponderance of white paint. Some of the many doors stood wide open with lads carrying sacks and buckets in and out, and some were half closed with horses' heads looking interestedly over the tops.

"We'd better do the colts' yard first," Flora said, "and the fillies' yard after, like Jack does, don't you think?"

"Absolutely," I agreed.

I knew about horses to the extent that I'd been brought up with them, as much after my father's death as before. My mother, wholly dedicated, seldom talked of much else. She had in her time ridden in point-to-point races and also adored to go hunting, which filled her life whenever my father was away on duty, and his as well when he was at home and not that minute racing. I had seen day after day the glowing enjoyment in their faces and had tried hard to feel it myself, but whatever enthusiasm I'd shown had been counterfeit, for their sakes. Galloping after hounds across muddy November fields I had thought chiefly of how soon one could decently go home, and the only part of the ritual I had actually enjoyed had been the cleaning and feeding of the horses afterward. Those great creatures, tired and dirty, were so uncritical. They never told one to keep one's heels down, one's elbows in, one's head up, one's spine straight. They didn't expect one to be impossibly brave and leap the largest fences. They didn't mind if one sneaked through gates instead. Closed into a box with a horse, humming while I brushed off dried mud and sweat, I'd felt a sort of dumb complete communion, and been happy.

After my father died my mother had hunted on with unfaltering zeal and had for the past ten years been joint master of the local hounds, to her everlasting fulfillment. It had been a relief to her, I often thought, when I had finally left home.

Jack Hawthorn's lads were halfway through the late afternoon program of mucking out, feeding and watering, a process known throughout the racing world as "evening stables." It was the custom for the trainer to walk round, usually with the head lad, stopping at every box to inspect the racer within, feeling its legs for heat (bad sign) and looking for a bright eye (good).

Jack's new head lad had greeted Flora's appearance with an exaggerated obsequiousness that I found distasteful and that seemed also to make Flora even less sure of herself. She introduced him as Howard, and told him Mr. Beach would be accompanying her on the rounds.

Howard extending the Uriah Heep manner to myself, we set off on what was clearly the normal pattern, and I listened attentively for Flora's sake to every Howard opinion.

Very little, it seemed to me, could have been different from the morning before, when Jack himself had been there. One horse had trodden on a stone out at exercise and was slightly footsore. Another had eaten only half of his midday feed. A third had rubbed skin off a hock, which would need watching.

Flora said "I see" and "I'll tell Mr. Hawthorn" at regular intervals and Howard ingratiatingly said that Flora could safely leave everything to him, Howard, until Mr. Hawthorn's return.

We came in turn to the Sheik's horses, still in residence, and also to Larry Trent's, bursting with health. They had been prolific winners all year, it seemed. Both the Sheik and Larry Trent had been excellent judges of potential, and were lucky as well.

"We'll be losing all of these horses, I suppose," Flora sighed. "Jack says it will be a heavy financial loss for us."

"What will happen to them?" I asked.

"Oh, I expect the Sheik's will be sold. I don't know. I don't know if he has any family. And Larry Trent's five, of course, will go back to their owners."

I raised my eyebrows slightly but because of Howard's unctuous presence said no more, and it wasn't until Flora and I were at length walking back toward my van that I asked her what she meant.

"Larry Trent's horses?" she repeated. "They weren't his own property. He leased them."

"Paid rent for them?" I asked.

"My dear, no. A lease is only an agreement. Say someone owns a horse but can't really afford the training fees, and someone else wants to have a horse racing in his name and can afford the training fees but not the cost of the horse itself, then those two people make an agreement, all signed and registered, of course. The usual terms are that when the horse earns any prize money it's divided fifty-fifty between the two parties. It's done quite often, you know."

"No, I didn't know," I said humbly.

"Oh, yes. Larry Trent always did it. He was pretty shrewd at it. He would lease a horse for a year, say, and if it turned out all right he might lease it for another year, but if it won nothing, he'd try another. You can lease a horse for as long as you like, as long as you both agree, for a year or a season or three months . . . whatever you want."

I found it interesting and asked, "How are the leases fixed up?"

"Jack has the forms."

"No, I meant, how does anyone know who has a horse they will lease but not sell?"

"Word of mouth," she said vaguely. "People just say. Sometimes they advertise. And sometimes one of our owners will ask Jack to find someone to lease their horse so they don't have to pay the training bills. Very often they do it with mares, so that they can have their horse back for breeding afterward."

"Neat," I said.

Flora nodded. "Larry Trent always liked it because it meant he could run five horses instead of owning only one outright. He was a great gambler, that man.''

"Gambler?"

"A thousand on this, a thousand on that. I used to get tired of hearing about it."

I gave her an amused glance. "Didn't you like him?"

"I suppose he was all right," she said dubiously. "He was always friendly. A good owner, Jack always said. Paid regularly and understood that horses aren't machines. Hardly ever blamed the jockey if he lost. But secretive, somehow. I don't really know why I think that, but that's how he seemed to me. Generous, though. He took us to dinner only last week at that place of his, the Silver Moondance. There was a band playing . . . so noisy." She sighed. "But of course you know about us going there. Jimmy said he told you about that whisky. I told him to forget it. Jack didn't want Jimmy stirring up trouble."

"Mm," I said. "The trouble got stirred, all the same, not that it matters."

"What do you mean?"

I told her of Jimmy's semiconscious wanderings and my visit with Detective Sergeant Ridger to the Silver Moondance saloon, and she said "Good heavens" faintly, with round eyes.

"Someone in that place had a great fiddle going," I said. "Whether Larry Trent knew or not."

She didn't answer directly, but after a long pause said, "You know, he did something once that I didn't understand. I happened to be at Doncaster Sales last year with some friends I was staying with. Jack didn't come, he was too busy at home. Larry Trent was there. He didn't see me, but I saw him across the sale ring, and he was bidding for a horse. It was called Ramekin." She paused, then went on. "The horse was knocked down to him and I thought good, Jack will be getting it to train. But it never came. Larry Trent never said a word. I told Jack, of course, but he said I must have been mistaken, Larry Trent never bought horses, and he wouldn't even ask him about it.''

"So who did train Ramekin afterward?" I asked.

"No one." She looked at me anxiously. "I'm not crazy, you know. I looked it up in the sale prices in the *Sporting Life* and it was sold for more than thirty thousand pounds. They didn't say who had bought it, but I'm absolutely certain it was Larry Trent because the auctioneer's man went right up to him to ask him his name when it had been knocked down to him, but after that nothing happened.''

"Well, someone must have him," I said reasonably.

"I suppose so. But he's not down in any trainer's list of horses-in-training. I checked, you know, because it would have been so annoying if Larry had sent the horse to someone else after all the races Jack's won for him, but Ramekin wasn't down anywhere, and he hasn't raced the whole season, I've been looking out for him. Ramekin just . . . really . . . vanished.''

SIX

FLORA TOOK ME INTO THE KITCHEN TO COLLECT THE glasses that were left whole: precisely nineteen.

"I'm sorry," she said.

I shrugged. "It's a wonder there are as many as that, considering. And don't worry, I'm insured."

She helped me slot the survivors into the box I'd brought, her kind round face looking worried.

"Insurance!" she said. "I've been hearing that word all morning. But who, I ask you, insures against such a tragedy? Of course we didn't have any insurance, not special insurance for the party. And those poor young things who own the horse trailer. I had Sally . . . that's the wife . . . on the telephone at lunchtime telling me over and over hysterically that Peter never never never left the hand-brake off and always always always left the horse trailer in gear, and that they're going to be ruined if the insurance companies can prove negligence. Poor things. Poor things." She glanced at me. "He didn't lock the doors, you know. I asked her. I'm afraid I made her angry. She said you don't lock the doors when you're at a friend's house."

I thought sourly of my stolen champagne and kept quiet.

"She said they came in the horse trailer only because they'd been to fetch a new hunter they'd just bought, and were on their way home. The hunter's still here, you know, in one of our spare trailers round the back. Sally says she never wants to see it again. She was totally, absolutely, distraught. It's all so awful."

Flora came with me as I carried the box of empty glasses out to the van, reluctant to let me go. "We didn't make that list for Jack," she said; so we returned to the kitchen and made it.

"If you still feel shaky tomorrow I'll come again for evening stables," I said. "I enjoyed it, to be honest."

"You're a dear, Tony," she said. "I'd love you to." And again she came out to the van to say goodbye.

"The police were here all morning swarming around the horse trailer," she said, looking over to the silent green monster. "Blowing dust all over it and shaking their heads."

"Looking for fingerprints, I suppose."

"I suppose so. Whatever it was they found, they didn't like it. But you know how they are, they didn't tell me a thing."

"Did you take a look, when they'd gone?" I asked.

She shook her head as if it hadn't occurred to her, but immediately set off toward the horse trailer across the grass. I followed, and together we made a rectangular tour, looking at a great deal of pinkish-grayish dust with smudges all over it.

"Hundreds of people must have touched it," Flora said resignedly.

Including the people with the crane, I thought, and the

people who'd released the horse, and any number of people before that.

On impulse I opened the passenger door, which was still not locked, and climbed up into the cab.

"Do you think you ought to, dear?" Flora asked anxiously.

"They didn't tell you to stay away, did they?"

"No, not today."

"Don't worry, then."

I looked around. There was a great deal more of the dust inside the cab, and also a great many fingerprints, but those inside were less smudged. I looked at them curiously but without expectation: it was just that I'd never actually seen the real thing, only dozens of representations in films.

Something about many of the prints struck me suddenly with a distinct mental jolt.

They were *tiny*.

Tiny fingerprints all over the vinyl surfaces of both front seats. Tiny fingerprints all over the steering wheel and on the gear lever and on the brake. Tiny . . .

I climbed down from the cab and told Flora, and I told her also about the investigator Wilson's interest when I'd mentioned a little boy and a dog.

"Do you mean," she said, very distressed, "it was a *child* who caused such horror?"

"Yes, I think so. You know how they love cars. They're always climbing into my van when I deliver things. Little wretches, if you don't watch them. I'd guess that that child released the brake and gear. Then when he'd run off with the dog the weight of the van eventually made it roll."

"Oh, dear." She looked increasingly upset. "Whose child?"

I described the boy as best I could but she said she didn't know everyone's children by sight, they changed so fast as they grew.

"Never mind," I said. "Wilson has addresses for all your guests. He'll find out. And dearest Flora, be grateful. If it was someone else's child who let off the brakes, your friends Peter and Sally won't be ruined."

"It wasn't their child. They haven't any. But that poor little boy!"

"If everyone's got any sense," I said, "which you can be sure they haven't, no one will tell him he killed eight people until he's long grown up."

On my way home from Flora's I got no further than the second delivery because my customer, a retired solicitor, was delighted (he said) that I had brought his order myself, and I must come in straightaway and share a bottle of Château Palmer 1970, which he had just decanted.

I liked the man, who was deeply experienced after countless holidays spent touring vineyards, and we passed a contented evening talking about the small parcels of miraculous fields in Pauillac and Margaux and about the universal virtues of the great grape cabernet sauvignon, which would grow with distinction almost anywhere on earth. Given poor soil, of course, and sun.

The solicitor's wife, it transpired, was away visiting relatives. The solicitor suggested cold underdone beef with the claret, to which I easily agreed, thinking of my own empty house, and he insisted also on opening a bottle of Clos St. Jacques 1982 to drink later.

"It's so seldom," he said to my protestations, "that I have anyone here with whom I can truly share my enthusiasm. My dear wife puts up with me, you know, but even after all these years she would as soon drink ordinary everyday Beaujolais or an undemanding Mosel. Tonight, and please don't argue, my dear chap, tonight is a treat.''

It was for me also. I drank my share of the Château Palmer and of the Clos St. Jacques, which I had originally tasted when I sold it to him a year earlier; and I greatly enjoyed discovering how that particular wine was satisfactorily changing color from purplish youth to a smooth deep burgundy red as it matured in excellence and power. It might well improve, I thought, and he said he would put it away for maybe a year. ''But I'm getting old, my dear chap. I want to drink all my treasures, you know, before it's too late.''

What with one thing and another it was nearly midnight before I left. Alcohol decays in the blood at a rate of one glass of wine an hour, I thought driving home, so with luck, after six glasses in five hours, I should be legitimately sober. It wasn't that I was unduly moral; just that to survive in business I needed a driving license.

Perhaps because of the wine, perhaps because of the tossing and turning I'd done the previous night, I slept long and soundly without bad dreams, and in the morning rose feeling better than usual about facing a new day. The mornings were in any case always better than the nights. Setting out wasn't so bad; it was going home that was hell.

My mother had advised me on the telephone to sell and live somewhere else.

''You'll never be happy there,'' she said. ''It never works.''

''You didn't move when Dad died,'' I protested.

''But this house was mine to begin with,'' she said,

surprised. "Inherited from my family. Quite different, Tony darling."

I wasn't quite sure where the difference lay, but I didn't argue. I thought she might possibly be right that I should move, but I couldn't. All my memories of Emma were alive there in the old renovated cottage overlooking the Thames, and to leave it seemed to be an abandonment of her: an ultimate unfaithfulness. I thought that if I sold the place I would feel guilty, not released, so I stayed there and sweated for her at nights and paid the mortgage and could find no ease.

The morning deliveries were widely scattered, which meant a fair amount of zigzagging, but free home delivering brought me so much extra business that I never minded.

Bad news travels as fast as the thud of jungle drums, and it was at only ten-fifteen, at my last port of call, that I heard about the Silver Moondance.

"Frightful, isn't it?" said a cheerful woman opening her back door to me on the outskirts of Reading. "Someone broke in there last night and stole every bottle in the place."

"Did they?" I said.

She nodded happily, enjoying the bad news. "The milkman just told me, five minutes ago. The Silver Moondance is just along the road from here, you know. He went in there as usual with the milk and found the police standing around scratching their heads. Well, that's what the milkman said. He's not overkeen on the police, I don't think."

I carried her boxes into the kitchen and waited while she wrote a check.

"Did you know the owner of the Silver Moondance

was killed in that accident on Sunday, the one with the horse trailer?'' she asked.

I said that I'd heard.

"Frightful, isn't it, people going in and looting his place as soon as he's dead?''

"Frightful," I agreed.

"Goodbye, Mr. Beach," she said blithely. "Wouldn't it be boring if everyone was good.''

The plundered Silver Moondance, so close to her house, lay on my own direct route back to the shop, and I slowed as I approached it, unashamedly curious. There was indeed a police car standing much where Ridger had parked the day before, and on impulse I turned straight into the driveway and pulled up alongside.

There was no one about outside, nor, when I went in, in the entrance hall. There were fewer lights on than before and even less air of anything happening. I pushed through the swinging Western doors to the saloon, but the black and scarlet expanse lay dark and empty, gathering dust.

I tried the restaurant on the opposite side of the entrance hall, but that too was deserted. That left the cellars, and I made my way as on the previous day along a passage to a door marked "Private" and into the staff area beyond. The cellars were not actually in a basement but consisted of two cool interconnecting windowless storerooms off a lobby between the dining room and what had been Larry Trent's office. The lobby opened onto a back yard through a door laden with locks and bolts, which now stood wide open, shedding a good deal of physical light onto the hovering figure of Sergeant Ridger, if no enlightenment.

The belted raincoat had been exchanged for an overcoat buttoned with equal military precision, and every hair was still rigidly in place. His brusque manner, too, was unchanged. "What are you doing here?" he demanded, stiffly, as soon as he saw me.

"Just passing."

He gave me a dour look but didn't tell me to leave, so I stayed.

"What was in here yesterday?" he asked, pointing to the open doors of the cellars. "The assistant manager is useless. But you saw what was here. You came here for that wine, didn't you, so what do you remember of the contents?" No "sir," I noticed, today. I'd progressed in his mind to "police expert," perhaps.

"Quite a lot," I said reflectively. "But what about the wine list? Everything was itemized on that."

"We can't find any wine lists. They seem to have gone with the wine."

I was astonished. "Are you sure?"

"We can't find any," he said again. "So I'm asking you to make a list."

I agreed that I would try. He took me into Larry Trent's office, which was plushly comfortable rather than functional, with a busily patterned carpet, several armchairs and many framed photographs on the walls. The photographs, I saw, were nearly all of the finishes of races, the winning post figuring prominently. Larry Trent had been a good picker, Flora had said, and a good gambler . . . whose luck had finally run out.

I sat in his own chair behind his mahogany desk and wrote on a piece of paper from Ridger's official notebook. Ridger himself remained standing as if the original occupant were still there to disturb him, and I thought fleetingly that I too felt like a trespasser on Larry Trent's privacy.

His desk was almost too neat to be believable as the

hub of a business the size of the Silver Moondance. Not an invoice, not a letter, not a billhead showing. No government forms, no cash book, no filing cabinets, no typewriter and no readily available calculator. Not a working room, I thought: more a sanctuary.

I wrote what I could remember of bins and quantities of wines and then said I could perhaps add to the list if I went into the cellars and visualized what I'd seen before. We transferred therefore into the first of the rooms, where the bulk of the wines had been kept, and I looked at the empty racks and partitioned shelving and added a couple more names to my list.

From there we went through the sliding inner door into the second cellar, which had contained stocks of spirits, liqueurs, canned beer and mixers. The beer and mixers remained: brandy, gin, vodka, whisky, rum and liqueurs were absent.

"They did a thorough job," I remarked, writing.

Ridger grunted. "They cleared the trolley in the dining room, besides."

"And the bar?"

"That too."

"Highly methodical," I said. "Head office must be fuming. What did your friend Paul Young have to say?"

Ridger looked at me broodingly and then glanced at the list, which I still held. "As a matter of fact," he said unwillingly, "the telephone number he gave me is unobtainable. I'm having it checked."

I blinked. "He wrote it down himself," I said.

"Yes, I know that." He slightly pursed his lips. "People sometimes make mistakes."

Whatever comment I might have made was forestalled by the arrival at the open door of the lobby of a young man in an afghan jacket who turned out to be a detective

constable in plain(ish) clothes. He reported briefly that
he'd finished peering into sheds with the assistant manager, and that there seemed to be nothing missing from
those. The assistant manager, he added, would be in the
manager's office, if required.

"Where's that?" Ridger asked.

"Near to the front door. Behind the door marked
'Staff only' in the entrance hall, so the assistant manager
said."

"Did you search in there?" Ridger asked.

"No, Sergeant, not yet."

"Get on with it, then," Ridger said brusquely, and
without expression the constable turned and went away.

The radio inside Ridger's coat crackled to life, and
Ridger pulled it out and extended its aerial. The metallic
voice that came from it reached me clearly in the quiet
cellar. It said, "Further to your inquiry timed ten-
fourteen, the telephone number as given does not exist
and has existed. Furthermore the address as given
does not exist. There is no such street. This message
timed ten-forty-eight. Please acknowledge. Over."

"Acknowledged," Ridger said grimly. "Out." He
pushed the aerial down and said, "I suppose you heard
that?"

"Yes."

"Shit," he said forcefully.

"Quite so," I agreed sympathetically, for which I received an absentminded glare. I handed him the completed list of what had all at once become not just the
simple tally of an opportunistic break-in but the evidence
of a more thorough and purposeful operation. His job,
however, not mine. "I'll be in my shop if you want me
again," I said. "I'll be glad to help."

"Very good, sir," he said vaguely, and then with more attention, "Right, then. Thanks."

I nodded and went back through the "Private" door into the entrance hall, glancing across at the inconspicuous "Staff only" door, which merged chameleonlike with the decor of the walls: and it was while I was supposing that the manager preferred not to be tracked down by grievance-bearing diners that the door itself opened and the assistant assistant manager reeled out backwards through the gap, staring at some sight cut off by the door swinging shut behind him.

The weakly inefficient man of the day before was now in a complete state of nonfunction, gasping and looking faint. I fairly sprinted across the entrance hall carpet and caught him as he sagged.

"What is it?" I said.

He moaned slightly, his eyes rolling upward, his weight growing heavier. I let him slide all the way to the carpet until he lay flat and spent a second or two pulling his tie loose. Then with a raised pulse and some shortening of my own breath I opened the door of the manager's office and went in.

It was here, I saw immediately, that the real business was done. Here in this office, very functional indeed, were all the forms, files and untidy heaps of paperwork in progress so conspicuously missing from Larry Trent's. Here there was a metal desk, old and scratched, with a plastic chair behind it and pots of pens among the clutter on its top.

There were stacks of miscellaneous stores in boldly labeled boxes all round; light bulbs, ashtrays, toilet rolls, tablets of soap. There was a floor-to-ceiling cupboard, open, spilling out stationery. There was a view through the single window to the sweep of drive outside, my van and Ridger's car in plain view. There was a sturdy safe the size of a tea-chest, its door wide, its interior bare: and there was the plainclothes constable sitting on the linoleum, his back against a wall, his head down between his knees.

Nothing in that place looked likely at first sight to cause mass unconsciousness. Nothing until one walked round to the chair behind the desk, and looked at the floor; and then I felt my own mouth go dry and my own heart beat suffocatingly against my ribs. There was no blood; but it was worse, much more disturbing than the accidental carnage in the tent.

On the floor, on his back, lay a man in gray trousers with a royal-blue padded jacket above. Its zip was fully fastened up the front, I noted, concentrating desperately on details, and there was an embroidered crest sewn on one sleeve, and he was wearing brown shoes with gray socks. His neck was pinkish red above the jacket, the tendons showing tautly, and his arms and hands, neatly arranged, were crossed at the wrists over his chest, in the classic position of corpses.

He was dead. He had to be dead. For head, above the bare stretched neck, he had a large white featureless globe like a giant puffball, and it was only when one fought down nausea and looked closely that one could see that from the throat up he had been entirely, smoothly and thickly encased in plaster of paris.

SEVEN

RETREATING SHAKILY I WALKED OUT OF THE OFFICE WITH every sympathy for the constable and the assistant assistant and leaned my back against the wall outside with trembling legs.

How could anyone be so barbaric, I wondered numbly. How could anyone do that, how could anyone think of it.

Sergeant Ridger emerged into the hall from the passage and came toward me, looking with more irritation than concern at the still prostrate assistant.

"What's the matter with him?" he said in his usual forceful way.

I didn't answer. He looked sharply at my face and said with more interest, "What's the matter?"

"A dead man," I said. "In the office."

He gave me a pitying look of superiority and walked purposefully through the door. When he came out he was three shades paler but still admirably in command and behaving every inch like a detective sergeant.

"Did you touch anything in there?" he asked me

sharply. "Any surface? Would your fingerprints be on anything?"

"No," I said.

"Certain?"

"Certain."

"Right." He pulled out his radio, extended the aerial and said he needed top priority technical teams in connection with the death in suspicious circumstances of a so-far-unidentified male.

The disembodied voice in reply said that his message was timed at ten-fifty-seven and would be acted upon. Ridger collapsed the aerial, put his head through the office door and crisply told his constable to come out of there, refrain from touching things and go outside for fresh air.

As much to himself as to me Ridger said, "It won't be my case from now on."

"Won't it?"

"Murder cases go to chief inspectors or superintendents."

I couldn't tell from his voice whether he was pleased or sorry and concluded he simply accepted the hierarchy without resentment. I said reflectively, "Is a man called Wilson anything to do with your force?"

"There are about four Wilsons. Which one do you mean?"

I described the hunch-shouldered quiet-mannered investigator and Ridger nodded immediately. "That's Detective Chief Superintendent Wilson. He's not at our station, of course. He's head of the whole district. Near retirement, they say."

I said that I'd met him at the Hawthorn accident, and Ridger guessed that Wilson had gone there himself because of the importance of the Sheik. "Not his job, normally, traffic incidents."

"Will he be coming here?" I asked.

"Shouldn't think so. He's too senior."

I wondered in passing why a man of such seniority should come to my shop to ask questions instead of sending a constable, but didn't get to mentioning it to Ridger because at that point the assistant to the assistant manager began to return to life.

He was disoriented after his long faint, sitting up groggily and looking blankly at Ridger and me.

"What happened?" he said; and then without us telling him, remembered. "Oh my God!" He looked on the point of passing out again but instead pressed his hands over his eyes as if that would shut sight out of memory. "I saw . . . I saw . . ."

"We know what you saw, sir," said Ridger without sympathy. "Can you identify that man? Is he the manager?"

The assistant assistant shook his head and spoke in a muffled voice through his hands. "The manager's fat."

"Go on," Ridger prompted.

"It's Zarac," said the assistant assistant. "It's his jacket."

"Who's Zarac?" Ridger said.

"The wine waiter." The assistant assistant rose unsteadily to his feet and transferred his hands to his mouth before departing with heaving stomach toward the door marked "Guys."

"The wine waiter," Ridger repeated flatly. "Might have guessed."

I pushed myself off the wall. "You don't actually need me here, do you? I should go back to my shop."

He thought it over briefly and agreed, saying he supposed he could find me easily if I were wanted. I left him standing virtual guard over the office door and went outside to my van, passing the constable, who had relieved himself of his breakfast onto the drive.

"Cripes," he said weakly in an endearing local accent, "I've never seen anything like that."

"Not an everyday sight," I agreed, taking refuge in flippancy: and I thought that I too had seen enough horrors since Sunday to last a lifetime.

I BOUGHT MORE GLASSES AT TUESDAY LUNCHTIME AND ferried them and the wines to the Thames Ladies for their fund-raising; and little else of note happened for the next three days.

The news media reported briefly on the man with the plaster topping, but no words, I thought, conveyed anything like the shock of actually seeing that football-head lying there blank and unhuman, attached to a human neck.

Cutting off the plaster at the autopsy had confirmed the identity of the victim: Feydor Zaracievesa, British born of Polish descent, succinctly known as Zarac. He had been employed as wine waiter for eighteen months at the Silver Moondance, which had itself been open for business for almost three years. An inquest would shortly be held, it was said, and meanwhile the police were pursuing their inquiries.

Good luck to them, I thought. Pursue away.

On Tuesday, Wednesday and Thursday Mrs. Palissey and Brian set off with the deliveries at four o'clock and at approximately four-thirty I stuck a notice on the shop door saying "Open 6:00–9:00 P.M." and scooted up the hill to go round the yard with Flora.

Shop hours as far as I was concerned were flexible,

and I'd found it didn't much matter what one did as long
as one said what one was doing. The pattern of when
most customers came and when they stayed away was
on the whole constant: a stream in the mornings, pre-
dominantly women, a trickle of either sex in the afternoons, a healthy flow, mostly men, in the evenings.

When Emma had been alive we had opened the shop
on Friday and Saturday evenings only, but since I'd been
alone I'd added Tuesday, Wednesday and Thursday, not
simply for the extra trade, but for the company. I enjoyed the evenings. Most of the evening people came
for wine, which I liked best to sell: a bottle to go with
dinner, champagne for a job promotion, a present on the
way to a party.

It was life on a small scale, I dared say. Nothing that
would change history or the record books. A passage
through time of ordinary mortal dimensions: but with
Emma alongside it had contented.

I had never had much ambition, a sadness to my
mother and a source of active irritation to my Wellington
schoolmasters, one of whom on my last term's report
had written acidly, "Beach's conspicuous intelligence
would take him far if only he would stir himself to
choose a direction." My inability to decide what I
wanted to be (except not a soldier) had resulted in my
doing nothing much at all. I passed such exams as were
thrust my way but hadn't been drawn to university.
French, my best subject, was scarcely in itself a career.
I didn't feel like a stockbroker or anything tidy in the
City. I wasn't artistic. Had no ear for music. Couldn't
face life behind a desk and couldn't ride boldly enough
for racing. My only real ability throughout my teens had
been a party trick of telling all makes of chocolate blind-

fold, which had hardly at that time seemed a promising foundation for gainful employment.

Six months after I left school I thought I might go to France for a while, ostensibly to learn the language better, but unhappily admitting to myself that it was to avoid being seen all too clearly as a disappointing failure at home. I could stand being a failure much better on my own.

By total chance, because of friends of friends of my despairing mother's, I was dispatched to live as a paying guest with a family in Bordeaux, and it had meant nothing to me at first that my unknown host was a wine-shipper. It was Monsieur Henri Tavel himself who had discovered that I could tell one wine from another, once I'd tasted them. He was the only adult I'd ever met who was impressed by my trick with the chocolate. He had laughed loudly and begun to set me tests with wine each evening, and I'd grown more confident the more I got them right.

It had still seemed a game, however, and at the end of the planned three months I'd returned home still with no idea of what to do next. My mother applauded my French accent but said it was hardly to be considered a lifetime's achievement, and I spent my days sneaking out of her sight as much as possible.

She had had to come looking for me the day the letter came, about a month after my return. She held it out in front of her, frowning at it as if it were incomprehensible.

"Monsieur Tavel suggests you go back," she said. "He is offering to train you. Train you in what, Tony darling?"

"Wine," I said, feeling the first pricking of interest for many a long day.

"You?" She was puzzled more than amazed.

"To learn the trade, I expect," I said.

"Good heavens."

"Can I go?" I asked.

"Do you want to?" she said, astonished. "I mean, have you actually found something you'd like to do?"

"I don't seem to be able to do anything else."

"No," she agreed prosaically: and she paid my fare again and my board and lodging with the family and a substantial fee to Monsieur Tavel for tuition.

Monsieur Tavel gave me a year's intensive instruction, taking me everywhere himself, showing me every stage of winemaking and shipping, teaching me rapidly what he'd spent a long lifetime learning, expecting me never to need telling twice.

I grew to feel at home in the Quai des Chatrons, where many doors into the warehouses were too narrow for modern trucks as a legacy from an ancient tax and where no wine could still be stored within a hundred yards of the street because it had been thought the vibration from horses' hooves on the quayside would upset it. In the de Luze warehouse, stretching nearly half a mile back, the staff went from end to end by bicycle.

In the city long buses had concertina central sections for turning sharp corners into narrow streets and in the country mimosa trees bloomed fluffily yellow in March, and everywhere, every day, all day, there was the talk and the smell of wine. By the time I left, Bordeaux was my spiritual home. Henri Tavel hugged me with moist eyes and told me he could place me with de Luze or one of the other top *négociants* if I would stay; and sometimes since then I'd wondered why I hadn't.

On my return to England, armed with a too-flattering Tavel reference, I'd got a job with a wineshipper, but I was too junior for much besides paperwork and after the intensities of Bordeaux grew quickly bored. Impulsively one day I'd walked into a wine shop that said "Help wanted" and offered my services, and in a short time began a brilliant nonstop career of lugging cases of booze from place to place.

"Tony works in a shop," my mother would say bravely. My mother was nothing if not courageous. Large fences had to be met squarely. She also, in due course, made me an interest-free loan for basic stock for a shop of my own and had refused to accept repayments once I could afford to start them. As mothers went, in fact, mine wasn't at all bad.

FLORA, IN ESSENCE A MORE MOTHERLY LADY, GREW DAY by day less exhausted and depressed. Jack's leg was doing well and Jimmy was tentatively out of danger, although with pierced lungs, it seemed, one couldn't be sure for a fortnight.

Jimmy, Flora said, couldn't remember anything at all of the party. He couldn't remember escorting the Sheik round the yard. The last thing he could remember was talking to me about the Laphroaig; and he had been very shocked to learn that Larry Trent was dead.

"And Jack's spirits?" I asked. "How are those?"

"Well, you know him, Tony dear, he hates to sit still, and he's growing more bad-tempered by the minute, which I suppose I shouldn't say, but you know how he is. He'll be home by the weekend, he says, and he won't sit in a wheelchair, he wants crutches, and he's quite a weight, you know, to support on his arms, and not as young as he was."

The daily reports, faithfully written by Flora and me, had not unduly cheered Jack, it appeared, because he thought we were keeping disasters from him; though as if in a burst of good luck after bad there had been fewer than usual sprains, knocks and skin eruptions among the string.

By Thursday the horse trailer had gone, also the remains of the tent and the matting, only the churned lawn and the gap in the rose hedge remaining.

"We'll never be able to walk on the grass without shoes," Flora said. "Not that we ever do, come to that. But everywhere you look there are splinters of glass."

She'd heard of course about the robbery and murder at the Silver Moondance and listened wide-eyed when I told her I'd been there again on the Tuesday morning. "How awful," she said, and "Poor Larry," and then with confusion, "Oh, dear, I'd forgotten for a minute. It's all so dreadful, so dreadful."

On Wednesday she told me that Sally and Peter now knew who had let off the brakes of their horse trailer. Sally had been again on the telephone, almost equally upset, telling Flora that the parents of the little boy were blaming Peter for leaving the doors unlocked and saying it was all Peter's fault, not their son's. They had denied at first that their child could have caused the accident and were very bitter about the fingerprints. Sally was saying they shouldn't have let their beastly brat run around unsupervised and should have taught it never to touch other people's property and especially never to get into strange cars or horse trailers and meddle.

"And who's right?" Flora asked rhetorically, sighing. "They used to be friends and now they're all so miserable." She shook her head sadly. "I wish we'd never had that party. We'll never have another, I don't suppose."

By Thursday afternoon she was almost back to her

old cozy self, handling the smarmy Howard on the stable round with sweet-natured assurance, and I said that unless she felt panic-stricken I wouldn't come the next day, Friday.

"Dear Tony, you've been such a rock, I can't tell you," and she gave me a warm kiss on the cheek when I left and said she would see me again soon, very soon.

FRIDAY PROCEEDED UP TO A POINT IN THE WAY OF MOST Fridays: morning extra-busy with customers and early afternoon spent making up the big load of orders for weekend delivery. Brian carried countless customers' goods for them personally to their parked cars and received their tips, beaming. Mrs. Palissey gave him six Mars bars when she thought I wasn't looking and told me brightly that we were running out of Coca-Cola.

Mrs. Chance came for her surreptitious gin. A wine-shipper telephoned that he'd reserved me fifty cases of Beaujolais Nouveau for November fifteenth, and did I want more? (November fifteenth was to the drinks trade what August twelfth was to the food: the race to be first with the new wine, as first with the grouse, was intense. I never waited for the Nouveau to be delivered but fetched it myself from the shipper very early on November fifteenth so as to be able to open my doors at practically dawn with it already displayed in the window. At least, I had done that for six years. Whether I would bother without Emma I wasn't sure. The fun had all gone.) Fifty cases would be fine, I said, considering Nouveau's short life: it was at its best sold and drunk before Christmas.

Mrs. Palissey set off with Brian soon after three on the extra-long delivery round and someone rang up in a

great fuss because I'd sent half the amount of beer ordered.

"Do you need it tonight?" I asked, apologizing.

"No, Sunday, for after the village football match."

"I'll bring it myself," I said. "Tomorrow morning at
nine o'clock."

In order not to forget I carried the beer immediately
out of the back door to the Rover, and found on my
return that I had a visitor in the shop in the quiet shape
of Detective Chief Superintendent Wilson.

"Mr. Beach," he said as before, extending his hand.

"Mr. Wilson," I said, trying to smother my surprise
and no doubt not succeeding.

"A bottle of wine," he said with a small smile. "For
dinner. What do you suggest?"

He liked full-bodied red, he said, and I offered him a
Rioja of distinction.

"Spanish?" he murmured dubiously, reading the label.

"Very well made," I said. "It's excellent."

He said he would take my word for it and punctiliously paid. I rolled the bottle in tissue and stood it on
the counter, but he was not, it appeared, in a hurry to
pick it up and depart.

"Your chair," he murmured. "Would it be available?"

I fetched it at once from the office and he sat gratefully as before.

"A question or two, Mr. Beach." His gaze unhurriedly rested on my face and then wandered vaguely
round the shop. "I heard that you called in at the Silver
Moondance last Tuesday morning, Mr. Beach."

"Yes," I said.

"And wrote a list of the stolen goods."

"As much as I could remember, yes."

"And on Monday last you went there with Detective Sergeant Ridger and tasted various whiskies and wines?"

"Yes," I said again.

"And you saw a certain Paul Young there?"

"Yes."

His slow gaze finished its wandering and came to rest tranquilly on my face. "Can you describe him, Mr. Beach?"

That's why he's here, I thought. For that.

"Sergeant Ridger . . ." I began.

"Sergeant Ridger made a full description," he said, nodding. "But two sets of eyes, Mr. Beach?"

I thought back and told him what I could remember of the man from the head office that didn't exist.

"A businessman," I said. "About fifty. Thickset, rather short, dark-haired, pale skin. Big pale fleshy hands. No rings. He wore glasses with black frames, but narrow frames, not heavy. He had . . . um . . . the beginnings of a double chin . . . and a hearing aid behind his right ear."

Wilson received the description benignly without giving me any indication of whether or not it was a carbon copy of Ridger's. "His voice, Mr. Beach?"

"No special accent," I said. "Plain English. I doubt if he'd been deaf from birth, he didn't sound toneless. He spoke ordinarily and heard everything anyone said. One wouldn't have known he was deaf without seeing the hearing aid."

"And his manner, Mr. Beach?"

"A bull," I said without hesitation. "Used to having people jump when he said so." I thought back. "He didn't seem like that at first sight, though. I mean, if he came in here now, he wouldn't seem aggressive, but he developed aggression very fast. He didn't like Sergeant Ridger's authority. He wanted to diminish him somehow." I smiled faintly. "Sergeant Ridger was pretty much a match for him."

Wilson lowered his eyes briefly as if to avoid showing whatever comment lay there and then with a few blinks raised them again. "Other impressions, Mr. Beach?"

I pondered. "Paul Young was definitely shocked to find so many bottles contained the wrong liquids."

"Shocked that they did, or shocked that anyone had discovered it?"

"Well, at the time I thought it was the first, but now . . . I don't know. He was surprised and angry, that's for sure."

Wilson rubbed his nose absentmindedly. "Anything else, Mr. Beach? Any insignificant little thing?"

"I don't know . . ."

A customer came in for several items at that point and wanted a detailed receipted bill, which I wrote for her, and the act of writing jogged a few dormant brain cells.

"Paul Young," I said when she'd gone, "had a gold-colored ball point with two wide black bands inset near the top. He wrote with his right hand, but with the pen between his first and second fingers and with the fingers curled round so that the pen was above what he was writing, not below. It looked very awkward. It looked how left-handed people sometimes write, but I'm sure he was right-handed. He wrote with the hand the same side as his hearing aid, and I was wondering why he didn't have the hearing aid incorporated into the frame of his glasses."

Wilson incuriously studied the tissue wrapping his waiting bottle.

"Did Paul Young seem genuine to you, Mr. Beach?"

"Oh, yes," I said. "He behaved very definitely as if the Silver Moondance belonged to an organization of which he was an executive of the highest rank. He seemed at first only to have come himself to deal with the crisis of Larry Trent's death because the manager was away and the assistant manager had flu. The third in line, the assistant to the assistant, was so hopeless that it seemed perfectly natural that head office should appear in person."

"Quite a long string of command, wouldn't you say?" murmured Wilson. "Trent himself, a manager, an assistant, an assistant to the assistant?"

"I don't know," I said, moderately disagreeing. "A place like that, open long hours, half the night sometimes, they'd need that number. And the assistant assistant struck me as just a general dogsbody in togs above his station, poor chap."

Wilson communed vaguely for a while with the South African sherries and then said, "Would you know Paul Young again, Mr. Beach? Could you pick him out in a roomful of people?"

"Yes," I said positively. "As long as I saw him again within a year. After that, I don't know. Maybe."

"And in a photograph?"

"Um, it would depend."

He nodded noncommittally and shifted on his chair.

"I've read Sergeant Ridger's reports. You've been most helpful all along, Mr. Beach."

"Sergeant Ridger did tell me," I said mildly, "who you are. I asked him if he knew of you, and he told me. And I've been surprised, you know, that you've come here yourself both times."

He smiled patiently. "I like to keep my hand in, Mr.

Beach, now and again. When I'm passing, you might say, for a bottle of wine.''

He stood up slowly, preparing to go, and I asked him the thing that had been on my mind since Tuesday.

"Was Zarac . . . the wine waiter . . . dead . . . before . . . ?"

I stopped in midsentence and he finished it for me. "Dead before the plaster was applied? Since you ask, Mr. Beach, no, he wasn't. Zarac died of suffocation."

"Oh," I said numbly.

"It is possible," Wilson said unemotionally, "that he had been knocked unconscious first. You may find that thought more bearable, perhaps."

"Is it true?"

"It's not for me to say before the coroner has decided."

There was a bleakness, I saw, behind his undemanding face. He had been out there for a long time in the undergrowth and found it easy to believe in all manner of horrors.

"I don't think," I said, "that I would like your job."

"Whereas yours, Mr. Beach," he said, his gaze again roving the bottles, "yours I would like very much."

He gave me the small smile and the unemphatic handshake and went on his way, and I thought of people bandaging all over a live man's head and then soaking the bandage with water to turn it to rock.

EIGHT

FLORA SENT GERARD MCGREGOR DOWN TO SEE ME: OR SO he said, that Friday evening, when he came into the shop.

He looked just as he had on Sunday when tunneling away and hauling trestle tables through under the canvas for roofs. Tall, in his fifties, going gray. Ultracivilized, with experienced eyes. Gerard with a soft J.

We shook hands again, smiling.

"My wife and I took Flora home to dinner with us yesterday evening," he said. "We insisted. She said it was chiefly thanks to you that she was feeling better."

"No," I said.

"She talked about you for hours."

"How utterly boring. She can't have done."

"You know how Flora talks." His voice was affectionate. "We heard all about you and Larry Trent and the goings-on at the Silver Moondance."

"I'm sorry," I said.

"Whatever for? Fascinating stuff."

Not for Zarac, I thought.

Gerard McGregor was looking around him with interest.

"We don't live so far from Flora," he said. "Five miles or so, but we shop in the opposite direction, not in this town. I've never been here before." He began to walk down the row of wine racks, looking at labels. "From what Flora said of the size of the trade you do, I somehow thought your shop would be bigger." His faintly Scottish voice was without offense, merely full of interest.

"It doesn't need to be bigger," I explained. "In fact large brightly lit expanses tend to put real wine-lovers off, if anything. This is just right, to my mind. There's room to show examples of everything I normally sell. I don't keep more than a dozen of many things out here. The rest's in the storeroom. And everything moves in and out pretty fast."

The shop itself was about twenty-five feet by thirteen, or eight by four if one counted in meters. Down the whole of one long side there were wine racks in vertical columns, each column capable of holding twelve bottles (one case), the top bottle resting at a slant for display. Opposite the wine racks was the counter with, behind it, the shelves for spirits and liqueurs.

More wine racks took up the farthest wall except for the door through to the office and storeroom, and on every other inch of wall space there were shelves for sherries, beers, mixers and Coke and all the oddments that people asked for.

At the end of the counter, standing at a slight angle into the main floorspace, was a medium-sized table covered to the ground with a pretty swagged tablecloth that Emma had made. A sheet of plate glass protected the top, and on it there stood a small forest of liqueur and aperitif and wine bottles, all opened, all available for customers to taste before buying. Coyly out of sight below the tablecloth stood open cartons of the same wines, ready to hand. We'd always sold a great deal because of the table: impulse buys leading to more and more repeat orders. Gerard fingered the bottles with interest, as so many did.

"Would you like to see behind the scenes?" I said, and he answered, "Very much."

I showed him my tiny office and also the tiny washroom, and the not-so-tiny storeroom beyond. "That door," I said, pointing, "opens outward to the yard where we park the cars and load and unload deliveries. I usually keep it bolted. Through here is the storeroom." I switched on the lights as the storeroom had no window, and he looked with interest at the columns of cases ranged all round the walls and in a double row down the center.

"I didn't always have as much stock as this," I said. "It was a terrible struggle to begin with. The storeroom was almost empty. Some weeks I'd buy things one afternoon, sell them the next morning and buy more with the same money again in the afternoon, and so on, round and round. Hair-raising."

"But not now, I see."

"Well, no. But it took us a while to get known, because this wasn't a wine shop before. We had to start from utter scratch."

"We?" he said.

"My wife."

"Oh yes, Flora said."

"Yes," I said flatly. "She died."

He made sympathetic motions with his hands, and we went back to the shop.

"When do you close?" he said, and suggested we might have dinner together.

"Is nine o'clock too late?"

Nine o'clock would do quite well, he said, and he returned at that time and drove me to a restaurant far outside my own catchment area. It seemed a long way to go, but he had reserved a table there, saying the food would be worth it.

We talked on the way about the accident and our excursions in the tent, and over dinner about Flora and Jack, and after that about the Silver Moondance and Larry Trent. We ate trout mousse followed by wild duck and he asked me to choose the wine. It was a pleasant enough evening and seemed purposeless; but it wasn't.

"What would you say," he said casually over coffee, "to a consultant's fee?"

"For what?"

"For what you're good at. Distinguishing one whisky from another."

"I wouldn't mind the fee," I said frankly. "But I'm not an expert."

"You've other qualities." His eyes, it seemed to me, were all at once concentrating on my face as if he could read every hidden response I might have. "Observation, resource and leadership."

I laughed. "Not me. Wrong guy."

"I'd like to hire your services," he said soberly, "for one particular job."

I said in puzzlement, "What sort of job?"

For answer he felt in an inner pocket and drew out a sheet of paper, which he unfolded and spread on the tablecloth for me to read: it was a photostat copy, I saw in some bewilderment, of a page from the yellow pages telephone directory.

"Detective Agencies," it said in capital letters at the top. Underneath were several boldly outlined box advertisements and a column of small firms. The word "investigation" figured prominently throughout.

"I am one of the management team of that concern," McGregor said, pointing to one of the bigger boxes.

"A private detective?" I asked, astounded. "About the last thing I'd have guessed."

"Mm." McGregor's tone was dry. "We prefer to be known as investigative consultants. Read the advertisement."

I did as he asked.

"Deglet Ltd.," it announced. "Comprehensive service offered in complete confidence to commercial clients. Experienced consultants in the fields of industrial counterespionage, fraud detection, electronic security, personnel screening. Business investigations of all sorts. International links."

At the bottom there was a London box number and telex and telephone numbers, but no plain address. Confidential to the bone, I thought.

"No divorce?" I asked lightly.

"No divorce," McGregor agreed easily. "No debt collecting and no private clients. Commercial inquiries only."

Any image one might have of mean streets didn't fit with McGregor. Boardrooms and country weekends, yes. Fistfights and sleazy night-life, no.

"Do you yourself personally . . ." I flicked a finger at the page, "go rootling around in factories?"

"Not exactly." He was quietly amused. "When we're approached by a prospective client I go along to size up what's happening and what's needed, and then either alone or with colleagues, according to the size of the problem, I plan how to get results.''

There was a pause while I thought over what he had and hadn't so far told me. I evaded all the head-on questions and in the end said only, ''Don't you have any better business cards than photostats of the phone book?''

Unruffled, he said, ''We don't advertise anywhere else. We have no pamphlets or brochures and carry only personal cards ourselves. I brought the photostat to show you that we exist, and what we do.''

''And all your business comes from the yellow pages?'' I asked.

He nodded. ''And from word of mouth. Also, of course, once-satisfied clients call upon us again whenever they need us, which believe me the larger corporations do constantly.''

''You enjoy your job?''

''Very much,'' he said. I listened to the quiet assurance in his depths and thought that I wasn't a hunter and never would be. Not I, who ducked through gates to avoid jumping fences, even if the fox escaped.

''Occasionally,'' he said conversationally, ''we're asked to investigate in areas for which none of our regular people are ideal.''

I looked at my coffee.

''We need someone now who knows whisky. Someone who can tell malt whisky from grain whisky, as Flora says you can.''

''Someone who knows a grain from the great gray green greasy Limpopo River?'' I said. ''The Limpopo River, don't forget, was full of crocodiles.''

''I'm not asking you to do anything dangerous,'' he said reasonably.

"No." I sighed. "Go on, then."

"What are you doing on Sunday?" he said.

"Opening the shop from twelve to two. Washing the car. Doing the crossword." Damn all, I thought.

"Will you give me the rest of your day from two o'clock on?" he asked.

It sounded harmless, and in any case I still felt considerable camaraderie with him because of our labors in the tent, and Sundays after all were depressing, even without horse trailers.

"O.K.," I said. "Two o'clock onward. What do you want me to do?"

He was in no great hurry, it seemed, to tell me. Instead he said, "Does all grain whisky taste the same?"

"That's why you need a real expert," I said. "The answer is no it doesn't quite, but the differences are small. It depends on the grain used and the water, and how long the spirit's been aged."

"Aged?"

"Newly distilled scotch," I said, "burns your throat and scrubs your tongue like fire. It has to be stored in wooden casks for at least three years to become drinkable."

"Always in wood?"

"Yes. Wood breathes. In wooden casks all spirit grows blander but if you put it in metal or glass containers instead it stays the same forever. You could keep newly distilled spirits a thousand years in glass and when you opened it it would be as raw as the day it was bottled."

"One lives and learns," he said.

"Anyway," I added after a pause, "practically no one sells pure grain whisky. Even the cheapest bulk whisky is a blend of grain and malt, though the amount of malt in some of them is like a pinch of salt in a swimming pool.''

"Flora said you told her some of the scotch at the Silver Moondance was like that,'' McGregor said.

"Yes, it was. They were selling it in the bar out of a Bell's bottle, and in the restaurant as Laphroaig.''

McGregor called for the bill. "This wasn't my case to begin with,'' he said almost absentmindedly as he sorted out a credit card. "One of my colleagues passed it on to me because it seemed to be developing so close to my own doorstep.''

"Do you mean,'' I asked, surprised, "that your firm was already interested in the Silver Moondance?''

"That's right.''

"But how? I mean, in what connection?''

"In connection with some stolen scotch that we were looking for. And it seems, my dear Tony, that you have found it.''

"Good grief,'' I said blankly. "And lost it again.''

"I'm afraid so. We're very much back where we started. But that's hardly your fault, of course. If Jack's secretary had been less fond of Laphroaig . . . if Larry Trent hadn't invited him to dinner . . . One can go back and back saying 'if,' and it's profitless. We were treading delicately toward the Silver Moondance when the horse trailer plunged into the marquee; and it's ironic in the extreme that I didn't know that the Arthur Lawrence Trent who owned that place had horses in training with Jack, and I didn't know he was at the party. I didn't know him by sight and I didn't know that he was one of the men we found dead. If I'd known he was going to be at the party I'd have got Jack or Flora to introduce me.'' He shrugged. "If and if.''

"But you were...um...investigating him?" I asked.

"No," McGregor said pleasantly. "The person we suspected was an employee of his. A man called Zarac."

I'm sure my mouth physically dropped open. Gerard McGregor placidly finished paying the bill, glancing with dry understanding at my face.

"Yes, he's dead," he said. "We really are totally back at the beginning."

"I don't consider," I said intensely, "that Zarac is a matter of no crocodiles."

I SPENT MOST OF SATURDAY WITH MY FINGERS HOVERING over the telephone, almost deciding at every minute to ring Flora and ask her for Gerard McGregor's number so that I could cancel my agreement for Sunday. If I did nothing he would turn up at two o'clock and whisk me off heaven knew where to meet his client, the one whose scotch had turned up on my tongue. (Probably.)

In the end I did ring Flora but even after she'd answered I was still shilly-shallying.

"How's Jack?" I said.

"In a vile temper, I'm afraid, Tony dear. The doctors won't let him come home for several more days. They put a rod right down inside his bone, through the marrow, it seems, and they want to make sure it's all settled before they let him loose on crutches."

"And are you all right?"

"Yes, much better every day."

"A friend of yours," I said slowly, "came to see me. Er . . . Gerard McGregor."

"Oh, yes," Flora said warmly. "Such a nice man. And his wife's such a dear. He said you and he together had helped a good few people last Sunday. He asked who you were, and I'm afraid, Tony dear, that I told him quite a lot about you and then about everything that happened at the Silver Moondance, and he seemed frightfully interested though it seems to me now that I did go on and on a bit.''

''I don't think he minded,'' I said soothingly. ''Um . . . what does he do, do you know?''

''Some sort of business consultant, I believe. All those jobs are so frightfully vague, don't you think? He's always traveling all over the place, anyway, and Tina . . . that's his wife . . . never seems to know when he'll be home.''

''Have you known them long?'' I asked.

''We met them at other people's parties several times before we really got to know them, which would be about a year ago.''

''I mean, has he always lived near here?''

''Only about five years, I think. They were saying the other evening how much they preferred it to London even though Gerard has to travel more. He's such a clever man, Tony dear, it just oozes out of his pores. I told him he should buy some wine from you, so perhaps he will.''

''Perhaps,'' I said. ''Er . . . do you have his telephone number?''

''Of course,'' Flora said happily, and found it for me. I wrote it down and we disconnected, and I was still looking at it indeterminately at nine o'clock when I closed the shop.

''I HALF EXPECTED YOU TO CRY OFF,'' HE SAID, WHEN HE picked me up at two the next day.

''I half did.''

''But?''

"Curiosity, I suppose."

He smiled. Neither of us pointed out that it was curiosity that got the Elephant Child into deep trouble with the crocodiles in the Limpopo River, though it was quite definitely in my mind, and Gerard, as he had told me to call him, was of the generation that would have had the Just So stories fed to him as matter of course.

He was dressed that afternoon in a wool checked shirt, knitted tie and tweed jacket, much like myself, and he told me we were going to Watford.

I sensed a change in him immediately; I'd committed myself and was too far literally along the road to ask him to turn back. A good deal of surface social manner disappeared and in its place came a tough professional attitude that I felt would shrivel irrelevant comment in the utterer's throat. I listened therefore in silence, and he spoke throughout with his eyes straight ahead, not glancing to my face for reactions.

"Our client is a man called Kenneth Charter," he said. "Managing director and founder of Charter Carriers, a company whose business is transporting bulk liquids by road in tankers. The company will transport any liquid within reason, the sole limiting factor being that it must be possible to clean the tanker thoroughly afterward, ready for a change of contents. Today's hydrochloric acid, for instance, must not contaminate next week's crop-sprayer."

He drove steadily, not fast, but with easy judgment of available space. A Mercedes, fairly new, with velvety upholstery and a walnut dash, automatic gears changing on a purr.

"More than half of their business," he went on, "is the transport of various types of inflammable spirit, and in this category they include whisky." He paused. "It's of course in their interest if they can arrange to pick up one load near to where they deliver another, the limiting factor again being the cleaning. They have steam cleaning facilities and chemical scrubbing agents at their Watford headquarters, but these are not readily available everywhere. In any case, one of their regular runs has been to take bulk gin to Scotland, wash out the tanker with water, and bring scotch back."

He stopped talking to navigate through a town of small streets, and then said, "While the scotch is in the tanker it is considered to be still in a warehouse. That is to say, it is still in bond. Duty has not been paid."

I nodded. I knew that.

"As Charter's tankers carry seven thousand five hundred gallons," Gerard said neutrally, "the amount of duty involved in each load is a good deal more than a hundred thousand pounds. The whisky itself, as you know, is of relatively minor worth."

I nodded slightly again. Customs and Excise duty, value added tax and income tax paid by the shopkeeper meant that three-quarters of the selling price of every standard bottle of whisky went in one way or another to the inland revenue. One quarter paid for manufacture, bottles, shipping, advertising, and all the labor force needed between the sowing of the barley and the wrapping in a shop. The liquid itself, in that context, cost practically nothing.

"Three times this year," Gerard said, "a tanker of Charter's hasn't reached its destination. It wouldn't be accurate to say the tanker was stolen, because on each occasion it turned up. But the contents of course had vanished. The contents each time were bulk scotch. The Customs and Excise immediately demanded duty, since the scotch was no longer in the tanker. Charter Carriers have twice had to pay up.''

He paused as if to let me catch up with what he was saying.

"Charter Carriers are of course insured, or have been, and that's where they've run into serious trouble. The insurers, notwithstanding that they rocketed their premiums on each past occasion, now say that enough is enough, they are not satisfied and are withholding payment. They also say no further cover will be extended. Charter's face having to raise the cash themselves, which would be crippling, but more seriously they can't operate without insurance. On top of that the Customs and Excise are threatening to take away their license to carry goods in bond, which would in itself destroy a large part of their business.'' He paused again for appreciable seconds. "The Excise people are investigating the latest theft, but chiefly because they want the duty, and the police also, but routinely. Charter's feel that this isn't enough because it in no way guarantees the continuation of their license or the reinstatement of their insurance. They're extremely worried indeed, and they applied to us for help.''

We were speeding by this time along the M40. Another silence lengthened until Gerard eventually said, "Any questions?''

"Well, dozens, I suppose.''

"Such as?''

"Such as why was it always the scotch that was stolen and not the gin? Such as was it always the same driver and was it always the same tanker? Such as what happened to the driver, did he say? Such as where did the tankers turn up? Such as how did you connect it all with Zarac?''

He positively grinned, his teeth showing in what looked like delight.

"Anything else?" he asked.

"Such as where did the scotch start from and where was it supposed to be going and how many crooks have you turned up at each place, and does Kenneth Charter trust his own office staff and why wasn't his security invincible third time around?"

I stopped and he said without sarcasm, "Those'll do to be going on with. The answers I can give you are that no it wasn't always the same driver but yes it was always the same tanker. The tanker turned up every time abandoned in Scotland in transport café carparks, but always with so many extra miles on the clock that it could have been driven as far as London or Cardiff and back."

Another pause, then he said, "The drivers don't remember what happened to them."

I blinked. "Don't remember?"

"No. They remember setting off. They remember driving as far as the English border, where they all stopped at a motorway service station for a pee. They stopped at two different service stations. None of them remembers anything else except waking up in a ditch. Never the same ditch." He smiled. "After the second theft Kenneth Charter made it a rule that on that run no one was to eat or drink in cafés. The drivers had to take what they wanted with them in the cab. All the same they still had to stop for nature. The police say the thieves must have been following the tanker each time, waiting for that. Then when the driver was out of the cab, they put in an open canister of gas, perhaps nitrous oxide, which has no smell and acts fast—it's what dentists use. When the driver climbed back in he lost consciousness before he could drive off."

"How regular was that run?" I asked.

"Normally twice a week."

"Always the same tanker?"

"No," he said contentedly. "Charter's keep four tankers exclusively for drinkable liquids. The other three made the run just as often, but weren't touched. It may be coincidence, maybe not."

"How long ago was the last load stolen?" I asked.

"Three weeks last Wednesday."

"And before that?"

"One in April, one in June."

"That's three in six months," I said, surprised.

"Yes, exactly."

"No wonder the insurers are kicking up a fuss."

"Mm." He drove quietly for a while and then said, "Every time the scotch was destined for the same place, a bottling plant at Watford, north of London. The scotch didn't however always come from the same distillery, or the same warehouse. The stolen loads came from three different places. The last lot came from a warehouse near Helensburgh in Dunbartonshire, but it set off from there in the normal way and we don't think that's where the trouble is."

"In the bottling plant?" I asked.

"We don't know, for sure, but we don't think so. The lead to the Silver Moondance looked so conclusive that it was decided we should start from there."

"What was the lead?" I said.

He didn't answer immediately but in the end said, "I think Kenneth Charter had better tell you himself."

"O.K."

"I should explain," he said presently, "that when firms call us in it's often because there are things they don't necessarily want to tell the police. Companies very often like to deal privately, for instance, with frauds. By no means do they always want to prosecute, they just want the fraud stopped. Public admission that a fraud was going on under their noses can be embarrassing.''

''I see,'' I said.

''Kenneth Charter told me certain things in confidence that he didn't tell the police or the Customs and Excise. He wants his transport firm to survive, but not if the price in personal terms is too high. He agreed I should bring you in as a consultant, but I'll leave it to him to decide how much he wants you to know.''

''All right,'' I said peacefully.

We left the motorway and Gerard began threading his way across the semisuburban sprawl to the north of London where one town ran into another without noticeable difference.

''You're an undemanding sort of man,'' Gerard observed after a while.

''What should I demand?''

''How much a consultancy fee is, perhaps. Conditions, maybe. Assurances.''

''Life's like the weather,'' I said wryly. ''What comes, comes. Even with a sunny forecast you can get wet.''

''A fatalist.''

''It rains. You can't stop it.''

He glanced at my face for almost the first time on the journey but I doubt if he read much there. I'd spoken not bitterly but with a sort of tiredness, result of failing to come to terms with my own private deluge. I was in truth quite interested in the stolen scotch and the tankers, but on a minor level, not down where it mattered.

As if sensing it he said, ''You'll do your best for me?''

"Such as it is," I assured him. "Yes."

He nodded as if a doubt had been temporarily stilled and turned off the road into an industrial area where small factories had sprung like recent mushrooms in a concrete field. The fourth on the right bore the words "Charter Carriers Ltd." in large red letters on a white board attached to the front, while down the side, like piglets to a sow, stretched a long row of silver tankers side by side, engines facing in, sterns out.

NINE

KENNETH CHARTER WASN'T IN THE LEAST WHAT I EX-
pected, which was I supposed a burly North Londoner
with a truculent manner. The man who came into the
entrance hall to greet us as we pushed through the glass
front door was tall, thin, reddish-haired and humorous
with an accent distinctly more Scottish than Gerard's
faint Highland.

"Is this the consultant?" he said with a lilt. He found
my youth more a matter of laughter than concern, it
seemed. "No graybeard, are you?" He shook my hand
firmly. "Come away in, then. And how are you today,
Mr. McGregor?"

He led the way into a square uninspiring cream-walled
office and waved us to two upright armless chairs facing
a large unfussy modern desk. There was a brown floor-
covering of utilitarian matting, a row of gray filing cabinets, a large framed map of the British Isles and a settled chill in the air, which might or might not have been
because it was Sunday. Kenneth Charter seemed not to
notice it and offered no comment. He had the Scots
habit, I suspected, of finding sin in comfort and virtue

in thrift and believing morality grew exclusively in a cold climate.

Gerard and I sat in the offered chairs. Kenneth Charter took his place behind his desk in a swiveling chair, which he tilted recklessly backward.

"How much have you told this bonny expert?" he said, and listened without visible anxiety to Gerard's recapitulation.

"Well, now," he said to me cheerfully at the end, "you'll want to know what liquid you're looking for. Or could you guess, laddie, could you guess?" His very blue eyes were quizzically challenging, and I did a quick flip and a turnover through past occasional nips in customers' houses and sought for a check against the memory from the bar of the Silver Moondance and said on an instinctive, unreasoned impulse, "Rannoch."

Charter looked cynical and said to Gerard, "You told him, then."

Gerard shook his head. "I didn't." He himself was looking smug. His consultant, it seemed, had come up trumps at the first attempt.

"I guessed," I said mildly. "I sell that make. I've tasted it quite a few times. There aren't so many whiskies that would be shipped in bulk and bottled in England. Rannoch just fitted."

"Very well, then." He opened a drawer in his desk and produced from it a full bottle of Rannoch whisky, the familiar label adorned with an imposing male kilted figure in red and yellow tartan. The seal, I noticed, was unbroken, and Charter showed no signs of altering that.

"A Christmas gift from the bottling company," he said.

"Last Christmas?" I asked.

"Of course last Christmas. We'll not be getting one this year, now will we?"

"I guess not," I said meekly. "I meant, it's a long time for the bottle to be full."

He chuckled. "I don't drink alcohol, laddie. Addles your brains, rots your gut. What's more, I can't stand the taste. We need someone like you because I wouldn't recognize that stolen load of firewater if it turned up in the pond in my garden."

The goldfish would tell him, I thought. They'd die.

"Did you have a profile of that load?" I asked.

"A what?"

"Um, its composition. What it was blended from. You could get a detailed list from the distiller, I should think. The profile is a sort of chemical analysis in the form of a graph. It looks something like the skyline of New York. Each different blend shows a different skyline. The profile is important to some people. The Japanese import scotch by profile alone, though actually a perfect-looking profile can taste rotten. Anyway, profiles are minutely accurate. Sort of like human tissue typing, a lot more advanced than just a blood test."

"All I can tell you is it was fifty-eight percent alcohol by volume," Charter said. "The same strength as always with Rannoch. It's here on the manifest." He produced from a drawer a copy of the Customs and Excise declaration and pushed it across for me to see. "I don't ask what's in the stuff, I just ferry it."

"We'll get on to the profile straightaway," Gerard murmured.

"The Customs people probably have already," I said.

"They'll have the equipment. A gas chromatograph." I had an uncomfortable feeling that Gerard was thinking

I should have told him about profiles on the way, but it hadn't crossed my mind.

"I mean," I said, "if they took a sample from the distillers and matched it with the sample the police took from the Silver Moondance, they would know for sure one way or another."

There was a silence. Finally Gerard cleared his throat and said, "Perhaps you might tell Tony how we were led to the Silver Moondance. Because at this moment," he looked straight at me, "there is no reason for the Customs to connect that place to the stolen tanker or to compare the samples. They aren't aware of any link."

I said "Oh" fairly vaguely and Kenneth Charter consulted the ceiling, tipping his chair back to where it should surely have overbalanced. He finally let his weight fall forward with a thud and gave me the full blast from the blue eyes.

"Promise of silence, laddie," he said.

I looked at Gerard, who nodded offhandedly as if such demands were an everyday business fact, which I supposed to him they were.

"Promise of silence," I said.

Kenneth Charter nodded his long head sharply as if taking it for granted that promises would be kept; then he pulled a bunch of keys from his pocket and unlocked the center drawer of his desk. The object within needed no searching for. He pulled out a small slim black notebook and laid it on the desk before him, the naturally humorous cast of his face straightening to something like grimness.

"You can trust this laddie?" he said to Gerard.

"I'd believe so."

Charter sighed, committed, turned to the page that fell open immediately in a way that spoke of constant usage.

"Read that," he said, turning the notebook round for me to see but retaining it under the pressure of his thumb.

"That" was a long telephone number beginning 0735, which was the code for the Reading area, with underneath it two lines of writing.

"Tell Z UNP 786 Y picks up B's Gin Mon. 10:00 A.M. approx."

"I've read it," I said, not knowing what exactly was expected.

"Mean anything?"

"I suppose it's the Silver Moondance number, and Z is Zarac."

"Right. And UNP 786 Y is the registration number of my tanker." His voice was cold; unemotional.

"I see," I said.

"Berger's Gin is where it set out from at 10:15 A.M. a month ago tomorrow. It went to Scotland, discharged the gin, was sluiced through in Glasgow and picked up the bulk scotch at Fairley's warehouse near Helensburgh, in Dunbartonshire. Wednesday morning it set off from there. Wednesday evening it didn't arrive at the bottling plant. By Thursday morning we know it was parked outside a drivers' café on the outskirts of Edinburgh, but it wasn't identified until Friday as its registration plates had been changed. The Customs and Excise have impounded it, and we haven't got it back."

I looked at Gerard and then again at Kenneth Charter.

"And you know," I said slowly. "You know who wrote the message."

"Yes, I do," he said. "My son."

Highly complicating, as Gerard had hinted.

"Um . . ." I said, trying to make my question as non-committal as Charter's own voice. "What does your son

say? Does he know where the bulk in the tanker vanished to? Because . . . er . . . seven thousand five hundred
gallons of scotch can't be hidden all that easily, and the
Silver Moondance wouldn't use three times that much
in six years, let alone six months, if you see.''

The blue eyes if anything grew more intense. ''I
haven't spoken to my son. He went to Australia two
weeks ago for a holiday and I don't expect him back for
three months.''

There was an element of good riddance in that statement, I thought. He wasn't so much grieving over his
offspring's treason as finding it thoroughly awkward. I
smiled at him faintly without thinking and to my surprise
he grinned suddenly and broadly back.

''You're right,'' he said. ''The little bugger can stay
there, as far as I'm concerned. I'm certainly not trying
to fetch him home. I don't want him charged and tried
and maybe flung in jail. I don't, I definitely don't want
any son of mine behind bars embarrassing the whole
family. Making his mother cry, spoiling his sister's wedding next spring, messing up his brother's chances of a
degree in law. If I have to sell up here, well, I will.
There'll be enough left for me to start something else.
And that's the end of the damage that sod will do. I
won't have him casting a worse blight on the family.''

''No,'' I said slowly. ''When was it, did you say, that
he went to Australia?''

''Two weeks ago yesterday, laddie. I took him to
Heathrow myself. When I got home I found this notebook on the floor of the car, fallen out of his pocket. I
guess he's sweating now, hoping like hell he dropped it
anywhere but at my very feet. I opened it to make sure
it was his.'' Charter shrugged, locking it back into the
desk drawer. ''It was his, all right. His writing. Nothing

much in it, just a few telephone numbers and lists of things to do. He always made lists of things to do, right from when he was small.''

Something like regret touched Kenneth Charter's mouth. Any son, I supposed, was loved when small, before he grew up a disappointment.

''The tanker's number sort of shouted at me,'' he said. ''I felt sick, I'll tell you. My own son! There were the police and the Customs and Excise chasing all over the place looking for the crook who tipped off the thieves, and he'd been right there in my own house.'' He shook his head in disgust. ''So then I took advice from a businessman I knew who'd had his troubles sorted out quietly, and I got on to Deglet's, and finally Mr. McGregor, here. And there you have it, laddie.''

Kenneth Charter's son, I was thinking, had gone to Australia ten days after the scotch had been stolen and a week before the horsebox had rolled into the marquee. If he was truly in Australia, he'd had nothing to do with the disappearance of the Silver Moondance's liquid assets or the murder of Zarac. For such small crumbs his father could be grateful.

''Would it be easy for your son to find out when exactly the tanker would be going to fetch whisky?'' I asked diffidently.

''Back in April, yes, easy. In June, not so easy. Last month, damned difficult. But there you are, I didn't know I had to defend myself so close to home.'' Kenneth Charter got to his feet, his big body seeming to rise forever. He grasped the frame of the map of the British Isles and gave it a tug, and the map opened away from the wall like a door, showing a second chart beneath.

The revealed chart was an appointments calendar with

registration numbers in a long column down the left-hand side, and dates across the top.

"Tankers," Charter said succinctly, pointing to the registration numbers. "Thirty-four of them. There's UNP 786 Y, sixth from the top."

All the spaces across from that number had a line drawn through: tanker out of commission. For many of the others some of the spaces across were filled with stuck-on labels of many colors, blue, green, red, yellow, gray, purple, orange, each label bearing a handwritten message.

"We use the labels to save time," Charter said. "Purple for instance is always hydrochloric acid. We can see at a glance which tanker is carrying it. On the label it says where from, where to. Gray is gin, yellow is whisky. Red is wine. Blue is sulphuric acid. Green is any of several disinfectants. And so on. My secretary, whom I trust absolutely, she's been with me twenty years, writes the labels and keeps the chart. We don't tell the drivers where they're going or what they're carrying until the moment they set out. They change tankers regularly. We often switch drivers at the last minute. Some of the loads could be dangerous, see, if they fell into the wrong hands. We have an absolute rule that all the tanker doors have to be locked if the drivers so much as set foot out of the cabs, and in all three stolen loads the drivers swore they did that, and found nothing to alarm them when they returned. We've been careful and until this year we've been fortunate." His voice was suddenly full of suppressed fury.

"It took my own son . . . my own son . . . to crack our system."

"He could come in here, I suppose," I said.

"Not often, he didn't. I told him if he wouldn't work

in the company, he could stay away. He must have sneaked in here somehow, but I don't know when. He knew about the chart, of course. But since the first two thefts I've not allowed the whisky labels to be written up, just in case the leak was in our own company. Yellow labels, see? All blank. So if he saw the yellow label for that tanker for the Wednesday, it wouldn't say where it was picking up. Gray for gin, on the Monday, that was written up, but only for the pickup, not the destination. If someone wanted to steal the return load of scotch they'd have to follow the tanker all the way from Berger's Gin distillery to find out where it was going.''

I frowned, thinking the theory excessive, but Gerard was nodding as if such dedication to the art of theft was commonplace.

"Undoubtedly what happened," Gerard said. "But the question remains, to whom did Zarac pass on that message? He didn't take part in the event himself. He wasn't away from the Silver Moondance long enough, and was definitely at his post both the Tuesday and Wednesday lunchtimes and also in the evenings until after midnight. We checked."

My mind wandered from the problem I didn't consider very closely my own (and in any case unanswerable) and I found my attention fastening on the few red labels on the chart. All the information on them had been heavily crossed out, as indeed it had on the gray labels as well. Kenneth Charter followed my gaze, his hairy Scots eyebrows rising.

"The wine," I said, almost apologetically. "Didn't you say red for wine?"

"Aye, I did. All those shipments have had to be canceled. Normally we fetch it from France and take it direct to the shippers near here, who bottle it themselves. We used to carry a lot more wine once, but they bottle more of it in France now. Half the bottling plants over here have been scratching round for new business. Hard times, laddie. Closures. Not their fault. The world moves on and changes. Always happening. Spend your life learning to make longbows, and someone invents guns.''

He closed the chart into its secrecy behind the map and dusted his hands on his trousers as if wiping off his son's perfidy.

''There's life in tankers yet,'' he observed. ''D'you want to see them?''

I said yes, please, as they were clearly his pride, and we left his office with him carefully locking the door behind us. He led the way not to the outside but down a passage lined on either side by office doors and through a heavier door, also locked, at the far end. That door led directly into a large expanse given to the maintenance and cleaning of the silver fleet. There was all the paraphernalia of a commercial garage: inspection pit, heavy-duty jacks, benches with vises, welding equipment, a rack of huge new tires. Also, slung from the ceiling, chains and machinery for lifting. Two tankers stood in this space, receiving attention from men in brown overalls who from their manner already knew Charter was around on Sunday afternoon and gave Gerard and myself cursory incurious glances.

''Over there,'' Charter said, pointing, ''down that side, inside that walled section, we clean the tanks, pumps, valves and hoses. The exteriors go through a carwash outside.'' He began walking down the garage, expecting us to follow. The mechanics called him Ken and told him there was trouble with an axle, and I looked

with interest at the nearest tanker, which seemed huge
to me, indoors.

The tank part was oval in section, resting solidly on
its chassis with what I guessed was a low center of gravity, to make overturning a minor hazard. There was a
short ladder bolted on at the back so that one could
climb onto the top, where there were the shapes of
hatches and loading gear. The silver metal was un-
painted and carried no information as to its ownership,
only the words FLAMMABLE LIQUID in small red
capitals toward the rear.

The paintwork of the cab, a dark brownish red, was
also devoid of name, address and telephone number. The
tanker was anonymous, as the whole fleet was, I later
saw. Kenneth Charter's security arrangements had kept
them safe for years from every predator except the traitor
within.

"Why did he do it?" Charter said from over my
shoulder, and I shook my head, not knowing.

"He was always jealous as a little boy, but we thought
he'd grow out of it." He sighed. "The older he got the
more bad-tempered he was, and sullen, and dead lazy. I
tried to speak kindly to him but he'd be bloody rude
back and I'd have to go out of the room so as not to hit
him sometimes." He paused, seeking no doubt for the
thousandth time for guilt in himself, where there was
none.

"He wouldn't work. He seemed to think the world
owed him a living. He'd go out and refuse to say where
he'd been, and he wouldn't lift a finger to help his
mother in the house. He sneered all the time at his
brother and sister, who are bonny kids. I offered him his
fare to Australia and some money to spend there, and
he said he'd go. I hoped, you know, that they'd knock

some sense into him over there." His tall body moved in a sort of shudder. "I'd no idea he'd done anything criminal. He was a pain in the arse. Didn't he know he would ruin me in this business? Did he care? Did he mean to?"

The son sounded irredeemable to me and for the sake of the rest of the Charter family I hoped he'd never come home, but life was seldom so tidy.

"Mr. McGregor may save your business," I said, and he laughed aloud in one of his mercurial changes of mood and clapped me on the shoulder. "A politician, Mr. McGregor, that's what you've brought me here. Aye, laddie, so he may, so he may, for the healthy fee I'm paying him."

Gerard smiled indulgently and we walked on through the length of the maintenance area and out through the door at the far end. Outside, as Charter had said, there was a tall commercial-sized carwash, but he turned away from that and led us round to the side of the building to where the fleet of tankers nestled in line.

"We've some out on the road," Charter said. "And I'm having to arrange huge insurance for every one separately, which is wiping out our profit. I've drivers sitting at home watching television and customers going elsewhere. We can't carry alcohol, the Customs won't let us. It's illegal for this company to operate if it can't pay its workforce and other debts. I reckon we can keep running on reserves for perhaps two weeks if we're lucky, but then we could be shut down in five minutes if the bank foreclosed on the tankers, which they will. Half of these tankers at any one time are being bought on loans, and if we can't service the loans, we're out." He smoothed a loving hand over one of the gleaming monsters. "I'll be bloody sorry, and that's a fact."

The three of us walked soberly along the imposing row until we were back at the entrance, and Gerard's car.

"Two weeks, Mr. McGregor," Kenneth Charter said. He shook our hands vigorously. "Hardly a sporting chance, would you say?"

"We'll try for results," Gerard assured him in a stockbroker voice, and we climbed into his car and drove away.

"Any thoughts?" he asked me immediately, before we'd even left the industrial estate.

"Chiefly," I said, "why you need me at all."

"For your knowledge, as I told you. And because people talk to you."

"How do you mean?"

"Kenneth Charter told you far more about his son than he told me. Flora says she talks to you because you listen. She says you hear things that aren't said. I was most struck by that. It's a most useful ability in a detective."

"I'm not . . ."

"No. Any other thoughts?"

"Well," I said, "did you see the rest of the son's notebook, when you were there before?"

"Yes, I did. Charter didn't want me to take it for some reason, so I used his photocopier to reproduce every page that was written on. As he said, there were just some telephone numbers and a few memos about things to do. We've checked on all the telephone numbers these last few days but they seem to be harmless. Friends' houses, a local cinema, a snooker club and a barber. No lead to how the son knew Zarac, if that's what you're thinking."

"Yes," I said.

"Mm. I'll show you the photostats presently. See if you can suggest anything we've missed."

Unlikely, I thought.

"Is he actually in Australia?" I asked.

"The son? Yes, he is. He stayed in a motel in Sydney the night he arrived. His father made the reservation, and the son did stay there. We checked. Beyond that, we've lost him, except that we know he hasn't used his return ticket. Quite possibly he doesn't know Zarac's dead. If he does, he's likely to drop even further out of sight. In any case, Kenneth Charter's instructed us not to look for him, and we'll comply with that. We're having to work from the Silver Moondance end, and frankly, since Zarac's murder, that's far from easy."

I reflected for a while and then said, "Can you pick the police's brains at all?"

"Sometimes. It depends."

"They'll be looking for Paul Young," I said.

"Who?"

"Did Flora mention him? A man who came to the Silver Moondance from what he said was head office. He arrived while I was there with Detective Sergeant Ridger, who took me there to taste the Laphroaig."

Gerard frowned as he drove. "Flora said one of the managers had come in when you were tasting the whisky and wine, and was furious."

I shook my head. "Not a manager." I told Gerard in detail about Paul Young's visit, and he drove more and more slowly as he listened.

"That makes a difference," he said almost absently when I'd finished. "What else do you know that Flora didn't tell me?"

"The barman's homosexual," I said flippantly. Gerard didn't smile. "Well," I sighed, "Larry Trent bought a horse for thirty thousand pounds, did she tell you that?''

"No. Is that important?''

I related the saga of the disappearing Ramekin. "Maybe the Silver Moondance made that sort of money, but I doubt it,'' I said. "Larry Trent kept five horses in training, which takes some financing, and he gambled in the thousands. Gamblers don't win, bookmakers do.''

"When did Larry Trent buy this horse?'' Gerard asked.

"At Doncaster Sales a year ago.''

"Before the whisky thefts,'' he said regretfully.

"Before those particular whisky thefts. Not necessarily before all the red wines in his cellar began to taste the same.''

"Do you want a full-time job?'' he said.

"No thanks.''

"What happened to Ramekin, do you think?''

"I would think,'' I said, "that at a guess he was shipped abroad and sold.''

TEN

At the rear of the row where my shop was located there was a service road with several small yards opening from it, leading to back doors, so that goods could be loaded and unloaded without one having to carry everything in and out through the front. It was into one of these yards that the bolted door next to my storeroom led, and it was in that yard that we commonly parked the van and the car.

Mrs. Palissey, that Sunday, had the van. The Rover was standing in the yard where I'd left it when Gerard picked me up. Despite my protestations, when we returned at six he insisted on turning into the service road to save me walking the scant hundred yards from the end.

"Don't bother," I said.

"No trouble."

He drove along slowly, saying he'd be in touch with me on the following day as we still had things to discuss, turning into the third yard on the left, at my direction.

Besides my car there was a medium-sized van in the yard, its rear doors wide open. I looked at it in vague surprise, as the two other shops who shared the yard with me were my immediate neighbor, a hairdresser, and next to that a dress shop, both of them firmly closed all day on Sundays.

My other immediate neighbor, served by the next yard, was a Chinese takeout restaurant, open always; the van, I thought in explanation, must have driven into my yard in mistake for his.

Gerard slowed his car to a halt as a man carrying a case of wine elbowed his way sideways out of the back door of my shop: the door I had left firmly bolted at two o'clock. I exclaimed furiously, opening the passenger door to scramble out.

"Get back in," Gerard was saying urgently, but I hardly listened. "I'll find a telephone for the police."

"Next yard," I said over my shoulder. "Sung Li. Ask him." I slammed the door behind me and fairly ran across to the intruding van, so angry that I didn't give my own safety the slightest thought. Extremely foolish, as everyone pointed out to me continually during the next week, a view with which in retrospect I had to agree.

The man who had walked from my shop hadn't seen me and had his head in the van, transferring the weight of the case from his arms to the floor, a posture whose mechanics I knew well.

I shoved him hard at the base of the spine to push him off balance and slammed both of the van's doors into his buttocks. He yelled out, swearing with shock and outrage, his voice muffled to all ears but mine. He couldn't do much to free himself: I'd got him pinned into the van by the doors, his legs protruding beneath, and I thought with fierce satisfaction that I could easily hold him there until Gerard returned.

I'd overlooked, unfortunately, that robbers could work in pairs. There was a colossal crunch against the small of my back that by thrusting me onto the van doors did more damage still, I should imagine, to the man half in the van, and as I struggled to turn I saw a second, very similar man, carrying another case of wine with which he was trying to bore a hole straight through me, or so it felt.

The man half in half out of the van was practically screaming. The urgency of his message seemed to get through to his pal, who suddenly removed the pressure from my back and dropped the case of wine at my feet. I had a flurried view of fuzzy black hair, a heavy black moustache and eyes that boded no good for anybody. His fist slammed into my jaw and shook bits I never knew could rattle, and I kicked him hard on the shin.

No one had ever taught me how to fight because I hadn't wanted to learn. Fighting involved all the scary things like people trying to hurt you, where I considered the avoidance of being hurt a top priority. Fighting led to stamping about with guns, to people shooting at you round corners, to having to kill someone yourself. Fighting led to the Victoria Cross and the Distinguished Service Order, or so it had seemed to my child mind, and the bravery of my father and grandfather had seemed not only unattainable but alien, as if they belonged to a different race.

The inexpert way I fought that Sunday afternoon had nothing to do with bravery but everything to do with rage. They had no bloody right, I thought breathlessly, to steal my property, and they damned well shouldn't, if I could stop them.

They had more to lose than I, I suppose. Liberty, for a start. Also I had undoubtedly damaged the first one rather severely around the pelvis, and as far as he was able he was looking for revenge.

It wasn't so much a matter of straight hitting with fists: more of clutching and kicking and ramming against hard surfaces and using knees as blunt instruments. At about the instant I ran out of enthusiasm the second man succeeded finally in what I'd been half aware he was trying to do, and reached in through the driver's door of the van, momentarily leaning forward in that same risky posture, which I would have taken advantage of if I hadn't had my hands full with robber number one. Too late I kicked free of him and went to go forward.

Number two straightened out of the front of the van, and the fight stopped right there. He was panting a little but triumphantly holding a short-barreled shotgun, which he nastily aimed at my chest.

"Back off," he said to me grimly.

I backed.

All my feelings about guns returned in a rush. It was suddenly crystal clear that a few cases of wine weren't worth dying for. I walked one step backward and then another and then a third, which brought me up against the wall beside my own back door. The door tended to close if not propped open, and was at that point shut but on the latch. If I could go through it, I thought dimly, I'd be safe, and I also thought that if I tried to escape through it, I'd be shot.

At the very second it crossed my mind that the man with the gun didn't know whether to shoot me or not, Gerard drove his car back into my yard. The man with the gun swung round toward him and loosed off one of the barrels and I yanked open my door and leaped to go through it. I knew the gun was turning back my way: I could see it in the side of my frantic vision. I knew also that having shot once he'd shoot again, that the moment of inhibition was past. At five paces away he was so close that the full discharge would have blown a hole in an ox. I suppose I moved faster in that second than ever before in my life, and I was jumping sideways through the doorway like a streak when he pulled the trigger.

I fell over inside but not entirely from the impact of pellets: mainly because the passage was strewn with more cases of wine. The bits of shot that had actually landed felt like sharp stings in my arm: like hot stabs.

The door swung shut behind me. If I bolted it, I thought, I would be safe. I also thought of Gerard outside in his car, and along with these two thoughts I noticed blood running down my right hand. Oh, well, I wasn't dead, was I? I struggled to my feet and opened the door enough to see what I'd be walking out to, and found that it wouldn't be very much, as the two black-headed robbers were scrambling into their van with clear intentions of driving away.

I didn't try to stop them. They rocketed past Gerard's car and swerved into the service road, disappearing with the rear doors swinging open and three or four cases of wine showing within.

The windscreen of Gerard's car was shattered. I went over there with rising dread and found him lying across both front seats, the top of one shoulder reddening and his teeth clenched with pain.

I opened the door beside the steering wheel. One says really such inadequate things at terrible times. I said, "I'm so sorry," knowing he'd come back to help me, knowing I shouldn't have gone in the yard in the first place.

Sung Li from next door came tearing round the corner on his feet, his broad face wide with anxiety.

"Shots," he said. "I heard shots."

Gerard said tautly, "I ducked. Saw the gun. I guess not totally fast enough." He struggled into a sitting position, holding on to the wheel and shedding crazed crumbs of windscreen like snow. "The police are coming and you yourself are alive, I observe. It could fractionally have been worse."

Sung Li, who spoke competent English, looked at Gerard as if he couldn't believe his ears, and I laughed, transferring his bewilderment to myself.

"Mr. Tony," he said anxiously as if fearing for my reason, "do you know you are bleeding also?"

"Yes," I said.

Sung Li's face mutely said that all English were mad, and Gerard didn't help by asking him to whistle up an ambulance, dear chap, if he wouldn't mind.

Sung Li went away looking dazed and Gerard gave me what could only be called a polite social smile.

"Bloody Sundays," he said, "are becoming a habit." He blinked a few times. "Did you get the number of that van?"

"Mm," I nodded. "Did you?"

"Yes. Gave it to the police. Description of men?"

"They were wearing wigs," I said. "Fuzzy black wigs, both the same. Also heavy black moustaches, identical. False, I should think. Also surgical rubber gloves. If you're asking would I know them again without those additions, then unfortunately I don't think so."

"Your arm's bleeding," he said. "Dripping from your hand."

"They were stealing my wine."

After a pause he said, "Which wine, do you think?"

"A bloody good question. I'll go and look," I said. "Will you be all right?"

"Yes."

I went off across the yard to my back door, aware of the warm stickiness of my right arm, feeling the stinging soreness from shoulder to wrist, but extraordinarily not worried. Elbow and fingers still moved per instructions, though after the first exploratory twitches I decided to leave them immobile for the time being. Only the outer scatterings of the shot had caught me, and compared with what might have happened it did truthfully at that moment seem minor.

I noticed at that point how the thieves had got in: the barred washroom window had been comprehensively smashed inward, frame, bars and all, leaving a hole big enough for a man. I went into the washroom, scrunching on broken glass, and picked up the cloth with which I usually dried the glasses after customers had tasted wines, wrapping it a few times round my wrist to mop up the crimson trickles before going out to see what I'd lost.

For a start I hadn't lost my small stock of really superb wines in wooden boxes at the back of the storeroom. The prizes, the appreciating Margaux and Lafite, were still there.

I hadn't lost, either, ten cases of champagne or six very special bottles of old cognac, or even a readily handy case of vodka. The boxes I'd fallen over in the passage were all open at the tops, the necks of the bottles showing, and when one went into the shop one could see why.

The robbers had been stealing the bottles from the racks. More peculiarly they had taken all the half-drunk wine bottles standing recorked on the tasting table, and all the opened cases from beneath the tablecloth.

The wines on and below the table had come from St.

Emilion, Volnay, Côtes de Roussillon and Graves, all red. The wines missing from the shop's racks were of those and some from St. Estèphe, Nuits St. Georges, Mâcon and Valpolicella; also all red.

I went back out into the yard and stooped to look at the contents of the case robber number two had jabbed me with and then dropped. It contained some of the bottles from the tasting table, four of them broken.

Straightening, I continued over to Gerard's car and was relieved to see him looking no worse.

"Well?" he said.

"They weren't ordinary thieves," I said.

"Go on, then."

"They were stealing only the sorts of wines I tasted at the Silver Moondance. The wines that weren't what the labels said."

He looked at me, the effort of concentration showing.

I said, "I bought those wines, the actual ones, at the Silver Moondance. Paid for them. Got a receipt from the barman. He must have thought I took them away with me, but in fact the police have them. Sergeant Ridger. He too gave me a receipt."

"You are saying," Gerard said slowly, "that if you'd brought those wines here to your shop, today they would have vanished."

"Yeah . . ."

"Given another half-hour . . . ." I nodded.

"They must be of extraordinary importance."

"Mm," I said. "Be nice to know why."

"Why did you buy them?"

We were both talking, I saw, so as to give a semblance of normality to the abnormal reality of two ordinary Englishmen quietly bleeding from shotgun wounds in a small town on a Sunday afternoon. I thought "this is bloody ridiculous" and I answered him civilly, "I bought them for the labels. To see if the labels themselves were forgeries. As a curio. Like collecting stamps."

"Ah," he said placidly.

"Gerard . . ."

"Yes?"

"I'm very sorry."

"So you should be. Stupid behavior."

"Yes."

We waited for a while longer until a police car rolled into the yard without haste, two policemen emerging inquiringly, saying they could see no evidence of any break-in at the wine shop, and did we know who had called them out.

Gerard closed his eyes. I said, "This is the back of the wine shop. The thieves broke in the back, not the front. If you look closely you'll see they smashed the washroom window, climbed in over the loo and unbolted the back door from the inside."

One of them said "Oh," and went to look. The other took out his notebook. I said mildly, "The thieves had a shotgun and . . . er . . . shot us. They were driving away in a gray Bedford van, brown lines along the sides, license number MMO 229Y, containing about four cases of red wine. They'll have gone ten miles by now, I shouldn't wonder."

"Name, sir?" he said blandly.

I wanted to giggle. I told him my name, however, and to do him justice he wasted no time once he realized that red wasn't in the original weave of Gerard's jacket. Gerard and I in due course found ourselves in the casualty department of the local major hospital where he was whisked off to regions unseen and I sat with my bare newly washed arm on a small table while a middle-aged nursing sister expertly and unemotionally picked pellets out with a glittering instrument reminiscent of tweezers.

"You look as if you've done this before," I observed.

"Every year during the shooting season." She paused. "Can you feel this?"

"No, not really."

"Good. Some of them have gone deep. If the local anaesthetic isn't enough, tell me."

"I sure will," I said fervently.

She dug around for a while until there were eleven little black balls like peppercorns rattling redly in the dish, each of them big enough to kill a pheasant; and to my morbid amusement she said I could take them with me if I liked, many people did.

Carrying my jacket and with a thing like a knitted tube over antiseptic patches replacing the shredded sleeve of my shirt I went to find Gerard, discovering him in a cubicle, sitting in a wheelchair, wearing a hospital-issue fawn dressing-gown over his trousers and looking abysmally bored. He had stopped bleeding both inside and out, it appeared, but several pellets were inaccessible to tweezers and he would have to stay overnight until the surgical staff returned in force in the morning. Life-and-death alone got seen to on Sundays, not small spheres of lead lodged behind collarbones.

He said he had telephoned to Tina, his wife, who was bringing his pajamas. Tina also would retrieve his car and get the windscreen fixed; and I wondered whether he had told Tina that the velvety upholstery that was where his head would have been if he hadn't thrown himself sideways was ripped widely apart with the stuffing coming out.

I went back to my shop in a taxi and checked that the police had, as they had promised, sent someone to board up the absent washroom window. I let myself in through the front door, switching on a light, assessing the extent of the mess, seeing it not now with anger but as a practical problem of repair.

For all that it wouldn't be permanently damaged I had an arm not currently of much use. Lifting cases of wine could wait a day or two. Likewise sweeping up broken glass. Thank goodness for Brian, I thought tiredly, and checked that the bolts were once again in position over the door and the sheet of plywood nailed securely in the washroom.

I left everything as it was, switched off the lights and went out again by the front door. Sung Li was emerging reluctantly from his restaurant, his forehead lined with worry.

"Oh, it is you, Mr. Tony," he said with relief. "No more burglars."

"No."

"You want some food?"

I hesitated. I'd eaten nothing all day but felt no hunger.

"It's best to eat," he said. "Lemon chicken, your favorite. I made it fresh." He gave me a brief bow. I bowed courteously in return and went in with him: between us there was the same sort of formality as between myself and Mrs. Palissey, and Sung Li, also, seemed to prefer it. I ate the lemon chicken seated at a table in the small restaurant section and after that fried shrimp and felt a good deal less lightheaded. I hadn't known I was lightheaded until then, rather like not knowing how ill one had been until after one felt well again, but, looking back, I imagined I hadn't been entirely ground-based since I'd looked into the business end of a shotgun and found my legs didn't reliably belong to my body. The euphoria of escape, I now saw, accounted for Gerard's and my unconcerned conversation in the yard and for my methodical checking of my losses. It was really odd how the mind strove to pretend things were normal . . . and there were good chemical reasons why that happened after injury. I'd read an article about it, somewhere.

I stood up, making a stiff attempt to pick my wallet out of my pocket, and Sung Li was at my side instantly, telling me to pay him in the morning. I asked if I could go out to my car in the yard through his kitchen door instead of walking all the way round and he was too polite to tell me I wasn't fit to drive. We bowed to each other again outside in the darkness, and I'd managed to grasp my keys pretty firmly by the time I reached the Rover.

I drove home. I hit nothing. The anaesthetic wore off my arm and the whole thing started burning. I swore aloud, most obscenely, half surprised that I should say such things, even alone. Half surprised I could think them.

I let myself into the cottage. The second Sunday in a row, I thought, that I had gone back there with blood on my clothes and my mind full of horrors.

Emma, I thought, for God's sake help me. I walked through the empty rooms, not really looking for her, knowing perfectly well she wasn't there, but desperately in need all the same of someone to talk to, someone to hold me and love me as she had done.

With the lights all brightly shining I swallowed some aspirin and sat in my accustomed chair in the sitting room and told myself to shut up and be sensible. I'd been robbed ... so what? Fought ... and lost ... so what? Been shot in the arm ... so what? So Emma ... my darling love ... help me.

Get a bloody grip on things, I told myself.

Switch off the lights. Go to bed. Go to sleep.

My arm throbbed unmercifully all night.

The new day, Monday, crept into the world at about the level of my perception of it: dull, overcast, lifeless. Stiffly I dressed and shaved and made coffee, averting my mind from the temptation to go back to bed and abdicate. Mondays were hard at the best of times. The shambles ahead beckoned with all the appeal of a cold swamp.

I put the aspirin bottle in my pocket. The eleven separate punctures, announcing themselves as unready to be overlooked, seemed to be competing against one another for my attention and various bruises were developing gingerly almost everywhere else. Bugger the lot of you, I thought: to little avail.

I drove to the shop and parked in the yard. Gerard's car stood exactly in the same place where he'd stalled it askew, stamping on the footbrake when he caught sight of the gun swinging round to his face. The keys weren't in the ignition and I couldn't remember who had them. One more problem to shelve indefinitely.

There was a police car already outside my door when I walked round to the front. Inside it, Detective Sergeant Ridger. He emerged at my approach, every button and hair regimentally aligned as before. He stood waiting for me and I stopped when I reached him.

"How are you?" he said. He cleared his throat. "I'm ... er ... sorry."

I smiled at least a fraction. Sergeant Ridger was becoming quite human. I unlocked the door, let us in and locked it again; then I sat in the tiny office slowly opening the mail while he walked round the place with a notebook, writing painstakingly.

He came to a halt finally and said, "You weren't trying to be funny, were you, with the list of missing property you dictated to the constable yesterday evening before you went off to the hospital?"

"No."

"You do realize it was almost identical with the red wines stolen from the Silver Moondance."

"I do indeed," I said. "And I hope you've got my Silver Moondance bottles tucked away safely in your police station. Twelve bottles of wine, all opened. My own property."

"I haven't forgotten," he said with a touch of starch. "You'll get them back in due course."

"I'd like one of them now," I said reflectively.

"Which one?"

"The St. Estèphe."

"Why that one particularly?" He wasn't exactly suspicious; just naturally vigilant.

"Not that one particularly. It was the first that came to mind. Any would do."

"What do you want it for?"

"Just to look at it again. Smell it, taste it again. You never know, it might just be helpful. To you, I mean."

He shrugged, slightly puzzled but not antagonistic. "All right. I'll get you one if I can, but I might not be able to. They're evidence." He looked around the tiny office. "Did they touch anything in here?"

I shook my head, grateful for that at least. "They were definitely looking for the wine from the Silver Moondance. The bottles they loaded first and succeeded in taking away with them in the van were all opened and recorked.'' I explained about the bottles missing from on and beneath the tasting table, and he went to have a further look.

"Anything you can add to the description you gave of the thieves?" he asked, coming back.

I shook my head.

"Could one of them have been the barman from the Silver Moondance?"

"No," I said definitely. "Not his sort at all."

"You said they wore wigs," Ridger said. "So how can you be sure?"

"The barman has acne. The robbers didn't."

Ridger wrote it down in his notebook.

"The barman knew exactly what you bought," he observed. "He spelled them out item by item on your receipt."

"Have you asked him about it?" I said neutrally.

Ridger gave me another of the uncertain looks that showed him undecided still about my status: member of the not-to-be-informed public or helpful-consultant-expert.

"We haven't been able to find him," he said eventually.

I refrained from impolite surprise. I said merely, "Since when?"

"Since . . ." he cleared his throat. "Not actually since you yourself last saw him leaving the bar last Monday after he'd locked the grille. Apparently he drove off immediately in his car, packed his clothes, and left the district entirely."

"Where did he live?"

"With . . . um . . . a friend."

"Male friend?"

Ridger nodded. "Temporary arrangement. No roots.

At the first sign of trouble, he was off. We'll look out for him, of course, but he'd gone by early afternoon that Monday.''

"Not suspected of killing Zarac," I suggested.

"That's right."

"The assistant assistant and the waitress both knew what I bought," I said thoughtfully. "But . . ."

"Too wet," Ridger said.

"Mm. Which leaves Paul Young."

"I suppose he wasn't one of the thieves." Hardly a question, more a statement.

"No," I said. "They were both younger and taller, for a start."

"You would obviously have said."

"Yes. Have you . . . er . . . found him? Paul Young?"

"We're proceeding with our inquiries." He spoke without irony: the notebook jargon came naturally to his tongue. He wasn't much older than myself; maybe four or five years. I wondered what he'd be like off duty, if such a structured and self-disciplined person were ever entirely off duty. Probably always as watchful, as careful, as ready to prickle into suspicion. I was probably seeing, I thought, the real man.

I looked at my watch. Nine-twenty. Mrs. Palissey and Brian should be arriving in ten minutes.

I said, "I suppose it's O.K. with you if I get all this mess cleared up? Replace the window, and so on?"

He nodded. "I'll just take a look round outside, though, before I go. Come and tell me what's different from before the break-in."

I got slowly to my feet. We went out into the littered passage and without comment Ridger himself unbolted the heavy door and opened it.

"My car was parked all day yesterday just about

where it is now," I said. "Gerard McGregor's car wasn't there, of course."

Ridger looked back through his notebook, found an entry, nodded, and flipped forward again. The door swung shut in its slow way. Ridger pushed it open and went out, looking over his shoulder for me to follow. I stepped after him into the raw cold air and watched him pacing about, measuring distances.

"The thieves' van was here?" he asked, standing still.

"A bit to your right."

"Where was the man with the shotgun standing when he fired at you?"

"About where you are now."

He nodded matter-of-factly, swung round toward Gerard's car and raised his arm straight before him. "He fired at the car," he said.

"Yes."

"Then . . ." he turned his body with the arm still outstretched until it was pointing at me. "He fired again."

"I wasn't actually standing here by that time."

Ridger permitted a smile. "Too close for comfort, I'd say." He walked the five steps separating us and ran his hand over the outside of the door. "Want to see what nearly hit you?"

The toughly grained wood was dark with creosote, the preservative recently applied against the coming winter. I looked more closely to where he pointed, to an area just below the latch, a few inches in from the edge of the door. Wholly embedded in the wood as if they were part of it were dozens and dozens of little black pellets, most of them in a thick cluster, with others making marks like woodworm holes in a wider area all around.

"There are three hundred of those in a normal cartridge," Ridger observed calmly. "The report we got from the hospital said they dug eleven of them out of your right arm.''

I looked at the deadly grouping of the little black shots and remembered the frenzied panic of my leap through the door. I'd left my elbow too far out for a split second too long.

The main cluster in the wood was roughly at the height of my heart.

ELEVEN

Mrs. PALISSEY AND BRIAN ARRIVED ON TIME AND FELL into various attitudes of horror, which couldn't be helped. I asked her to open the shop for business and asked Brian to start clearing up, and I stayed out in the yard myself, knowing it was mostly to postpone answering their eagerly probing questions.

Ridger was still pacing about, estimating and making notes, fetching up finally at a dark red stain on the dirty concrete.

He said, frowning, "Is this blood?"

"No. It's red wine. The thieves dropped a case of bottles there. Some of them smashed in the case and seeped through onto the ground."

He looked around. "Where's the case now?"

"In the sink in the washroom. Your policemen carried it there yesterday evening."

He made a note.

"Sergeant?"

"Yes?" He looked up with his eyes only, his head still bent over the notebook.

"Let me know, would you, how things are going?"

"What things, for instance?"

"Whether you find that van. Whether you find a lead to Paul Young."

He looked up fully and soberly, not refusing at once. I could almost feel his hesitation and certainly see it; and his answer when it came was typically ambivalent.

"We could perhaps warn you that you might be needed at some future date for identification purposes."

"Thank you," I said.

"Not promising, mind." He was retreating into the notebook.

"No."

He finished eventually and went away, and Mrs. Palissey enjoyed her ooh/ahh sensations. Mrs. Palissey wasn't given to weeping and wailing and needing smelling salts. Mrs. Palissey's eyes were shining happily at the news value of the break-in and at the good isn't-it-awful gossip she'd have at lunchtime with the traffic warden.

Brian with little change to his normal anxious expression swept and tidied and asked me what to do about the case in the sink.

"Take out the whole bottles and put them on the draining board," I said, and presently he came to tell me he'd done that. I went into the washroom to see, and there they were, eight bottles of St. Emilion from under the tablecloth.

Brian was holding a piece of paper as if not knowing where to put it.

"What's that?" I said.

"Don't know. It was down in the case." He held it out to me and I took it: a page from a notepad, folded across the center, much handled, and damp and stained all down one side with wine from the broken bottles. I read it at first with puzzlement and then with rising amazement.

In a plain strong angular handwriting it read:

FIRST
All opened bottles of wine.
SECOND
All bottles with these names.
St. Emilion.
St. Estèphe.
Volnay.
Nuits St. Georges.
Valpolicella.
Mâcon.
IF TIME
Spirits, etc. Anything to hand.
DARKNESS 6:30. DO NOT USE LIGHTS.

"Shall I throw that away, Mr. Beach?" Brian asked helpfully.

"You can have six Mars bars," I said.

He produced his version of a large smile, a sort of sideways leer, and followed me into the shop for his reward.

Mrs. Palissey, enjoyably worried, said she was sure she could cope if I wanted to step out for ten minutes, in spite of customers coming and almost nothing on the shelves, seeing as it was Monday. I assured her I valued her highly and went out and along the road to the office of a solicitor of about my age who bought my wine pretty often in the evenings.

Certainly I could borrow his photocopier, he said. Any time.

I made three clear copies of the thieves' shopping list

and returned to my own small lair, wondering whether to call Sergeant Ridger immediately and in the end not doing so.

Brian humped cases of whisky, gin and various sherries from storeroom to shop, telling me each time as he passed what he was carrying, and each time getting it right. There was pride on his big face from the accomplishment; job satisfaction at its most pure. Mrs. Palissey restocked the shelves, chattering away interminably, and five people telephoned with orders.

Holding a pen was unexpectedly painful, arm muscles stiffly protesting. I realized I'd been doing almost everything left-handedly, including eating Sung Li's chicken, but writing that way was beyond me. I took down the orders right-handedly with many an inward curse, and when it came to the long list for the wholesaler, picked it out left-handed on the typewriter. No one had told me how long the punctures might take to heal. No time was fast enough.

We got through the morning somehow, and Mrs. Palissey, pleasantly martyred, agreed to do the wholesaler run with Brian in the afternoon.

When they'd gone I wandered round my battered domain thinking that I should dredge up some energy to telephone for replacement wines, replacement window . . . replacement self-respect. It was my own silly fault I'd been shot. No getting away from it. It hadn't seemed natural, all the same, to tiptoe off and let the robbery continue. Wiser, of course. Easy in retrospect to see it. But at the time . . .

I thought about it in a jumbled way, without clarity, not understanding the compulsive and utterly irrational urge that had sent me running toward danger when every scared and skin-preserving instinct in my life had been to shy away from it.

Not that I'd been proud of that, either. Nor ashamed of it. I'd accepted that that was the way I was: not brave in the least. Disappointing.

I supposed I had better make a list of the missing wines for the insurance company, who would be getting as fed up with my repeated claims as Kenneth Charter's insurers were with his. I supposed I should, but I didn't do it. Appetite for chores, one might have said, was at an extremely low ebb.

I took some aspirin.

A customer came in for six bottles of port and relentlessly brought me up to date on the family's inexhaustible and usually disgusting woes. (Father-in-law had something wrong with his bladder.)

Sung Li appeared, bowing, with a gift of spring rolls. He wouldn't be paid for my previous evening's dinner, he said. I was an honored and frequent customer. When I was in need, he was my friend. I would honor him by not offering payment for yesterday. We bowed to each other, and I accepted.

He had never seen China, but his parents had been born there and had taught him their ways. He was a most punctilious neighbor and because of his roaringly successful but unlicensed takeout business I sold much wine in the evenings. Whenever I could without offending him I gave him cigars, which he smoked on sunny afternoons sitting on a wooden chair outside his kitchen door.

At three Sergeant Ridger returned carrying a paper bag from which he produced a bottle, setting it on the counter.

St. Estèphe: just as I'd asked. Uncorked and sealed

with sticky tape, untouched since its departure from the Silver Moondance.

"Can I keep it?" I said.

He gave one brief sharp nod. "For now. I said you'd been helpful, that it would be helpful for you to have this. I obtained permission from the chief inspector in charge of the Silver Moondance murder investigations." He dug into a pocket and produced a piece of paper, holding it out. "Please sign this chit. It makes it official."

I signed the paper and returned it to him.

"I've something for you, as well," I said, and fetched for him the thieves' shopping list. The original.

His body seemed to swell physically when he understood what it was, and he looked up from it with sharply bright eyes.

"Where did you find it?"

I explained about Brian clearing up.

"This is of great significance," he said with satisfaction.

I agreed. I said, "It would be particularly interesting if this is Paul Young's handwriting."

His staring gaze intensified, if anything.

"When he wrote his name and address," I said, "do you remember, he held his pen awkwardly? He wrote in short sharp downward strokes. It just seemed to me that this list looked similar, though I only saw his name and address very briefly, of course."

Sergeant Ridger, who had looked at them long and carefully, stared now at the thieves' list, making the comparison in his mind. Almost breathlessly he said, "I think you're right. I think they're the same. The chief inspector will be very pleased."

"A blank wall, otherwise?" I suggested. "You can't find him?"

His hesitation was small. "There are difficulties, certainly," he said.

No trace at all, I diagnosed.

"How about his car?" I suggested.

"What car?"

"Well, he didn't come to the Silver Moondance that day on foot, would you think? It's miles from anywhere. But when we went out with the boxes of drinks, there wasn't an extra car in the carpark. He must have parked round at the back where the cars of the staff were. Round by that door into the lobby where Larry Trent's office is, and the wine cellars. So Paul Young must have been to the Silver Moondance some other time . . . or he would have parked out front. If you see what I mean."

Detective Sergeant Ridger looked at me long and slowly. "How do you know the staff parked round at the back?"

"I saw cars through the lobby window when I went to fetch the bottles of wine. It seemed common sense to assume those were the staff's cars . . . barman, assistant assistant, waitress, kitchen staff and so on. They all had to get to work somehow, and the front carpark was empty."

He nodded, remembering.

"Paul Young stayed there after we left," I said. "So maybe the assistant or the waitress . . . or somebody . . . remembers what car he drove away in. Pretty long shot, I suppose."

Ridger carefully put the folded shopping list into the back of his notebook and then wrote a sentence or two on a fresh page. "I'm not of course in charge of that investigation," he said eventually, "and I would expect this line of questioning has already been thoroughly explored, but I'll find out.''

I didn't ask again if he would tell me the results, nor did he even hint that he might. When he left, however, it was without finality: not so much goodbye as see you later. He would be interested, he said, in anything further I could think of in connection with the bottle of wine he had brought. If I came to any new conclusions, no doubt I would pass them on.

''Yes, of course,'' I said.

He nodded, shut the notebook, tucked it into his pocket and collectedly departed, and I took the bottle of St. Estèphe carefully into the office, putting it back into the bag in which Ridger had brought it so that it should be out of plain sight.

I sat down at the desk, lethargy deepening. Still a load of orders to make up to go out on the van; couldn't be bothered even to start on them. Everyone would get their delivery a day late. Goblets and champagne needed for a coming-of-age on Thursday . . . by Thursday I mightn't feel so bone weary and comprehensively sore.

Women's voices in the shop. I stood up slowly and went out there, trying to raise up a smile. Found the smile came quite easily when I saw who it was.

Flora stood there, short, plump and concerned, her kind eyes searching my face. Beside her, tall and elegant, was the woman I'd seen fleetingly with Gerard after the horsebox accident: his wife, Tina.

''Tony, dear,'' Flora exclaimed, coming down the shop to meet me, ''are you sure you should be here? You don't look well, dear. They really should have kept you in hospital, it's too bad they sent you home.''

I kissed her cheek. ''I wouldn't have wanted to stay.'' I glanced at Mrs. McGregor. ''How's Gerard?''

"Oh, dear," Flora said. "I should introduce . . . Tina, this is Tony Beach . . ."

Tina McGregor smiled, which was noble considering that her husband's predicament was my fault, and in answer to my inquiry said Gerard had had the pellets removed that morning, but would be staying one more night for recovery.

"He wants to see you," she said. "This evening, if you can."

I nodded. "I'll go."

"And Tony, dear," Flora said, "I was so wanting to ask you . . . but now I see how dreadfully pale you look I don't suppose . . . It would be too much, I'm sure."

"What would be too much?" I said.

"You were so frightfully kind coming round the stables with me, and Jack's still in hospital, they still won't let him come home, and every day he gets crosser . . ."

"You want me to visit Jack too, after Gerard?" I guessed.

"Oh, no!" She was surprised. "Though he would love it, of course. No . . . I wondered . . . silly of me, really . . . if you would come with me to the races." She said the final words in a rush and looked of all things slightly ashamed of herself.

"To the races?"

"Yes, I know it's a lot to ask, but tomorrow we've a horse running that has a very awkward owner and Jack insists I must be there and honestly that owner makes me feel so flummoxed and stupid, I know it's silly, but you were so good with that horrible Howard and I just thought you might enjoy a day at the races and I would ask you. Only that was before Tina rang me and told me about last night. And now I can see it wouldn't be a pleasure for you after all."

A day at the races . . . well, why not? Maybe I'd feel better for a day off. No worse, at any rate.

"Which races?" I said.

"Martineau."

Martineau Park, slightly northeast of Oxford, large, popular and not too far away. If ever I went to the races it was either to Martineau Park or to Newbury, because I could reach either track inside forty minutes and combine the trip with shop hours, Mrs. Palissey graciously permitting.

"Yes, I'll come," I said.

"But Tony dear, are you sure?"

"Yes, sure. I'd like to."

She looked greatly relieved and arranged to pick me up at one o'clock the next day, promising faithfully to return me by six. Their runner, she explained, was in the big race of the day at three-thirty, and the owner always expected to talk for hours afterward, analyzing every step and consequence.

"As if I can tell him anything," Flora said despairingly. "I do so wish the horse would win, but Jack's afraid he won't, which is why I've got to be there. Oh, dear, oh, dear."

The Flat racing season was due to end in two or three weeks and none too soon, I judged, from Jack Hawthorn's point of view. No stable could long survive the absence of both its main driving forces, left as it was in the hands of a kind unbusinesslike woman with too little knowledge.

"Listen to the owner with respect and agree with everything he says and he'll think you're wonderful," I said.

"How very naughty, Tony dear," she said, but looked more confident all the same.

I took them out to the yard, as Flora had chiefly brought Tina to retrieve Gerard's car. It appeared that Tina herself had the ignition key: Gerard had given it to her the previous evening. Tina gazed without comment for a while at the shattered windscreen and the exploded upholstery and then turned toward me, very tall and erect, all emotions carefully straightjacketed.

"This is the third time," she said, "that he's been shot."

I WENT TO SEE HIM IN THE EVENING AND FOUND HIM propped against pillows in a room with three other beds but no inmates. Blue curtains, hospital smell, large modern spaces, shiny floors, few people about.

"Utterly boring," Gerard said. "Utterly impersonal. A waiting room to limbo. People keep coming to read my notes to see why I'm here, and going away again, never to return."

His arm was in a sling. He looked freshly shaved, hair brushed, very collected and in control. Hung on the foot of the bed was the clipboard of notes to which he'd referred, so I picked them off and read them also.

"Your temperature's ninety-nine, your pulse seventy-five, you're recovering from birdshot pellets, extracted. No complications. Discharge tomorrow."

"None too soon."

"How do you feel?"

"Sore," he said. "Like you, no doubt."

I nodded, put the notes back and sat on a chair.

"Tina said this was the third time for you," I said.

"Huh." He smiled lopsidedly. "She's never totally approved of my job. An embezzler took a pot at me once. Very unusual, that, they're normally such mild people. I suppose it was true to form that he wasn't altogether successful even at murder. He used too small a pistol and shot me in the thigh. Couldn't hold the thing steady. I'd swear he shut his eyes just before he fired.''

"He didn't fire again?''

"Ah. Well I was rushing him, you know. He dropped the pistol and started crying. Pathetic, the whole thing.''

I eyed Gerard respectfully. Rushing someone intent on killing you wasn't my idea of pathos.

"And the other time?'' I asked.

He grimaced. ''Mm. Much closer to home. Touch and go, that time. Tina wanted me to promise to do office work only after that, but one can't, you know. If you're hunting out criminals of any sort there's always the outside chance they'll turn on you, even the industrial spies I'm normally concerned with.'' He smiled again, ironically. ''It wasn't anyway the disloyal little chemist who sold his company's secrets to their chief rival who shot me, it was his father. Extraordinary. Father wouldn't believe his precious son guilty. He telephoned about six times, shouting I'd sent the most brilliant man of a generation to jail out of spite and ruined his career to cover up for someone else. He was obsessed, you know. Mentally disturbed. Anyway, he was waiting for me one day outside the office. Just walked across the pavement and shot me in the chest.'' He sighed. ''I'll never forget his face. Evil triumph . . . quite mad.''

"What happened to them?'' I asked, riveted.

"The father's in and out of padded cells. Don't know what's happened to the son, though he'll have been out of jail long ago. Sad, you know. Such a clever young man. His father's pride and joy.''

I was interested. ''Do you ever try to find out what becomes of the people you catch . . . afterwards?''

"No, not often. On the whole they are vain, greedy,

heartless and cunning. I don't care for them. One can feel sorry for them, but it's with their victims my sympathies normally lie.''

"Not like the old joke," I said.

"What old joke?"

"About the man who fell among thieves, who beat him and robbed him and left him bleeding and unconscious in the gutter. And along came two sociologists who looked down upon him lying there and said, the one to the other, 'The man who did this needs our help.'"

Gerard chuckled and made a face, putting his free hand to his shoulder.

"You mustn't think," he said, "that my record for injury is the norm. I've been unlucky. Only one other man in our firm has ever been wounded. And most policemen, don't forget, go through their entire careers uninjured."

Some didn't, I thought.

"Your bad luck this time," I apologized, "was my stupidity."

He shook his head stiffly, with care. "Don't blame yourself. I drove back into the yard of my own accord. Let's leave it at that, eh?"

I thought gratefully that he was generous but I felt nonetheless still guilty. Absolution, it had always seemed to me, was a fake. To err was human, to be easily forgiven was to be sentimentally set free to err again. To be repeatedly forgiven destroyed the soul. With luck, I thought, I wouldn't do anything else to incur Gerard's forgiveness.

The word that best described Gerard, I thought, was decent. As a detective he wasn't "colorful" as understood in fiction: that's to say a womanizer, unshaven and drunk. Goodness, easy enough to perceive, was as quick-silver to define, but that most difficult of virtues lived in the strong lines of his face. Serious, rational, calm, he seemed to be without the mental twitches that af-flicted many: the bullying pleasure in petty power, the self-regarding pomposity, the devouring anxiety of the insecure, all the qualities I saw at work daily not only among customers but in people to whom others had to go in trust, officials and professional people of all sorts. One never knew for certain: Gerard might indulge in secret sins galore, locking his Hyde in a closet; but what I saw, I liked.

I told him about Brian finding the thieves' shopping list and gave him one of the photostats out of my pocket, explaining about its being very likely in Paul Young's own handwriting.

"Great God," he said, reading it. "He might as well have signed a confession."

"Mm."

"But you can see why the robbers needed a written list," he said. "All those French names. They needed a visible check actually in their hand. They'd never have been sure to take the right things without."

"Not unless they knew the right labels intimately."

Gerard looked up from the list. "You mean, the men who broke in are therefore not the designers of the swin-dle."

"If they were they wouldn't have needed the list."

"Right." He smiled slightly. "How would they grab you as the murderers of Zarac?"

I opened my mouth and shut it again: then when the small shock had passed, I slowly and undecidedly shook my head.

"I don't know," I said. "They were rough, but there

was a moment, when the bigger one picked the gun out of the van, that he pointed it at me and visibly hesitated. If he'd already helped to kill Zarac, wouldn't he have killed me then?''

Gerard considered it. ''We can't tell. Zarac died out of earshot of a Chinese takeout restaurant. The hesitation may have been because of the more public nature of the yard. But people who take shotguns to robberies have at least thought of killing, never forget.''

I wouldn't forget, I thought.

''What made you become a detective?'' I asked curiously.

''Don't say detective. Tina doesn't like it.''

''Investigating consultant, then.''

''I was baby-snatched from college while detection still seemed a glamorous idea to my immature mind,'' Again the lopsided self-mocking smile. ''I'd done an accountancy course and was at business school but not much looking forward to making a living at what I'd learned. Rather dismayed, actually, by my prospects. I mentioned to an uncle of mine one day that I thought I'd like to join the police only the family would have mass heart attacks, and a friend of his who was there said why didn't I join the business police. I didn't know what he meant, of course, but he steered me to an agency and I think spoke in their ear. They offered me a trial year and started to teach me how to investigate white-collar crime. It was a different agency, not Deglet's. Deglet's took us over, and I was part of the furniture and fittings.''

''And you've never regretted it?''

He said thoughtfully, ''It's fashionable to explain away all crime as the result of environment and upbringing, always putting the blame on someone else, never the actual culprit. No one's born bad, all that sort of thing. If it weren't for poor housing, violent father, unemployment, capitalism, et cetera et cetera. You'll have heard it all, over and over. Then you get a villain from a good home with normal parents who's in a job and can't keep his fingers out of the till. I've seen far far more of those. They're the ones I investigate. Sometimes there's a particular set of circumstances you can point to as the instigation of their thieving or spying or betraying of confidence, but so many of them, I find, simply have an urge to be dishonest. Often not out of dire need, but because that's how they get their kicks. And whichever way you look at them, as poor little victims of society or as marauding invaders, they damage everyone in their path.'' He shifted against his pillows. ''I was brought up to respect that most old-fashioned concept, fair play. Even the present weary world tends not to think all's fair in war . . . I seek to restore fair play . . . I only achieve a bit here and there and the next trickster with a computer is being born every minute . . . What did you ask me?''

''You've answered it,'' I said.

He ran his tongue round his lips as if they were dry. ''Pass me that water, will you?'' he said.

I gave him the glass and put it down when he'd drunk.

Be grateful for villainy, I thought. The jobs of millions depended on it, Gerard's included. Police, lawyers, tax inspectors, prison warders, court officials, security guards, locksmiths and people making burglar alarms. Where would they be the world over but for the multiple faces of Cain.

''Gerard,'' I said.

''Mm?''

''Where does my consultancy start and end?''

"How do you mean?"

"Well, there wasn't a tankerful of scotch at the Silver Moondance. That Rannoch scotch is still about somewhere masquerading perhaps as Laphroaig but more likely as Bell's."

Gerard saw the smile twisting the corners of my mouth and gave another painful chuckle.

"You mean you might find it," he said, "if you drank at every hostelry from here to John O'Groat's?"

"Just Berkshire and Oxfordshire and all the way to Watford. Say fifty thousand places, for starters. A spot of syncopation. Syncopation, as you know, is an uneven movement from bar to bar."

"Please be quiet," he said. "Laughing hurts."

"Mm," I said. "Cirrhosis, I love you."

"All the same."

"I was only joking."

"I know. But as you said."

"Yeah. Well, I'll drink scotch at every opportunity, if not every bar. But I won't find it."

"You never know. Some dark little pub in a Reading backstreet."

I shook my head. "Somewhere like the Silver Moondance with smoke and noise and dancing and a huge turnover."

His glance grew thoughtful. "It depends how much Kenneth Charter wants to spend. As you say, it's an incredibly long shot, but I'll put it to him. Incredibly long shots sometimes pay off, and I've known them to happen at worse odds than fifty thousand to one."

I hadn't expected him to take me seriously and it made what I had chiefly been going to say sound unimportant. "I persuaded Sergeant Ridger to let me have one of the Silver Moondance wine bottles. The label might be informative. I know it's nothing on the face of it to do with Kenneth Charter's tankers, but . . . er, if you found out more about the wine it might lead you back to the scotch.''

He looked at the photostat lying on the sheet. "To Paul Young, do you mean?''

"I suppose so, yes.''

He said calmly, "Information about wine labels very definitely comes under the heading of consultancy. Getting too close to Paul Young does not.''

TWELVE

HENRI TAVEL IN HIS ROBUST FRENCH ASKED ME TO GIVE his felicitations to my dear mother.

I said I would.

He said he was delighted to hear my voice after so many months and he again regretted infinitely the death of my dear Emma.

I thanked him.

He said I would have enjoyed the harvest, it had been an abundant crop of small excellent grapes full of flavor: everyone in Bordeaux was talking of equaling 1970.

I offered congratulations.

He asked if I could spare time to visit. All his family and my many friends would welcome it, he said.

I regretted that my shop prevented an absence at present.

He understood. *C'est la vie*. He hoped to be of help to me in some way, as I had telephoned.

Thus invited and with gratitude I explained about the substitute wine and the existence of various labels.

"Alas," he said. "This is unfortunately too common. A matter of great annoyance."

"If I describe one of the labels, could you find out for me if it's genuine?" I asked.

"Certainly," he agreed. "Tomorrow, my dear Tony."

I was telephoning from the office in the shop with the St. Estèphe bottle in front of me.

I said, "The label is of a château in the region of St. Estèphe, a village you know so well."

"The home of my grandparents. There is no one there of whom I cannot inquire."

"Well, this label purports to come from Château Caillot." I spelled it for him. "Do you know of it?"

"No, I don't, but don't forget there must be two hundred small châteaux in that part of Haut Médoc. I don't know them all. I will find out."

"Great," I said. "The rest of the label reads: '*Mis en bouteilles par W. Thiery et Fils, négociants à Bordeaux.*'" Henri Tavel's suspicions came clearly down the line. "I know of no *W. Thiery et Fils*," he said. Monsieur Tavel, *négociant à Bordeaux* himself, was more likely to be aware of a fellow wineshipper than of a château seventy kilometers to the north. "I'll find out," he said again.

"Also the label bears the year of vintage," I said.

"Which year?"

"Nineteen seventy-nine."

He grunted. "Plentiful and quite good."

"It's an attractive label altogether," I said. "Cream background with black and gold lettering, and a line drawing of an elegant château. The château reminds me of somewhere . . . . I wish you could see it, you might recognize it."

"Soak it off, my dear Tony, and send it."

"Yes, I might."

"And the wine under the label," he asked. "What of the wine?"

"At a guess, mostly Italian. Blended with maybe Yugoslav, blended again with anything handy. Impossible, I would think, to distinguish its origins, even for a master of wine. It's light. Not much body. No finish. But pleasant enough. Palatable. No one would think it undrinkable. Wherever it came from it wasn't abused too much before it was bottled."

"Bordeaux bottled," he said thoughtfully.

"If the château doesn't exist, the wine could have been bottled anywhere," I said. "I kept the cork. It looks pretty new and there is no lettering on it."

The row of six corks stood before me on the desk, all identical. When châteaux bottled their own wine in their own cellars they stamped the corks with their name and the year of vintage. Anyone ordering a château-bottled wine would expect to see the cork, consequently a swindler would be less likely to present his work as château-bottled: too great a risk of a clued-up customer knowing what he wasn't being given.

Whoever had chosen the Silver Moondance labels had chosen well: all familiar-sounding respected names, all saleable at a substantial price. At a guess the wine itself, part of the great European wine lake, might have cost the bottler one fiftieth of what Larry Trent's diners had been charged.

I asked Henri Tavel when I could telephone again.

"Tomorrow night, again at this time. I will inquire at once in the morning."

I thanked him several times and we disconnected, and I pictured him as I'd so often seen him, sitting roundly at his big dining table with its lace cloth, drinking ar-

magnac alone after the evening meal and refusing to
watch television with his wife.

Flora collected me from the shop at one the following day as arranged and drove me in Jack's opulent
car to Martineau Park races. She talked most of the way
there out of what seemed a compulsive nervousness,
warning me about what not to say to Orkney Swayle,
the owner she felt cowed by.

Flora, I thought, had no need to be cowed by anybody. She had status in the racing world, she was pleasant to look at in a motherly middle-aged way and she
was dressed for action in tailored suit and plainly expensive shoes. Self-confidence had to come from within,
however, and within Flora one could discern a paralyzed
jelly.

"Don't ask him why he's called Orkney," she said.
"He was conceived there."

I laughed.

"Yes, but he doesn't like it. He likes the name itself
because it has grandeur, which he's always looking for,
and Tony dear, if you can be a bit grand like Jimmy it
will do very well with Orkney. Put on your most upper-
class voice like you do sometimes when you aren't
thinking, because I know you damp it down a bit in the
shop so as not to be intimidating to a lot of people, if
you see what I mean."

I was amused and also rueful at her perception. I'd
learned on my first day of sweeping and carrying as
general wine shop dogsbody that my voice didn't fit the
circumstances, and had altered my ways accordingly. It
had been mostly a matter, I'd found, of speaking not far
back in the throat but up behind the teeth, a reversal of

the way I'd just painstakingly learned to speak French like a Frenchman.

"I'll do my best Jimmy imitation," I promised. "And how is he, by the way?"

"Much better, dear, thank goodness."

I said I was glad.

"Orkney thinks he owns Jack, you know," she said, reverting to what was more immediately on her mind. "He hates Jack talking to other owners." She slowed for a roundabout and sighed. "Some owners are dreadfully jealous, though I suppose I shouldn't say so, but Orkney gets quite miffed if Jack has another runner in Orkney's race."

She was driving well and automatically, her mind far from the road. She told me she usually drove Jack to meetings: he liked to read and think on the way there and sleep on the way back. "About the only time he sits still, dear, so it has to be good for him."

"How old is this Orkney?" I asked.

"Getting on for fifty, I should think. He manufactures some frantically unmentionable undergarments, but he'll never say exactly what. He doesn't like one to talk about it, dear." She almost giggled. "Directoire knickers, do you think?"

"I'll be careful not to ask," I said ironically. "Directoire knickers! Do even great-grannies wear them anymore?"

"You see them in those little advertisements on Saturdays in the newspapers," Flora said, "along with things to hold your shoulders back if you're round-shouldered and sonic buzzers that don't actually say what they're for, and all sorts of amazing things. Haven't you noticed?"

"No," I said, smiling.

"I think sometimes of all the people who buy all those things," she said. "How different everyone's lives are."

I glanced at her benign and rounded face, at the tidy graying hair and the pearl earstuds, and reflected not for the first time that the content of what she said was a lot more acute than her manner of saying it.

"I did tell you, dear, didn't I, that Orkney has a box at the races? So we'll be going up to it when we get there and we'll have to stay after the race for ages and ages; he does go on so. He'll probably have a woman there. I'm just telling you, because she's not his wife and he doesn't like people to talk about that either, so don't ask if they're married, will you, dear?"

"There's an awful lot he doesn't like talking about," I said.

"Oh, yes, dear, he's very awkward, but if you stick to horses it will be all right. That's all he really likes to talk about and he'll do that all night, and of course that's just what I can't do, as you know."

"Any other bricks I might drop?" I asked. "Religion, politics, medical history?"

"Yes, well, Tony dear, you're teasing me." She turned into the entrance of Martineau Park, where the gateman waved her through with welcoming recognition. "Don't forget his horse is called Breezy Palm and it's a two-year-old colt, and it's run nine times this season and won twice, and once it smashed its way out of the stalls and nearly slaughtered the assistant starter so maybe you'd better not mention that too much either."

She parked the car but didn't get out immediately, instead pulling on a becoming hat and adjusting the angle in the driving mirror.

"I haven't asked you how your arm is, dear," she said, "because it's perfectly obvious it's hurting you."

"Is it?" I said, slightly dismayed.

"When you move it, dear, you wince."

"Oh."

"Wouldn't it be better in a sling, dear?"

"Better to use it, I should think."

The kind eyes looked my way. "You know, Tony dear, I think we should stop at the first-aid room and borrow one of those narrow black wrist-supporting slings that the jumping jockeys use when they've broken things, and then you won't have to shake hands with people, which I noticed you avoided doing with Tina yesterday, and other people won't bang into you if they see they shouldn't."

She left me speechless. We went to the first-aid room, where by a mixture of charm and bullying she got what she wanted, and I emerged feeling both grateful and slightly silly.

"That's better, dear," she said, nodding. "Now we can go up to Orkney's box." All her decisiveness in the first-aid room vanished. "Oh, dear, he makes me feel so stupid and clumsy and as if I'd never stepped out of the schoolroom."

"You look," I said truthfully, "poised, well-dressed and anybody's match. Stifle all doubts."

Her eyes, however, were full of them and her nervousness shortened her breath in the elevator going up to the fourth floor.

The Martineau Park grandstands were among the best in the country, the whole lot having been designed and built at one time, not piecemeal in modernization programs as at many other courses. The old stands having decayed to dangerous levels around 1950, it had been decided to raze the lot and start again, and although one could find fault about wind tunnels (result of schools of architecture being apparently ignorant of elementary physics), the cost-cutting disasters of some other places had been avoided. One could nearly everywhere, for instance, if one wanted to, watch the races from under cover and sitting down, and could celebrate afterward in bars large enough for the crush. There was a warmed (or cooled) glass-walled gallery overlooking the parade ring and a roof above the unsaddling enclosures (as at Aintree) to keep all the back-slapping dry.

The two long tiers of high-up boxes were reached by enclosed hallways along which, when we came out of the elevator, waitresses were pushing trolleys of food: a far cry from Ascot, where they tottered with trays along open galleries, eclairs flying in the wind. Martineau Park, in fact, was almost too comfortable to be British.

Flora said "This way," and went ahead of me with foreboding. Orkney Swayle, I thought, simply couldn't be as intimidating as she made out.

The door of his box stood open. Flora and I reached it together and looked in. A sideboard scarcely groaning with food and drink stood against one wall. Three small tables with attendant chairs filled the floorspace, with glass doors to the viewing balcony beyond. To the right of the entrance door was a small serving pantry, clean and uncluttered. Orkney's, unlike some of the boxes we'd passed, wasn't offering lunch.

A man sat alone at one of the tables, head bent over racing newspaper and form book, pen at the ready for making notes.

Flora cleared her throat, said "Orkney?" waveringly and took three tentative steps into the box. The man at the table turned his head without haste, an inquiring expression raising his eyebrows. Even when he saw Flora he was in no rush to stand up. He finally made it, but as if the politeness were something he'd belatedly thought of, not an instinctive act of greeting.

He was tall, sandy-haired, wore glasses over pale blue eyes, smiled with reluctance.

"This is Tony Beach, Orkney," Flora said.

Orkney looked me calmly up and down, gaze pausing briefly on the sling. "Jack's assistant?" he asked.

"No, no," Flora said, "a friend."

"How do you do?" I said in my best Jimmy manner, and got a nod for it, which seemed to relieve Flora, although she still tended to shift from foot to foot.

"Jack asked me to tell you he's had good reports about Breezy Palm from the head lad," she said valiantly.

"I talked to Jack myself," Orkney said. After a noticeable pause he added, "Would you care for a drink?"

I could sense Flora about to refuse so I said "Yes, why not?" in a Jimmy drawl, because a stiffener might be just what Flora needed.

Orkney looked vaguely at the sideboard, upon which stood a bottle of gin, a bottle of scotch, an assortment of mixers and several glasses. He picked up an empty glass that had been near him on the small table, transferred it to the sideboard and stretched out his hand to a Seagram's bottle.

"Gin and tonic, Flora?" he offered.

"That would be nice, Orkney."

Flora bought gin from me to give to visiting owners, saying she didn't much care for it herself. She watched apprehensively as Orkney poured two fingers worth and barely doubled it with tonic.

"Ice? Lemon?" he asked, and added them without waiting for an answer. He handed her the glass while looking mostly at me. "And you . . . er . . . same for you?"

"Scotch," I said. "Most kind."

It was Teacher's whisky, standard premium. He poured the two fingers and hovered a hand between ginger ale and soda, eyebrows elevated.

"Just as it comes," I said. "No ice."

The eyebrows rose higher. He gave me the glass, recapped the whisky and returned to the gin for himself. Two and a half fingers. Very little tonic. Two chunks of ice.

"To luck," I said, taking a sip. "To . . . ah . . . Breezy Palm."

"Oh, yes," Flora said. "Breezy Palm."

The blended flavors trickled back over my tongue, announcing their separate presences, grain, malt and oakwood, familiar and vivid, fading slowly to aftertaste. I maybe couldn't have picked Teacher's reliably from a row of similar blends, but one thing was certain: what I was drinking wasn't Rannoch.

"Hurt your arm?" Orkney asked.

"Er . . ." I said. "Had an accident with a door."

Flora's eyes widened but to my relief she refrained from rushing in with details. Orkney merely nodded, acknowledging life's incidental perils. "Too bad," he said.

A waitress appeared at the doorway, pushing a trolley. A quick glance at Flora's face showed me one couldn't expect too much from this, and the reality turned out to be three moderately large plates bearing respectively crustless sandwiches, cheese with biscuits and strawberry tartlets, all tautly covered with Saran Wrap. The waitress asked if she could liberate the modest feast but Orkney said no, he would do it later, and there it all sat, mouth-wateringly out of reach.

"In the good old days," Flora told me later, "one used to be able to take one's own food and drink to one's box, but now the caterers have an absolute stranglehold and everyone has to buy everything from them, and for some things they are frightfully expensive, absolutely exorbitant, my dear, and Orkney resents it so much that he buys the absolute minimum. He's not really so mean as he looks today, it's just his way. He told us once that the caterers charge bar prices in the boxes, whatever that means, and that it made him very angry."

"Bar prices?" I said. "Are you sure?"

"Is that so bad, dear?"

"Judging from race meeting bar prices, about a hundred and fifty percent profit on a bottle of scotch."

Flora worked it out. "So Orkney has to pay in his box more than double what the same bottle costs in your shop?"

"Yes, a good deal more than double."

"My dear," she said, "I'd no idea drinks in the boxes cost so much."

"A pound barely wets the glass."

"You're teasing me."

"Not entirely," I said.

"No wonder Orkney resents having to pay that much when he used to take his own."

"Mm," I said reflectively. "The caterers do have big overheads, of course, but to charge by the tot in the boxes . . ."

"By the tot, dear?"

"Thirty-two tots to a bottle. That's the single measure for spirits in all bars, racing or not. Two centiliters. One large mouthful or two small."

Flora hardly believed me. "I suppose I don't often

buy drinks in bars, dear,'' she said, sighing. "Jack does it, you see.''

In hindsight Orkney Swayle's hand on the bottles had been lavish: generosity well disguised by a cold demeanor. And the external manners, I came to see during the afternoon, were not intentionally rude, but a thoughtless habit, the sort of behavior one could inherit in ultrareserved families. He appeared not to be aware of the effect he had on others and would perhaps have been astonished to know he reduced Flora to quivers.

Orkney made inroads in his gin with his regard impassively on my face.

"Are you knowledgeable about horses?" he asked.

I began to say "marginally" but Flora didn't want any sort of modest disclaimers on my part, she wanted Orkney to be impressed. "Yes of course he is, Orkney, his mother is a master of hounds and his father was a colonel and the greatest amateur rider of his generation and his grandfather was also a colonel and nearly won the Grand National.''

The faintest of gleams entered and left Orkney's eyes and I thought with surprise that somewhere deep down he might have after all a sense of humor.

"Yes, Flora," he said. "Those references are impeccable.''

"Oh.'' She fell silent, not knowing if he were mocking her, and went pink round the nose, looking unhappily down at her drink.

"Breezy Palm," Orkney said, oblivious, "is by Desert Palm out of Breezy City, by Draughty City, which was a half-brother to Goldenburgh whose sire won the Arc de Triomphe, of course."

He paused as if expecting comment so I obligingly said, "What interesting breeding," which seemed to

cover most eventualities, including my own absolute ignorance of all the horses involved.

He nodded judiciously. "American blood, of course.
Draughty City was by Chicago Lake out of a dam by
Michigan. Good strong hard horses. I never saw
Draughty City of course, but I've talked to people who
saw him race. You can't do better than mixed American
and British blood, I always say."

"I'm sure you're right," I said.

Orkney discoursed for several further minutes on
Breezy Palm's antecedents with me making appropriate
comments here and there and Flora, on the edge of my
vision, slowly beginning to relax.

Such progress as she had made was however ruined
at that point by the arrival from the powder room of the
lady to whom Orkney wasn't married, and it was clear
that however much Orkney himself made Flora feel
clumsy, his lady did it double.

Compared with Flora she was six inches taller, six
inches slimmer and approximately six years younger.
She also had strikingly large gray eyes, a long thin neck
and luminous makeup and was wearing almost the same
clothes but with distinctly more chic: tailored suit, good
shoes, neat felt hat at a becoming angle. An elegant,
mature, sophisticated knockout.

To the eye it was no contest. Flora looked dumpy
beside her, and knew it. I put my arm round her shoulder
and hugged her and thought for one dreadful second that
I'd reduced her to tears.

"Flora," Orkney said, "of course you and Isabella
know each other . . . Isabella, my dear, this is Flora's
walker . . . er . . . what did you say your name was?"

I told him. He told Isabella. Isabella and I exchanged

medium hello smiles and Orkney returned to the subject of American forebears.

The races came and went: first, second, third. Everyone went down each time to inspect the horses as they walked round the parade ring, returning to the box to watch the race. Orkney gambled seriously, taking his custom to the bookmakers on the rails. Isabella flourished fistfuls of Tote tickets. Flora said she couldn't be bothered to bet but would rather check to make sure everything was all right with Breezy Palm.

I went with her to find Jack's traveling head lad (not the unctuous Howard but a little dynamo of a man with sharp restless eyes) who said cryptically that the horse was as right as he would ever be and that Mrs. Hawthorn wasn't to worry, everything was in order.

Mrs. Hawthorn naturally took no heed of his good advice and went on worrying regardless.

"Why didn't you tell Orkney what really happened to your arm, dear?" she asked.

"I'm not proud of it," I said prosaically. "Don't want to talk about it. Just like Orkney."

Flora the constant chatterer deeply sighed. "So odd, dear. It's nothing to be ashamed of."

We returned in the elevator to the box where Flora wistfully eyed the still-wrapped food and asked if I'd had any lunch.

"No," I said. "Did you?"

"I should have remembered," she sighed, "but I didn't." And she told me then about Orkney's hate reaction to the caterers.

Orkney had invited no other guests. He appeared to expect Flora and myself to return to the box for each race but didn't actually say so. An unsettling host, to say the least.

It was out on the balcony when we were waiting for the runners in the third race to canter down to the start that he asked Flora if Jack had found anyone else yet to lease his mare: he had forgotten to ask him on the hospital telephone.

"He'll do it as soon as he's home, I'm sure," Flora said placatingly, and to me she added, "Orkney owns one of the horses that Larry Trent leased."

Orkney nodded austerely. "My good filly by Fringe. A three-year-old, good deep heart room, gets that from her dam, of course."

I thought back. "I must have seen her in Jack's yard," I said. Four evenings in a row, to be precise.

"Really?" Orkney showed interest. "Liver chestnut, white blaze, kind eye."

"I remember," I said. "Good bone. Nice straight hocks. And she has some cleanly healed scars on her near shoulder. Looked like barbed wire."

Orkney looked both gratified and annoyed. "She got loose one day as a two-year-old. The only bit of barbed wire in Berkshire and she had to crash into it. Horses have no sense."

"They panic easily," I agreed.

Orkney's manner to me softened perceptibly at that point, which Flora noted and glowed over.

"Your filly did well for Larry Trent," I said.

"Not bad. Won a nice handicap at Newbury and another at Kempton. Both Larry and I made a profit through the books, but I was hoping for black print, of course."

I caught Flora starting to look anxious. "Of course," I said confidently; and she subsided. "Black print" had come back just in time as an echo from childhood. Races of prestige and high prizes were printed in heavy black type in auction catalogues: black print earned by a broodmare upped the price of her foals by thousands.

"Will you keep her in training next year?" I asked.

"If I can get someone else to lease her." He paused slightly. "I prefer to run two-year-olds myself, of course. I've had four in training with Jack this year. I sell them on if they're any good, or lease them, especially fillies, if they're well bred, so that I can either breed from them later or sell them as broodmares. Larry often took one of my fillies as a three-or four-year-old. Good eye for a horse, Larry had, poor fellow."

"Yes, so I hear."

"Did you know him?"

"No." I shook my head. "I saw him at the party, but that was all." In my mind's eye I saw him alive and also lifeless, the man whose death had started so many worms crawling.

"I didn't go to the party," Orkney said calmly. "Too bad he was killed."

"You knew him well?" I asked.

"Pretty well. We weren't close friends, of course. Just had the mutual interest in horses."

Orkney's voice clearly announced what his lips hadn't said: Larry Trent hadn't been, in Orkney's estimation, Orkney's social equal.

"So . . . er . . ." I said, "you didn't go to his place . . . the Silver Moondance?"

The faintest spasm crossed Orkney's undemonstrative face. "I met him there, once, yes, in his office, to discuss business. We dined afterward. A dinner dance, Larry said. Very loud music . . ." He left the sentence hanging, criticism implied but not uttered.

"What did you think of the wine?" I asked.

"Wine?" He was surprised.

"I'm a wine merchant," I said.

"Oh, really?" Wine merchants, it seemed, were in Orkney's world provisionally O.K. "Interesting. Well, as far as I remember it was perfectly adequate. For a dinner dance, of course."

Perfectly adequate for a dinner dance brilliantly summed up the superior plonk in all those suspect bottles. There wasn't any point, I thought, in asking Orkney about the scotch; he was a gin man himself.

The horses for the third race emerged onto the track and cantered past the stands. Orkney raised a massive pair of binoculars and studied his fancy, a flashy-looking bay with a bounding impatient stride like an impala and sweat already on his neck.

"Fighting his jockey," Orkney muttered. "Losing the race on the way down." He lowered the race-glasses and scowled.

"Larry Trent sometimes bought horses at the sales," I said casually, watching the runners. "Not for you?"

"No, no. For his brother." Orkney's eyes and attention were anywhere but on me. "Horses in training. Three-year-olds, or four or five. Shipped them abroad, that sort of thing. No, no, I buy yearlings—on bloodstock agents' advice, of course."

Flora, listening, wore an expression that changed rapidly from surprise to comprehension. The disappearing Ramekin had been explained in the most mundane unmysterious way. She wasn't exactly disappointed but in the comprehension there was definite anticlimax.

"Look at that!" Orkney exclaimed crossly. "The damn thing's bolting."

His fancy had won the battle with his jockey and was departing into the distance at a flat gallop. Orkney raised his binoculars and folded his mouth into a grim and almost spiteful line as if he would have wrung the jockey's neck if he could have caught him.

"Did you know Larry Trent's brother?" I asked.

"What? No. No, never met him. Larry just said . . . Look at that! Bloody fool ought to be fined. I saw Larry buying a good horse for around fifty thousand at the sales. I said if he had that sort of money, why did he prefer leasing? It was his brother's cash, he said. Out of his league. But he could pick horses, he said, and his brother couldn't. The one thing his brother couldn't do, he said. Sounded envious to me. But there you are, that's people. Look at that bloody boy! Gone past the start. It's too bad! It's disgraceful!" Ungovernable irritation rose in his voice. "Now they'll be late off, and we'll be rushed for Breezy Palm."

THIRTEEN

HE WAS RIGHT. THEY WERE LATE OFF. ORKNEY'S FANCY finished dead tired and second to last and we were indeed rushed for Breezy Palm.

Orkney was seriously displeased. Orkney became coldly and selfishly unpleasant.

I dutifully walked Flora down to the saddling boxes, though more slowly than our angry host had propelled his lady. ("You didn't mind him calling you my walker, did you, dear?" Flora asked anxiously. "Not at all. Delighted to walk you anywhere, any time." "You're such a comfort, Tony dear.") We reached the saddling boxes as the tiny saddle itself went on over the number cloth, elastic girths dangling.

Breezy Palm, a chestnut with three white socks, looked as if he had a certain amount of growing still to do, particularly in front. Horses, like children, grow at intervals with rests in between: Breezy Palm's forelegs hadn't yet caught up with the last spurt in the hind.

"Good strong rump," I said, in best Jimmy fashion.

The brisk traveling head lad, busy with girth buckles, glanced at me hopefully but Orkney was in no mood for flattery. "He's coming to hand again at last," he said sourly. "He won twice back in July, but since then there have been several infuriating disappointments. Not Jack's fault, of course . . ." His voice all the same was loaded with criticism. ". . . Jockeys' mistakes, entered at the wrong courses, frightened in the starting gate, needed the race, always something."

Neither the head lad nor Flora looked happy, but nor were they surprised. Orkney's prerace nerves, I supposed, were part of the job.

"Couldn't you have saddled up sooner?" Orkney said crossly. "You must have known the last race was delayed."

"You usually like to see your horses saddled, sir."

"Yes, yes, but use some common sense."

"Sorry, sir."

"Can't you hurry that up?" Orkney said with increasing brusqueness as the head lad began sponging the horse's nose and mouth. "We're damned late already."

"Just coming, sir." The head lad's glance fell on the horse's rug, still to be buckled on over the saddle for warming muscles on this cool October day. There was a pot of oil also for brushing gloss onto the hooves. And a prize to the lad, it said in the racecard, for the best-turned-out horse.

"It's too bad," Orkney said impatiently. "We should be in the parade ring already." He turned away sharply and stalked off in that direction, leaving Isabella, Flora and me to follow as we would.

Isabella looked stoically unaffected. Flora began to scurry after Orkney but I caught her abruptly by the arm, knowing he'd think less of her for hurrying, not more.

"Slow down, slow down, the jockeys aren't out yet."

"Oh. All right, then." She looked guilty as much as

flustered, and walked with small jerky steps between the long-legged Isabella and myself as we joined Orkney in the parade ring, no later than any other owner-trainer group.

Orkney was still in the grip of his outburst of bad temper, which failed to abate when Breezy Palm finally appeared in the ring looking polished. The jockey, approaching it seemed to me unsmilingly out of past experience, was sarcastically told not to leave his winning run as bloody late as last time and not to go to sleep in the stalls, if he didn't mind.

The featherweight jockey listened expressionlessly, his gaze on the ground, his body relaxed. He's heard it all before, I thought, and he simply doesn't care. I wondered, if I'd been a jockey, whether I would have ridden my heart out for owners who spoke in that way, and concluded that possibly not. Breezy Palm's uncertain prospects developed a certainty for me at that moment; and I wondered what Orkney would be like in defeat when he was so obnoxious in hope.

The bell rang for the jockeys to mount. Breezy Palm's jockey nodded to Orkney and went away with Orkney still telling him that if he used his whip too much he'd have him in in front of the stewards.

Flora was standing so close to me she was virtually clinging. When Orkney turned and strode out of the parade ring without waiting for Isabella or to see his horse mounted she said to me shakily, "Jack manages him, but I can't. Jack stops him being so rude to the jockeys. One of them refused to ride his horses. Can you imagine?"

"Mm," I said. "Do we have to go up to the box to watch the race?"

"Oh, my goodness, yes," she said emphatically. "At

least . . . I mean . . . you don't have to . . . I could go alone.''

"Don't be silly.''

I looked around for the decorative Isabella, but she too had disappeared.

"They've both gone to bet,'' Flora said, sighing. "Jack said the opposition was stiff. I'm so afraid Breezy Palm won't win.''

We went up in the elevator to the empty box. The sandwiches and tartlets were still wrapped, but the gin level had dropped considerably since we had arrived. Gin itself, I reflected, was a notorious inducer, in some people, of catty ill-humor.

Flora and I went onto the balcony to see the runners go down to the start, and Orkney arrived breathlessly, moving in front of us without apology, raising his binoculars to see what sins his jockey might already be committing. Isabella collectedly arrived with her clutched tickets and I glanced at the flickering lights of the Tote board to see Breezy Palm's odds. Seven to one; by no means favorite but fairly well backed.

There were eighteen runners, several of them past winners. Breezy Palm, well drawn, went into the stalls quietly and showed no signs of reassaulting the assistant starter. Orkney's slightly frantic agitation stilled suddenly to concentration and in the six-furlong distance the dark green starting gates opened in unison and spilled out their brilliant accelerating rainbow cargo.

Flora raised her own small race-glasses but I doubted if she could see much for trembling. Three-quarter-mile straight races were in any case difficult to read in the early stages as the runners were so far away and coming straight toward one, and it took me a fair time myself to sort out Orkney's jockey in red and gray. The commentator, rattling off names, hadn't mentioned Breezy Palm at all by the time they reached halfway but I could see him there, bobbing along in the pack, making no move either forward or backward, proving merely at that stage that he was no better and no worse than his opponents.

Flora gave up the struggle with the race-glasses, lowered them, and watched the last two furlongs simply with anxiety. The bunch of runners that had seemed to be moving so slowly was suddenly perceived to be flying, the tiny foreshortened distances from first to last stretching before one's eyes to gaps of a length, to definite possibles and positive losers. The young colts stuck out their necks and strove to be first as they would have done in a wild herd on an unrailed plain, the primeval instinct flashing there undiluted on the civilized track. The very essence of racing, I thought. The untamed force that made it all possible. Exciting, moving . . . beautiful.

Breezy Palm had the ancient instinct in full measure. Whether urged to the full by his jockey or not he was straining ahead with passion, legs angular beneath the immature body, stride hurried and scratchy, the compulsion to be first all there but the technical ability still underdeveloped.

The trick of race-riding, my father had once said, was to awaken a horse's natural panic fear and then control it. My father, of course, had had no doubt at all that he could do both. It was I, his son, who couldn't do either. Pity . . .

Breezy Palm's natural panic, jockey controlling it to the extent of letting it have its head and keeping it running straight, was still lustily aiming a shade beyond his ability. Orkney watched in concentrated silence. Flora

seemed to be holding her breath. Isabella behind me was
saying "Come on, you bugger, come on, you bugger,"
continuously under her breath, her most human reaction
to date. Breezy Palm, oblivious, had his eyes fixed on
the three horses still in front of him and over the last
hundred yards ran as if the great god Pan were at his
very heels.

Horses can only do their best. Breezy Palm's best on
that day couldn't overhaul the winner, who went ahead
by a length, or the second, who left clear space behind
him, but he flashed over the line so close to the third of
the leaders that from the angle of Orkney's box it was
impossible to tell the exact placings. The judge, announced the loudspeaker, was calling for a photograph.

Orkney, still silent, lowered his glasses and stared up
the track to where his hepped-up colt was being hauled
back into the twentieth century. Then still saying nothing
he turned and hurried away, again leaving his compan-
ions to fare for themselves.

"Come on, dear," Flora said, tugging my sleeve.
"We must go down too. Jack said to be sure to. Oh,
dear . . ."

The three of us consequently made the downward
journey as fast as possible and arrived to find Breezy
Palm stamping around in the place allotted to the horse
that finished fourth, the jockey unbuckling the girths and
Orkney scowling.

"Oh, dear . . ." Flora said again. "The jockeys always know. He must have been beaten for third after
all."

The result of the photograph, soon announced, confirmed it: Breezy Palm had finished fourth. Distances;
length, two lengths, short head.

Flora, Isabella and I stood beside Orkney, looking at

the sweating, tossing, skittering two-year-old and making consoling and congratulatory remarks, none of which seemed to please.

"Ran extremely well in a strong field," I said.

"The wrong race for him," Orkney said brusquely. "I've no idea why Jack persists in entering him in this class. Perfectly obvious they were too good for him."

"Only just," Isabella said reasonably.

"My dear woman, you know nothing about it."

Isabella merely smiled; fortitude of an exceptional nature.

It struck me that she herself was totally uncowed by Orkney. He treated her rudely: she ignored it, neither embarrassed nor upset. Subtly, somewhere in their relationship, she was his equal . . . and both of them knew it.

Flora said bravely, "I thought the horse ran splendidly," and received a pitying glance from on high.

"He fought to the end," I said admiringly. "Definitely not a quitter."

"Fourth," Orkney said repressively, as if fourth in itself bespoke a lack of character, and I wondered if he cared in the least how graceless he sounded.

The signal was given for the horses to be led away and Orkney made impatient movements, which everyone interpreted as his own type of invitation to return to the box. There at last he busied himself with removing the wrappings from the overdue sandwiches, but without much method, finally pushing the plates toward Isabella for her to do it. Orkney himself poured fresh drinks as unstintingly as before and indicated that we might all sit down round one of the tables, if we so wished. All of us sat. All of us ate politely, hiding our hunger.

As a postrace jollification it would have done a funeral proud, but gradually the worst of Orkney's sulks wore off and he began to make comments that proved he had at least understood what he'd seen, even if he took no joy in it.

"He's lost his action," he said. "Back in July, when he won, he had a better stride. Much more fluent. That's the only trouble with two-year-olds. You think you've got a world-beater and then they start developing unevenly."

"He might be better next year," I suggested. "Won't you keep him? He could be worth it."

Orkney shook his head. "He's going to the sales next week. I wanted a win today to put his price up. Jack knew that." The echo of grudge was still strong. "Larry Trent might have leased him. He thought, as you seem to, that his action might come back once he'd finished growing, but I'm not risking it. Sell, and buy yearlings, that's my preference. Different runners every year. More interesting."

"You don't have time to grow fond of them," I said neutrally.

"Quite right," he nodded. "Once you get sentimental you throw good money down the drain."

I remembered the friendships my father had had with his steeplechasers, treating each with camaraderie over many years, getting to interpret their every twitch and particularly loving the one that had killed him. Money down the drain, sure, but a bottomless pleasure in return such as Orkney would never get to feel.

"That damned jockey left his run too late," Orkney said, but without undue viciousness. "Breezy Palm was still making up ground at the end. You saw that. If he'd got at him sooner . . ."

"Difficult to tell," I said, drawling.

"I told him not to leave it too late. I told him."

"You told him not to hit the horse," Isabella said calmly. "You can't have it both ways, Orkney."

Orkney could, however. Throughout the sandwiches, the cheese and the strawberry tartlets he dissected and discussed the race stride by stride, mostly with disapproval. My contention that his colt had shown great racing spirit was accepted. Flora's defense of the jockey wasn't. I grew soundly tired of the whole circus and wondered how soon we could leave.

The waitress appeared again in the doorway asking if Orkney needed anything else, and Orkney said yes, another bottle of gin.

"And make sure it's Seagram's," he said. The waitress nodded and went away, and he said to me, "I order Seagram's just because the caterers have to get it in specially. They serve their own brand if you don't ask. They charge disgraceful prices and I'm not going to make life easy for them if I can help it."

Flora's and Isabella's expressions, I saw, were identical in pained resignation. Orkney had mounted his hobby horse and would complain about the caterers for another ten minutes. The arrival of the fresh bottle didn't check him, but at the end he seemed to remember my own job and said with apparently newly reached decision, "It's local people like you who should be providing the drinks, not this huge conglomerate. If enough people complain to the Clerk of the Course, I don't see why we couldn't get the system put back to the old ways. Do you?"

"Worth a try," I said noncommittally.

"What you want to do," he insisted, "is propose yourself as an alternative. Give these damn monopolists a jolt."

"Something to think about," I murmured, not meaning to in the least, and he lectured me at tiresome length on what I ought to do personally for the box-renters of Martineau Park, not to mention for all the other racecourses where the same caterers presided, and what I should do about the other firms of caterers who carved up the whole country's racecourses between them.

"Er . . . Orkney," Flora said uncertainly, when the tirade had died down, "I do believe, you know, that at a few courses they really have finished with the conglomerates and called in local caterers, so perhaps . . . you never know."

Orkney looked at her with an astonishment that seemed to be based less on what she'd said than on the fact of her knowing it. "Are you sure, Flora?"

"Yes, I'm sure."

"There you are then," he said to me. "What are you waiting for?"

"I wouldn't mind shuttling the drinks along," I said. "But what about the food? This food is good, you'd have to admit. That's where these caterers excel."

"Food. Yes, their food's all right," he said grudgingly.

We'd finished every crumb and I could have eaten the whole lot again. Orkney returned to the subject of Breezy Palm and two drinks later had exhausted even Isabella's long-suffering patience.

"If you want me to drive you home, Orkney, the time is now," she said. "You may not have noticed that they ran the last race ten minutes ago."

"Really?" He looked at his watch and surprisingly took immediate action, standing up and collecting his papers. "Very well then. Flora, I'll be talking to Jack on the telephone . . . and, er . . ." he made an effort to remember my name as the rest of us stood up also. "Good to have met you ... er ... Tony." He nodded twice in lieu of shaking hands. "Any time you're here with Flora ... glad to have you."

"Thank you, Orkney," I said.

Isabella bent to give Flora a kiss in the air an inch off her cheek and looked vaguely at my sling, finding like Orkney that hands unavailable for shaking left goodbyes half unsaid.

"Er ..." she said. "So nice ..."

They went away down the hallway and Flora sat down again abruptly.

"Thank goodness that's over," she said fervently. "I'd never have got through it without you. Thank goodness he liked you."

"Liked?" I was skeptical.

"Oh, yes, dear, he asked you back, that's practically unheard of."

"How did Isabella," I asked, "get him to go home?"

Flora smiled the first carefree smile of the day, her eyes crinkling with fun. "My dear, they will certainly have come in her car, and if he didn't go when she says she would drive off and leave him. She did it once. There was a terrible fuss and Jack and I had to put him on a train. Because as you've noticed, dear, he likes his gin and a few months ago he was breathalyzed on the way home and lost his license ... but he doesn't like one to talk about that either."

AFTER THE RACES, DURING THE EVENING SHIFT IN THE shop, I telephoned again to Henri Tavel in Bordeaux and listened without much surprise to his news.

"*Mon cher* Tony, there is no Château Caillot in St. Estèphe. There is no Château Caillot in Haut Médoc.

There is no Château Caillot in the whole region of Bordeaux."

"One thought there might not be," I said.

"As for the *négociant Thiery et Fils* . . ." the heavy Gallic shrug traveled almost visibly along the wires, "there is no person called Thiery who is *négociant* in Bordeaux. As you know, some people call themselves *négociants* who work only in paper and never see the wine they sell, but even among these there is no Thiery."

"You've been most thorough, Henri."

"To forge wine labels is a serious matter."

His voice, vibrating deeply, reflected an outrage no less genuine for being unsurprised. To Henri Tavel, as to all the château owners and wineshippers of Bordeaux, wine transcended religion. Conscious and proud of producing the best in the world, they worked to stiff bureaucratic criteria that had been laid down in Médoc in 1855 and only fractionally changed since.

They still spoke of 1816, a year of undrinkable quality, as if it were fresh in their memory. They knew the day the grape harvest had started every year back beyond 1795 (September twenty-fourth). They knew that wine had been made uninterruptedly in their same vineyards for at least two thousand years.

Every single bottle of the five hundred and fifty million sent out from the region each year had to be certified and accounted for: had to be worthy of the name it bore: had to be able to uphold the reputation for the whole of its life. And the life of a Bordeaux red wine could be amazing. With Henri Tavel I had myself tasted one ninety years old that still shone with color and sang on the palate.

To forge a Bordeaux château label and stick it on an

amorphous product of the European wine lake was a heresy of burning-at-the-stake proportions. Henri Tavel wanted assurances that the forgers of Caillot would feel the flames. I could offer only weak-sounding promises that everyone would do their best.

"It is important," he insisted.

"Yes, I know it is. Truly, Henri, I do know."

"Give my regards," he said, "to your dear mother."

LIFE CONTINUED NORMALLY ON THE NEXT DAY, WEDNES-day, if a disgruntledly itching arm could be considered normal. I was due to take it back to the hospital for inspection the following afternoon and meanwhile went on using the sling much of the time, finding it comfortable and a good excuse for not lifting the cases. Brian had become anxiously solicitous at the sight of it and carefully took even single bottles out of my grasp. Mrs. Palissey was writing down the telephone orders to save me the wincing. I felt cosseted and amused.

She and Brian left early with the deliveries because there were so many: some postponed and some in advance, including the glasses and champagne for the next day's coming-of-age. I kept shop, smiling, ever smiling as usual, and thinking, when I could.

Shortly after eight in the evening Gerard walked in looking gray and tired and asking if I could shut the damned place and come out and eat. Somewhere quiet. He wanted to talk.

I looked at the fatigue lines in his face and the droop of his normally erect body. I was twenty years younger than he and I hadn't had a general anaesthetic, and if in spite of taking things fairly easy I still felt battered and weak, then he must feel worse. And maybe the cause wasn't simply the profusion of little burning stab wounds but the residue also from the horse trailer . . . the frissons of nearness to death.

"We could take Sung Li's food home to my house," I suggested diffidently, "if you'd like."

He would like, he said. He would also buy the food while I fiddled with the till and locked up, and how soon would that be?

"Half an hour," I said. "Have some wine."

He sighed with resignation, sat on the chair I brought from the office and ruefully smiled at our two slings.

"Snap," he said.

"Flora's idea, mine."

"Sensible lady."

"I'll get the wine."

In the office I poured some genuine wine from St. Estéphe and some of the Silver Moondance version into two glasses and carried them out to the counter.

"Taste them both," I said. "Say what you think."

"What are they?"

"Tell you later."

"I'm no expert," he protested. He sipped the first, however, rolling it round his gums and grimacing as if he'd sucked a lemon.

"Very dry," he said.

"Try the other."

The second seemed at first to please him better, but after a while he eyed it thoughtfully and put the glass down carefully on the counter.

"Well?" I asked.

He smiled. "The first is demanding. The second is pleasant . . . but light. You're going to tell me that the first is more expensive."

"Pretty good. The second one, the pleasant but light one, came from the Silver Moondance. The first is near enough what it should have tasted like, according to the label."

He savored the various significances. "Many might prefer the fake. People who didn't know what to expect."

"Yes. A good drink. Nothing wrong with it."

He sipped the genuine article again. "But once you know this one, you grow to appreciate it."

"If I had any just now I'd give you one of the great St. Estèphes . . . Cos d'Estournel, Montrose, Calon Ségur . . . but this is a good cru bourgeois . . . lots of body and force."

"Take your word for it," he said amiably. "I've often wished I knew more about wine."

"Stick around."

I tasted both the wines again myself, meeting them as old friends. The Silver Moondance wine had stood up pretty well to being opened and refastened, but now that I'd poured the second sample out of the bottle, what was left would begin to deteriorate. For wine to remain perfect it had to be in contact with the cork. The more air in the bottle the more damage it did.

I fetched and showed him both of the bottles, real and fake, and told him what Henri Tavel had had to say about forgeries.

He listened attentively, thought for a while, and then said, "What is it about the fake wine that seems more significant to you than the fake whisky? Because it does, doesn't it?"

"Just as much. Equally."

"Why, then?"

"Because . . ." I began, and was immediately interrupted by a row of customers wanting to know what to drink inexpensively with Sung Li's crispy Peking duck, hot and sour prawns and beef in oyster sauce. Gerard listened with interest and watched them go one by one with their bottles of Bergerac and Soave and Côtes du Ventoux.

He said, "You sell knowledge, don't you, as much as wine?"

"Yeah. And pleasure. And human contact. Anything you can't get from a supermarket."

A large man with eyes awash shouldered his way unsteadily into the shop demanding beer loudly, and I sold him what he wanted without demur. He paid clumsily, belched, went on his weaving way; and Gerard frowned at his departing back.

"He was drunk," he said.

"Sure."

"Don't you care?"

"Not as long as they're not sick in the shop."

"That's immoral."

I grinned faintly. "I sell escape also."

"Temporary," he objected disapprovingly, sounding austerely Scots.

"Temporary is better than nothing," I said. "Have an aspirin."

He made a noise between a cough and a chuckle. "I suppose you've lived on them since Sunday."

"Yes, quite right." I swallowed two more with some St. Estèphe, in itself a minor heresy. "I'm all for escape."

He gave me a dry look that I didn't at first understand, and only belatedly remembered my rush down the yard.

"Well, as long as I'm not being robbed."

He nodded sardonically and waited through two more sales and a discussion about whether Sauternes would go with lamb chops, which it wouldn't; they would each taste dreadful.

"What goes with Sauternes, then? I like Sauternes."

"Anything sweet," I said. "Also perhaps curry. Or ham. Also blue cheese."

"Good heavens," said Gerard when he'd gone. "Blue cheese with sweet wine . . . how odd."

"Wine and cheese parties thrive on it."

He looked round the shop as if at a new world. "Is there anything you can't drink wine with?" he said.

"As far as I'm concerned . . . grapefruit."

He made a face.

"And that's from one," I said, "who drinks wine with baked beans, who practically scrubs his teeth in it."

"You really love it?"

I nodded. "Nature's magical accident."

"What?"

"That the fungus on grapes turns the sugar in grape juice to alcohol. That the result is delicious."

"For heaven's sake . . ."

"No one could have invented it," I said. "It's just there. A gift to the planet. Elegant."

"But there are all sorts of different wines."

"Oh, sure, because there are different sorts of grapes. But a lot of champagne is made from black-skinned grapes . . . things may not be as they seem, which should please you as a detective."

"Hm," he said dryly. His glance roved over the racks of bottles. "As a detective what pleases me is proof . . . so what's proof?"

"If you mix a liquid with gunpowder and ignite it, and it burns with a steady blue flame, that's proof."

He looked faintly bemused. "Proof of what?"

"Proof that the liquid is at least fifty percent alcohol.

That's how they proved a liquid was alcohol three centuries ago when they first put a tax on distilled spirits. Fifty percent alcohol, one hundred percent proved. They measure the percentage now with hydrometers, not gunpowder and fire. Less risky, I dare say.''

''Gunpowder,'' he said, ''is something you and I have had too much of recently.'' He stood up stiffly. ''Your half hour is up. I'll get the food.''

FOURTEEN

GERARD FOLLOWED ME HOME IN HIS MENDED MERCEDES and came into the house bearing Sung Li's fragrant parcels.

"You call this a cottage?" he said skeptically, looking at perspectives. "More like a palace."

"It was a cottage beside a barn, both of them falling to pieces. The barn was bigger than the cottage . . . hence the space."

We had joyfully planned that house, Emma and I, shaping the rooms to fit what we'd expected to be our lives, making provision for children. A big kitchen for family meals; a sitting room, future playroom; a dining room for friends; many bedrooms; a large quiet drawing room, splendid for parties. The conversion, done in three stages as we could afford it, had taken nearly five years. Emma had contentedly waited, wanting the nest to be ready for the chicks, and almost the moment it was done she had become pregnant.

Gerard and I had come into the house through the kitchen, but I seldom ate there anymore. When the food was reheated and in dishes we transferred it to the sitting room, putting it on a coffee table between two comfortable chairs and eating with our plates balanced on our knees.

It was in that warm-looking room with its bookshelves, soft lamplight, television, photographs and rugs that I mostly lived. It was there that I now kept a wine rack and glasses lazily to hand and averted my mind from chores like gardening. It was there, I daresay, that my energy was chronically at its lowest ebb, yet it was there also that I instinctively returned.

Gerard looked better for the food, settling deep into his chair when he'd finished with a sigh of relaxation. He put his arm back in its sling and accepted coffee and a second glass of California wine, a 1978 Napa cabernet sauvignon I'd been recently selling and liked very much myself.

"It's come a long way," Gerard observed, reading the label.

"And going further," I said. "California's growing grapes like crazy, and their best wine is world class."

He drank a little and shook his head. "It's pleasant enough but I honestly couldn't tell it from any old plonk. A terrible admission, but there you are."

"Just what the Silver Moondance ordered, customers like you."

He smiled. "And I'd guess I'm in the majority."

"It doesn't matter. Liking wine at all is the main thing."

He said, "You were going to tell me why the substitute wines were equally as important as the substitute scotch at the Silver Moondance."

I glanced at him, hearing the hardening tone in the soft Scottish voice and seeing the same change in him as there had been in the car the previous Sunday: the shedding of the social shell, the emergence of the investigator. His eyes were steady and intent, his face concentrated, the mouth unsmiling: I answered to this second man with recognition and relief, dealing in facts and guesses dispassionately.

"People who steal scotch whisky," I said, "usually go for a shipment of bottles in cases. The proceeds are ready to sell; the receiver's probably already lined up. There's no difficulty. It's all profit. But if you steal a tankerful of the liquid in bulk you have the trouble and expense in bottling it. Cost of bottles, cost of labor, all sorts of incidentals."

"Right," he said, nodding.

"There were seven thousand five hundred gallons of scotch at roughly fifty-eight percent alcohol content in each of Kenneth Charter's three lost loads."

"Right."

"Each load was of a higher concentration than is ever sold for drinking. When they received the tankerload the Rannoch people would have added water to bring the scotch down to retail strength, around forty percent alcohol by volume."

Gerard listened and nodded.

"At that point they'd have enough scotch to fill approximately fifty thousand bottles of standard size."

Gerard's mouth opened slightly with surprise. "Kenneth Charter never said that."

"He shifts the stuff, he doesn't bottle it. He maybe never did the arithmetic. Anyway, with three tankersful we're talking about one hundred and fifty thousand bottles in six months, and that's not something you can mess about with in the back yard."

He was silent for a while thinking about it, and then said merely, "Go on."

"On each occasion the whole load was pumped out of the tanker pretty fast, as the tanker was found empty on the following day."

"Right."

"So unless the point of the operation was simply to ruin Kenneth Charter, in which case it's conceivable the loads were dumped in ditches like the drivers, the scotch was pumped from the tanker into some sort of storage."

"Yes, of course."

"So the logical place for the tanker to be unloaded was at a bottling plant."

"Yes, but it never reached there."

"It never reached Rannoch's bottling plant. There's a difference."

"All right." His eyes smiled. "Go on."

"Fifty thousand bottles three times over isn't going to keep any reasonable plant in operation for anything like six months. Small châteaux bottle that much themselves in a few weeks without blinking. So . . . um . . . what if in between times the whisky bottling changed over to wine . . . to Silver Moondance wine, to be precise."

"Ah." It was a deep note, an acknowledgment that we'd arrived at the center of things. "Carry on."

"Well, with a bottling plant it would be easy to fill any shape of bottle from a single source of wine . . . and the shapes of the bottles at the Silver Moondance fitted the labels: claret bottles for claret labels, burgundy bottles for burgundy labels and so on. The very fact that there were both scotch and wine under false labels at the Silver Moondance . . . well, for the simplest explanation I'd bet you a pea to a case of Krug they were bottled in the same place."

Gerard drank some of his wine absentmindedly.

"Where?" he said succinctly.

"Mm. That's the rub."

"Any ideas?"

"It did occur to me that it might be in one of those plants that Kenneth Charter described, that got into difficulties or went bust when the French started bottling more of their own wines. I mean, suppose someone came to you if you were on the verge of bankruptcy and offered you work. Even if you knew it was crooked you might do it and keep quiet. Or suppose a bottling plant was for sale or lease at a ridiculous price, which they're bound to have been . . . if the game looked worth it . . . if it was going to go on maybe for years . . ."

"Yes," Gerard said. "It's possible." He gave it about five seconds' thought. "So provisionally we're looking for a bottling plant. Now let's shelve that for a moment." He paused again, considering, and then said, "In Deglet's we often work in pairs, discussing a case, bouncing ideas off each other, coming up sometimes with things neither of us had considered on our own. It's a way that I'm used to, that I like . . . but my usual partner's in London, and frankly I'm too tired to go there. Meanwhile you're here on the doorstep loaded to the hairline with specialist knowledge, so do you mind letting me talk my ideas to you? And be sure to speak out if I start something in your thoughts. That's where the value of these sessions lies. Bouncing ideas back. Do you mind?"

"No, of course not. But I—"

"Just listen," he said. "Stop me if you've a comment. That's all there is to it."

"All right."

"And honestly . . . do you have any brandy?"

I smiled. "Yes, I do. What would you like?"

"Anything."

I gave him some Hine Antique, which he sighed over as if putting on friendly old shoes. I poured some for myself also on the grounds that the people who said it had medicinal qualities weren't joking. If queasy, drink brandy; if tired, drink brandy; if suffering from green shivers and cold shakes, drink brandy.

"All right, then," he said, cradling his glass in the palm of one hand. "First, review the status quo. Under that heading we have the prime and never-to-be-forgotten fact that our number-one aim is to save Kenneth Charter's business without landing his son in jail. That's what we're being paid for. Justice and other considerations are secondary."

He sipped his drink.

"Fact number two," he went on, "Kenneth Charter's son . . . whose name is also Kenneth, to be awkward, so we'll call him Kenneth Junior . . . Kenneth Charter Junior made the theft of the scotch possible by telling Zarac of the Silver Moondance where to find the tanker." He paused. "We still have the unanswered question."

"How did Kenneth Junior know Zarac."

"Yes. Anyway, I've brought the photostats of the pages of Kenneth Junior's notebook." He pulled a well-filled business-sized envelope from an inner pocket and laid it on the table. "I'll leave these with you . . . see if you make anything from them that we haven't."

He saw the doubt in my face. "You'll try?" he said almost severely, and I without apology said, "Yes."

"Right, then. Fact three: Zarac passed on the message and wasn't present when the tanker was stolen. Fact four: scotch was being sold under the wrong labels at the Silver Moondance, which Zarac as wine waiter must have known. Supposition arising: the substitute scotch was part of an earlier load stolen from Charter's tankers. Any comment?''

I shook my head.

"Second supposition arising: Larry Trent knew his whisky and wines were cheating the customers.''

He stopped, waiting for an opinion. I said, "I agree with that, yes. I'd say it was definite.''

"Supposition three: Larry Trent organized the theft of the tankers.''

I frowned.

"You don't think so?''

"I don't know," I said. "I never talked to him . . . can't make a first-hand guess. He certainly did have in his hands a great deal more cash than he would have made out of the Silver Moondance, but he said it was his brother's.'' I told Gerard precisely what Orkney Swayle had told me at Martineau Park. "Larry Trent was buying horses and shipping them abroad to be sold. As sweet a way as one can imagine of turning illegal money pure white.''

Gerard drank some brandy.

"Did you believe in the brother?'' he asked.

"You mean, was it a case of the hypothetical friend? My friend has a problem, give me advice?''

He nodded.

"I would have thought so," I said, "except for one thing that rang humanly true. Orkney told me that Larry Trent said he, Larry, was buying the horses for his brother because his brother couldn't tell good from bad. About the only thing his brother couldn't do, he said. Orkney Swayle said Larry was envious. That sort of grudge sounds like a real brother to me. Or at any rate a real person. Partner, maybe.''

A small silence. We both thought about the partner

who might or might not be a brother, and finally Gerard gave him his name. The name, anyway, that we knew him by.

"Paul Young."

I agreed.

"Supposition four," Gerard said. "When Larry Trent was killed, Paul Young came to the Silver Moondance to take over, unaware that the police were investigating the drinks and unaware that Charter's tanker thefts had been linked with Zarac."

"Those are certainties, not suppositions. I saw him arrive myself. He had no idea he was walking into trouble."

"Right. And I'll add in a few certainties of my own at this point. I've spent all day interviewing people from the Silver Moondance, especially the waitress and the wet little assistant who were both there with you in the bar. They say that soon after you left Paul Young told them to go home, the waitress until told to return and the assistant until the following day. Paul Young said he would discuss with the police about a reopening date, and run the place himself until the manager returned from holiday. After that, head office would appoint a replacement for poor Mr. Trent. None of the staff saw anything odd in his manner or proposals. Very sensible, they thought him, considering how angry he was about the drinks. He then sent the kitchen staff home, telling them also to return when told. The waitress said Zarac arrived for work just as she was leaving, and Paul Young told him to go into Larry Trent's office and wait for him."

I was fascinated. "Did she remember exactly what they said to each other?"

Gerard smiled thinly. "She's used to remembering orders. An excellent ear. She said they knew each other. Paul Young called him Zarac without being told.''

"And the other way round?"

"She said Paul Young said 'I'm Paul Young,' which she thought silly because Zarac looked as if he knew him perfectly well."

"Telling Zarac his alias."

"Exactly. The waitress said Paul Young looked very angry with Zarac, which she thought natural, and she thought Zarac was going to get a right ticking off, which she was sorry about because Zarac was all right with the waitresses and kept his hands to himself, unlike some others she could mention.''

I appreciated the verbatim reporting. "And who were those?"

"The manager, mostly."

"Not Larry Trent?"

"No. Always the perfect gent, she said.'' He paused. "She said the police sergeant had been round before me, asking the same questions. She said he asked her about Paul Young's car."

I was amused. "What else did she say?"

"She said it was a Rolls."

"Really?"

"Her exact words were 'a black Roller with them tinted windows.' She said it had to be Paul Young's because it was in the staff carpark and it didn't belong to the regular staff, and it hadn't been there when she came to work an hour earlier."

"Observant girl."

Gerard nodded. "I went to the wet assistant's home after I left the waitress and asked him mostly the same questions. He said he didn't know what car Paul Young had come in. He couldn't even describe Paul Young. Useless.''

"And the barman hoofed it.'' I relayed Ridger's half-hearted search. "I guess he knew he wasn't selling the right stuff, but you wouldn't get him to admit it, even if you found him.''

"No,'' he agreed. "So now we come to supposition . . . where are we? five? . . . supposition five: that Paul Young and Zarac spent the afternoon deciding what to do and organizing the removal of all the wines and spirits to look like burglary.''

"It would have taken them hours if they did it themselves.''

"And they would have needed a van.''

"Large,'' I said, nodding. "There were dozens of cases.''

He put his head on one side. "They had all day and all night, I suppose.''

"Do we know when Zarac actually died?'' I asked.

Gerard shook his head. "There was an opening inquest last Friday, adjourned for a week. The police aren't giving out much publicity on Zarac, but I've a friend behind the forensic scenes and I'll hear everything the police know about times and so on by this Friday.''

"He suffocated,'' I said with revulsion.

"It bothers you?''

"Like bricking up someone alive.''

"Much quicker,'' he said prosaically. "Supposition six: Paul Young and Zarac weren't the greatest of buddy-buddies.''

"A fair conclusion,'' I said dryly.

"Supposition seven: Zarac was in some way a terrible threat to Paul Young.''

"Who solved the problem permanently.''

"Mm," he reflected. "So far, that seems reasonable. Any questions?"

"Yes. How did Paul Young happen to have plaster of paris bandage with him on what he expected to be simply an organizational outing?"

"You mean it might be significant?"

"Something to add to what we know of him, anyway."

"And why use it? Why not smash in his head?"

"Well, why?" I said.

"A warning to others, perhaps. Or genuine psychosis. Very nasty, in any case." He drank some brandy. A brain alive above a flagging body. "Our Mr. Young is a middle-aged businessman with a hearing aid, a black Rolls and a reason for carrying plaster of paris. Pity we can't, as they say, run that lot through the computer."

"Any self-respecting computer would come up with a consultant surgeon, ear, nose and throat."

Gerard was startled. "You don't suppose . . . ? No, most unlikely."

"Computers only spit out what you feed in."

"Whereas you can feed countless facts into a human being and get no connections at all." He sighed resignedly. "All right, then. Work arising. Find out if Larry Trent had a brother. Search further to know how Kenneth Junior knew Zarac. Sort out bottling plants. And Rannoch, by the way, have mailed to us profile analyses of the loads they sent in Charter's tankers. If you can wheedle a sample from the Silver Moondance out of your pal Ridger, I can get the comparison made. For proof rather than speculation." He paused. "Anything else?"

"Well . . ." I hesitated.

"Go on."

"Ramekin, then. The horse Flora saw Larry Trent buy at Doncaster Sales a year ago. If Ramekin was shipped abroad, someone shipped it. There aren't so very many shippers. They'd have Ramekin in their records . . . race-horses have passports, like people. Masses of export documents, besides. If we could find the shipper we'd know the destination. Larry Trent might always have used the same shipper and sold all the horses through one agent at the same destination . . . If you've set up a line, so to speak, you carry on using it. The agent at the far end might know . . . just might know . . . whose cash had bought the horses. The real owner, for whom Larry Trent was acting."

Gerard listened intently, but he said, "That's stretching it."

"I suppose so."

"I'll see how much is involved."

"Do you want me to do it?"

He shook his head. "We'll do it in the office, if at all. We have country-wide phone books and our staff are used to that sort of routine. They make it sound enormously official and get the most surprising results. They'll do the bottling plant sales and leases first; a long job but more promising."

"I suppose it would be too simple . . ." I began diffidently.

"What would?"

"I mean . . . you could try them first . . . nothing to lose . . ."

"Do get on," he said.

I felt foolish. I said, "The plants to which Kenneth Charter took red wine in his tankers."

Gerard looked at me levelly for a while with unblinking eyes. "Right," he said eventually, without inflection. "We'll start with those. As you say, nothing to lose." He looked at his watch and took the second-to-last mouthful of his brandy. "Tina will be locking me out."

"Come any time," I said.

I didn't mean to sound lonely, but maybe that's what he heard. He looked at the photograph of Emma and myself on our wedding day that stood on a table near him in a silver frame. We were laughing in a shower of bubbles from a shaken-up champagne bottle in the hands of my best man, and Emma had liked the picture for its informality. "Most brides and grooms look like waxworks," she'd said. "At least you can tell we were alive."

"You were a good-looking couple," Gerard said neutrally. "And happy."

"Yes."

"How did she die?"

He asked it straightforwardly, without emotion, and after a moment I answered him similarly, as I had learned to do, as if it happened to someone else.

"She had a sub-arachnoid hemorrhage. Something called Berry's aneurysm. In effect a blood vessel split in her brain."

"But . . ." his gaze slid to the photograph, ". . . how old was she?"

"Twenty-seven."

"So young."

"Apparently it can happen at any age."

"I'm so sorry."

"She was pregnant," I said, and surprised myself. I normally didn't say that. Normally I said the absolute minimum. But to Gerard, after months of silence, I found myself slowly telling it all, wanting to and not wanting to, trying to keep my voice steady and not cry . . . for God's sake don't cry.

"She'd been having headaches on and off for ages. Then she had backaches. Nothing specific. Just aches in her spine. Everyone put it down to her being pregnant. And it passed off . . . until next time. Every week or so, for a day or two. One Sunday when she was nearly six months pregnant she woke up with one of those headaches, a fairly bad one. She took some aspirins but they never did much good. It got worse during the morning and when I went to do the midday stint in the shop she said she would go to bed and sleep it off. But when I got back she was crying . . . moaning . . . with pain. I tried to get a doctor . . . but it took ages . . . it was Sunday afternoon . . . Sunday . . . an ambulance finally came for her but by then she was begging me . . . begging me somehow to knock her out . . . but how could I? I couldn't. We were both terrified . . . more than frightened . . . it was so implacable . . . she was in awful agony in the ambulance . . . hitting her head with her fists . . . nothing I could do . . . couldn't even hold her . . . she was yelling, rolling, jerking with pain. At the end of the journey she went slowly unconscious, and I was glad for her, even though by then I feared . . . Well, I feared."

"My dear man."

I sat for a while looking back to the past, and then swallowed and told him the rest of it coldly.

"She was in a coma for four days, going deeper . . . I stayed with her. They let me stay. They said they couldn't save the baby, it was too soon. In another month, perhaps . . . They told me the blood vessel must have been leaking for ages . . . it was the blood leaking into her brain and down her spinal nerves that had given her the headaches and backaches . . . but even if they'd diagnosed the trouble earlier they couldn't have done much . . . it would have split open more one day, as it did . . . so perhaps it was better we didn't know.''

I stopped. No tears. All I couldn't have borne at that point was sympathy, and Gerard didn't offer it.

"Life's most unfair," he said calmly.

"Yes."

He didn't say I would get over it, or that time was a great healer. He didn't say I would find another girl. Marry again. I approved of Gerard more and more.

"Thank you for telling me," he said.

"I don't usually," I said apologetically.

"No. Flora told me. You clam up, she said, if anyone asks."

"Flora chatters."

"Chattering does good, sometimes."

I was silent. What I felt, having told him about Emma, was a sort of release. Chattering helped. Sometimes.

He finished his brandy and stood up to go. "If you have any more thoughts, telephone."

"O.K."

He walked toward the door and stopped by a side table upon which stood three or four more photo frames among Emma's collection of shells.

"Your mother?" he asked, picking up the lady on horseback with hounds. "Most handsome."

"Mother," I nodded.

He put her down. Picked up another. "Father?"

"Father."

He looked at the strong amused face above the colonel's uniform with its double row of medal ribbons, at the light in the eyes and the tilt of the chin, at the firm half-smiling mouth.

"You're like him," Gerard said.

"Only in looks." I turned away. "I loved him when I was small. Adored him. He died when I was eleven."

He put the picture down and peered at the others. "No brothers or sisters?"

"No." I grinned faintly. "My birth interfered with a whole season's hunting. Once was enough, my mother said."

Gerard glanced at me. "You don't mind?"

"No, I never did. I never minded being alone until I got used to something else." I shrugged abruptly. "I'm basically all right alone. I will be again, in the end."

Gerard merely nodded and moved on out into the hall and from there to the kitchen and beyond to the rear door, where neither of us shook hands because of the slings.

"A most productive and interesting evening," he said.

"I enjoy your company."

He seemed almost surprised. "Do you? Why?"

"You don't expect too much."

"Like what?"

"Like . . . er . . . Chinese takeout on your knees." It wasn't what I truly meant, but it would do.

He made an untranslatable noise low in his throat, hearing the evasion and not agreeing with it. "I expect more than you think. You underestimate yourself." He smiled sardonically. "Good night."

"Good night."

He drove away and I locked the doors and went back through the house to fetch the supper dishes, to stack them in the dishwasher. I thought of what I'd said to him about being all right alone, hearing in memory in the accumulated voices of years of customers the sighs and sadnesses of the bereaved. They talked of the common experience that was freshly awful for each individual. Two years, they said, was what it took. Two years before the sun shone. After two years the lost person became a memory, the loss itself bearable. I'd listened to them long before I thought of needing their wisdom, and I believed them still. Grief couldn't be escaped, but it would pass.

I finished tidying downstairs and went up to bed, to the room where Emma and I had made love.

I still slept there. She often seemed extraordinarily near. I woke sometimes in the early hours and stretched out for her, forgetting. I heard the memory of her giggle in the dark.

We had been lucky in love; passionate and well matched, equal in satisfaction. I remembered chiefly her stomach flat, her breasts unswollen, remembered the years of utter fun, her gleeful orgasms, the sharp incredible ecstasy of ejaculation. It was better to remember that.

The room was quiet now. No unseen presence. No restless spirit hovering.

If I lived with ghosts, they were within me: Emma, my father and the titanic figure of my grandfather, impossibly brave. They lived in me not condemning but unconsoling. I struggled forever to come to terms with them, for if I didn't I was sunk, but all three of their shadows fell long.

Pregnancy might recently have raised Emma's blood pressure, they'd said. It was quite common. Higher blood pressure would have put too much strain on the slow leak, opening it wider . . . too wide.

Pregnancy itself, they'd said, had tipped the scales toward death. Although we had both wanted children, the seed that I'd planted had killed her.

FIFTEEN

I LET MYSELF INTO THE SHOP THE NEXT MORNING WONdering what I could trade with Sergeant Ridger for a sample of the Silver Moondance scotch, and he solved the problem himself by appearing almost immediately at my door as if transported by telekinesis.

"Morning," he said, as I let him in. Raincoat belted, shoes polished, hair brushed. Hadn't he heard, I wondered, that plainclothes policemen these days were supposed to dress in grubby jeans and look unemployed?

"Good morning," I replied, shutting the door behind him. "Can I sell you something?"

"Information." He was serious, as always, coming into the center of the shop and standing solidly there with his feet apart.

"Ah. Yes, well fire away."

"Is your arm worse? You didn't have a sling last time I came."

"No worse." I shook my head. "More comfortable."

He looked not exactly relieved but reassured. "Good. Then . . . I'm making an official request to you to aid us in our inquiries."

"What aid? What inquiries?"

"This is a direct suggestion from Detective Chief Superintendent Wilson."

"Is it?" I was interested. "To me personally?"

"He suggested you himself, yes." Ridger cleared his throat. "It is in connection with our inquiries into complaints received about goods supplied by licensed premises other than the Silver Moondance."

"Er . . ." I said. "Sergeant, would you drop the jargon?"

Ridger looked surprised. What he'd said had been obviously of crystal clarity to his notebook mind. He said, "In the course of our investigations into the murder of Zarac it was suggested that we should follow up certain other complaints of malpractice throughout the whole area. There was a top-level regional conference yesterday, part of which I attended as the officer first on the spot in the drinks fraud, and Chief Superintendent Wilson requested me directly to enlist your help as before. He said if we could find another place passing off one whisky as another, and if such whisky were similar or identical to that in the Silver Moondance, we might also find a lead to Zarac's supplier and murderer. It was worth a try, the chief said, as there were so few other lines of inquiry. So, er, here I am."

I gazed at him in awe. "You're asking me to go on a pub crawl?"

"Er . . . if you must put it like that, yes."

Beautiful, I thought. Stunning. Fifty thousand bars between home and Watford with the known bad apples offered on the platter of a police list.

"Would you be driving me, like last time?" I asked.

"I've been assigned to that duty." He showed no feelings either for or against. "Can I take it you will be available?"

"You can," I said. "When?"

He consulted his bristling wristwatch. "Ten-fifteen."

"This morning?"

"Of course. I'll go back now and report and return for you later."

"All right," I said. "And, Sergeant, when you return, would you bring with you the Bell's whisky bottle from the Silver Moondance bar?"

He looked concentratedly doubtful.

"I'd like to taste its contents again," I explained. "It's ten days since that morning in the Silver Moondance. If more of that scotch is what you're all looking for in these inquiries, I'll have to learn the taste well enough to recognize it anywhere."

He saw the logic. "I'll request it."

"Mm . . . say it's a requirement. I can't do what you're asking without it."

"Very well." He pulled out the notebook and wrote in it, rolling his wrist for another time check and adding nine-fourteen punctiliously.

"How many places are we going to?" I asked.

"It's quite a long list." He spoke matter-of-factly. "It's a big area, of course. My chief inspector's hoping we can complete the inquiry within two weeks."

"Two weeks!"

"Working from ten-thirty to two o'clock daily in licensing hours."

"Is this an official appointment with pay?"

He checked internally before he answered. "It was being discussed."

"And?"

"They used to have an available consultant expert,

but he's just retired to live in Spain. He was paid. Sure to have been.''

''How often was he consulted?''

''Don't rightly know. I only saw him once or twice. He could tell things by taste like you can. The Customs and Excise people use instruments, same as Weights and Measures. They're concerned with alcohol content, not flavor.''

''Did they check any of the places on your list?''

He said ''All of them,'' disapprovingly, and I remembered what he'd said before about someone in one of those two departments tipping off the Silver Moondance that investigators were on their way.

''With no luck?'' I asked.

''No prosecutions have resulted.''

Quite so. ''All right, Sergeant. You drive, I'll drink, and I've got to be sober and back here by three to get my arm checked at the hospital.''

He went away looking smug and at nine-thirty to the half-minute Mrs. Palissey arrived with Brian. I explained that I would be away every midday for a while and said I would get her some help by tomorrow if she could possibly manage that morning on her own.

''Help?'' She was affronted. ''I don't need help.''

''But your lunch hour . . .''

''I'll bring our lunch and we'll eat it in the back,'' she said. ''I don't want strangers in here meddling. Brian and I will see to things. You go off and enjoy yourself, you're still looking peaky.''

I was about to say that I wasn't doing police work to enjoy myself but then it occurred to me that I probably was. I'd had no hesitation at all in accepting Ridger's— or Wilson's—invitation. I was flattered to be thought an expert. Deplorable vanity. Laugh at yourself, Tony. Stay human.

For an hour the three of us restocked the shop, made lists, took telephone orders, served customers, swept and dusted. I looked back when I left with Ridger: to a clean, cozy, welcoming place with Mrs. Palissey smiling behind the counter and Brian arranging wine boxes with anxious care. I wasn't an empire builder, I thought. I would never start a chain. That one prosperous place was enough.

Prosperous, I knew, against the odds. A great many small businesses like mine had died of trying to compete with chains and supermarkets, those giants engaged in such fierce undercutting price wars that they bled their own profits to death. I'd started that way and began losing money, and, against everything believed and advised in the trade, had restored my position by going back to fair, not suicidal prices. The losses had stopped, my customers had multiplied, not deserted, and I'd begun to enjoy life instead of waking up at night sweating.

Ridger had brought the Bell's bottle with him in his car; it sat upright on the back seat in the same box in which it had left the Silver Moondance, two-thirds full, as before.

"Before we go," I said, "I'll take that whisky into the shop and taste it there."

"Why not here?"

"The car smells of petrol." A gift, I thought.

"I've just filled up. What does it matter?"

"Petrol smells block out scotch."

"Oh. All right." He got out of his car, removed the box and methodically locked his doors although the car was right outside the shop and perfectly visible through the window; then he carried the box in and set it on the counter.

Casually I slipped my wrist out of the sling, picked up the Bell's bottle, took it back to the office, and with a clink or two poured a good measure through a funnel into a clean small bottle I'd put ready, and then a very little into a goblet. The small bottle had a screw-on cap, which I caught against the thread in my haste, but it was closed and hidden with the funnel behind box-files in an instant, and I walked unhurriedly back into the shop sipping thoughtfully at the glass, right wrist again supported.

Ridger was coming toward me. "I'm not supposed to let that bottle out of my sight," he said.

"Sorry." I gestured with the glass. "It's just on the desk in the office. Perfectly safe."

He peered into the recess to make sure and turned back nodding. "How long will you be?"

"Not long."

The liquid in my mouth was definitely Rannoch, I thought. Straightforward Rannoch. Except that . . .

"What's the matter?" Ridger demanded; and I realized I'd been frowning.

"Nothing," I said, looking happier. "If you want to know if I'll recognize it again, then yes, I will."

"You're sure?"

"Yes."

"Why are you smiling?"

"Sergeant," I said with exasperation, "this is a collaboration, not an inquisition. Let's take the bottle and get the show on the road."

I wondered if Sergeant Ridger ever achieved friendship: if his suspicious nature ever gave him a rest. Certainly after all our meetings I found his porcupine reflexes as sensitive as at the beginning, and I made no attempt to placate him, as any such attempt would in itself be seen as suspicious.

He drove away from the curb saying that he would visit the nearest places first, with which I could find no quarrel, and I discovered that by nearest he meant nearest to the Silver Moondance. He turned off the main road about a mile before we reached it, and stopped in a village outside a country pub.

As an inn it had been old when Queen Anne died, when coaches had paused there to change horses. The building of the twentieth-century highway had left the pub in a backwater, the old coaching road a dead end now, an artery reduced to an appendix. Emma and I had stopped a few times, liking the old bulging building with the windows leaning sideways and the Stuart brickwork still in the fireplaces.

"Not here!" I said, surprised, as we stopped.

"Do you know it?"

"I've been here, but not for a year."

Ridger consulted a clipboard. "Complaints of whisky being watered, gin ditto. Complaints investigated, found to be unfounded. Investigations dated August twenty-third and September eighteenth last."

"The landlord's a retired cricketer," I said. "Generous. Loves to talk. Lazy. The place needs a facelift."

"Landlord: Noel George Darnley."

I turned my head, squinting down at the page. "Different man."

"Right." Ridger climbed out of the car and carefully locked it. "I'll have a tomato juice."

"Who's paying?"

Ridger looked blank. "I haven't much money . . ."

"No instructions?" I asked. "No police float?"

He cleared his throat. "We must keep an account," he said.

"O.K.," I said. "I'll pay. We'll write down at each place what I spend and you'll initial it."

He agreed to that. Whether the police would reimburse me or not I didn't know, but Kenneth Charter very likely would, if not. If neither did, no great matter.

"And what if we find a match?" I asked.

He was on surer ground. "We impound the bottle, sealing it, labeling it, and giving a receipt."

"Right."

We walked into the pub as customers, Ridger as relaxed as guitar strings.

The facelift, I saw at once, had occurred, but I found I preferred the old wrinkles. True, the worn Indian rugs with threadbare patches had needed renewing, but not with orange and brown stripes. The underpolished knobbly oak benches had vanished in favor of smooth leather-look vinyl, and there were shiny modern brass ornaments on the mantel instead of antique pewter platters.

The new landlord's new broom had resulted, however, in a much cleaner-looking bar, and the landlord himself, appeared from the rear, wasn't fat, sloppily dressed and beaming, but neat, thin and characterless. In the old days the pub had been full: I wondered how many of the regulars still came.

"A Bell's whisky, please," I said. I looked at his row of bottles. "And a second Bell's whisky from that bottle over there, and a tomato juice, please."

He filled the order without conversation. We carried the glasses to a small table and I began on the unlikely task with a judicious trial of the first tot of Bell's.

"Well?" Ridger asked, after fidgeting a full minute. "What have we got?"

I shook my head. "It's Bell's all right. Not like the Silver Moondance."

Ridger had left his clipboard in the car, otherwise I was sure he would have crossed off mine host there and then.

I tried the second Bell's. No luck there either.

As far as I could tell, neither bottle had been watered: both samples seemed full strength. I told Ridger so while he was making inroads into the tomato juice, which he genuinely seemed to enjoy.

I left both whiskies on the table and wandered to the bar.

"You're new here?" I said.

"Fairly." He seemed cautious, not friendly.

"Settling in well with the locals?" I asked.

"Are you here to make trouble?"

"No." I was surprised at the resentment he hadn't bothered to hide. "What do you mean?"

"Sorry, then. It was you ordering two whiskies from different bottles and tasting them carefully, as you did. Someone round here made trouble with the Weights and Measures, saying I gave short measures and watered the spirits. Some of them round here don't like me smartening up the place. But I ask you, trying to get me fined or lose my license . . . too much."

"Yes," I agreed. "Malicious."

He turned away, still not sure of me, which was fair enough, considering. I collected Ridger, who was wiping red stains from his mouth, and we went outside leaving the unfinished whiskies on the table, which probably hardened the landlord's suspicions into certainty, poor man.

Ridger ticked off the pub on the clipboard and read out the notes of our next destination, which proved to be a huge soulless place built of brick in the thirties and run for a brewery by a prim-looking tenant with a passion for fresh air. Even Ridger in his raincoat shivered before the open windows of the bar and muttered that the place looked dull. We were the first customers, it was true, but on a grayly chilly morning there were no electric lights to warm and welcome thirsty strangers.

"Tomato juice, please," I said. "And a Bell's whisky."

The puritan landlord provided them, stating the price in a tight-lipped way.

"And could we have the windows closed, please?"

The landlord looked at his watch, shrugged, and went round closing October out with ill grace. I wouldn't sell much in my shop, I reflected, with that scowl: everyone sought to buy more than the product they asked for and it was the intangible extra that repelled or attracted a return. The whisky in that place might be fine, but I'd never go back out of choice.

"Well?" Ridger said, initialing the cost on our list. "What is it?"

"Bell's."

Ridger nodded, drinking this time barely a mouthful from his glass. "Shall we go, then?"

"Glad to."

We left the landlord bitterly reopening his windows and Ridger consulted his clipboard in the car.

"The next place is a hotel, the Peverill Arms, on the Reading to Henley road. Several complaints of thin or tasteless whisky. Complaints investigated, September twelfth. Whisky found to be full strength in random samples."

His voice told something more than the usual dry information: a reservation, almost an alarm.

"You know the place?" I asked.

"I've been there. Disturbances." He fell silent with determination and started the car, driving with disapproval quivering in the stiffness of his neck. I thought from these signs that we might be on the way to a rowdy rendezvous with Hell's Angels, but found to my amusement on arrival that Ridger's devil was a woman.

A woman moreover of statuesque proportions, rising six feet tall with the voluptuous shape of Venus de Milo, who had forty-two-inch hips.

"Mrs. Alexis," Ridger muttered. "She may not remember me."

Mrs. Alexis indeed gave our arrival scarcely a glance. Mrs. Alexis was supervising the lighting of logs in the vast fireplace in the entrance lounge, an enterprise presently producing acrid smoke in plenty but few actual flames.

Apart from the haze below the ceiling the hall gave a lift to the entering spirit: clusters of chintz-covered armchairs, warm colors, gleaming copper jugs, an indefinable aura of success. Across the far end an extensive bar stood open but untended, and from the fireplace protruded the trousered behind of the luckless firelighter, to the interest and entertainment of scattered armchaired guests.

"For God's sake, Wilfred, fetch the bloody bellows," Mrs. Alexis said distinctly. "You look idiotic with your arse in the air puffing like a beetroot."

She was well over fifty, I judged, with the crisp assurance of a natural commander. Handsome, expensively dressed, gustily uninhibited. I found myself smiling in the same instant that the corners of Ridger's mouth turned down.

The unfortunate Wilfred removed his beetroot-red face from the task and went off obediently, and Mrs. Alexis with bright eyes asked what we wanted.

"Drinks," I said vaguely.

"Come along then." She led the way, going toward the bar. "It's our first fire this winter. Always smokes like hell until we get it going." She frowned upward at the drifting cloud. "Worse than usual, this year."

"The chimney needs sweeping," Ridger said.

Mrs. Alexis gave him a birdlike look from an eye as sharp and yellow as a hawk's. "It's swept every year in the spring. And aren't you that policeman who told me if I served the local rugger team when they'd won I should expect them to swing from the chandeliers and put beer into my piano?"

Ridger cleared his throat. I swallowed a laugh with difficulty and received the full beam from the hawk eyes.

"Are you a policeman too?" she asked with good humor. "Come to cadge for your bloody ball?"

"No," I said. I could feel the smothered laugh escaping through my eyes. "We came for a drink."

She believed the simple answer as much as a declaration of innocence from a red-handed thief, but went around behind her bar and waited expectantly.

"A Bell's whisky and a tomato juice, please."

She pushed a glass against the Bell's optic and waited for the full measure to descend. "Anything else?"

I said no thank you and she steered the whisky my way and the tomato juice toward Ridger, accepting my money and giving change. We removed ourselves to a pair of armchairs near a small table, where Ridger again initialed our itemized account.

"What happened with the rugger club?" I asked interestedly.

His face showed profound disapproval. "She knew there'd be trouble. They're a rowdy lot. They pulled the chandeliers clean out of the ceiling with a lot of plaster besides and she had them lined up against the wall at gunpoint by the time we got here."

"Gunpoint?" I said, astonished.

"It wasn't loaded, but the rugger club weren't taking chances. They knew her reputation against pheasants."

"A shotgun?"

"That's right. She keeps it there behind the bar. We can't stop her, though I'd like to, personally, but she's got a license for it. She keeps it there to repel villains, she says, though there isn't a local villain who'd face her."

"Did she send to you for help with the rugger club?"

"Not her. Some of the other customers. She wasn't much pleased when we turned up. She said there wasn't a man born she couldn't deal with." Ridger looked as if he believed it. "She wouldn't bring charges for all the damage, but I heard they paid up pretty meekly."

It would be a brave man, I reflected, who told Mrs. Alexis that her Bell's whisky was Rannoch: but in fact it wasn't. Bell's it was; unadulterated.

"Pity," Ridger said, at the news.

I said thoughtfully, "She has some Laphroaig up there on the top shelf."

"Has she?" Ridger's hopes were raised. "Are you going to try it?"

I nodded and returned to the bar, but Mrs. Alexis had departed again toward the fireplace where Wilfred with the bellows was merely adding to the smog.

"The chimney seems to be blocked," he said anxiously, exonerating himself.

"Blocked?" Mrs. Alexis demanded. "How could it be?" She thought for barely two seconds. "Unless some bloody bird has built a nest in it, same as three years ago."

"We'd better wait until it's swept again," Wilfred suggested.

"Wait? Certainly not." She strode toward the bar. "I'll be with you in a moment," she said, seeing me waiting there. "Birds building their bloody nests in my chimney. They did it once before. I'll shift the little buggers. Give them the shock of their lives."

I didn't bother to point out that nests in October were bound to be uninhabited. She was certain to know. She was also smiling with reckless mischief and reappeared from behind the bar carrying the fabled shotgun and feeding a cartridge into the breech. My own feelings at the sight seemed to be shared by most of the people present as she walked toward the fireplace, but no one thought of stopping her.

Ridger's mouth opened in disbelief.

Mrs. Alexis thrust the whole gun up inside the vast chimney and at arm's length unceremoniously pulled the trigger. There was a muffled bang inside the brickwork and a clatter as she dropped the gun on the recoil onto the logs. The eyes of everyone else in the place were popping out but Mrs. Alexis calmly picked up her fallen property and returned to the bar.

"Another Bell's?" she asked, stowing the shotgun lengthways under the counter. "Another tomato juice?"

"Er . . ." I said.

She was laughing. "Fastest way to clear a chimney. Didn't you know?"

"No."

"It's an old gun ... the barrel's not straight. I wouldn't treat a good gun like that." She looked toward the fireplace. "The damn smoke's clearing, anyway."

It appeared that she was right. Wilfred, again on his knees with the bellows, was producing smoke that rose upward, not out into the room. The eyes of the onlookers retreated to their accustomed sockets and the mouths slowly closed: even Ridger's.

"Laphroaig," I said. "Please. And could I look at your wine list?"

"Anything you like." She stretched for the Laphroaig bottle and poured a fair measure. "You and the policeman, what are you here for?" The bright eyes searched my face. "That policeman wouldn't come here just for a drink. Not him. Not tomato juice. Not early."

I paid for the Laphroaig and took the wine list that she held out. "We're looking for some scotch that turned up in a Bell's bottle at the Silver Moondance," I said. "More of the same, that is."

The sharp gaze intensified. "You won't find any here."

"No, I don't suppose so."

"Is this because of those complaints last month?"

"We're here because of them, yes."

"You've shown me no authority." No antagonism, I thought: therefore no guilt.

"I haven't any. I'm a wine merchant."

"A wine ... ?" She considered it. "What's your name?"

I told her, also the name of my shop.

"Never heard of you," she said cheerfully. "Would you know this scotch if you tasted it?"

"That's the general idea. Yes."

"Then good luck to you." She gave me an amused and shining glance and turned away to another customer, and I carried my glass across to Ridger expecting the Laphroaig to be Laphroaig and nothing else.

"She's disgraceful," Ridger said. "I should arrest her."

"On what charge?"

"Discharging a firearm in a public place."

"The inside of a chimney is hardly a public place."

"It's no laughing matter," he said severely.

"The smoke's clearing," I said. "The shot worked."

"I would have thought you'd had enough shooting for one lifetime."

"Well, yes."

I drank the Laphroaig: smoky, peaty, oak-aged historic Laphroaig, the genuine thing.

Ridger bit on his disappointment, complained about the price and fidgeted unhelpfully while I read the wine list, which was handwritten and extensive. All the familiar Silver Moondance names were there along with dozens of others, but when I pointed this out to him he said stiffly that his brief was for whisky only.

I took the wine list thoughtfully back to the bar and asked Mrs. Alexis for a bottle of St. Estèphe.

She smiled. "By all means. Do you want it decanted?"

"Not yet." I went through the rest of the list with her, picking out St. Emilion, Mâcon, Valpolicella, Volnay and Nuits St. Georges.

"Sure," she said easily. "Do you want all of them?"

"Yes, please."

She disappeared briefly and came back with a partitioned basket containing the six asked-for wines. I picked each bottle up in turn to read the labels: all the right names but none from the right year.

"We've sold all we had of 1979," she explained patiently when I pointed it out. "We constantly update the wine list, which is why we don't have it printed. We're writing another at the moment. These present wines are better. Do you want them, then, or not?"

"Sorry," I said. "Not."

She put the basket of bottles without comment on the floor near her feet and smiled at me blandly.

"So you know the Silver Moondance?" I asked.

"Heard of it. Who hasn't, round here? Never been there. Not my style. I'm told it's a tube job, anyway."

"A tube . . . ?"

"Down the tubes," she said patiently. "The bank's foreclosing on the mortgage. As of this morning the staff have been sacked. I had one of the chefs telephoning to ask for a job." She spoke with amusement as if the closure were comic, but she'd worn the same expression all the time we'd been there, her cheek muscles seeming to be permanently set into tolerant mockery.

"At the Silver Moondance," I said mildly, "they were selling one single wine under six different labels."

Her expression didn't change but she glanced down at her feet.

"Yes, those," I said. "Or rather, not those."

"Are you insulting me?"

"No, just telling you."

The brilliant eyes watched me steadily. "And you're looking for that wine as well as the scotch?"

"Yes."

"Sorry I can't help you."

"Perhaps it's as well," I said.

"Why?"

"Well, I don't think it's too utterly safe to know much about that wine. The wine waiter of the Silver Moondance undoubtedly knew what he was selling ... and he's dead."

Nothing altered in her face. "I'm in no danger," she said. "I can promise you that. Do you want anything else?"

I shook my head. "We'll be on our way."

Her gaze slid past me to rest on Ridger and still without any change of expression she said, "Give me a man who'll swing from a chandelier. Give me a goddamn *man*." Her glance came back to my face, the mockery bold and strong. "The world's a bloody bore."

Her abundant hair was a dark reddish brown gleaming with good health and hair dye, and her nails were hard and long like talons. A woman of vibrating appetite who reminded me forcibly of all the species where the female crunched her husband for breakfast.

Wilfred (currently on the menu?) was still on his knees to the fire god when Ridger and I eventually made our way to the door. As Ridger went out ahead of me there was a sort of soft thudding *flump* from the direction of the chimney and a cloud of dislodged shot-up soot descended in a sticky billowing mass onto logs, flames and man beneath.

Transfixed, the armchair audience watched Wilfred rise balefully to his feet like a fuzzily inefficient demon king, scattering black rain and blinking great eyes slowly like a surprised owl on a dark night.

"I'll sue that bloody sweep," Mrs. Alexis said.

SIXTEEN

WE WENT TO FOUR MORE PUBS ON THAT FIRST DAY AND I grew tired of the perpetual taste of neat Bell's. Ridger methodically annotated his clipboard and showed not the slightest disappointment as glass after glass proved genuine. The pub crawl was a job to him like any other, it seemed, and he would phlegmatically continue until instructed otherwise.

He was a man without rebellion, I thought, never questioning an order nor the order of things; living at the opposite end of the spectrum from that mean kicker-over-of-traces, Kenneth Charter's son. Somewhere between the two lay the rest of us, grousing, lobbying, enduring and philosophical, making what best we could of our imperfect evolution.

Toward the end I asked him if they'd found any trace of the Bedford van used in the robbery at my shop, and perhaps because by that time he had provisionally accepted me as a full colleague he answered without any of his usual reservations.

"No, we haven't found it," he said. "And we don't expect to."

"How do you mean?" I asked.

"It belonged to a firm called Quality House Provisions who hadn't noticed it was missing until one of our PCs went there early Monday asking about it. Dozy lot. They'd got several vans, they said. It's now on the stolen-vehicle list marked urgent because of its tie-in with Zarac's murder, but a hot van like that's sure to be dumped somewhere already, probably in a scrap yard miles away with the number plates off. No one will find it except by luck, I shouldn't think."

"Cheerful."

"Fact of life."

He drove me back toward the shop, saying he would return in the morning with tomorrow's list of suspicious premises.

"Can't you bring the whole list instead of in bits?" I asked.

"It's still being compiled. We started today with our own patch, but we may have to wait for information from others."

"Mm—Do you have a first name, Sergeant?"

He looked faintly surprised. "John," he said.

"In the pubs tomorrow, do you mind if I use it? I damn nearly called you Sergeant twice in front of barmen today."

He considered it. "Yes. All right. Do you want me to call you Tony?"

"It would make more sense."

"All right."

"What do you do off duty?" I asked.

"Garden," he said. "Grow vegetables, mostly."

"Married?"

"Yes, been married fourteen years. Two daughters, proper little madams." An indulgence in his face belied the sharpness in his voice. "Your wife died, they say."

"Yes."

"Sorry about that."

"Thank you, Sergeant."

He nodded. John was for business, a temporary intimacy that wouldn't commit him to friendship. I could sense his approval, almost his relief, at my avoidance of John in private.

He left me outside my door and drove tidily away, directional signal blinking, carefully efficient to the last. Mrs. Palissey had been rushed off her feet, she was glad to say, and was I sure I was fit to drive myself to the hospital because to be honest, Mr. Beach, I did smell a wee bit of drink.

I reflected that I'd ordered, paid for and swallowed a good deal of a dozen neat whiskies and if I still felt sober it was an illusion. I went to the hospital by taxi and received disgusted sniffs from the nursing sister (the same one), who stripped off the tube bandage to see what was cooking underneath.

"People who drink heal more slowly," she said severely.

"Do they?"

"Yes."

With her head not far from mine she one by one unstuck the antiseptic patches she'd applied the previous Sunday, and I tried to breathe shallowly through my nose in the opposite direction. Without much success, it seemed, judging from the offended twitch of her nostrils.

"Most of these are healing better than you deserve," she said finally. "Three are inflamed and another looks troublesome. Do they hurt?"

"Well, sort of."

She nodded. "One should expect it. Several were

more than an inch deep." She began sticking on new patches. "I'll put a stitch in this bad one up here on your biceps, to hold it together. And keep off alcohol. There are much better painkillers."

"Yes, ma'am," I said dryly, and thought of the boozy tomorrow and of fifty thousand pubs to Watford.

Back in the shop I saw Mrs. Palissey and Brian off with the deliveries and dealt with some paperwork, and in the lull between late-afternoon customers eventually got dutifully around to looking at the photostats of Kenneth Junior's notebook.

Gerard's firm had made a good job of their deciphering and checking and my respect for his organization consolidated from vague expectation into recognition that Deglet's were experts in a way I hadn't appreciated.

Gerard's fat envelope contained an explanatory note and about fifteen sheets of typing paper. The center of each sheet bore the stat of one page of the small notebook, and from each entry in the notebook a fine straight line led to explanation in the margin.

Gerard's note was typewritten:

Tony,

All the inquiries were done by telephone, not in person. Answers were given freely by Kenneth Charter himself, also by his wife and daughter and elder son, although with them as with friends and shops our questions had to be cautious, as Kenneth Charter forbade us to represent Kenneth Junior in a criminal light.

The sheets are numbered in the order in which the pages occurred in the notebook. Kenneth Charter dates the first page as having been written at the beginning of August as it refers to Mrs. Charter's birthday on August eighth. One may assume that the entries were written consecutively after that, but it is not certain, and there are no other positive dates, as you will see.

Please write down immediately any thoughts that cross your mind as you read. Don't leave such thoughts until afterward as they are apt to evaporate.

G.

I turned to the first of the notebook pages and found that the first entry of all read:

Buy card for Mum's birthday next week.

A fine straight line led to the marginal note: August eighth.

Kenneth Junior's handwriting was inclined to shoot off at both forward-and backward-sloping angles in the same word, but was otherwise distinctly formed and easy to read. The Deglet's annotator had written in neat fine black script, utterly different but equally legible. I could hardly complain that Gerard had set me a technically difficult task.

The second entry on the first page read:

Go to D. N.'s for w.g.

The marginal note said: D. N. is David Naylor, Kenneth Junior's only close friend. It is thought the letters w.g. stand for war games, as they are David Naylor's hobby.

The first page also read:

Collect trousers from cleaners.

Ask Dad for cash.

Tell B. T. to fuck off.

The line from the last entry led to: B. T. is probably Betty Townsend, a girl Kenneth Junior had been seeing.

Mrs. Charter says she was a nice girl but clinging.

Poor Betty Townsend.

I turned to page two and found a list of telephone numbers, each with an identification in the margin, along with an address.

Odeon cinema. (Local.)

Diamond snooker club. (Local.)

David Naylor. (Friend. Unemployed.)

Clipjoint. (Barber's shop, local.)

Lisa Smithson. (Occasional girlfriend. Unemployed.)

Ronald Haleby. (Friend. Works as doorman at local disco.)

The next many pages contained entries that were only understandable because of the telephone numbers and spoke eloquently of a drifting purposeless life. Kenneth Junior's lists were almost a diary, embracing such revelations as "Snort with R. H. Sunday, take cash" and "Get abortion number for L. S." but were mainly on the more mundane level of "Tell Mum to buy toothpaste," "Play snooker at Diamond's" and "Rewire plug on stereo."

One later page read:

Haircut.

Go to Halifax.

Buy tank for w.g., Phone D. N.

Get keys of N. T. for duplicates.

Meet R. H. in Diamond's.

Pay L. S. for abortion.

Deglet's annotations were:

(1) Clipjoint say Kenneth Junior went there at about ten-day intervals for shampoo and styling. He bought expensive products and tipped lavishly.

(2) Kenneth Junior is most unlikely to have been to the town of Halifax. Suggest this reference means Hal-

ifax Building Society, though his parents don't know if he had an account there. Kenneth Charter thought that apart from unemployment benefit his son had no money except what he himself gave him, but this cannot be right as Charter did not give him enough extra for co-caine and abortions.

(3) Tank must be toy tank for war games.

(4) Not traced.

I frowned for a while over the letters N. T. but could make no more of them than Deglet's had. What did one need keys for? House, car, suitcase, drawer, locker, desk, mail box, deposit box . . . infinitum. N. T. was perhaps a person. Person unknown.

On the next page there was a single entry, the one that had started the bushfire.

The Reading telephone number followed by:

Tell Z UNP 786 Y picks up B's Gin Mon. 10:00 A.M. approx.

I made a wry face over the bald and still disturbing treachery and turned over to what was left: three more pages very much like the others, with only a few new themes.

Go with D. N. for w.g. with S. N.! bore the Deglet explanation: S. N. is Stewart Naylor, David Naylor's father. Stewart Naylor lives alone after divorce. David Naylor visits his father occasionally. Stewart Naylor is noted for skill in war games, which probably accounts for the exclamation mark.

On the last page of all it said:

Get visa for Australia.

Ask R. H. about pushers in Sydney.

Pay L. S. That's her lot.

Go to Halifax.

Remember to ask Dad for cash.

Collect keys from Simpers and send them off.

There was a final Deglet explanation: Simpers is a hardware shop that duplicates keys. They have no record of work done for Kenneth Junior or anyone else in the family. They normally cut keys immediately, while you wait, but not if they don't keep the blanks in stock and have to send away for them. In that case they ask for an address and a deposit. If Kenneth Junior obtained keys in that way from Simpers he gave a name and address not his own.

I shuffled the pages together and put them back in the envelope, looking dubiously at the very few thoughts and comments I'd jotted down for Gerard; and half an hour later, when he telephoned, I offered them reluctantly and apologetically.

"Just say what occurred to you," he said a touch impatiently. "Anything at all may be helpful."

"Well, those keys."

"What about them?"

"Well . . . what sort of keys do the tankers have?"

There was utter silence from Gerard.

"Are you still there?" I asked.

"Yes, I am." Another pause. "Go on talking."

"Um . . . I wondered at the beginning about it always being the same tanker that was stolen, and I thought it might be because of something dead simple, like that one being the only one for which the thieves had keys. Because they would have needed the keys to unlock the cab door when the driver was in the service stations, in order to put the gas in there, and lock the door again so the driver found nothing suspicious when he got back."

"Hm," Gerard said. "The police assumed the thieves used lock-pickers."

"The right key would be quicker."

"I agree."

"Kenneth Junior had easy access to Charter's office and everywhere else in the place before the first theft. You might ask Charter Senior where the tanker keys are kept."

"Yes, I will."

"It struck me that maybe it was keys to a second tanker that Kenneth Junior was having cut. I mean, N. T. might stand for Next Tanker or New Tanker or something. Anyway, it might be worth taking some tanker keys to Simpers and seeing if they keep those blanks in stock or if they'd need to send away for them. And it might be as well to warn Kenneth Charter that someone, somewhere, might have the keys to another of his tankers . . . if any of this is right, of course."

"Right or wrong, I'll warn him."

"I'm afraid that's all," I said. "I didn't think of much else. Except . . ."

"Except?"

"Except that to himself Kenneth Junior didn't seem so bad. He sold information for presumably spot cash and he banked it in something ultraconservative like a building society. He might have enjoyed his snort with the disco doorman but he wasn't addicted. He paid for the girl's abortion. That's none of it heavy villainy."

"No. A moderately stable personality. I thought so too. Staying at home, buying a birthday card for his mother, being impressed by his friend's father . . . but totally without loyalty to his own."

"Teenage rebellion gone a step too far."

"Right," Gerard said. "Untrustworthy little bugger. But there you are, he's earning us money. Life's full of such ironies."

I said with a smile in my voice, "Want another?

We're now looking for that scotch courtesy of the police."

I told him about my day's journeyings with Ridger and raised a chuckle on account of Mrs. Alexis.

"I wasn't sure about Mrs. Alexis," I said. "She did have all those wines on her wine list. She says she's sold them all. She wears such a knowing expression the whole time that you can't tell if she knows anything specific. Maybe I'll go back."

"She sounds an utter dragon."

"Very good value," I said. "She likes men who swing from chandeliers."

"But you don't. You're not the type."

"No. I should be safe."

He laughed. "How was your arm? I have to go myself tomorrow."

"Not bad. And good luck."

RIDGER RETURNED PUNCTUALLY IN THE MORNING AND we set off to cover a territory in and around Henley-on-Thames, where every July the rowing regatta brought the sleepy town to bulging expensive life. In late October, in a cold drizzle, it was quiet. Ducks swam silently on the gray river and shoppers huddled head-down under umbrellas. Ridger and I went into bar after bar brushing off raindrops and I lost count after a while of the Bell's.

All of the Bell's rang true. Not a cracked note among them.

One of the barmen gave us short change, slapping down coins in a handful while sloshing water onto the counter top, so that I should snatch them up without checking, but Ridger said that that didn't rate a clipboard entry. He produced his badge, however, and warned the barman, who scowled. As the high spot of the morning it didn't rate much, but one couldn't expect a Mrs. Alexis every day of the week.

Some of the pubs had two bars. One had three. My friend John insisted on making sure of every Bell's bottle in sight.

Awash with tomato juice he returned me to my shop at two-thirty and I sat heavy-headed in my office regretting the whole enterprise. I would simply have to take something to spit into, I thought, even if spitting alerted the barman and disgusted the other customers. Getting half sloshed every lunchtime was no joke.

Mrs. Palissey drove Brian away with a big load of deliveries and between each sporadic afternoon customer I sat down and felt thick with sleep. When the door buzzer roused me for the fifth time I went into the shop yawning.

"That's no way to greet manna from heaven," my customer said.

Mrs. Alexis stood there, larger than life, bringing out her own sun on a wet afternoon. I shut my mouth slowly, readjusted it to a smile, and said, "I was coming to see you again at the first opportunity."

"Were you now," she said, mockery in full swing. "So this is where our little wine merchant dwells." She peered about her good-humoredly, oblivious to the fact that her "little" wine merchant stood a fraction under six feet himself and could at least look her levelly in the eyes. Nearly all men, I guessed, were "little" to her.

"I was passing," she said.

I nodded. Amazing, the number of people who said that.

"No, I bloody well wasn't," she amended explosively. "I came here on purpose." She lifted her chin almost defiantly. "Does that surprise you?"

"Yes," I said truthfully.

"I liked the look of you."

"That surprises me too."

"Bloody cool, aren't you?"

I was still half drunk, I thought. Almost a third of a bottle of scotch on an empty stomach, whichever way you looked at it. Ulcer land.

"How's the chimney?" I asked.

She grinned, showing teeth like a shark.

"Bloody Wilfred hasn't forgiven me."

"And the fire?"

"Burning like Rome." She eyed me assessingly. "You're young enough to be my bloody son."

"Just about."

"And do you want to know about those bloody wines or don't you?"

"Yes, I do indeed."

"I wasn't going to tell that police sergeant. Wouldn't give him the satisfaction. Pompous little killjoy."

I said "Mm" noncommittally.

"I bought them, all right," she said. "But I damn soon sent them back."

I breathed in deeply, trying to do nothing to distract her.

"I ran short of Bell's," she said. "So I phoned across to the pub opposite to borrow some. Nothing odd in that, we always help each other out. So he brings a whole unopened bloody case over, saying it came from a new supplier who offered good discounts, especially on wine, which was more my sort of thing than his. He gave me a phone number and told me to ask for Vernon."

I looked at her.

"Should have known better, shouldn't I?" she said

cheerfully. "Should have suspected it had all fallen off the back of a bloody lorry."

"But you telephoned?"

"That's right. Very good wines, just a shade under normal price. So I said right, shunt along a case of each, I'd put them on the wine list and see if anyone liked them."

"And did they?"

"Sure." She gave me the shark smile. "Shows how much some of these so-called wine buffs really know."

"And then what?"

"Then I got someone in the bar one day kicking up a fuss and saying he'd been given the wrong whisky. I'd given it to him myself out of a Bell's bottle, one I'd got from my neighbor. I tasted it but I don't like the stuff, can't tell one from another. Anyway I gave him some Glenlivet free to placate him and apologized and when he'd gone I rang up my neighbor pretty damn quick, but he said he was certain it was O.K., Vernon worked for a big firm."

"Which big firm?"

"How the hell do I know? I didn't ask. But I'll tell you, I wasn't taking any risks so I poured the rest of the case of Bell's down the drain and chalked it up to experience. Damn good thing I did, because the next bloody day I got the Weights and Measures people round with their little measuring instruments following a strong complaint from a customer. And that damned man drank my Glenlivet, too, and still reported me."

"And I don't suppose he's been back," I said, smiling.

"I'd've strangled him."

"If it hadn't been him, it would have been someone else."

"You don't have to be so bloody right. Anyway, after that I asked a man I know who buys for a wine society to come out straightaway and taste those splendid wines, and when he told me they were all the same I rang up that bloody Vernon and told him to collect what was left and repay me for the whole lot or I'd give his bloody phone number to the police."

"And what happened?" I asked, fascinated.

"The same man who delivered them came back with my cash and took his wines away, what wasn't already drunk. He said he wasn't Vernon, just a friend of his, but I'll bet it was Vernon himself. He said Vernon hoped I'd keep my word about the phone number because if not something very nasty would happen to me." She grinned, superbly unconcerned. "I told him if Vernon tried anything with me, I'd eat him."

I laughed. "And that was that?"

"That was bloody that. Until you came round yesterday snooping."

"Well," I said, "do you still have the phone number?"

Her brilliant eyes shone yellowly. "Yes, I do. How much is it worth to you? A case of Krug? Case of Pol Roger? Dom Pérignon?"

I reflected. "Case of Bell's?" I suggested.

"Done." She picked a piece of paper without ceremony out of her handbag and gave it to me.

"If you carry it," I said.

She glanced at the sling I still wore. "Hurt your arm?"

"Shotgun pellets . . . I wouldn't tell anyone, if I were you, that you'd been here to see me. I got shot at because of that wine. Vernon might not be pleased to know you'd given me his phone number."

Her eyes opened wide and the mockery for once died right out of her face.

"I came here," she said flatly, "because of the wine waiter at the Silver Moondance. Murder's going too far. But you didn't say . . ."

I shook my head. "I'm sorry. There seemed no need. I had no idea you would come here. And I'm sure you'll be O.K. if you just keep quiet. After all, others must have Vernon's number. Your neighbor, for one."

"Yes." She thought it over. "You're damn right." Her face lightened back into its accustomed lines. "Any time you're passing, my little wine merchant, call in for dinner."

She came with me into the storeroom to collect her trophy, which she bore easily away under her arm, diving out into the drizzle with the teeth and eyes gleaming against the gray sky.

GERARD SAID "THAT'S GREAT," AND PROMISED TO RING back as soon as his firm had traced the number.

"It's somewhere near Oxford," I said.

"Yes," he agreed. "Oxford code."

His voice for all his enthusiasm sounded tired and when I asked after his shoulder he merely grunted without comment, which I took to mean no good news.

"I'll call you back," he said, and within half an hour did so, but not to say he had located Vernon's number.

"Thought you'd like to know . . . The office has checked with the Doncaster auctioneers. Ramekin was bought for actual cash. Banknotes. They've no record of who bought it. The office did a quick check also on transporters and sure enough, as you said, Ramekin was in their books. He was shipped to California to a well-known bloodstock agent. The agent is away traveling in

Japan and no one in his office will release information
in his absence. He's expected home next Thursday night.
Ramekin's shipment costs were paid in cash by a Mr.
A. L. Trent, who has sent several other horses to California via the same shipper to the same agent. So there
we are. The laundered cash is in California, either
banked or still on the hoof.''

"Banked, I'd bet a million.''

"Yes, I'd think so. But a dead end until Friday.''

"Pity.''

"We're making progress,'' he said. "And you might
also like to know about the tanker keys.''

"What about them?''

"I talked to Kenneth Charter. He says there's nothing
exceptional about the keys to the cab or the ignition keys
but he has special keys for the valves into the segments
in his tankers. Part of his security arrangements. There
are nine separate segments in those big tankers. He says
it's so the tanker can carry several different liquids in
small loads on the same journey, if necessary. Anyway,
each segment has its own particular key, to avoid mistakes with unloading, so the scotch tankers each have a
bunch of nine valve keys. With goods in bond Charter
has always posted a set of keys in advance to both shipper and destination so that they are never carried on the
tanker itself, for security.''

"Most prudent,'' I said.

"Yes. So Kenneth Charter went to the Simpers' shop
himself this afternoon, and sure enough they said they'd
twice made a set of nine keys like that, and both times
they'd had to send away for the blanks. The young man
who'd ordered them had given his name as Harrison
each time. Kenneth Charter is spitting mad as of course
the shop has no record of the shapes they cut into the

blanks, and he doesn't know which of his tankers is now at risk.''

"Awkward."

"He says if he loses the whole business it won't matter a damn. What upset him most was Kenneth Junior going to such lengths.''

"Does he know how Kenneth Junior got hold of the keys?" I asked.

"He says they're usually kept in his office, but when the tankers' valves are being steam-cleaned the keys are out in the workshop. He reckons Kenneth Junior took them from there.''

"Cunning little beast.''

"Absolutely. Incidentally, both Kenneth Charter and Deglet's have now received from Rannoch the profile analyses of all three of the stolen loads of scotch. Apparently they are all slightly different because they were blends from more than one distillery. Too technical for me. Anyway, they're in our office ready, if we find anything to match.''

"Mm. I wonder if Mrs. Alexis's neighbor still has any.''

"What a thought! Get onto her pronto.''

"Pity she poured hers down the drain.''

Gerard and I disconnected and I got through to Mrs. Alexis, who sounded breezily unaffected and said she would find out at once; but she called back within ten minutes to say her neighbor had sold the lot some time ago and couldn't get any more at that price because Vernon had discontinued the discount, but she thought Vernon must have got the wind up after his brush with her and had closed down altogether in her area.

Damn, I thought, and told Gerard.

"Whenever we get near that stuff it seems to recede from us like a phantom," he said wearily.

"Maybe I'll find it tomorrow."

He sighed. "It's a very big haystack."

SEVENTEEN

FLORA CAME BREATHLESSLY INTO THE SHOP SOON AFTER I'd opened it on the Saturday morning, saying she was on her way to fetch Jack home and wanted to thank me again for my help with Howard and Orkney Swayle.

"There's no need. I enjoyed it."

"All the same, Tony dear, I want you to have this." She put a gift-wrapped parcel on the counter, and when I opened my mouth to protest said, "Now don't argue, Tony dear, it's for you and it's not enough, it's very small and I expect you have one already, but I'll have my hands full when Jack's home so I thought I'd bring it for you now."

She patted my hand in motherly fashion and I bent to kiss her cheek.

"You're very naughty," I said. "But thank you."

"That's right, dear. Where's your sling?"

"I forgot it this morning. It's at home."

"Don't tire yourself, dear, will you? And we'll need some more drinks whenever you've time." She fished in her handbag and produced a list. "After Jack's home the owners will start coming again and some of them drink like fish, though I shouldn't say it, and Jack says he's going to add it on their bills as medicine for the horses, which you can't blame him for, can you, dear?''

''Er . . . no.''

She put the list on the counter beside the present, and, saying she had a thousand things to do on her way to the hospital, went light-footedly away.

I unwrapped the parcel curiously and found that although it was small in size it couldn't have been in price. The box inside the glazed white paper had come from a jeweler in Reading, and it contained, in a nest of red velvet, a silver penknife.

Not one that would necessarily gladden the hearts of Boy Scouts. Not knobbly with thirteen blades and a hook for taking stones out of horses' hooves, like the one that had been the pride of my childhood. A slim elegantly tooled affair with a sharp steel cutting blade tucked into one side and a second blade on the other that turned out to be a screwdriver. I liked both the look and the feel, and although it was true I already had a knife, it was old and blunt. I took the old knife out of my pocket and replaced it with the new, and thought friendly thoughts of Flora all morning.

Ridger added to my pleasure by telephoning to say there would be no more pub crawls for a few days as he had been assigned to other duties, but we would resume on Wednesday and he would be along for me then at ten-fifteen.

I suppose I should have told him about Mrs. Alexis and the mysterious Vernon with his telephone number, but I didn't. It seemed odd to me to find that my allegiance was to Gerard rather than to the police. I had caught from him quite thoroughly, it seemed, the belief that the paying client's interests came first, with public justice second.

I did actually half jokingly ask Ridger who I should tell if I came across the suspect scotch when I wasn't in his own company, and he answered seriously, after earnest thought, that I'd probably better tell Chief Superintendent Wilson straightaway, as Ridger himself, along with many of the county's police, was having to go up north to help deal with some ugly picketing, which made a change, and he couldn't tell who'd be on duty while he was away.

"How would I reach the chief superintendent?" I asked.

He told me to wait a moment and came back with a number that would reach the Zarac investigation room direct. Night or day, he said. Priority.

"Would the Silver Moondance scotch be priority?"

"Of course," he said.

"O.K., Sergeant. See you on Wednesday."

He said he hoped so, and goodbye.

Relieved at being let off the drinking I sold a lot of wine to a flood of customers, with Mrs. Palissey busily beaming and Brian carrying the loads out to the cars, and it seemed as if it would be for once a normal day until Tina McGregor telephoned at eleven.

"Gerard's gone up to the office," she said. "I wish he wouldn't on Saturdays and particularly as he's not right yet from last Sunday, but it's like arguing with a bulldozer . . . Anyway, he asked me to tell you they've traced the number you gave him yesterday and it doesn't look too promising. It's the number of the big caterers at Martineau Park racecourse. He says if you'd care to go along there you might ask them if Vernon—is that right?—still works for them. He says if you should see

Vernon yourself he'll leave it up to you to decide whether or not to ask him where he got the scotch and wines. Is that all right?''

"Yes, fine," I said. "How's his shoulder?"

"He's being utterly tight-lipped about it and they've put him on antibiotics."

"It's infected?" I asked, alarmed.

"He didn't say. I just wish he'd slow down."

She sounded neither anxious nor angry, but one could never tell Tina's reactions from her voice. I said weakly, "I'm sorry," and she answered "No need to be" in the same calm tone, and said Gerard would like me to telephone him at his home later to let him know how I got on at Martineau Park.

It was odd, I reflected, putting down the receiver, to think that I had been at Martineau Park races so long on Tuesday afternoon totally oblivious of the existence of Vernon among the caterers Orkney Swayle so much detested. Life, as Gerard said, was full of ironies.

Mrs. Palissey, geared to my planned absence with Ridger, took my substitute trip to Martineau Park in her stride. "Of course, Mr. Beach. No trouble at all."

Grudge-and-spite might be the prevailing social climate but Mrs. Palissey rose gloriously above it. Mrs. Palissey was a noninterfering do-gooder, heaven reward her. I said I would make it up to her later, and she said, "Yes, yes," as if it didn't matter one way or the other.

I drove to Martineau Park wondering if in fact there would be anyone there. It wasn't a race day. There would be no crowds. I hadn't before been to a racecourse on a nonracing day and didn't know what level of activity to expect in the way of managers, maintenance, groundsmen or cleaners. The whole catering department would very likely be locked. I would quite likely be turning round to drive straight back.

The gates into the members' carpark at least stood open, unguarded. I drove through them and across the unpopulated expanses of cindery grass, leaving the Rover at the end of a short row of cars near the entrance to the paddock. That gate too was open and unattended, where on race days watchful officials checked the admittance badges of the throng streaming through.

It was eerie, I thought, to see the place so deserted. Without people the bulky line of buildings seemed huge. Bustling human life somehow reduced their proportions, filled their spaces, made them friendlier, brought them to comfortable size. I hadn't realized how big the place was in all the days I'd been there.

There was no one about around the weighing room area, though the doors there too were open. I went curiously inside, looking at the holies from where racegoers were normally barred, peering with interest at the scales themselves and at the flat pieces of lead used for packing weight-cloths. I went on into the jockeys' changing rooms and looked at the rows of empty pegs, empty benches, empty racks for saddles: all echoingly bare with no scrap of personal life remaining. When the racing circus moved on, it took all with it but the dust.

Gerard might consider the detour a waste of time, but I would probably never get such an opportunity again. I peered for good measure into a room marked Stewards, which contained merely a table, six undistinguished chairs and two pictures ditto. No mementos, no records of the make-or-break inquiries held there.

Returning to fresh air and the allotted task I came to a door marked Clerk of the Course, which stood slightly ajar. I pushed it open tentatively and found a man there sitting at a desk, writing. He raised a smooth head and bushy eyebrows and said in a civilized voice, "Can I help you?"

"I'm looking for the caterers," I said.

"Delivery entrance?"

"Er . . . yes."

"You'll want to go along the back of the stands to the far end. You'll find the Tote building facing you. Turn right. You'll see the Celebration Bar there alongside the Tote, but the door you want is to your right again before you get there. A green door. Not conspicuous. There are some empty beer crates just outside, unless they've moved them as I asked."

"Thank you."

He nodded civilly and bent to his writing, and I walked to the far end of the stands and found the green door and the beer crates, as he'd said.

I found also that deliveries were at that moment taking place. A large dark van had been drawn up outside the closed front of the Celebration Bar, a van with its rear doors opened wide and two workmen in brown overalls unloading a shipment of gin from it onto a pallet on a forklift truck.

The green door itself stood open, propped that way by a crate. I walked through it behind the two men in overalls as they trundled inward the make of gin that Orkney had refused to have in his box.

The door, I saw, represented the outward end of a very dimly lit passage about six feet wide, which stretched away into the distance as far as one could see, and I realized that it must run under the whole length of the main stands, an inner spinal thoroughfare, the gut life of the building, unseen from outside.

The gin-handlers walked onward past three closed green painted doors marked Stores A, Stores B, and

Stores C, and past an open one, Stores D, which revealed only a half dozen of the sort of deep trays used by bakers.

A few paces beyond that the gin turned abruptly to the left, and I, turning after it, found myself in a wider side passage aiming for an open but heavy and purposeful-looking door. Beyond the door were brighter lights and more people in what was clearly a larger area and I went in there wondering whether Vernon was a first name or surname, and whether there was the slightest chance of his being at work on a Saturday.

Immediately through the heavy door there was a large storeroom stacked head-high with dense-packed beer crates like those outside, only these were full. To the left was a partitioned section, walls of wood to waist height, glass above, containing a desk, files, calendar, paperwork. To the right an inner door led into a still larger storeroom, a miniwarehouse where cases of bottles rose nearly to the ceiling and advanced into the central space in deep blocks. Martineau Park, I reflected, was due to hold its Autumn Carnival jump-racing meeting near the beginning of November and was stocking up accordingly. At the Cheltenham Festival in March, one wine merchant told me, the jump-racing crowd had in three days, apart from beer by the lakeful, dispatched six thousand bottles of champagne in addition to nine thousand bottles of other wines and four thousand bottles of spirits. At Martineau, by the look of things, at least double that was expected.

The gin went through into the inner warehouse to be added to a huge stack already growing there, and I again followed. One large man with a clipboard was checking off quantities and another with a black felt pen put a mark on each box as it was unloaded.

No one paid me any attention. I stood there as if invisible to all of them, and it slowly struck me that each set thought I belonged to the other. The two delivery men disengaged the forklift from the pallet they'd brought in, picked up an empty one from a low stack and began wheeling back to the door. The man with the pen heaved the cases into their new positions, putting his mark on each, and the man with the clipboard watched and counted.

I thought I'd better wait until they'd finished before I interrupted, and looking back it seems possible that that brief hesitation saved my life.

The telephone rang in the office section, raucously loud.

"Go and answer that, Mervyn," the man with the clipboard said, and his henchman with the marker went off to obey. Then the clipboard man frowned as if remembering something, looked sharply at his watch, and called out, "Mervyn, I'll answer it. You go and shift those beer cases like the man says. Put them in Store D. Wait outside until I tell you to come back. And tell those men not to bring in the next load until I'm off the phone, right?" His gaze flicked over me, scarcely reaching my face. "Your job, of course," he said. "You tell them."

He strode away fast in the direction of the office leaving me flat-footed in his wake, and presently I could hear his voice answering the telephone and could see a portion of his back view through the glass.

"Yes, speaking. Yes, yes. Go on."

Before I'd consciously decided whether to retire or eavesdrop another and different voice spoke loudly from the passage outside, a voice accompanied by firm approaching footsteps.

"Vernon? Are you there?"

He came straight through the doorway and veered immediately to his left toward the office: and to my startled eyes he was unmistakable.

Paul Young.

"Vernon!"

"Yes, look, I'll be with you . . ." Vernon of the clipboard put the palm of his hand over the telephone and began to turn toward the newcomer, and while neither of them was looking my way I stepped backward out of their line of sight.

Paul Young.

My mind seemed stuck; my body of lead.

To reach the outside world I would have to go past the office section and with all that glass around Paul Young would be sure to see me. He might not have taken particular note of me on that Monday morning in the Silver Moondance saloon but he'd certainly thought of me a good deal since. The assistant assistant would have told him who I was. He'd sent the thieves to my shop with his list. He must know how that sortie had ended. He must also know it hadn't achieved its main purpose. I thought that if he saw me now he would know me, and the idea of that filled me with numbing, muscle-paralyzing fright.

Neither Vernon nor Paul Young at that exact moment seemed to be moving, but impelled no doubt by the atavistic burrowing instincts of the hunted and trapped, I sought in that brightly lit warehouse for a dark place to hide.

There were no soft nooks or crannies, just solid blocks and columns of cases of drink. There were narrow spaces between some of the blocks into which I could squeeze . . . and where anyone glancing in as they walked past would easily see me. Down the far end, I thought in panicky fashion. They might not go right down there.

But I'd have to get there, and at any second, any second . . . It was too far. Something else . . . Something fast.

I climbed.

I climbed the highest and most extensive stack, which happened to be of nonvintage champagne. I lay flat on my stomach along the top of it, at the back against the wall. The ceiling was eighteen inches above my head. The cases stretched beyond my feet at one end and beyond my head at the other. I could see nothing but cardboard. No floor. No people. My heart bounced around like a rubber ball and I wanted to shut my eyes on the ostrich principle that if I didn't look I wouldn't be seen.

Consultancy did not include getting too close to Paul Young.

What a hollow bloody laugh.

If he found me on top of the champagne it would be a crocodile job for sure. Did he take plaster of paris with him always in his Rolls?

Why hadn't I run for it? If I'd run, he might not have caught me. I ought simply to have sprinted. It would have been better. There were people around. I'd have been safe. And now here I was, marooned eight feet up on a liquid mountain and feeling more frightened than I'd ever been in my life.

They left the office and came into the main storeroom. I clenched my teeth and sweated.

If they searched for me . . . if they knew I was there . . . they would certainly find me.

"I'm not satisfied. I want to see for myself."

It was Paul Young's own hard voice, full of aggressive determination and so close that he might have been speaking to me directly. I tried not to tremble, not to rustle against the cardboard . . . not to breathe.

"But I've told you . . ." the clipboard man said.

"I don't give a sod what you've told me. You're a twisty bastard, Vernon. You'd lie as soon as spit. I've warned you twice and I don't trust you. By my reckoning you should still have twenty-four cases of scotch left here and I've written down on this list how much you should have under each wine label. And I'm telling you, Vernon, you'd better show me just that much because if I find you've been selling any more on your own account and pocketing the proceeds, you're out."

Vernon said sullenly, "Your list won't be up to date. I sold a lot to that wine bar in Oxford."

"How many labels?" Paul Young asked sharply.

"Two."

"That'd better be right. You can show me the invoices."

Vernon said combatively, "You make selling them too difficult, not letting more than two go to each place. No one ever says they're the same. How many complaints have we had, tell me that? Your brother's been selling all six for years and no one's ever said they aren't what's on the labels."

Paul Young said heavily, "Someone must have complained, otherwise why was that snooping wine merchant there tasting everything and telling the police? I'm not risking all six together anymore, not for anyone. If you want to stay in business, Vernon, you'll do what I tell you and don't get too greedy. It's greed that puts people behind bars, Vernon, and don't you forget it. Now let's check on the stocks, and you'd better not have been cheating me, Vernon, you'd better not."

"It's all down the far end," Vernon said glumly, and

their voices faded and became less distinct as they moved away down the long room.

At the far end . . . and I'd have gone down there to hide, if I'd had time. Great God Almighty.

I wondered if they would see my feet. I thought of escape but knew my first movement would alert them. I thought that if the worst came to the worst I could defend myself by throwing champagne bottles. Champagne bottles were reinforced because if they broke they were like minigrenades exploding with gas into cutting knives of glass. Flying glass was lethal, which people tended to forget because of actors crashing out harmlessly through windows in television sagas: but that fictional glass was made of sugar to safeguard the stuntmen. In real life little children had been killed by dropped soda bottles . . . and I'd fight with champagne if I had to.

They were down at the far end for several minutes, their voices still muffled. When they came back, nothing between them had improved.

"You had all the Silver Moondance scotch back here," Paul Young said furiously. "I brought it myself. What have you done with it?"

Silence from Vernon.

"I put a red circle on every box from there when Zarac and I loaded it. You didn't notice that, I suppose? I didn't trust you, Vernon. I was sodding right not to trust you. You've been useful to me, I'm not saying different. But you're not the only stores manager who can shuffle a bit of paper. You're greedy and you're not safe. The party's over, Vernon. You're short a total of twenty-eight cases by my reckoning and I won't have people steal from me. You've had a fair cut. Very fair. But enough's enough. We're through. I'll remove the rest of my stock tomorrow afternoon in one of the vans, and you'll be here with the keys of this place to see to it."

With defensive anger and no caution at all Vernon said explosively, "If you break with me I'll see you regret it."

There was a small intense silence, then in a deadly voice Paul Young said, "The last person who threatened me in that way was Zarac."

Vernon made no reply. I felt my own hairs rising, my breath stifling, my skin chilling to cold.

I had heard too much.

If I'd been at risk before, it was now doubled. And it wasn't just the threat of death that terrified, but the manner of it . . . the nightmare of a soft white bandage over one's nose and mouth, turning to rock, choking off breath . . . coming my way if Paul Young knew what I'd heard . . . or so it seemed to me, lying in fear, trying to prevent tremor or twitch from creaking through the unstable columns of boxes.

Vernon must have known what had become of Zarac. He made no reply at all, nor did Paul Young find it necessary to spell out his meaning at more length. I heard his strong gritty footsteps move away toward the doorway to the office, and after them, hesitant, shuffling, the footfalls of Vernon.

I heard Vernon's voice saying loudly, angrily, "What are you doing? I told you not to bring that lot in until I was ready," and with the sublime disrespect for orders shown by a certain type of British workman the two men in brown overalls pushed their forklift truck resolutely past him into the warehouse.

I couldn't see them, but I heard them plainly. One of them said truculently, "Time and a half or no time and a half, we knock off at twelve-thirty, and if this isn't unloaded by then we'll take it back with us. We can't ponce about waiting for your private phone calls.''

Vernon was flustered. I heard him outside calling, ''Mervyn, Mervyn, get back here''; and when Mervyn returned it was with news that made my precarious position much worse.

''Did you know Bakerton's van's here? They've brought fifty more cases of Pol Roger White Foil.''

Pol Roger White Foil was what I was lying on.

If they were busy with Pol Roger someone would be bound to see me. They could hardly avoid it. Delivery men wouldn't exactly ignore a man lying on top of their boxes. They would for instance remark on it. Who wouldn't?

Vernon said disorganizedly, ''Well if they've brought it . . . Go out and count what they unload, they left us short two cases last time. And you there with the gin, stack that lot separately, it's not checked.''

Paul Young's decisive voice cut through the hurrying orders. ''Tomorrow afternoon, Vernon. Two o'clock sharp.''

Vernon's reply was drowned as far as I was concerned by the gin handlers heating up an argument about football six paces from my toes. I could no longer hear Paul Young either. I heard too much about a questionable foul and the eyesight of the referee.

Staying on top of the champagne was hopeless, though the temptation to remain invisible was almost overwhelming. Discovery on my stomach, discovery on my feet . . . one or the other was inevitable.

There must be a safety of sorts, I thought, in the presence of all those delivery men.

On my feet, then.

I slithered backwards and dropped down into the narrow gap between the bulk of the Pol Roger and the smaller block of Krug beyond.

I was trembling. It wouldn't do. I stepped from the champagne shelter numb with fright and went down to the men with the gin.

One of them broke off his denunciation of a deliberate kick at a kneecap and said, "Blimey, where did you come from?"

"Just checking," I said vaguely. "Have you finished?"

"Near enough." They expertly off-loaded the last few cases. "That's the lot. You want to sign our chit?"

One of them picked a yellow folded paper from his top overall pocket and held it out.

"Er . . ." I said, fishing for a pen. "Yes."

I opened the yellow paper, leaned it against a case of gin, signed it illegibly in the space provided and gave it back to them.

"Right. We'll be off."

They left the forklift truck where it was in the middle of the wide central aisle, and set off for the door. Almost without thought I grasped the truck's handle and pushed it along in their wake, and it was in that way that I came face to face with Vernon.

There was sweat on his forehead. He looked harassed, small eyes anxious above a flourishing moustache, mouth open, breath hurried and heavy.

He gave me the smallest frown. He was accompanying an incoming load of white boxes. I let go of the truck I was pushing and walked past Vernon and the Pol Roger and was out into the passage with no sign of Paul Young, no shouts, no scalding pursuit.

I followed the brown-overalled gin men round the turn into the main passage with only a short way to go to the free open air . . . and there he was, Paul Young, outside the green entrance, lit by daylight, standing as if waiting, solid, shortish, unremarkable, a man without pity.

I glanced back the way I'd come. Vernon had peeled off from the champagne and was advancing after me, appearing undecided, inquiring, on the verge of suspicious.

"You, there," he said. "I didn't see you come in."

"Maintenance," I said briskly. "Just checking."

Vernon's frown deepened. Paul Young remained at the outer door motionless and in plain sight, watching something outside.

I turned toward the only alternative, the long passage leading deep under the stands. Vernon glanced to where I'd been looking and saw Paul Young, and his mouth tightened. I gave him no more time to crystallize his suspicions of me but set off down the long passage as if every step of the way was familiar. When I looked back after about fifteen paces Vernon was still there, still staring after me. I gave him a wave. Beyond him Paul Young still blocked the way out. I continued to walk onward, trying to control a terrible urge to run. At all costs, I told myself, don't look back again. Vernon would begin to follow.

Don't look back.

Don't actually run.

I went faster and deeper to I didn't know where.

EIGHTEEN

THE PASSAGE ENDED IN KITCHENS: VAST CAVERNOUS halls with stainless steel growing everywhere in monstrous mixing bowls and sinklike trays.

Empty, cold, clean, grayly gleaming: a deserted science fiction landscape that on Tuesday must have been alive with warmth and smells and food and bustle. There were a few lights on, inadequate for the area, but no sign that anyone was working. I glanced back against all my good intentions as I turned away from the passage and saw that Vernon had indeed followed; that he was almost halfway along.

I waved again as I stepped out of his sight, a brief and I hoped reassuring signal.

Vernon was not apparently reassured. I heard his voice shouting loudly from the distance, "Hey!"

He didn't know who I was, but he was alarmed that I could have overheard what I had. His unease sprang from guilt and his persistence in following me from a wholly accurate instinct. If he thought I was a danger to him, he was right.

Damn him, I thought. He was a better prospect than

Paul Young, but not much. I might be able to talk myself
free of him with something like saying I was checking
electric wiring. Or I might not. Better by far to vanish
as inexplicably as I'd appeared.

The ovens were big enough to crawl into, but they
had glass doors and gas jets inside. Where else?

Another way out. There had to be a way out for food.
They wouldn't push it along that passage into possible
rain. There would be a way into bars, into dining rooms.
Exit doors, somewhere.

I sped round two corners. More stainless steel monsters. Sinks like bathtubs for dishwashing. Floor-to-
ceiling racks of trays. No doors out.

Nowhere to hide.

"Are you there?" Vernon's voice shouted. "Hey,
you. Where are you?" He was much nearer. He sounded
determined now, and more belligerent. "Come out of
there. Show yourself."

I went desperately round the furthest possible corner
into a small space that looked at first like a short blank
corridor leading nowhere. I began to turn to go back the
way I'd come, feverishly trying to remember electri-
cians' terms to flourish around like interrupted resistance
and circuit overload and other such nonsense when I saw
that one wall of the corridor wasn't blank.

It contained a row of four small elevators, each about
a yard high, a yard wide, a yard deep. Constructed without fronts, they were of the sort especially designed for
transporting food upward from downstairs cooks. Dumb-
waiters the Victorians had called them. Beside each elevator, selector buttons: 1, 2, 3.

I scrambled into the nearest elevator, pressed button
3, not by choice but because my unsteady fingers hit it

first, and wondered what on earth I would say now if Vernon at that moment appeared.

He didn't. I heard him still round a corner or two, calling angrily, "Hey you. Answer me." Then the food elevator rose smoothly, quietly, taking me far upward like a sandwich.

When it stopped I spilled hurriedly out, finding myself in a serving area high up in the stands. There was daylight from large windows and a row of food trolleys parked end to end along a wall.

No one about. No sound from below, but Vernon might have heard the elevator's electric hum and be on his way. He knew every cranny; he belonged there. Out of a muddled thought that if the elevator returned to the kitchens before he saw it had gone he might not think I'd used it, I pressed the down button and saw it disappear as fast as I'd come up.

Then I scorched out of the serving area and at any other time might have laughed, because I was up on the level of Orkney Swayle's box. Up where the waitresses had ferried the food whose origins I hadn't imagined.

I ran at last: softly but with terrible fear still at my heels. Ran past the big passenger elevators that might go down from there to the ground floor, but would go slowly with flashing lights announcing their progress and might deliver me to Vernon waiting in anticipation at the doors. Ran past them to Orkney's box, because I knew it. Prayed the door wouldn't be locked.

None of the boxes was locked.

Marvelous.

Orkney's was ten or more along the glassed-in gallery, and I reached it at an Olympic sprint. I went in there and stood in the corner that couldn't be seen from the passage because of the out-jutting serving section just inside the door, and I made my breathing shallow and almost silent, and couldn't stop the noisy thump of my heart.

Nothing happened for a long long time.

Nothing at all.

There was no more voice shouting "Hey . . ."

No Vernon appeared like Nemesis in the doorway.

I couldn't bring myself to believe he'd given up. I thought that if I took a step into the gallery he would pounce on me. That somewhere, round a turning, he would be lying in wait. As in a childhood game I strained deep into a hiding place cringing from the heart-stopping moment of capture . . . but this time for real, with a penalty beyond facing.

I wasn't good at this sort of thing, I thought miserably. I felt sick. Why couldn't I have courage like my father?

I stood in my corner while time stretched agonizingly and silently out . . . and I'd almost got to the point of thinking it would perhaps be safe to move, when I saw him. He was down below in front of the stands out on the far edge of the tarmac where the bookmakers raised their tempting racket on race days. He had his back to the racecourse rails. He was scanning the length of stands, searching for movement, searching for a sight of me.

Beside him, looking upward, was Paul Young.

To them I must have been in darkness because I could see them through glass, through the glass of the doors leading from the box to the steps on the balcony.

I stood frozen, afraid almost to blink. It was movement they would see, not a stock-still shadow in the angle of two walls.

Why ever, I thought hopelessly, had I dived into such a small dead end so close to the elevators, so easy to

track down and find. Why hadn't I searched for a staircase and run downward. Going upward was fatal . . . one
could run out of up. I'd always thought it stupid for
fugitives in films to start climbing, and now I'd done it
myself. Escape always lay downward. I thought it and
knew it, and couldn't bring myself to move even though
if I ran fast enough and if I could find the way, I might
escape down the stairs and be away through some exit
before they came in from the tarmac.

Very slowly I turned my head to look along to where
my car was parked by the paddock entrance. I could see
it all right, elderly and serviceable, ready to go. I could
see also a car parked next to it, where no car had stood
when I arrived.

My eyes ached with looking at the newly arrived car
with its noble unmistakable lines and its darkened glass
and sable paint.

Black Rolls Royce . . . "a black Roller with them
tinted windows" . . . next to my way out.

Reason told me that Paul Young didn't know the car
next to his was mine. Reason said he didn't know it was
I he was looking for, and that the urgency of his search
must be relative. Reason had very little to do with lurch-
ing intestines.

The two men gave up their raking inspection and
walked toward the stands, going out of my line of sight
below the outer edge of the balcony. If I'd been rushing
downstairs I could have run straight into them. If they
started searching methodically, and I didn't move, they
would find me. Yet I didn't move. I couldn't.

For a whole hour I saw nothing, heard nothing.

They were waiting for me, I thought.

Listening for my footfall on a stairway, for the whine
of an elevator, for a door stealthily opening. The tension

in my body went screaming along like a roller-coaster, winding up as soon as it began to die down, kept going only by my own wretched thoughts.

Cat and mouse.

This mouse would stay a long time in his hole.

Orkney's box, I thought; where the tartlets had waited so long in their wrapping and Flora had flushed uncomplainingly for Jack's sake. The sideboard was emptier than ever. Orkney's bad temper rested sourly in the memory. Breezy Palm had run in panic and lost. Dear heavens . . .

When I'd been in Orkney's box for two hours, Paul Young returned to his Rolls and drove it out of the carpark.

I should have been reassured that it no longer stood next to my Rover, but I wasn't. I feared that he'd driven out, round and back through a service entrance from the main road, where the delivery vans must come in and out. I feared that he was still down there below me, claws ready.

When I moved in the end it was out of a sort of shame. I couldn't stand there quivering forever. If the cat was waiting right outside Orkney's door, then all the same I'd have to risk it.

I looked most delicately out . . . and there was no one in sight. Breathing shallowly with a racing pulse I stepped slowly into the gallery and looked down from the windows there into the wide tarmacked area behind the stands along which I'd walked to find the green door.

The green door itself was round a corner out of sight, and from my angle I couldn't see any delivery vans or any Rolls Royce.

No one was out in the rear area looking up to the gallery, but I crabbed along it with my back against the

walls of the boxes, sliding past their open doors nervously, ready at any moment to stop, to dive into any
shelter, to freeze.

No sound. I reached the place where the gallery
opened into a wider concourse, and in the last yard of
window and with my last glance downward I saw Vernon walk into sight.

He was still looking around him. Still looking upward.
Still unsatisfied, still worried, still persistent.

I watched him breathlessly until he began to walk
back toward the buildings, then I ran through the concourse because at least he couldn't see me at that point,
and at the far end with trepidation approached the stairs
to the next-lower level; and I went down them in a blue
funk and from there out to the huge viewing balcony
where tiered rows of seats stretched away on each side,
turning their blank tipped-up bottoms to the empty track.

I walked along behind the top row of seats in the
direction of the winning post and saw no one, and at the
end hopped over a railing into a similar enclosure labeled firmly Owners and Trainers Only. Not an owner
or trainer in sight. Nor Vernon, nor Paul Young.

From the ''Owners and Trainers'' a small staircase
led downward into the main bulk of the stands, and
down there I went, heart thudding, trying to make myself
believe that the smaller the place I was in, the less likely
it was that I would be spotted from a distance.

The Owners and Trainers staircase led into the Owners and Trainers bar. There were rattan armchairs, small
glass-topped tables, sporting murals, not a bottle or glass
in sight: and at the far end, a wide tier of steps allowed
one to see through a wall of glass to the parade ring.
Outside and to the left, before one reached the parade
ring, lay the weighing room and the office of the Clerk

of the Course. Beyond the parade ring lay the gate to
the carpark and to freedom.

I was there. Nearly there. A door at the bottom of the
Owners and Trainers' enclosed viewing steps led straight
out to the area in front of the weighing room, and if only
that door, like every one else in the building, were unlocked, I'd be out.

I approached the steps thinking only of that, and along
from behind the stands, barely twenty paces away from
me, marched Vernon.

If he had walked up to the glass and looked through
he would have seen me clearly. I could see even the
brown and white checks of his shirt collar over his
zipped leather jacket. I stood stock still in shuddering
dismay and watched him walk along to the Clerk of the
Course's office and knock on the door.

The man who had been writing there came outside. I
watched them talking. Watched them both look across
to the stands. The man from the office pointed to the
way he'd told me to go to find the caterers. Vernon
seemed to be asking urgent questions but the office man
shook his head and after a while went back indoors; and
with clearly evident frustration Vernon began to hurry
back the way he'd come.

The door at the bottom of the Owners and Trainers
bar steps proved to be bolted on the inside, top and bottom. I undid the bolts, fumbling. The door itself . . . the
knob turned under my hand and the door opened inward
toward me when I pulled, and I stepped out.

No one was there. I shut the door behind me and
started walking with unsteady knees. The man from the
office came out of his door and said, "I say, do you
know the caterer's store manager is looking for you?"

"Yes," I said. It came out as a croak. I cleared my

throat and said again, "Yes. I just met him along there."
I pointed to the way Vernon had gone . . . and I feared
he would come back.

"Did you? Righto." He frowned at me, puzzled. "He
wanted to know your name. Most odd, what? I said I
didn't know, but mentioned that it was hours since you'd
asked the way to his door. I'd have thought he would
have known."

"Most odd," I agreed. "Anyway, he knows now. I
told him. Er . . . Peter Cash. Insurance."

"Ah."

"Not a bad day," I said, looking at the sky. "After
yesterday."

"We needed the rain."

"Yes. Well, good day."

He nodded benignly over the civility and returned to
his lair, and I went shakily onward past the parade ring,
down the path, through the still open entrance gate and
out to the Rover; and no one yelled behind me, no one
ran to pounce and clutch and drag me back at the last
moment. No one came.

The keys went tremblingly into the locks. The engine
started. There were no flat tires. I pushed the old gear
lever through the ancient gears, reverse and forward, and
drove away over the cindery grass and through the main
gates and away from Martineau Park with Pan at my
shoulder fading slowly into the shadows on the journey.

When I went into the shop it was still only twenty-
one minutes to four, although I felt as if I had lived
several lifetimes. I headed straight through to the washroom and was sick in the washbasin and spent a long
time wretchedly on the loo and felt my skin still clammy
with shivers.

I splashed water on my face and dried it, and when I

eventually emerged it was to worried inquiries from Mrs. Palissey and open-mouthed concern from Brian.

"Something I ate," I said weakly, and took a brandy miniature from the shelves, and dispatched it.

MRS. PALISSEY AND BRIAN HAD BEEN TOO BUSY WITH customers to make even a start on the telephone orders. I looked at the pile of numbered lists carefully written in Mrs. Palissey's handwriting and felt absolutely incapable of the task of collecting each customer's requirements into cartons for delivery.

"Are any of these urgent?" I asked helplessly.

"Don't you worry," Mrs. Palissey said comfortingly. "Only one and Brian and I will see to it."

"I'll make it up to you."

"Yes, yes," she said, nodding. "I know that. I do really."

I went and sat in the office and dialed Gerard's number.

Tina answered. Gerard had left his office to go home but would still be on his way to the train. He would telephone, she said, when he came in; and could it wait until after a shower and a drink?

"Preferably not."

"All right. I'll tell him. He'll be tired." It was more a warning than a plea, I thought.

"I'll be brief," I said, and she said, "Good," and put her receiver down decisively.

Mrs. Palissey and Brian left at four-thirty and I locked the shop door behind them, retreating out of sight to my desk while I returned physically to normal and mentally to the accustomed morass of no self-respect.

Gerard, when he telephoned, sounded very tired indeed.

"How did you get on?" he said, stifling a yawn. "Tina said it wouldn't wait."

I told him what I'd heard of the conversation between Vernon and Paul Young and where I'd been when I heard it: everything in detail to that point but very little after.

"Paul Young?" he said aghast.

"Yes."

"Good grief. Look, I'm sorry."

"Whatever for?"

"I shouldn't have sent you there."

"You couldn't have known," I said, "but I'm afraid we're no nearer discovering who Paul Young is or where he came from. Vernon didn't call him by name from start to finish."

"We now know for sure he's Larry Trent's brother," Gerard pointed out. "But that's not much help. Someone in our office traced Larry Trent's birth certificate yesterday afternoon. He was illegitimate. His mother was a Jane Trent. Father unknown."

"What are you going to do?" I asked. "Do you want me to tell the police?"

"No, not yet. Let me think it over and call you back. Will you be in your shop all evening?"

"Until nine, yes."

"Right."

I opened my doors again at six, trying and failing to raise genuine interest in the customers' needs. I felt limp and unsteady as if after illness and wondered how Gerard had survived a working lifetime of chasing villains with every nerve coolly intact.

He didn't telephone again until almost closing time, and by then he sounded exhausted.

"Look . . . Tony . . . Can you meet me in the morning at nine at Martineau Park?"

"Er . . ." I said feebly. "Well . . . yes." Going back there, I thought, was so low on my priority list as to have dropped off the bottom.

"Good," Gerard said, oblivious. "I've had a good deal of trouble finding the proprietor of the caterers at Martineau. Why does everyone go away at weekends? Anyway, he's meeting us there tomorrow morning. We both agree it's best to find out just what's been going on before we say anything to the police. I said I'd bring you because you'd be able to check out the scotch and the wine if you tested them, and he agreed you were essential. He himself is no expert, he says."

Gerard made the expedition sound perfectly regular. I said, "You won't forget Paul Young's going there tomorrow afternoon, will you?"

"No. That's why we must go early, before he removes anything."

"I meant the police could arrest him and find out who he is."

"Once we're sure the stolen whisky is at Martineau, we'll alert them." He spoke patiently but there were reservations in his voice. He would do the police's work only when his own was completed.

"Can I count on you?" he said, after a pause.

"Not to tell them anyway?"

"Yes."

"I won't," I said.

"Good." He yawned. "Goodnight, then. See you in twelve hours."

HE WAS WAITING IN HIS MERCEDES OUTSIDE THE MAIN gates when I arrived, and sleep had clearly done a poor job of restoration. Gray shadows lay in his lean cheeks, with puffed bags under his eyes and lines of strain everywhere, aging him by years.

"Don't say it," he said as I approached. "Antibiotics make me feel lousy." He was still wearing his sling, I saw, for everything except actual driving. He yawned. "How do we get into this place?"

We went in the way I'd gone the day before, all the gates again standing open, and walked as far as the Clerk of the Course's office before being challenged. At that point the same man as on the previous day came out with bushy eyebrows rising and asked civilly if he could help us.

"We've come to meet Mr. Quigley, the caterer."

"Ah."

"I'm Gerard McGregor," Gerard said. "This is Tony Beach."

The busy eyebrows frowned. "I thought you said Cash," he said to me. "Peter Cash."

I shook my head. "Beach."

"Oh." He was puzzled, but shrugged. "Well, you know the way."

We smiled, nodded, walked on.

"Who's Peter Cash?" Gerard asked.

"No one." I explained about Vernon searching for me the day before. "I didn't want him to know it was Tony Beach who was there. Peter Cash was the first name that came into my head."

"Do you mean," he said, alarmed, "that this Vernon chased you all over the stands?"

"Hardly chased."

"It must have felt like it to you."

"Mm."

We reached the green door, which on this occasion

was firmly locked. Gerard looked at his watch, and almost immediately a proprietor-sized car appeared from round the far end of the Tote building, pulled up near us outside the Celebration Bar, and disgorged a proprietor-shaped occupant.

He had black hair, a moustache and a paunch. First impressions also included an air of importance, a touch of irritability and a liking for white silk scarves worn cravat-style under nautical blazers.

"Miles Quigley," he announced briefly. "Gerard McGregor?"

Gerard nodded.

"Tony Beach," I said.

"Right." He looked us over without cordiality. "Let's see what all this is about, shall we? Although I'll tell you again as I told you last night, I'm certain you're wrong. Vernon has worked for our family for years."

I could almost feel Gerard thinking of a hundred clients who had said and believed much the same.

"Vernon who?" he said.

"What? No, Vernon's his last name. He's always called Vernon."

The keyhole in the green door was round and uninformative. The key Miles Quigley produced was six inches long. The one inside the other turned with a good deal of pressure and the multiple click of a heavy mortise lock.

"That's the first locked door I've seen on this racecourse," I said.

"Really?" Miles Quigley raised his eyebrows. "They do tend to open everything for easy maintenance between meetings in the daytime but I assure you everything's locked at night. A security guard comes on duty after dark. We're very security-conscious of course, because of all the alcohol stored here.''

The green door opened outward like the one to my own storeroom: more difficult to break in. Miles Quigley pulled it wide and we went into the passage, where he importantly turned on the lights by slapping a double row of switches with his palm. Yesterday's all-too-familiar scene sprang to life, the long corridor stretching away dimly to the bowels of the kitchens.

In the wider passage leading to the drinks store Quigley opened a small cupboard marked First Aid and applied to the contents a second key, not as large as the first but equally intricate.

''Security alarm,'' he explained with superiority. ''A heat-sensitive system. If anyone goes into the store when the system is on, an alarm rings in the security office here on the racecourse and also in the main police station in Oxford. We test the system regularly. I assure you it works.''

''Who has keys?'' Gerard asked, and Quigley's irritated look was its own reply.

''I'd trust Vernon with my life,'' he said.

Not me, I thought. I wouldn't.

''Only Vernon and yourself have keys?'' Gerard persisted.

''Yes, that's right. Keys to the alarm and the store, that is. The racecourse has a key to the outer door, the green one.''

Gerard nodded noncommittally. Quigley turned his back on the problem and produced a third and a fourth key to undo the heavy door into the actual store, each key having to be turned twice, alternately: and considering the value of the liquor stacked inside, I supposed the vaultlike precautions weren't unjustified.

"Can your keys be duplicated?" Gerard asked.

"What? No, they can't. They can be obtained only from the firm who installed the system, and they wouldn't issue duplicates without my say-so."

Quigley was younger than I first thought. Not mid-forties, I judged, standing near him in the brighter storeroom lights: more like mid-thirties aping the manner of fifty.

"A family firm, did you say?" I asked.

"Basically, yes. My father's retired."

Gerard gave him a dry look. "He's still chairman, I believe, your father?"

"Presides over board meetings, yes," Quigley said patronizingly. "Makes him feel wanted. Old people need that, you know. But I run things. Have done for three years. This is a big firm, you know. We don't cater only for this racecourse, but for many other sporting events and also for weddings and dances. Very big, and growing."

"Do you keep everything here?" I asked. "Your linen, tableware, glasses, things like that?"

He shook his head. "Only the liquor here, because of the high security of this place. Everything else is at our central depot two miles away. Equipment, food stores and offices. We ship everything from there by van daily as required. It's a very big operation, as I said." He sounded vastly self-satisfied. "I have streamlined the whole business considerably."

"Were spirits by the tot in the private boxes here your own idea?" I asked.

"What?" His eyebrows rose. "Yes, of course. Got to fall in line with other racecourse caterers. Much more profitable. Got to answer to shareholders, you know. Shareholders are always with us."

"Mm," I said.

He heard doubt in my tone. He said sharply, "Don't forget it's to the box-holder's advantage. When only a little has been used, we don't insist on them buying the whole bottle."

"True," I said neutrally. A Quigley—Swayle face-to-face could draw blood: diverting prospect. "Your strawberry tartlets are excellent."

He looked at me uncertainly and explained to Gerard that all the paperwork to do with wines, beer and spirits passed through the small office to our left. Vernon, he said without happiness, was wholly in charge.

"He chooses and orders?" Gerard said.

"Yes. He's done it for years."

"And pays the bills?"

"No. We have a computerized system. The checked invoices go from here to the office two miles away to be paid through the computer. Saves time. I installed it, of course."

Gerard nodded, ignoring the smugness.

"We keep beer in here, as you see," Quigley said. "This is just back-up. Normally we get suppliers to deliver on the day of need."

Gerard nodded.

"Outside in the passage . . . we've just passed it . . . is the one passenger lift that comes down here. We transfer all the drinks to the bars and the boxes in that lift. Early on race days we are extremely busy."

Gerard said he was sure.

"Through here are the wines and spirits," Quigley said, leading the way into the main storeroom. "As you see."

Gerard saw. Quigley walked a few steps ahead of us and Gerard said quietly, "Where were you, yesterday?"

"Lying up there . . . on the Pol Roger."

He looked at me with curiosity. "What's the matter?"

"What do you mean?"

"You look . . . it can't be right . . . you look of all things ashamed."

I swallowed. "When I was up there . . . I was frightened sick."

He looked round the storeroom; at the possibilities and limitations of concealment; and he said judiciously, "You'd have been a fool not to be scared stiff. I don't think there's much doubt Paul Young would have killed you if he'd found you. Killing the second time is easier, I'm told. Fear in a fearful situation is normal. Absence of fear is not. Keeping one's nerve in spite of fear is courage."

He had a way, I thought, of speaking without sympathy while giving incredible comfort. I didn't thank him, but in my heart I was profoundly grateful.

"Shall we start?" he said as we rejoined Quigley. "Tony, you said the suspect cases are somewhere at the far end?"

"Yes."

We all moved through the central canyon between the piled-high city blocks of cartons until we reached the end wall.

"Where now?" Quigley demanded. "I see nothing wrong. This all looks exactly the same as usual."

"Always keep Bell's whisky at the end here?"

"Of course."

The size of the Bell's block would have shamed the wholesaler I regularly bought from. Even Gerard looked daunted at the possibility of having to open the whole lot to find the bad apples, which was nothing to the vision of paralytic drunkenness crossing my own imagination.

"Er ..." I said. "There may be marks of some sort on the boxes. Someone was putting black felt tip squiggles on the gin when it was being checked in."

"Mervyn, probably," Quigley said.

"Yes, that's right."

I walked back to the gin and looked at Mervyn's handiwork: a hasty curling cross with two diagonals almost joined in a circle on the right side. The only problem was that it appeared also on every Bell's case in sight. No other distinguishing mark seemed to be on any that we could see without dismantling the whole mountain.

"Vernon must have been able to tell one from another, easily," Gerard said. "He wouldn't risk not knowing his stuff at a glance."

"I don't believe all this," Quigley announced irritably. "Vernon's a most efficient manager."

"I don't doubt it," Gerard murmured.

"Perhaps we could find the wine," I suggested. "It might be less difficult."

Wine was stacked in narrower blocks on the opposite wall from the spirits, the quantity in each stack less but the variety more: and I found St. Estèphe and St. Emilion six deep behind a fronting wall of unimpeachable Mouton Cadet.

Quigley consented to the opening of a case of St. Estèphe, which laid bare the familiar false label in all its duplicity.

"This is it," I said. "Shall we taste it to make sure?"

Quigley frowned. "You can't be right. It's come from a respectable supplier. Vintners Incorporated. There's their name stamped on the box."

"Taste the wine," Gerard said.

I produced my corkscrew, opened a bottle and went back to the office section to search for a glass. All I could find were throwaway expanded polystyrene beakers that would have given Henri Tavel a fit: but even in the featherweight plastic the bottle's contents were unmistakable.

"Not St. Estèphe," I said positively. "Shall I try St. Emilion?"

Quigley shrugged. I opened a case and a bottle, and tasted.

"It's the same," I said. "Shall we look for the other four?"

They were all there, all hidden behind respectable facades of the same sort of wine: the Mâcon behind Mâcon, and so on. The contents of all were identical, as at the Silver Moondance: and all six wines had been supplied, according to the cases, by Vintners Incorporated.

"Um," Gerard said thoughtfully. "Do Vintners Incorporated supply Bell's whisky also?"

"But they're a well-known firm," Quigley protested.

"Anyone," Gerard pointed out, "can cut a stencil and slap the name Vintners Incorporated onto anything."

Quigley opened his mouth and then slowly closed it. We returned to the Bell's and immediately found a section at the back of the block with Vintners Incorporated emblazoned obviously on the side.

"I can't believe it," Quigley said. Then, "Oh, very well. Taste it."

I tasted it. Waited. Let aftertaste develop. Beyond that let nuances linger in mouth, throat and nose.

"He can't tell," Quigley said impatiently to Gerard. "There's nothing wrong with it. I told you."

"Have you ever had complaints?" I asked eventually.

"Of course we have," he said. "What caterer hasn't? But none of them has been justified."

I wondered if Martineau Park would turn up on Ridger's lists. No hope of finding out until he came back on Wednesday.

"This isn't Bell's," I said. "Too much grain, hardly any malt."

"Sure?" Gerard said.

"It's what we're looking for," I said, nodding.

"What do you mean?" Quigley asked, and then without waiting for an answer said aggrievedly, "How could Vernon possibly be so disloyal?"

His reply came through the doorway in the shape of the man himself: Vernon in his leather jacket, large, angry and alarmed.

"What the bloody hell is going on in here?" he shouted, advancing fast down the storeroom. "What the hell do you think you're doing?"

He stopped dead when Gerard moved slightly, disclosing the presence of Quigley.

He said, "Oh . . . Miles . . . I didn't expect . . ."

He sensed something ominous in our stillness. His gaze shifted warily from Quigley to Gerard and finally to me: and I was a shock to him of cataclysmic proportions.

NINETEEN

"LET'S STRAIGHTEN THIS OUT," GERARD SAID MATTER-OF-factly in the office section, to which we had all moved. "The fraud as I see it is as follows."

His voice was as unhurried and unemotional as an accountant summing up an unexciting audit and was having a positively calming effect on Quigley if not on Vernon.

"It appears to me from a preliminary inspection of the invoices at present to hand in this office that the following sequence of events has been taking place. And perhaps I should explain to you," he said directly to Vernon, "that the unraveling of commercial fraud is my constant occupation."

Vernon's small intense eyes stared at him blackly and under the large drooping moustache the mouth moved in twitches, tightening and loosening with tension. He half stood, half sat, his bulk supported by the desk on which he had done his constructive paperwork, and he had folded his arms across his chest as if not accepting in the least the accusations now coming his way. The fine dew, however, stood again on his forehead, and I guessed that all he could be grateful for was that this present inquisitor was not his dangerous friend Paul Young.

"A supplier proposed to you the following scheme," Gerard said. "You as liquor manager here would order extensively from him and in return receive a sizable commission. A kickback. You were to sell what he provided as if it were part of your firm's regular stock. However, what he provided was not as described on the invoice. Your firm was paying for Bell's whisky and fine wines and receiving liquor of lower quality. You certainly knew this. It considerably increased your payoff."

Quigley, standing by the doorway, rocked slowly on his heels as if disassociating himself from the proceedings. Gerard, seated on the only chair, dominated the moment absolutely.

"Your provider," he said, "chose the name of a respectable supplier with whom you didn't already do business and sent you everything stenciled 'Vintners Incorporated.' You received normal-looking invoices from your supplier with that heading and your treasurer's department sent checks normally in return. They were perhaps negligent in not checking that the address printed on the invoice heading was truly that of Vintners Incorporated, as you have just heard me doing on the telephone, but no doubt Mr. Quigley's firm as a whole deals with dozens of different suppliers and has no habit of checking each one." He broke off and turned his head toward Quigley. "I always advise firms to check and keep checking. Such a simple matter. When an address has been entered once into a computerized system such as yours, it's seldom ever checked. The computer goes on sending payments without question. Invoices may indeed be routinely paid without the goods ever being delivered.'' He turned back to Vernon. "On how many occasions did that happen?''

"Rubbish,'' Vernon said.

"Vernon,'' Quigley said, and it was a shattered word of disillusion, not of disbelief. "Vernon, how could you? You've been with the family for years.''

Vernon gave him a look in which contempt was clearly a component. Vernon might have remained loyal to the father, I thought, but had been a pushover under the son.

"Who is this provider?'' Quigley said.

I saw Gerard wince internally: it wasn't a question he would have asked except obliquely, trying to squeeze out a name by finesse.

Vernon said, "No one.''

"He's coming here this afternoon,'' I said.

Vernon stood up convulsively and unfolded his arms.

"You bloody spy,'' he said intensely.

"And you're afraid of him,'' I said. "You don't want to follow Zarac to the cemetery.''

He glared at me. "You're not Peter Cash,'' he said suddenly. "I know who you are. You're that interfering bloody wine merchant, that's who you are. Beach, bloody Beach.''

No one denied it. No one asked him, either, how he knew anything about any bloody interfering wine merchant called Beach. He could only have known if Paul Young had told him.

"Who's Peter Cash?'' Quigley asked, lost.

"He told the racecourse people his name was Peter Cash,'' Vernon said violently. "Insurance.'' He nearly spat. "He didn't want us knowing who he was.''

"Us?'' Gerard asked.

Vernon shut his mouth tight under the curtain of moustache.

"I'd guess," I said slowly, "that you turned up this early today because you intended to take all the 'Vintners Incorporated' cases out of here and be long gone before your provider arrived at two."

Vernon said "Rot," but without conviction, and Quigley shook his head despairingly.

"It's possible," Gerard said with authority, "that Mr. Quigley wouldn't himself press charges against you, Vernon, if you cared to answer some questions."

Quigley stiffened. I murmured "Shareholders?" at his elbow and felt his opposition falter and evaporate. With the faintest twitch of humor to his mouth Gerard said, "For instance, Vernon, how close were your ties with Zarac at the Silver Moondance?"

Silence. The dew on Vernon's forehead coagulated into visible drops and he brushed the back of one hand over the moustache in evident nervousness. The struggle within him continued for a lengthening time until his doubts forced a way out.

"How can I know?" he said. "How can I be sure he wouldn't get the police here the minute I said anything?" He, it appeared, was Miles Quigley. "Keep the trap shut and stay out of trouble, that's what I say," Vernon said.

"Wise advice, if we were the police," Gerard said. "But we're not. Whatever you say here won't be taken down and used in evidence. Mr. Quigley can give you an assurance and you can believe in it."

Mr. Quigley looked as if he were well on the way from injured sorrow to vengeful fury at Vernon's defection, but still had enough of an eye to the annual general meeting to see that swallowing the unpalatable now could save him corporate indigestion later on.

"Very well," he said rigidly. "No prosecutions."

"On condition," Gerard added, "that we consider your answers to be frank."

Vernon said nothing. Gerard neutrally repeated his question about Zarac, and waited. "I knew him," Vernon said at length, grudgingly. "He used to come here for wine if they ran out at the Silver Moondance."

"Your provider's wine?" Gerard said. "The 'Vintners Incorporated' labels?"

"Yes, of course."

"Why of course?"

Vernon hesitated. Gerard knew the answer: testing him, I thought.

Vernon said jerkily, "Larry Trent was his brother."

"Zarac's brother?"

"No, of course not. My . . . well . . . provider's."

"His name?"

"Paul Young." Vernon had less trouble with that answer, not more. He sounded glib, I thought. He was lying.

Gerard didn't press it. He said merely, "Paul Young was Larry Trent's brother, is that it?"

"Half-brother."

"Did you know Zarac before this Paul Young persuaded you to join his scheme?"

"Yes, I did. He came here for regular wine like restaurants do sometimes and said he knew of a good fiddle, no risks, for someone in my position. If I was interested, he would let me in."

Gerard pondered. "Did the Silver Moondance normally get its wine straight from, er, Paul Young?"

"Yes, it did."

"Did you know Larry Trent?"

"I met him." Vernon's voice was unimpressed. "All he cared about was horses. His brother was bloody good to him, letting him strut about pretending to own that place, giving him money by the fistful for his training fees and gambling. Too bloody good to him by half, Zarac said."

I heard in memory Orkney Swayle saying Larry Trent was jealous of his brother; the brother who gave him so much. Sad world; ironic.

"What was the relationship between Larry Trent and Zarac?"

"They both worked for his brother. For Paul Young." Again the unfamiliarity over the name. Gerard again let it go.

"Equal footing?"

"Not in public, I don't suppose."

"Why did Paul Young kill Zarac?"

"I don't know," Vernon said, indistinctly, very disturbed. "I don't know."

"But you knew he did kill him?"

"Jesus . . ."

"Yes," Gerard said. "Go on. You do know, and you can tell us."

Vernon spoke suddenly as if compelled. "He said Zarac wanted the Silver Moondance. Wanted it given to him on a plate. Given to him or else. Sort of blackmail."

Vernon was a sweating mixture of fear, indignation, sympathy and candor and had begun to experience the cathartic release of confession.

I watched in fascination. Gerard said smoothly, "He justified the killing to you?"

"Explained it," Vernon said. "He came here with the Silver Moondance liquor piled up in his Rolls. He said he was loading it with Zarac's help. He made three trips.

There was so much. The third time he came he was different. He was flushed . . . excited . . . very strong. He said I would hear Zarac was dead, and to keep my mouth shut. He said Zarac had wanted power over him, and he couldn't have that. And then I heard later how he'd killed him. Made me vomit. Zarac wasn't a bad guy. Jesus, I never meant to get mixed up in murder. I didn't. It was supposed to be just an easy fiddle for good money . . .''

"And for how long," Gerard said flatly, "has the fiddle been in progress?"

"About fifteen months."

"Wine and whisky all the time?"

"No. Just wine to start with. Whisky these past six months."

"Always Bell's?"

"Yes."

"Where did the fake Bell's whisky go from here?"

"Where?" Vernon took a moment to understand. "Oh. We sold it in the bars here all the time. Sometimes in the boxes too. Also it went to the other sports events Quigley's cater, and to weddings and dances. All over."

Quigley's face went stiff and blank with almost comical shock.

"Anywhere you thought no one would notice the difference?" Gerard asked.

"I suppose so. Most people can't. Not in a crowded place, they can't. There's too many other smells. Zarac told me that, and he was right."

Wine waiters, I knew, were cynics. I also thought that but for Orkney's anticaterer obsession and his refusal to accept what they routinely offered, I might even have found the Rannoch/Bell's in his box.

"Do you know what precise whisky you were selling in Bell's bottles?" Gerard asked.

Vernon looked as if he hadn't considered it very closely. "It was scotch."

"And have you heard of a young man called Kenneth Charter?"

"Who?" Vernon said, bewildered.

"Return to Paul Young," Gerard said without visible disappointment. "Did he plan with you the robbery at Mr. Beach's shop?"

Vernon wasn't so penitent as not to be able to afford me a venomous glance. "No, not really. He just borrowed one of our vans. I lent him the keys."

"What?" Quigley exclaimed. "The van that was stolen?"

Quigley . . . Quality House Provisions. I picked up one of the printed catering pricelists from the desk beside Gerard and belatedly read the heading: Crisp, Duval and Quigley Ltd., incorporating Quality House Provisions. Quigley's own van outside my back door.

"They meant to bring it back," Vernon said defensively. "They didn't expect that bloody man to turn up on a Sunday teatime." He glared at me balefully. "They said he might have seen the number plate and they'd keep the van for a while but we'd get it back eventually. When the heat died down they'd dump it somewhere. They told me to report it missing, but I didn't get a chance, the police were round at the office before you could sneeze."

"They," Gerard said calmly. "Who are they?"

"They work for . . . Paul Young."

"Names?"

"Don't know."

"Try again."

"Denny. That's all I know. One's called Denny. I was just told Denny would pick up the van. They were going to bring the wines here from the shop for me to sort through but they didn't come although I waited until nine. Then I heard *he* turned up," Vernon jerked his head in my direction, "and something happened to put them off so they never came here. I heard later they got the wrong stuff anyway, so it was all a bloody muddle for nothing."

"Did anyone tell you what it was that happened to put them off?" Gerard asked casually.

"No, except they panicked or something because something happened they didn't expect, but I didn't hear what."

Both Gerard and I believed him. He couldn't have stood there so unconcernedly disclaiming knowledge in front of us if he'd known that the something that had happened was our being shot.

"How well do you know them?" Gerard asked.

"I don't. Denny drives the delivery van that brings the stuff here. The other comes sometimes. They never talk much."

"How often do they deliver?"

"About once a week. Depends."

"On how much you've sold?"

"Yes."

"Why didn't they use that van to rob Mr. Beach's shop?"

"It's big . . . it's got Vintners Incorporated on the door . . . it was in for repairs, or something."

"And can you describe Denny and his mate?"

Vernon shrugged. "They're young."

"Hair style?"

"Nothing special."

"Not frizzy black Afro?"

"No." Vernon was positive and slightly puzzled. "Just ordinary."

"Where do they come from? Where do they bring the wine from?"

"I don't know," Vernon said. "I never asked. They wouldn't have said. They're not friendly. They work for Paul Young, that's all I know."

He had said Paul Young this time far more easily. Getting accustomed, I thought.

"When did you first meet Paul Young?"

"Right when I started. When I told Zarac I was interested. He said the boss would come to check me out and explain what he wanted, and he came. He said we'd get on well together, which we did mostly."

Until Vernon started in business on the side, stealing from his master: but he wasn't confessing that, I noticed.

"And what is Paul Young's real name?" Gerard asked.

The open doors of the confessional slammed rapidly shut.

Vernon said tightly, "His name is Paul Young."

Gerard shook his head.

"Paul Young," Vernon insisted. "That's what his name is."

"No," Gerard said.

Vernon's sweat ran from his forehead across his temple and down to his jaw. "He told me the police had seen him in the Silver Moondance when he went there unawares after his brother died, and that was the name he gave them because he didn't want to be investigated because of the drinks, and he said they'd be looking for him now because of Zarac. He said if ever, if ever anyone came here asking, which he said he was certain they wouldn't, but if ever . . . I was to call him Paul Young. And my God, my God, that's what I'm calling him and I'm not telling you his real name, he'd kill me somehow . . . and I'm not joking, I know it. I'll go to jail, but I'm not telling you.''

He'd spoken with total conviction and in understandable fear, but all the same I was slightly surprised when Gerard didn't press him, didn't lean on him further.

He said merely, ''All right.'' And after a pause, ''That's all then.''

Vernon for a wild moment seemed to think he had been let off all hooks, straightening up with a returning echo of burly authority.

Quigley instantly deflated him, saying in pompous outrage, ''Give me your keys, Vernon. At once.'' He held out his hand peremptorily. ''At once.''

Vernon silently brought a ring of keys from his pocket and handed them over.

''Tomorrow you can look for another job,'' Quigley said. ''I'll stick to my agreement. I won't prosecute. But you'll get no reference. I'm disappointed in you, Vernon, I don't understand you. But you'll have to go, and that's it.''

Vernon said blankly, ''I'm forty-eight.''

''And you had a good job here for life,'' Gerard said, nodding. ''You blew it. Your own fault.''

As if for the first time Vernon seemed to be looking realistically at his doubtful future. New lines of worry deepened round his eyes.

''Do you have a family?'' Gerard said.

Vernon said faintly, ''Yes.''

''Unemployment is preferable to imprisonment,'' Gerard said austerely, as no doubt he had said to many a detected cheat: and Quigley as well as Vernon and myself heard the iron in his voice. Actions had to be accounted for and responsibility accepted. Consequences had to be faced. Constant forgiveness destroyed the soul . . .

Vernon shivered.

WITH QUIGLEY'S PERMISSION, AFTER VERNON HAD gone, Gerard and I loaded into his Mercedes (driven round to the green door) a case of "Vintners Incorporated" Bell's and a case each of the "Vintners Incorporated" wines. In effect Gerard and Quigley watched while I shifted the cases. Back to my normal occupation, I thought with a sigh, and let the forklift truck take most of the strain off my mending muscles.

"What do I do with the rest?" Quigley said helplessly. "And how are we going to cope with the Autumn Carnival without Vernon? No one else knows the routine. He's been here so long. He *is* the routine . . . he developed it."

Neither Gerard nor I offered solutions. Quigley gloomily set about double-double-locking his treasure house and switching on the alarm, and we made the final reverse trip to the outer world.

"What should I do?" Quigley asked, fastening the green door. "I mean . . . about that murder?"

Gerard said, "Vernon told you his version of what Paul Young told him, which was itself no doubt only a version of the facts. That's a long way from first-hand knowledge."

"You mean I could do nothing?"

"Act as your judgment dictates," Gerard said pleasantly and unhelpfully, and for once in his life I guessed Quigley was searching his self-importance and finding only doubt and irresolution.

Gerard said, "Tony and I will tell the police that Paul Young may arrive here at any time from now on. After that, it's up to them."

"He said he was coming at two o'clock," Quigley corrected.

"Mm. But he might suspect Vernon would do what Vernon did mean to do, in other words clear off with the loot before Paul Young got here. Paul Young could be here at any minute." Gerard seemed unconcerned but he was alone in that. Quigley made his mind up to leave as soon as possible and I felt very much like following.

"He won't be able to get in as I have all the keys," Quigley said. "I suppose I must thank you, Mr McGregor. I don't like any of this. I can only hope that with Vernon gone we'll have no more trouble."

"Certainly hope not," Gerard said blandly, and we both watched Quigley drive away with hope already straightening the shoulders and throwing forward the chin. "He might be lucky, he might not," Gerard said.

"I don't want to be here when Paul Young arrives," I said.

He half smiled. "More prudent not. Get in my car and we'll fetch your car first and then find a telephone box."

We both drove for five miles and stopped in a small village where he made the call from a public telephone outside the post office. I gave him the priority number Ridger had told me, and I listened to his brief message.

"It's possible," he said to the police, "that the man known as Paul Young may arrive at the caterers' entrance in the grandstands of Martineau Park racecourse at any time today from now onward." He listened to a reply and said, "No. No names. Goodbye."

Smiling, he replaced the receiver. "O.K.," he said. "Duty done."

"To some extent," I said.

"Everything's relative." He was cheerful although still looking far from well. "We know where Kenneth Charter's scotch is."

"Some of it," I said. "Enough."

"But not where it went between the tanker and the Vintners Incorporated deliveries."

"To a bottling plant, as you said."

He was leaning against his car, arm in sling, looking frail, a recuperating English gentleman out for a harmless Sunday morning drive in the country. There was also a glimmer of humor about him and the steel core looking out of the eyes, and I said abruptly, "You know something you haven't told me."

"Do you think so? What about?"

"You've found the bottling plant!"

"Found *a* bottling plant, yes. Somewhere to start from anyway. I thought I'd go and take a look this afternoon. Preliminary recce."

"But it's Sunday. There'll be no one there."

"That's sometimes an advantage."

"You don't mean . . . break in?"

"We'll see," he said. "It depends. Sometimes there's a caretaker. I'm good at government inspectors, even on Sundays."

Slightly aghast I said, "Well, where is it?"

"Roughly twenty-five miles this side of Kenneth Charter's headquarters." He smiled slightly. "By Friday afternoon we had concluded in the office that your idea of looking first at the plants to which Charter's tankers took wine had been good but wrong. There were five of them. We screened them all first, and all of them were rocksolid businesses. Then some time during last night . . . you know how things float into your head while you're half asleep . . . I remembered that one of them had had two links with Charter, not just one, and that maybe, just maybe, that second link is more important than we thought.''

"Tell me," I said.

"Mm. I don't want to be too positive."

"For heaven's sake . . ."

"All right then. We established right at the beginning of our bottle-plant inquiries that one of the plants is owned by a man called Stewart Naylor. It was at the top of the list that Charter gave us, and the first we checked."

"Stewart Naylor?" I thought. "He's . . . he's . . . um . . . isn't he mentioned in Kenneth Junior's notebook? Oh yes, the father who plays war games. David Naylor's father."

"Top of the class. Stewart Naylor owns Bernard Naylor Bottling. Started by his grandfather. Old respectable firm. I woke up with that word Naylor fizzing like a sparkler in my head. I telephoned Kenneth Charter himself early this morning and asked him about his son's friendship with David Naylor. He says he's known the father, Stewart Naylor, for years: they're not close friends but they know each other quite well because of their business connection and because of their sons like each other's company. Kenneth Charter says David Naylor is the only good thing in Kenneth Junior's lazy life, he keeps Kenneth Junior off the streets. War games, Kenneth Charter thinks, are a waste of time, but better than glue-sniffing."

"His words?" I asked, amused.

"Aye, laddie."

"Do you really think . . . ?"

"Kenneth Charter doesn't. He says Bernard Naylor Bottling is twenty-four carat. But we've found no other leads at all, and we've been checking bottling plants up and down the country until the entire staff are sick at the sound of the words. Three days' concentrated work, fruitless. A lot of the plants have gone out of business. One's a library now. Another's a boot and shoe warehouse."

"Mm," I said. "Could Stewart Naylor have an illegitimate half-brother?"

"Anyone can have an illegitimate half-brother. It happens to the best."

"I mean . . ."

"I know what you mean. Kenneth Charter didn't know of one." He shrugged. "Naylor's plant's a long shot. Either a bullseye or a case for apology. I'll go and find out."

"Right now?"

"Absolutely right now. If Stewart Naylor is by any chance also Paul Young, he should be safely going to or from Martineau Park this afternoon, not stalking about among his bottles."

"Did you ask Kenneth Charter what he looked like?"

"Yes. Ordinary, he said."

All these ordinary men. "Is he deaf?" I asked.

Gerard blinked. "I forgot about that."

"Ask him," I said. "Telephone now, before you go."

"And if Stewart Naylor is deaf, don't go?"

"Quite right. Don't go."

Gerard shook his head. "All the more reason to go."

"It's flinging oneself into the Limpopo," I said.

"Perhaps. Only perhaps. Nothing's certain." He returned to the telephone, however, and dialed Kenneth

Charter's house and then his office, and to neither attempt was there a reply.

"That's it, then," he said calmly. "I'll be off."

"Have you ever been in a bottling plant?" I said despairingly. "I mean . . . do you know what to look for?"

"No."

I stared at him. He stared right back. In the end I said,
"I spent a year in and out of bottling plants in Bordeaux."

"Did you?"

"Yes."

"Tell me, then, what to look for."

I thought of pumps and machinery. I thought of vats
and what might be in them. I said hopelessly, "You need
me with you, don't you?"

"I'd like it," he said. "But I won't ask. It's on the
very edge of consultancy . . . and maybe beyond."

"You wouldn't know the wine if you fell into it,
would you?" I said. "Nor the scotch?"

"Not a chance," he agreed placidly.

"Bloody sodding hell," I said. "You're a bugger."

He smiled. "I thought you'd come, really, if I told
you."

TWENTY

I PUT A NOTICE ON MY SHOP DOOR SAYING "CLOSED. VERY sorry. Staff illness. Open Monday 9:30 A.M."

I'm mad, I thought. Crazy.

If I didn't go, he would go on his own.

My thoughts stopped there. I couldn't let him go on his own when it was I who had the knowledge he needed. When he felt tired and ill and I was well and almost as strong as ever.

I sat at my desk and wrote a note to Sergeant John Ridger saying I'd been told to look in the Bernard Naylor bottling plant for the Silver Moondance scotch, and I was going there with Gerard McGregor (I gave his address) to check. I sealed the note in an envelope and wrote on it an instruction to Mrs. Palissey: take this to the police station if you haven't heard from me by ten this morning and tell them to open it.

I wedged the envelope on the till where she couldn't miss it and hoped she would never read it. Then with a last look round I locked my door and drove away, and tried not to wonder if I would ever come back.

Half the time I thought Kenneth Charter must know

his man. Stewart Naylor was true blue. Half the time I trusted Gerard's fizzler in the night. Intuition existed. Solutions came in sleep.

It would probably turn out to be an anticlimax of a journey not worth melodramatic notes to policemen or all this soul-searching. We would drive to the bottling plant, we would not break in, there would be plentiful evidence of legal prosperity and we would drive sedately home. It would not be another day of Sunday bloody horrors.

Gerard met me in a carpark we had agreed on, he having meanwhile been home to leave the Martineau Park spoils in his garage. From there we went toward London in his Mercedes, but with me driving this time.

"Suppose you were Stewart Naylor," Gerard said. "Suppose you'd spent your entire working life learning to run the family bottling business and then because of the French changing their regulations found the wine flood drying to a trickle."

"Longbows," I said, nodding.

"What? Oh, yes. Kenneth Charter was wrong, you know, in point of fact. It was the crossbow that put paid to the longbow. Well, never mind. Crossbows, guns, whatever, from no fault of your own you're going out of business. Kenneth Charter confirmed this morning that he hardly takes a fifth of what he used to to the Naylor plant, but it's still quite a lot. More than to anywhere else. He says that's how he knows that Naylor's is healthy while others struggle."

"Huh."

"Yes, indeed. Suppose you are Stewart Naylor and you look anxiously around for other things to bottle . . . tomato sauce, cleaning fluid, whatever . . . and you find everyone else in your line of business is in the same boat and doing the same. Ruin raises its ugly head and gives you a good long threatening glare.'' He paused as I passed a truck, then went on, ''We supposed earlier that at that point a convenient crook came along offering salvation in return for dishonesty and that our beleaguered bottler accepted. But suppose it wasn't like that. Suppose Stewart Naylor needed no seducing but without help thought up his own crooked scheme.''

''Which was,'' I said, ''to buy wine himself instead of bottling for others. To bottle it and label it as better than it was, and then sell it.'' I frowned. ''And at that point you get discovered and prosecuted.''

''Not if you have a half-brother who likes horses. You set him up on bank money in a Silver Moondance, and you take him your wine to sell. It sells well and for about twenty times more than it cost you, even including the bottles. Money starts flowing in, not out. And that's when the greed complex hits you.''

''The greed complex?'' I asked.

''Addiction,'' Gerard said. ''The first step is the huge one. The decision. To snort cocaine or not to. To borrow the Christmas Club's money, just once. To sell the first secret. To design a label of a nonexistent château and stick it on a bottle of wine-lake. The first step's huge, the second half the size, by the sixth step it's a habit. Suppose our Stewart Naylor begins to think that if he could arrange other outlets he could double and redouble his receipts.''

''O.K.,'' I said. ''Suppose.''

''At this point we have to suppose a henchman called Zarac, who is conveniently installed as wine waiter at the Silver Moondance. One of his duties is to cast about for possibilities of expansion and in due course he arrives on Vernon's doorstep at Martineau Park. He reports back to Paul Young ... er ... Paul Young query Stewart Naylor ... who goes to see Vernon and hey presto, the fake wine business takes a deep breath and swells to double size. Money now rolls in to the extent that concealing it is a problem. Never mind. Half-brother Larry is a whiz at horses. Pass Larry the embarrassing cash, magic-wand it into horseflesh, ship it to California, convert it again at a profit if possible and bank it ... intending, I daresay, to collect it one day and live in the sun. In my experience the last chapter seldom happens. The addiction to the crime becomes so integral to the criminal that he can't give it up. I've caught several industrial spies because they couldn't kick their taste for creeping about with cameras.''

"Clean up and clear out," I suggested.

"Absolutely. Almost never done. They come back for a second bite, and a third, and just one more ... and whammo, one too much.''

"So Stewart Naylor turned his ideas to scotch?"

"Ah," Gerard said. "Suppose when your son visits his divorced father one day he brings his friend Kenneth Junior with him. Or suppose he's often brought him. Stewart Naylor knows Kenneth Junior's father quite well. Kenneth Charter's tankers have brought wine to Naylor's plant for many years. Suppose our crime-addicted Stewart casts an idle eye on Kenneth Junior and reflects that Charter's tankers carry scotch and gin as well as wine, and that whereas the wine profits are healthy, from stolen scotch they would be astronomical.''

"But he couldn't ask Kenneth Junior outright to sell his dad's tankers' routes and destinations and timetables. Kenneth Junior might have gone all righteous and buzzed home to spill the beans ...''

"But he does think Kenneth Junior is ripe for a spot of treason as he's probably heard him bellyaching about his life with father . . ."

"So he sends Zarac to recruit him," I said. "Sends Zarac perhaps to the Diamond snooker hall? Or the disco? Somewhere like that? And Zarac says here's a lot of money, kid. Get me a tanker's keys, get me a tanker's route, and I'll give you some more cash. And three month's later he pays again. And again. And then says get me another tanker's keys, kid, the first one's too hot."

"Don't see why it couldn't have happened that way, do you?"

"No," I said. "I don't."

"Zarac," Gerard said thoughtfully, "held a very strong hand anyway when it came to blackmail."

I nodded. "Too strong for his own good."

We came to the end of the motorway and turned off into narrower streets to thread the way to Ealing.

"Do you know how to find this plant?" I said. "Or do we ask a policeman?"

"Map," Gerard said succinctly, producing one from the glove compartment. "It shows the roads. When we reach the road, drive slowly, keep the eyes skinned."

"Fair enough."

"And drive straight past," he said. "When we see what's what, we'll decide what to do."

"All right."

"If you turn left a mile ahead we'll be about five miles from target. I'll steer you."

"Right."

We turned left at a major intersection onto a dual carriageway through sleepy suburbs where in countless ovens Sunday roasts spluttered to lunchtime.

"We'll get a profile done tomorrow of that scotch we took from Martineau," Gerard said.

"And of the sample I took from the Silver Moondance bottle."

"They should be the same."

"They will be."

"You're exceedingly positive."

I grinned. "Yes."

"Go on, then. What's the joke?"

"Well, you know that the tankerful of scotch set off from Scotland every time at fifty-eight percent alcohol? And that at Rannoch's own bottling plant they would have added water to dilute it to forty?"

"Yes," he nodded.

"Have you any idea how much water that entails?"

"No, of course not. How much?"

"About three thousand four hundred gallons. More than ten tons by weight."

"Good grief!"

"Well," I said, "Rannoch's would be careful about that water. They'd use pure spring water of some sort, even if it hadn't actually come from a Scottish loch. But I'll swear that Charter's stolen loads have been diluted from an ordinary tap."

"Is that bad?"

I laughed. "It sure is. Any Scottish distiller would have a fit. They say that Scotch whisky is only the way it is because of the softness and purity of loch water. When I tasted the Silver Moondance scotch again in my shop I could sort of smell chemicals very faintly in the aftertaste. A lot of tap water isn't too bad, but some is awful. Makes disgusting tea. Ask the residents around here."

"Here?" he exclaimed.

"Western parts of London. Notorious."

"Good grief."

"It will turn up in the profile, too."

"Water?"

"Mm. Purifying chemicals. There shouldn't be any in neat scotch."

"But won't tap water spoil the scotch profile? I mean, will we still be able to prove our samples are identical with the original sent off from Scotland?"

"Yes, don't worry. Tap water won't affect the whisky profile, it'll just show up as extra components."

"Will it matter that the scotch is diluted?"

"No," I said. "The gas chromatograph just shows up the presence of things, not their quantity."

He seemed relieved. "Turn right at the next traffic lights. Could the gas chromatograph tell where any particular sample of tap water came from?"

"I don't know."

"Amazing."

"What is?"

"There's something you don't know."

"Yeah . . . Well, I don't know the dynasties of China or how to say no thanks in fifteen languages or the way to this bottling plant." And I'd like to turn straight round and go home, I thought. The nearer we got to Naylor's the more my nervousness increased. I thought of my father, brave as brave, setting off into battlefields, inspiring his men . . . and why couldn't I be like him instead of feeling my mouth go dry and my breath shorten before we were even in the heartland of deepest Ealing.

"Turn left here," Gerard said. "Then the third on the right. That's our road."

He was totally calm. No strain or anxiety in voice or face. I consciously unclenched my fingers from their grip on the steering wheel and tried without noticeable success to relax to Gerard's level.

Hopeless. Even my teeth were tightly together when we turned into the third on the right and went slowly along.

"There it is," Gerard said matter-of-factly. "See?"

I glanced to where he indicated and saw a pair of very tall entrance gates, shut, set in a length of very tall brick wall. On the gates in faded white lettering were the words "Bernard Naylor Bottling," with below them a padlock the size of a saucer.

We wouldn't be able to get in, I thought. Thank goodness for that.

"Turn left at the end," Gerard said. "Park there if you can."

It was one of those suburbs built before zoning where light industries sat among dwelling houses as an integral part of the community. When I'd parked the Mercedes at a curbside among a row of residents' wheels we walked past lace curtains and shrubby front gardens to get back to the high wall. Eating their roast beef, I thought, and the Yorkshire puddings and the gravy. Ten minutes past lunchtime and my stomach fluttering with enough butterflies to stock a Brazilian rain forest.

We walked slowly as if out for a stroll and in the short street there was only one other pedestrian, an elderly man waiting patiently for his dog at lampposts.

When we reached the gates, eight feet high, dark green sun-faded paint, Gerard stopped and faced them, head back as if reading the big white letters spreading across.

"There's broken glass embedded in the top of those walls," I said. "Barbed wire along the top of the gates. Don't tell me you can pick that half-ton padlock."

"No need," Gerard said placidly. "Open your eyes. In many massive gates conspicuously bolted there's a smaller door inset, wide enough for one person only. There's one right ahead of us in the left-hand gate with quite an ordinary-looking spring lock, and if I can't let us in through there I've been wasting the best years of my life."

He stopped his apparent reading of the legend on the gates and resumed his stroll, glancing as if casually at the small gate cut in the large.

"Do you smoke?" he said.

"No," I said in surprise.

"Tie a shoelace."

"Sure," I said, understanding, and bent down obligingly to pretend to tie bows on my laceless slip-ons.

"A doddle," Gerard said, above my head.

"What?"

"Step in."

I saw to my astonishment that the narrow door was already swinging open. He'd been fast. He was tucking a piece of clear plastic into his top pocket and glancing down to where the dog was again detaining his master.

Gerard stepped through the gate as if belonging there and with a rapid acceleration of heartbeats I went after him. He pushed the gate shut behind me and the spring lock fell into place with a click. He smiled faintly, and I saw with incredulity that beneath the tiredness and the malaise he was quietly enjoying himself.

"There may be people here," I said.

"If there are, we found the gate open. Curiosity."

We both looked at the insides of the very large gates. The padlock outside had been at least partly for show: on the inside there were thick bolts into the ground and a bar let into sockets waist-high so that no amount of direct pressure from outside could force the gates open.

"Factories often cut that hole in their defenses," Gerard said, waving at the way we had come in. "Especially old ones like this, built in the age of innocence."

We were in a big paved yard with a high brick building running the whole length of it on our right: small square barred windows pierced the walls in two long rows, one up, one down. At the far end of the yard, facing us, was a one story modern office building of panel-like construction, and on our immediate left was a gatehouse, which on busy days would have contained a man to check people and vehicles in and out.

No gatekeeper. His door was shut. Gerard twisted the knob, but to no avail.

Alongside the door was a window reminiscent of a ticket office, and I supposed that on working days that was where the gatehouse keeper actually stood. Gerard peered through it for some time at all angles, and then readdressed himself to the door.

"Mortise lock," he said, inspecting a keyhole. "Pity."

"Does it matter?" I said. "I mean, there wouldn't be much of interest in a gatehouse."

Gerard glanced at me forgivingly. "In old factories like this it's quite common to find the keys to all the buildings hanging on a board in the gatehouse. The gatekeeper issues keys as needed when employees arrive."

Silenced, I watched with a parched mouth while he put a steel probe into the keyhole and concentrated on feeling his way through the tumblers, his eyes unfocused and unseeing, all the consciousness in his fingers.

The place was deserted. No one came running across the yard demanding impossible explanations. There was a heavy click from the gatehouse door and Gerard with a sigh of satisfaction put his steel probe away and again twisted the doorknob.

"That's better," he said calmly, as the door opened without protest. "Now let's see."

We stepped into a wooden-floored room that contained a chair, a time-punch clock with barely six cards in a slot-holder designed for a hundred, a new-looking fire extinguisher, a poster announcing Factory Act regulations and a shallow unlocked wall cupboard. Gerard opened the cupboard and it was just as he'd said: inside there were four rows of labeled hooks, and upon all the hooks, labeled keys.

"All there," Gerard said with immense satisfaction. "There really is no one here. We have the place to ourselves." He looked along the labels, reading. "We'll start with the offices. I know more about those. Then . . . what?"

I read the labels also. "Main plant. Bottle store. Label room. Vats. Dispatch. How long have we got?"

"If Stewart Naylor is Paul Young and does what he said, he'll be on his way now to Martineau Park. If the police detain him there we've at least two or three hours."

"It doesn't feel like that," I said.

"No. Always scary, the first few times."

He left me again speechless. He took the keys he wanted from the hooks and indicated that I should do the same. Then we left the gatehouse, closing the door (unnecessarily, I thought) behind us and walked on into the main part of the yard.

Another large brick building was revealed to the left; and any residual hopes I might have had of our establishing Stewart Naylor's innocence and retreating in prudence were canceled at that point. Tucked into the lefthand corner of the yard stood a gray Bedford van, brown lines down the sides, devoid of number plates. I went across and looked through its windows but it held nothing: no wine, no fuzzy wigs, no shotgun.

"God in heaven," Gerard said. "That's the very one, isn't it?"

"Identical, if not."

He sighed deeply and glanced round the yard. "There's no big delivery van here marked Vintners Incorporated. It's probably on its way to Martineau. Let's take the offices, then, and . . . er . . . try not to leave any trace of our having been here."

"No," I said weakly.

We walked across the concrete, our shoes scrunching it seemed to me with alarming noise, and Gerard unlocked the main door of the office building as if he were the manager arriving in pinstripes.

As revealed by the time-punch cards, the plant for its size was almost unstaffed. There were six small offices in the office block, four of them empty but for desk and chair, two of them showing slight paperwork activity: beyond those a locked suite of rooms marked Managing Director on the outer door said in smaller letters underneath, Knock and Enter.

We entered without knocking, using the appropriate key from the gatehouse. Inside, first of all, was a pleasant-looking office, walls lined with calendars, charts and posters of wine districts in France. There were two desks, one managerial, one secretarial, both clearly in everyday use. In-trays bore letters, receipts were spiked, an African violet bloomed next to a pot of pens.

I left Gerard reading invoices with concentration and went through into the next room, which was furnished with an expensive leather-topped desk, green leather armchairs, carpet, brass pot with six-foot-high evergreen, cocktail cabinet, framed drawings of Bernard Naylor and his bottling plant fifty years earlier and a door into a luxurious washroom.

On the far side of the plushy office another door led into what had probably been designed as a boardroom, but in there, with daylight pouring through the skylights, the whole center space was taken by a table larger than a billiard table upon which someone appeared to have been modeling a miniature terrain of hills, valleys, plains and plateaux, all of it green and brown like the earth, with a winding ribbon of pale blue stuck on in a valley as a river.

I looked at it in awe. Gerard poked his head round the door, glanced at the table, frowned and said, "What's that?"

"War games," I said.

"Really?" He came closer for a look. "A battlefield. So it is. Where are the soldiers?"

We found the soldiers in a cupboard against one wall, tidily stacked in trays, hundreds of them in different uniforms, many hand-painted. There were also ranks of miniature tanks and gun carriages of all historical ages and fierce-looking missiles in pits. There were troop-carrying helicopters and First-World-War biplanes, baby rolls of barbed wire, ambulances and small buildings of all sorts, some of them bombed-looking, some painted red as if on fire.

"Incredible," Gerard said. "Just as well wars aren't fought on the throw of dice. I've thrown a six, I'll wipe out your bridgehead."

We closed the cupboard and in giving the table a last interested look I brushed my hand lightly over the contours of the nearest range of mountains.

They moved.

Slightly horrified I picked them up to put them back into place and stood looking at the hollowed-out interior in absolute surprise. I picked up another hill or two. Same thing.

"What is it?" Gerard said.

"The mountains are white inside."

"What of it?"

"See what they're made of?"

I held the mountains hollow side up so that he could see the hard white interior. "It's plaster of paris," I said. "Look at the edges . . . like bandage. I should think he's modeled that whole countryside in it."

"Good grief."

"Not an ear, nose and throat surgeon. A war games fanatic. Simple material, easily molded, easily colored, sets hard as rock."

I put the hills and the mountains carefully back in position. "There must be a fair few rolls of the stuff on this table. And if you don't mind . . . let's get out of here."

"Yes," Gerard agreed. "I suppose he'd just bought some more, the day he went to the Silver Moondance. Just happened to have it in his Rolls."

People didn't just happen to wrap people's heads in it. To do that, people had to have seriously vengeful thoughts and psychotic malice. Paul Young had gone a long way from where Stewart Naylor set out.

We closed the war games room door, crossed the green leather office, returned to the business sector.

"There's just enough legitimate trade going on to give an appearance of tottering a fraction this side of bankruptcy," Gerard said. "I can't find anything out of place. There were deliveries via Charter Carriers up to a month ago. Nothing since. No invoices as from Vintners Incorporated, no delivery notes, nothing. This office is for accountants and inspectors. Depressingly clean except for many samples of the Young-Naylor handwriting. Let's try the plant itself.''

He locked our way out of the office block and raised his eyebrows for a decision from me.

"Let's try over there," I said, pointing to the building by the Bedford van. "See what's in there first."

"Right."

There were two sets of double doors set into the long blank wall, and having tried "bottle store" and "vats" I found the key marked "dispatch" opened one of them.

The hinges creaked as I pulled the door open. My body had almost given up on separate nervous reactions: how could one sweat in some places while one's mouth was in drought? We went into the building and found it was the store for goods already bottled and boxed ready for sending out.

There was a great deal more space than merchandise. There were three lonely pallets laden with cases marked House Wine Red, addressed to a restaurant in Surrey, and four other pallets for the same place marked House Wine White: and that was all.

"The paperwork for that lot is in the office," Gerard said. "The restaurant bought and shipped the wine, Naylor bottled it. Regular consignments, it looked like."

We went back into the yard and locked the dispatch doors.

"Main plant," I said, looking at the high building opposite. "Well, let's see what it's like."

The key duly let us in. The building was old, it was clear at once, built by grandfather Naylor sturdily to last for generations. Internal walls were extensively tiled in white to shoulder height, cream-painted (long ago) above. From the central entrance some stairs on the left wound upward, and Gerard chose to go that way first as his paper-oriented mind looked instinctively for most enlightenment aloft: so we went upstairs and to a great extent he was right.

Upstairs, among much unused and dusty space, we found a locked door to further reaches, a door that opened like Sesame to the "label room" key.

"Great heavens," Gerard said. "Is all this usual?"

We stood looking at an expanse of floor covered with heaps of bundles of labels, thousand upon thousand of them altogether, in an apparent muddle but no doubt in some sort of order.

"Quite usual," I said. "No one ever tries to order exactly the right number of labels needed for any particular job. You always have to have more, for contingencies. The unused ones just tend to be dumped, and they pile up."

"So they do."

"Labels in constant use are probably in those small drawers over there. The ones looking like safe deposit boxes. Some of those drawers have labels on the front. They'll have those labels in the drawers."

"What we want are St. Estèphe and all the rest, and Bell's."

"Mm."

We both set to, but none of the fake labels turned up, very much to our dismay.

"We need something," Gerard said. "We need proof."

We didn't find it in the label room.

At the back of the label room a closed door led presumably to another room beyond, and I suggested taking a look through there, on the off chance.

"All right," Gerard said, shrugging.

The door was locked and the "label room" key didn't fit. Gerard diagnosed another mortise job and took what seemed to be an age with his probe turning the mechanism, but eventually that door too yielded to him, and we went through.

Inside that room there was a printing press. A clean, oiled, sleek modern machine capable of turning out impeccable labels.

Some of the press's recent work was still in uncut sheets: rows and rows of Bell's upon Bell's, brilliant in color, indistinguishable from the real thing.

Neither Gerard nor I said a word. We turned instead to the cupboards and boxes stacked around the walls, and we found them all, the neatly printed oblongs saying St. Estèphe, St. Emilion, Valpolicella, Mâcon, Volnay and Nuits St. Georges.

"It's the Château de Chenonceaux," I said suddenly.

"What is?"

"On this St. Estèphe label. I knew I'd seen it somewhere. It's the Château de Chenonceaux on the Loire without its bridge."

"I'm glad you know what you're talking about."

He was taking one each of all the fake labels and stowing them tenderly in his wallet, tucking them away in his jacket. We left everything else as it was but on the way out to my relief he didn't stop to relock the door. We went down again to the hall and from there to a door on the left which unlocked to "vats."

One could immediately smell the wine; a warm rosy air-filling aroma like a lungful of earthy fruit. Gerard lifted his head in surprise and to me it felt like coming home.

"I'd no idea," he said.

A small lobby opened into two long halls, the larger, on the left, containing a row of ten huge round vats down each side. Each vat, painted dark red, was eight feet high, six feet in diameter, and sat eighteen inches above ground level on thick brick pillars. Each vat, on its front, had large valves for loading and unloading, a small valve for testing, a quantity gauge, and a holder into which one could slot a card identifying the present contents.

"They're vast," Gerard said.

"Kenneth Charter's tanker would fill four of these. That size vat holds nearly nineteen hundred gallons. You can get them bigger."

"Thanks."

I smiled. "Let's see what's in them."

We read the contents cards. Most of them said EMPTY, the quantity gauges reading zero. The three nearest the entrance on the left side bore "Keely house wine, shipped October first," and another further along, "Dinzag private cuvé, shipped September twenty-fourth." Two together on the opposite side said "Linakket, shipped September tenth"; and all of the occupied vats were only three quarters full.

"They're all in the office paperwork," Gerard said regretfully.

"Let's try the empties, then," I said. "Quantity gauges can be disconnected."

I started at the far end under the premise that if Paul Young stacked his loot as far from the entrance as possible at Martineau Park then he might have done so on his own territory: and he had. The very first trickle that came out onto my fingers as I turned the small testing valve bore the raw volatile smell of scotch.

"Bloody bingo," I said. "I'll find a bottle and we'll take a sample, if you like."

"Later. Try the others."

"All of them?"

"Yes."

I loosed the small valves on all the EMPTY monsters, and we found scotch in five of them and wine in three. There was no way of telling how many gallons were in each, but to neither of us did that seem to matter. The wine as far as I could tell from sucking it from my palm was similar to our old friend "St. Estèphe," and the scotch was Rannoch already mixed with tap. Gerard looked like a cat in cream as I straightened from testing the last EMPTY (which was in fact empty) and said we'd seen everything now except the actual bottling department, and where would that be?

"Follow the hoses," I said.

He looked at the three or four hoses that were lying on the ground, fat lightweight gray ridged plastic hoses like giant earthworms as thick as a wrist, some in coils, some straightened out and running the length of the room between the vats.

I said, "Those connectors at the end of the hoses lock into the valves on the vats. One of them is connected to one of the so-called 'empty' vats we found the wine in, see? The wine is pumped from the vats to the bottling plant, so to find the plant, follow the hoses."

The hoses snaked round a corner into another wide hall, which this time contained only two vats, both painted a silvery white, taller, slimmer, and with several upright pipes attached from top to bottom of their sides.

"White wine?" Gerard said flippantly.

"Not really. They're refrigeration vats."

"Go on then, what are they for?"

I went over to the nearest, but it was switched off, and so was the other, as far as I could see. "They use them to clear cloudy particles out of spirits and white wine. If you drop the temperature, the bits and pieces fall to the bottom, and you run off the cleared liquid from higher up."

The hoses ran straight past the refrigeration vats and through another wide doorway, and through there we found what Gerard was looking for, the long light and airy hall, two stories high, where the liquids were fed into the bottles and stoppered by corks, where the caps and the labels were applied and the bottles packed into cases.

There were four separate lines of filling, corking, labeling, and capping machines, a capacity way beyond the jobs in hand. The machines themselves, like the vats and hoses, were new compared with the buildings. It all looked bright, clean, orderly, spacious and well run.

"I somehow expected something dark and Dickensian," Gerard said. "Where do we look?"

"Those big wooden slatted crates standing around probably contain empty bottles," I said, "but some might have full ones ready for labeling. Look in those."

"What are those glass booth things?"

"The actual bottling machines and corking machines and automatic labelers are enclosed with glass for safety and they don't work unless the glass doors are shut. One set of the machines looks ready to go. See the corks in that transparent hopper up there? And up there," I pointed, "on that bridge, see those four vats? The wine or whatever is pumped along from those huge storage vats in the long hall through the hoses up into these vats on the bridge, then it feeds down again by gravity into the bottles. The pumps for those vats look as if they're up on the bridge. I'll go up and see if there's anything in those feeder vats, if you like.''

Gerard nodded and I went up the stairs. The bridge, stretching from side to side of the bottling hall, was about twelve feet wide, railed at the sides, with four feeder vats on it standing taller than my head, each with a ladder bolted to its side so that one could go up to the entry valves on top.

There were four electric pumps on the bridge, one for each feeder vat, but only one was connected to hoses. In that one case a hose came up from the floor below and a second hose ran from the pump to the top of one of the feeder vats. In that vat I thought I might find more of the "St. Estèphe," and I squatted at the base of it and released a few drops through the small valve there.

Gerard was rattling bottles in the slatted wooden crates, looking for full ones. The crates were about five feet square, four feet high, very heavy, constructed of rows of timber rather like five barred gates. One could see the bottles inside glinting between the slats, hundreds in each crate.

I had become so at home in my more or less natural surroundings that I'd forgotten to be frightened for the past ten minutes: and that was a fundamental mistake because a voice suddenly spoke from directly beneath me, harsh, fortissimo and threatening.

"What the hell do you think you're doing? Back off, put your hands up and turn round.''

TWENTY-ONE

H<small>E WAS SPEAKING NOT TO ME BUT TO GERARD.</small>

He advanced from below the bridge into my vision, young, bullish, dressed in jeans and padded jacket, carrying a short-barreled shotgun. He had his back to me and he hadn't seen me, and I crouched on the bridge in a frozen state, incapable of movement, muscles locked, with the old clammy chill of abject fear sweeping over my skin and settling in my gut.

He was the one, I was intuitively certain, who had shot us before.

He was probably Denny. I called him Denny in my mind.

Gerard turned slowly toward him and raised one hand, the other being still in its sling. He didn't look up to the bridge. He could have seen me perhaps if he had, even though I was down behind the railings and between two vats. He did nothing, said nothing, then or later, to let Denny suspect I was there.

"Stand still," Denny said, "or I'll blast you."

Another voice said, "Who is it? Is it Beach?" and that was worse. I knew that voice too well.

Paul Young's voice. Stewart Naylor.

"That's not Beach," he said.

He appeared from below me and stood beside Denny.

I could see the black hair, the heavy shoulders, the glint of glasses, the hearing aid behind his ear.

"Who is it, then?" Denny said.

"The one who was with him. Older, grayer, wearing a sling. That's him. Some name like Gregg, Lew said."

Who was Lew . . .

"What's the sling for?" Stewart Naylor demanded.

Gerard didn't answer. After a silence Naylor said, "You said you hit someone in a car at Beach's shop. Was this him?"

Denny said, "I couldn't see who it was."

"I don't want him shot in here," Naylor said forcefully. "Too much sodding mess. You just keep your sodding finger off the trigger. And you, Gregg, take your arm out of that sling and turn your back to me and put both your hands on the top rail of that bottle container crate, and you do just what I tell you or you'll get shot again, mess or not."

Gerard did as he was told. I've got to do something, I thought, and couldn't think what. Couldn't think. Listened in hopeless horror.

Stewart Naylor walked to Gerard and patted him all over, looking for weapons. Gerard didn't move. Naylor reached round into Gerard's jacket and pulled out his wallet, stepping back a few paces to look at the contents.

"Gerard McGregor," Naylor said, reading. "Where's your friend Beach?"

"Don't know," Gerard said, shrugging.

"How the hell did he turn up here?" Denny said. "I don't like it."

With suddenly spurting alarm and anger Naylor viciously said, "He'll sodding wish he hadn't!"

I watched in despair. He had found in the wallet the fake labels from upstairs. He was holding them out as if in disbelief.

"He's seen the press," he said furiously. "He knows too bloody much. We'll kill him and dump him. He'll have had no chance yet to tell what he's seen. We'll be all right." He sounded convinced of it.

Gerard's apparently untroubled voice rose as if in courteous discussion. "I did of course leave word of where I was going. If I don't return safely you'll find the police at your door."

"They always say that in movies," Denny said. "It's never bloody true."

After a pause Naylor said, "Hold him there, Denny. I'll be straight back," and he turned and walked under the bridge and out of the bottling hall, and I thought about trying to jump down onto Denny . . . who was too far away for it to be practicable. He would whirl when he heard me move and he would shoot while I was climbing the railings to launch myself far enough out to have a hope of reaching him in one jump. He would shoot either Gerard or me for sure before we could overpower and disarm him. I didn't see what else to do and I was certain that that jump would be literally fatal perhaps for both of us, and I was worrying also and cringing inside with fear that the reason I didn't move was fear. Not caution, just cowardice. One could fling one's life away trying to prove to oneself one was brave . . . and maybe for some people it was worth it, but not to me.

Stewart Naylor came back carrying a small package, which he zipped open as he walked.

The contents were wide white bandage.

I felt sick.

I should have jumped, I thought. I should have risked it while I had the chance. Why hadn't I?

Because I would now be lying dead or dying on the floor.

Common sense, emotion, logic, bravado . . . they could whirl through the mind in a jumbled mess, and how could one tell which was right.

Naylor walked over to Gerard and with great speed tied the wrist of his injured arm to the rail with the bandage. A strong tremor ran visibly through Gerard's body and he turned away from the crate, trying to tug himself free, trying to escape. The lines of his face were set rigid, the eyes hollowly dark.

He's afraid too, I thought. He knows what that bandage is. He's as human as I am . . . and he's terrified.

He didn't look up to the bridge.

Something, I thought. I must do something. I had no weapon. Nothing. Gerard. Plaster of paris.

What did I have . . .

I had knowledge.

Naylor hit Gerard's face a swiping blow with his fist and when he had him off balance he tied the second wrist to the railing, and although I could then see only his back the desperation in Gerard's body was like a shout.

In my mind I was begging, "No, don't do it, no, no . . . ," and Naylor wound the bandage once round Gerard's neck.

Knowledge.

The bandage went round twice and three times. Naylor was intent on the work. So was Denny, his back to me, the barrel of the gun drooping.

Gerard was kicking backward and not reaching Naylor's legs, yelling to him, screaming that what he was doing was useless, useless, people knew he was there and would come looking.

Neither Naylor nor Denny believed him. They were intent . . . enjoying the wrapping of a living head . . . to turn it to rock.

The weapon I had was knowledge.

I moved. My muscles felt stiff. I slid jerkily round behind the vat I'd tested for St. Estèphe and climbed its ladder.

Go on yelling, Gerard, I thought. Go on filling the hearing aid of the deaf man. Go on kicking. Keep them looking your way.

My hands grasped the locking nut that connected the hose to the valve at the top of the feeder vat. Usually I could turn them easily without a wrench. My hands slipped with sweat. I'd got to unlock it. Only chance. Had to have the hose off the vat.

Had to have the hose free at that end.

On top of the vat I strained with almost fury and felt the locking nut turn and turn again and come loose. I lifted the hose off the vat and carried the end of it with me down the short ladder, trying to do it all silently, making small noises that sounded frightful to me but brought no dreaded shouts from the floor.

I was down the ladder. By the pump. From the pump the main long hose ran down to the ground and away into the distance, going to the great storage vat in the main hall. Long hose, holding a good deal of wine.

I switched on the pump. Begging. Praying. Sick.

The pump went smoothly about its business, efficient beyond dreams. Wine gushed out of the hose I held like red force-driven water out of a fire hose. I directed it straight at Naylor, drenching Denny on the way. I propped the spurting nozzle between the railings. I climbed over the railings myself and made the flying leap that had been so illogical, so impossible, so deadly. I landed on Denny, who couldn't see for wine, and grabbed his shotgun from him and hit him hard with it on the head.

Naylor, totally surprised, tried to clutch me. I felt such anger for him that he would have needed twice his strength. I caught him by his clothes and pushed him until he was under the gushing wine, and I pulled his head back by the hair until the wine was running full onto his face, onto his glasses and up his nose and into his opening mouth until he was beginning to choke.

I was drowning him, I thought.

Perhaps I shouldn't.

He was gagging for breath. Waving his arms about. Helpless.

I half pulled, half pushed him back to the crate Gerard was tied to and propped him chest forward against it, holding him there by leaning on his back.

He really was choking. Not breathing.

I hit him very hard with my palm below the shoulder blades and the air trapped in his lungs rushed out through the wine blockage in his trachea, and he began to breathe again in wild gasps like whooping cough, air fighting against wine in his bronchial tubes.

He had dropped the plaster of paris bandage at Gerard's feet. I picked up the roll, wet and soggy and pink now with wine, and unwound the layers from Gerard's throat.

Naylor hadn't had any scissors. The bandage led from Gerard's neck down to one wrist and from there to the other. Tight knots on his wrists beyond undoing.

Something to cut with, to free him.

Old blunt penknife. I felt in my pocket for it and with some astonishment came up with Flora's new sharp silver present. Blessed Flora.

I cut the roll of bandage off at Gerard's wrist and then cut the bandages tying his wrists to the crate. Even when his wrists were no longer fixed there he held on to the rail for a few moments, and in that time I'd wound the end of the bandage roll about eight times around one of Naylor's wrists instead, and fastened it similarly to the crate.

Naylor leaned over the crate, retching, coughing, his glasses opaque with wine, his body jerking with the effort of drawing breath. He seemed hardly to notice, much less fight, when I fastened his other wrist to the rail.

Denny on the floor returned to life. I looked down from tying knots and watched fuzzy thoughts begin to straighten out in his eyes, and I took one of the empty bottles out of the crate and hit him again with it on the head.

The bottle broke. A claret bottle, I remotely noticed. The pieces fell into the wine that was still flooding out in a red lake all over the floor, curling round corners, making rivers, pulsating down from the open hose. The smell of it filled the senses; heavily sensuous, headily potent.

So much wine. The main valve on the huge storage vat must be open, I thought. The whole thing must be emptying through the pump. Nineteen hundred gallons . . .

Denny was lying facedown in it. I hauled him over to the crate, turned him onto his back, pulled his arms up, and with soggy pink bandage tied each of his wrists separately to one of the sturdy lower slats.

Wine swirled through his hair. If there was blood there also, I couldn't see.

Gerard watched, leaning against the crate.

When I'd finished the essential tying there was still some bandage left in the roll. I wound some more of it round each of Naylor's wrists, joining them in more and more layers to the crate, and then used the last of it to do the same for Denny.

The gypsum in the bandage had been already released to some extent by the wine so that my fingers were covered with pale pink slime. I picked an empty bottle from the crate and held it under the spurting hose until it was half filled and then I carefully poured wine over each tied wrist until the bandages were soaked right through.

Gerard watched throughout, speechless.

Finally I went up the stairs and switched off the pump.

The gusher stopped. The only sound suddenly was the labored wheezing of Naylor fighting for breath.

I looked down for a moment at the scene below: at so much floor redly awash, at Denny lying on his back with his hands tied above his head, at Naylor heaving over the crate, at the shotgun lying in the wine, and the broken claret bottle and the bottles in the crates.

The only thing that might cut through hardening plaster of paris was broken glass.

I went down the stairs and carefully removed the broken bottle from anywhere near Denny, and took enough bottles out of the crate to make sure Naylor couldn't reach any.

I pushed the shotgun well out of their reach with my foot.

What else?

Nothing else.

I was myself, like Naylor and Denny, soaked from

head to foot with wine: jacket, trousers, shirt, socks, shoes, all dark red against dark red skin. Gerard alone, though copiously splashed, was relatively dry.

I said to him, "Could you fetch your car round to the gate? I'll drive from there, but I'm not quite sure that I'm what they'd expect in this neighborhood."

"What about them?" he said, looking at our captives.

"We'll send the posse. I'd like to get away from here first. Denny has a partner somewhere."

"Right. Yes, I'll get the car." He sounded exhausted and very subdued, and looked anywhere but at my face.

Denny stirred and groaned. Naylor wheezed. In a very few minutes the bandages round their wrists would be pink rock, and it would take a saw to release them.

We left without locking anything. Gerard brought the car to the gates and I drove from there on, apologizing as I got in for the stains I would be leaving on the upholstery. He said stains were secondary. He said little else.

We stopped again as in the morning at a nearby public telephone and this time I got through myself to the priority number, reversing the charges. I said to the answering voice that I wanted an urgent message to reach Detective Chief Superintendent Wilson from Tony Beach.

Hold on, he said. I held. A smooth well-known voice came on the line and said, "Mr. Beach? Is that you?"

"Yes, Mr. Wilson."

"And was it you earlier, who directed us to Martineau Park?"

"Not exactly."

"Mr. McGregor, was it?"

"Yes. How do you know?"

"A man at the racecourse. The deputy clerk of the

course who is present there on Saturdays and Sundays while the gates and doors are unlocked, he told our men that a Mr. Beach had been to the caterer's section yesterday and again today with a Mr. McGregor.''

"What happened?" I asked.

"Paul Young hasn't gone there, Mr. Beach." He spoke partly regretfully, partly with faint reproof.

"Has anyone?" I asked.

"A man called Lew Smith arrived a short while ago in a van from Vintners Incorporated. Our men surrounded him, accompanied by the deputy clerk of the course. Lew Smith could give no good reason for being there, but neither was he Paul Young. There seemed to be no grounds for detaining him on the basis of an anonymous telephone call, and our men let him go. And now, Mr. Beach, could you give me an explanation? Why did you expect Paul Young to go to Martineau Park?''

"Mr. Wilson," I said. "I do know where Paul Young is now. Do you want him?"

"Don't be facetious, Mr. Beach."

I told him exactly where to find his quarry. I said, "You'll find a printing press if you go upstairs, complete with Bell's labels and also the same fake wine labels found in the Silver Moondance. You'll find stolen whisky in the vats. If you apply to Rannoch whisky distillers you'll get a profile match. The scotch was stolen from tankers belonging to a firm called Charter Carriers. You'll find another branch of the police investigating those thefts and you'll find plaster of paris in Paul Young's office. He's Larry Trent's half-brother and his name is Stewart Naylor."

"Mr. Beach . . ."

"Goodbye, Mr. Wilson," I said. "Please don't waste time. Lew Smith might drive there and free him. And oh, yes, you remember Gerard McGregor and I were shot at by the robbers outside my shop? You'll find one of those thieves tied up with Naylor. I think his name's Denny. His gun's there too. Lew Smith was probably his partner. Worth a try, anyway.''

I put the receiver down although I could hear him still talking and got back into the car with Gerard.

"There will be endless questions," he said.

"Can't be helped."

I restarted the engine and we angled our way sedately out of Ealing, crossed the hinterland, made it safely back to the high road home.

Neither of us talked again for a long way. There was none of the euphoria of the Sunday before with the pellets burning in our bodies and our spirits high with escape. Today had been grimmer, dark with real horror, dark as wine.

Gerard shifted in his seat and sighed and said eventually, "I'm glad you were with me."

"Mm."

Five minutes later he said, "I was afraid."

"Yes, I know. Well, so was I."

He turned his head, glanced finally at my face and then looked forward again through the windscreen.

"That plaster . . .'' He shuddered. "I was screaming . . . I've never been so craven in my life."

"Fear in a fearful situation is normal. Absence of fear is not."

He swallowed. "I also feared you wouldn't rescue me."

"Wouldn't? Do you mean couldn't, or wouldn't try?"

"Couldn't, of course." He seemed surprised at the question. "It would have been pointless to do anything useless like throwing your life away to make a gesture."

"Die in the attempt?"

"Dying in the attempt," he said somberly, "has always seemed to me the height of incompetence."

"Or plain bad luck."

"All right," he said. "I'll allow bad luck."

Another silence lengthened. We turned off the motorway and would soon be back where we'd left my car.

"Are you all right to drive home?" I said.

"Yes, perfectly."

He looked no better than when we'd set off, but not worse either. Still gray, still strained, but still also with apparently endless reserves of stamina.

I had known him for two weeks. Fifteen days, to be accurate, since we had rescued guests from under the tent at Flora's party. With him and through him I had looked newly into many internal mirrors and was coming to understand what I saw there. I owed him a great deal and didn't know how to tell him.

I stopped his car beside mine. We both got out. We stood looking at each other, almost awkwardly. After such intensity there seemed to be no suitable farewell.

"I'm in your debt," he said.

I shook my head. "Other way round."

He smiled faintly, ruefully. "Call it quits."

He stepped quietly into his wine-stained car, gave me the briefest of waves, drove away.

I watched him go until he was out of sight. Then in similar peace I unlocked my own door and motored ordinarily home.

THE SUN WAS BREAKING THROUGH CLOUDS WHEN I reached the cottage, shining with the heavy golden slant of a late October teatime.

I went into the hall and looked into the real mirror

there. My hair was spiky and sticky with wine. The stains all over my head and face had dried to purple, but in the sun's rays they still seemed to glow red. My eyes shone pale gray in a burnished landscape.

I smiled. My teeth gleamed. I looked like a red devil, I thought. A bloody red devil from the far side of terror.

I was filled quite suddenly with a sort of restless exultation.

I went through my sun-filled house shouting aloud, "Emma ... Emma ... Emma ... Emma ..." and my voice bounced off the walls, reverberating.

I didn't shout for lack of her but from wanting to tell her ... wanting to shout to her to make her hear ... that for once I felt I had done what I should, that I hadn't been forever a coward, that I knew I hadn't failed her memory ... or myself ... or anything I thought I ought to be ... and that I felt comforted and whole and at one with her, and that if I wept for her from now on it would be for what she had missed ... the whole of life ... the unborn child ... and not for my own loss, not from loneliness ... not from guilt.

TWENTY-TWO

Fragments of information floated my way for days like debris from a shipwreck.

Chief Superintendent Wilson came himself to tell me the police had had to saw through the crate and transport Naylor and Denny to a hospital to get their unorthodox handcuffs removed. He seemed deeply amused and also content, and took away a bottle of wine for dinner.

Sergeant Ridger returned with a cut forehead from his scuffle with the pickets and told me that the racecourse bars at Martineau Park had been on the police list of whisky complaints. He said we would have gone there on the next race day and our pub crawl would have been successful: and I didn't like to tell him that it already had been, thanks to Mrs. Alexis.

Mrs. Alexis asked me to lunch. I went, laughed a lot, and came away with a commission to choose and supply wine for her restaurant. Wilfred had survived the soot and the sweep got the sack.

Gerard fed me with constant news, mostly good.

The scotch in the big storage vats had been profile matched and had proved to be the third load stolen from the tanker. The Martineau Park and Silver Moondance scotch was all from the second load. The first load had presumably been sold and drunk.

Rannoch's were refusing to collect or accept their scotch because of the tap water. Customs and Excise were pressing all and sundry for the duty. Kenneth Charter's insurers were insisting that as the whisky was Rannoch's, Rannoch's should pay. Rannoch's said Naylor should pay. Kenneth Charter's suggestion that they run the stuff away down a drain and forget it was not being treated seriously.

The best news was that the insurers had agreed to reinstate Charter's policies in full: the tanker fleet would stay in business.

Kenneth Junior's part was so far unknown to the police and would with luck remain so. Kenneth Junior wrote to his father from Australia asking for more money, which Kenneth Senior sent him along with advice to stay far away until parental disgust had abated.

Mission accomplished, Gerard said with satisfaction. Deglet's were sending Charter their account.

Into Deglet's office came news also from the Californian bloodstock agent: he regularly sold the horses shipped by Larry Trent and paid the proceeds as instructed into three bank accounts in the name of Stewart Naylor.

He had met Mr. Naylor, who had been over once to open the accounts. The horses were good and had won races for their new owners. Everything was straightforward, he was sure.

Flora came to tell me she and Jack were going to Barbados for a month to lie in the sun.

"We go every year, dear, but you know Jack, never still for five minutes except that this time his leg will slow him up nicely, won't it? Of course half the racing world goes to Barbados in the winter. Did you know they call it Newmarket-on-Sea?'' And later she sent me a postcard saying Orkney Swayle and Isabella were staying in the same hotel and one couldn't have everything, dear, could one?

Miles Quigley telephoned, full of importance, to offer me Vernon's job, starting immediately, as liquor manager to his firm. Double Vernon's salary, he said, and managerial status and a seat on the board; and I reflected while politely declining that if he'd given Vernon those rewards Vernon might have stayed loyal for life.

Quigley said he was sticking to his agreement not to prosecute and Vernon was cooperating with the police. Cooperating? I asked. Vernon, Quigley said, would be a prosecution witness, chattering in return for immunity. Was I sure about the job?

I was sure. Perfectly certain, thanks all the same.

I would stay with my shop, I thought, because for me it was right. The scale of its life was my scale. We fitted.

I would stay with good-natured gossipy Mrs. Palissey and maybe one day teach Brian to write his own name. I would eat Sung Li's dinners and bow to him; and I would listen to my customers and sell them comfort.

Ordinary life would go on.

I went home one night after closing at nine and found the postman had left a package from my mother.

She seldom wrote; mostly telephoned. The note inside the package was characteristically short.

Darling,

Turned out some very old boxes. Found these oddments of your father's. If you don't want them, throw them away.

The oddments were from a long way back, I thought, looking through them. One of a pair of military gold cuff links. A bronze belt buckle with his regimental crest. A leather jotter with a slot for a pencil, but no pencil.

I riffled through the pages of the jotter. Nothing but memos about things like duty rosters; notes about the day-to-day running of the regiment. It was only by chance that I came upon the page where he had written something else.

I stared at the page, transfixed. It was a scrawl, a *cri de coeur*, hurried, barely punctuated, ending without a question mark. I knew my mother wouldn't have sent it, if she'd seen it. It too nearly destroyed the myth.

I felt nearer to him than ever before. I felt his true son.

He had written . . . at not quite my present age, he had written:

> The battle must be soon now. It is essential not
> to show fear to the men, but God, I fear
> Why can't I have the courage of my father

Somewhere in the battle, I thought, he had found it.

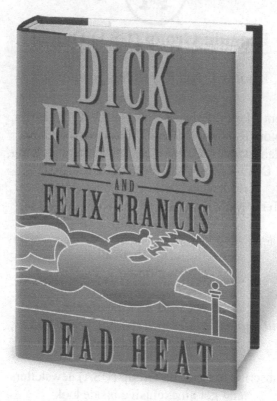